ILARIA TUTI lives in Friuli, in the far north-east of Italy. *The Man in the Woods* (previously *Flowers Over the Inferno*), the first book in the Teresa Battaglia trilogy, was a *Times* 'Crime Book of the Month' and a top ten bestseller on publication in Italy. Her second novel *Painted in Blood* was published in Italy in 2019 and became an instant top five bestseller.

EKIN OKLAP was born in Turkey, and grew up in Italy. She is a graduate of the University of Cambridge and the School of Oriental and African Studies, and currently lives in London, where she works as a literary agent. As a translator, she was short-listed for the 2016 Man Booker International Prize.

PAINTED
IN
BLOOD

ILARIA TUTI

Translated from the Italian by
EKIN OKLAP

Printed and bound in Great Britain by Clays Ltd, Elcograf

WEIDENFELD & NICOLSON

First published in Great Britain in 2020
by Weidenfeld & Nicolson
This paperback edition published in Great Britain in 2021
by Weidenfeld & Nicolson
an imprint of The Orion Publishing Group Ltd
Carmelite House, 50 Victoria Embankment
London EC4Y 0DZ

An Hachette UK Company

1 3 5 7 9 10 8 6 4 2

Originally published as *Ninfa dormiente*
in Italian in 2019 by Longanesi & C.

Longanesi & C. © 2019
Gruppo editorial Mauri Spagnol
English Translation © Ekin Oklap 2020

A CIP catalogue record for this book is
available from the British Library.

ISBN (Paperback) 978 1 4746 0963 0
ISBN (eBook) 978 1 4746 0964 7

Typeset by Input Data Services Ltd, Somerset

S.p.A.

For Jasmine and Sarah.
For our foremothers, for the women of today and of tomorrow.
For the men who honour them.

Tempus volat, valet, velat

I am all that has been,
and is,
and shall be,
and my robe no mortal has yet uncovered.
Isis and Osiris, Plutarch

The End

Teresa often thinks of death. But she never pictured hers like this, or the cruel irony of being unable to remember the very thing that could save her.

A fire about to break out, victims waiting to be rescued, yet here she is, motionless.

Her mind has abandoned her. Her state of confusion is a grotesque addition to the last act of this tragedy. Those eyes are watching her, brimming with terror and despair, as she does the only thing she is capable of in that moment: nothing at all. Teresa is sure she will die with this vacant expression on her face. She will die helpless and inept, her arms hanging at her sides, her armour gone after a lifetime spent as a warrior.

A warrior? A police officer, just about. A sixty-year-old woman, and a sick one at that, trying to play the hero when she can no longer remember what things are called.

She could try guessing. It feels like lately that's all she's been able to do to survive: guess which road to take, where to look, what words to say and which shadows to be wary of.

Even the knowledge of her own name has been corroded by doubt, as has the killer's – the killer who is with her now, or perhaps in a different room, but certainly inside that house, that hell on the verge of exploding in the blackness of the valley. All because Teresa dared to confront the secret that was hidden within its walls, sheltered by the mountains.

Teresa *knows*, but her mind still can't remember.

Who among the victims about to be sacrificed to the fire is innocent and who has shown the savage force required to tear a man's beating heart out of his chest?

Whom do I save?

Then there's *him*, who looks at her like the son Teresa never had. His name is still just the trace of a whisper on her lips, but their connection is visceral. Teresa can feel it in her gut, in the burn of a scar, in the red liquid rippling through her veins.

It feels like the walls are closing in on her, crackling like the whispers that have been tormenting her for days. The sound of all of her worst fears.

The name of the killer is . . . The name of the killer is . . .

She is face to face with death, yet all Teresa can think of is a riddle – heard who knows where and when.

She hears a scream, an inhuman sound that breaks through the petrified torpor that has imprisoned her and brings her back to the world.

Then, suddenly, the scream – his scream – stops.

'We've found it,' she hears him say, whispering as if to save the words for the two of them alone. His pupils are dilated. 'We've found Evil. It's here. Waiting for us.'

The words trickle and drip out of him like the beads of a diabolical rosary. He lifts his arm through the ropes that bind him and points his index finger towards a corner of the room where the darkness seems to be pulsating in time with their fear.

'We've found it. *It's not human.*'

He screams again, so loud that something inside Teresa shatters.

She remembers his name now.

The time has come to find out how far Teresa is willing to go.

The time has come to find out if Teresa is willing to trade Massimo Marini's life for that of an innocent, if she is willing to kill the man who looks at her like the son she never had, and who is shaking now as if he has seen the devil himself over in that corner, dancing in the dark.

The Beginning

The haematite chalk glides across the paper, shaping arabesques into familiar curves, drawing valleys that blossom into open lips. It traces tender arcs and soft, smudged lines. A delicate profile. Long dark hair. The paper, like her skin, a luminous white.

The redness overflows and seeps into the fibres of the sheet until colour and paper are one. Fingers press and spread the hue out, soak and colour the paper, desperate to capture the image before its beauty vanishes.

The fingers tremble, they smooth and caress. The eyes weep and their tears mix with the redness, dilute it, reveal unexpected crimson hues.

The heart of the world suspends its beat. The fronds and the birdsong fall silent. The pale petals of wild anemones cease to thrum with the breeze and the stars seem too abashed to show themselves in the twilight. The whole mountain is leaning in to watch the miracle unfolding in the valley, on a bend in the gravelly river where the water comes to a quiet rest.

The *Sleeping Nymph* takes shape beneath the painter's hands. She is brought into the world, as red as passion and love.

I

The sun cut sideways into Massimo Marini's face, drawing out a blaze of colour as it filtered through his brown eyelashes. He was walking with nervous steps down a street flanked by hidden gardens, kept out of sight by thick walls. Petals from the taller branches of the trees behind the walls had fallen onto the street. It was like treading on something that was still alive, a carpet of dying creatures.

It was a drowsy, placid spring afternoon, but the roiling black mass at the edge of his line of sight announced an upheaval. The air crackled with electricity, a contagious force that made the inspector restless.

The entrance to *La Cella* art gallery was marked by a brass plaque on the coarse plaster exterior of a building from the 1600s. Reflected on the metal, Massimo's eyes looked as twisted as his mood. He rolled down his shirtsleeves and put on his jacket before ringing the doorbell. The lock clicked open. He pushed the studded knocker and entered.

The day's warmth reached no further than the threshold. The moment he stepped through the door, a wet weight seemed to settle on him. The floor was chequered black and white, and a stairway of veined marble curved upwards towards the second floor. Light filtered through some of the high windows onto a chandelier made of Murano glass, launching emerald shimmers into the semi-darkness of the ground floor. There was a smell of lilies in the air. It reminded Massimo of incense, the inside of a gloomy church, endless litanies and the stern look on his father's face whenever Massimo – then still a child – dared show any sign of boredom.

His head began to pound.

His mobile phone vibrated with an incoming call and in the silence of that solemn place, the sound seemed to belong to another universe.

He took out his phone from his breast pocket. It writhed in his palm like a cold, flat artificial heart, but Massimo knew that on the other end of the line was a real heart in which love wrestled with rage and disappointment with pain. His phone had been ringing with that number for weeks now, often several times a day, relentless.

He ignored the call, his mouth pasty with a sickening mixture of remorse and guilt. He let the call ring out and switched his phone off. Circumventing the marble stairway, he descended a set of wrought-iron steps that spiralled ivy-like into the basement. Muffled voices floated through the gloom. A hallway dimly lit by lamps set into the floor, a door made of pebbled glass and beyond, the gallery.

La Cella, finally. The vaulted ceiling of coarse tiles stood above a smooth slate floor. Along the walls, most of the plaster had been scraped off to reveal the original stonework beneath. Each splash of light fell precisely onto each of the pieces on display, drawing them out like jewels from the shadows. Bronze sculptures, glass vases and dazzlingly colourful abstract paintings were the characters on that spare underground stage.

The inspector followed the murmur of voices to a cluster of people standing in the most spacious room in the gallery. A pair of uniformed policemen stood guard along the edges. Past them, Marini recognised Parisi and de Carli, both in plain clothes. Olive-skinned, muscular Parisi was talking quietly on the phone, while de Carli – as skinny and ungainly as a teenager – watched and occasionally intervened. They had become Marini's team ever since he had requested a transfer from the city to this small local precinct. He had thought – or at least hoped – that this change in trajectory might be a way to find solace and perhaps start over. He had ended up finding a whole lot more than he'd expected, but solace remained a fire-breathing chimera that burned him every time he reached out to grasp it.

He walked up to his team.

'What's going on?' he asked de Carli.

De Carli pulled up his jeans, which had slid down his thighs.

'God knows. They haven't told us a thing yet. It's all a big mystery.'

'Then why did you tell me it was urgent?'

Parisi covered the phone with his hand and tilted his chin towards the opposite side of the room.

'Because she needs us. And you.'

Marini's eyes searched for the person who had made every minute of his life hell over the past few months, but in doing so, had brought him back to life.

At first he only saw her feet, glimpsed between the legs of two officers. She was wearing wedge trainers and kept shifting her weight from one leg to the other; every now and then she stood on the balls of her feet to give her legs a rest.

She's tired, he thought. And although he had no idea why the team had been dispatched to the *Cella*, he knew she would be the last person to leave that day.

Then the two officers moved and he could finally see the rest of her, standing between a bronze sculpture of a half-liquefied heart and an installation of Perspex wings hanging from the ceiling. Heart and soul, just like her.

And determination, a vitality that sometimes threatened to crush those closest to her, but that always managed, at the very last moment, to pick them up and push them beyond what they thought possible.

It so happened that she was also a bit of a bitch.

There was a raggedness in her appearance, which had less to do with her age – sixty – than with some inner torment that Massimo could not yet name and that only seemed to find release in the notebook she kept permanently clasped in her hands, filling it with frenzied notes at every opportunity.

He walked up to her and noticed the single blink with which she registered his arrival. She didn't even turn round. She was holding one of the arms of her reading glasses between her lips and chewing nervously on a sweet.

'I hope it's sugar-free,' he said.

She finally looked at him, though for barely a second.

'And that is your business because . . . ?'

Her voice was hoarse and dry, and leavened with a note of amusement.

'You're diabetic, Superintendent. And supposedly a lady, too . . .' he muttered, ignoring the curse that followed.

It was a familiar game they played, one he almost never won.

She stopped gnawing at her glasses.

'Isn't this supposed to be your day off, Inspector?' she asked, boring into him with those terrible eyes of hers, so adept at seeing well below the surface.

Massimo gave her a half-smile.

'And haven't you just finished your shift?'

'All this diligence won't compensate for your recent lapses, Marini.'

Massimo decided to avoid the minefield of a possible response. Already, she appeared to have lost interest in him. He watched her closely, this woman whose head didn't even reach his chest but who could crush his ego in the blink of an eye. She was almost twice his age, but frequently left him behind, exhausted, well before her own energies were spent. Her manner was often brutal and her hair, styled in a bob that framed her face, was dyed such an artificial shade of red that it was almost embarrassing. Or at least it would have been on anyone else but her.

Teresa Battaglia could bark, and there were some who swore they had seen her bite, too – quite literally.

'So? Why are we here? What's with all the mysteries?' he asked in a bid to draw her back to the hunt – that territory she could navigate better and faster than anyone else.

Teresa Battaglia was staring straight ahead as if she were

looking at someone, her eyes narrowed, black thoughts lodged in her furrowed brow.

'Singular, Inspector, not plural. There's only ever one mystery.'

Superintendent Battaglia wiped the lenses of her reading glasses, as she did every time she was thinking. She was putting her thoughts in order.

'Why else would we be here, if not to solve the mystery of death?'

2

'Cold case.'

That was how Deputy Public Prosecutor Gardini had described it not even an hour ago when he'd summoned her to the *Cella*. Two words, followed by something Superintendent Teresa Battaglia had heard him say countless times before: 'I want you and your team on this.'

Cold case. Teresa had been relieved to hear that; it meant no killer on the loose to hunt down, no potential further victims to save, no immediate threat. Only the echo of something that had happened long ago and somehow resurfaced today.

She could handle it. She was not going to lose control of this case and even if she did, there would be no harm done – except perhaps to her ego.

You're a fool if you think they won't notice what's happening to you.

What was happening to her had a name so powerful it could crush her, but Teresa had not retreated from the word on her medical record, had not stepped aside and let it take over her world. Instead, she had locked it away where all our most terrible fears like to settle: in the depths of her soul – and in the diary she always carried with her. Her paper memory.

Massimo Marini was another problem in an already complicated situation. He kept looking at her as if he suspected something, as if he had access to her very thoughts. She found it difficult to keep him at arm's length; in fact, his closeness had started to feel normal, almost welcome, and she had begun to worry that this urge to seek each other out might become a dangerous habit for them both.

Prosecutor Gardini emerged from a room that had been cordoned off. He looked anxious, as always. A lanky man with permanently dishevelled hair and scruffy tie – as if he'd just been swept over by a gust of wind – Gardini was an accomplished magistrate who worked himself to the bone, his appearance symptomatic of the unrelenting rhythm of his life.

He was accompanied by a noticeably tanned man of rather eccentric appearance. His brown hair had been lightened by the sun along the sides of his head, leading Teresa to deduce that his tan, too, must be natural, the kind people who practised outdoor sports tended to get. There was a certain elegance about him, a refinement reflected in the clothes he wore, classic cuts in vibrant colours: flamboyant yet entirely tasteful.

Teresa leafed through the most recent notes in her diary but found no description of the man. Her memory was not failing her: they had never met before. But she did have an idea of who he might be.

Gardini walked towards her, holding his arm out for a hand-shake. They had been friends for many years, but work was work and they had to act in accordance with their respective positions.

'Thank you for coming, Superintendent. I'm sorry to have troubled you at the end of your shift,' he said, addressing her in unusually formal fashion. 'This is Gianmaria Gortan, the owner of this gallery. Mr Gortan, this is Superintendent Battaglia. I intend to put her in charge of the investigation.'

Teresa smiled briefly.

'This is Inspector Marini, my right hand man,' she said.

They all shook hands. Teresa noticed that the art dealer's palm was clammy. A hint of unease that clashed with the polished image he projected.

'It was Mr Gortan who called us in,' Gardini was saying. 'We have a rather unusual case here.'

He hadn't given her any kind of hint, but Teresa had spent the past few minutes watching the forensics team in the art gallery going in and out of the room she hadn't yet seen. A camera attached to a photodetector was clicking incessantly, its powerful flash piercing the dim light. If this was a cold case, then something wasn't quite right. The volume of resources and personnel that had been deployed did not square with what she'd expected to find: no one really cared about deaths that happened a long time ago. After the blood dries up, Justice is never in any rush to strike her sword: the scales of her balance remain suspended, and her blindfold falls just loose enough for her to look around and find fresher tragedies to set her hounds on.

'Did someone die in there?' asked Marini.

'Not recently.' Gardini sighed. 'Come with me; I'll show you.'

The sealed room was a laboratory equipped with instruments, most of which Teresa had never seen before. A digital microscope gave off a metallic glint under the flashing cameras and she recognised some colleagues from the public prosecutor's office – Gardini's men – who were busy collecting evidence.

'We use this equipment to conduct authenticity tests,' the art dealer explained. 'For dating and valuation purposes. We have an expert who analyses the artwork brought to us on consignment, or by people who simply wish to establish the market value of a piece they've inherited – or found in the attic.'

Teresa flipped her notebook open and quickly noted down the date, time and situation, with particular emphasis on the names, physical appearance and role of those around her. Her recurring nightmare, her most pressing fear, was that she wouldn't be able to recognise people she knew. She noticed Marini trying to see what she was doing, so she turned the page and doodled something obscene for his benefit. He blushed furiously and retreated.

Teresa gave her surroundings a quick once-over. Everything seemed to be obsessively in order. As she'd expected, there weren't any mummified remains sticking out of some interstice in the wall or a hiding place under the floor.

'Are we going to need that microscope to find the body?' Marini – back to being her shadow – whispered in her ear.

She batted him away and looked questioningly at Gardini.

'Give us a minute, please,' the deputy prosecutor told the forensics team.

The activity inside the room died down as everyone except the four of them walked out. Teresa saw a pool of light that had previously been hidden from her view.

Gardini motioned at Teresa to come closer and she took a few steps forwards. She was taken aback by something in the deputy public prosecutor's expression, a kind of trepidation mixed with anticipation – the latter somewhat surprising to see, considering the circumstances. She followed his gaze.

There was a table with an unframed drawing on it, laid out over a glass surface and held flat with small metal weights at each corner. It was the portrait of a woman. It appeared to be roughly fifteen inches in height and perhaps just under that in width. The paper was thick, almost coarse in appearance.

Teresa walked up to it and when she leant over to examine it, she found she was unable to look away. She stood like that, motionless and wide-eyed with wonder.

True art needs no explanation, she thought to herself, remembering the words of an old high-school teacher. And right here was the proof. She put on her reading glasses, attached to a thin chain dangling over her chest, and looked closer.

The portrait seemed to spring up from the paper. There was a fullness, a three-dimensionality to it that was astonishing. It depicted the face of a young woman, a face of such singular grace that it caught you off guard. Her eyes were closed, her long eyelashes lowered onto her cheeks, her lips just slightly parted. She had an air of the exotic about her, but it would have been difficult to describe how. Her moonlike complexion was framed by her dark hair, falling down to her chest and fading out into the edges of the paper.

It was a magnetic, sublime beauty.

Teresa finally tore her eyes away from the face in search of other details.

On the lower right corner of the paper was a date scrawled in shaky handwriting: 20 April 1945. But there was no signature.

More than seventy years stood between that day and this moment now, when Teresa's eyes basked in the result. Almost a century – yet time was not a measure that applied to this image in any way. In fact, it seemed to have transcended time, eliminated it altogether.

Over her shoulder, Marini was barely breathing. He, too, had been ensnared by the spell the painting had cast over them all.

'Who is it?' she heard him ask. She herself had been on the verge of asking the same thing. Marini had clearly had the same feeling that had already lodged itself in Teresa's chest: the sensation of having come face to face with a living creature.

'It's the *Sleeping Nymph*,' replied the dealer, surveying the painting. 'It was believed to have been lost, but it turned up in an attic among some old paperwork. At least that's how the artist's nephew tells it. He brought it to the gallery to have it authenticated, as there's no signature. But of course it's purely a formality; there's no doubt that the artist is his great-uncle Alessio Andrian.'

Teresa had never heard that name before. She couldn't figure out why Gardini wanted her help with the preliminary investigation. What was she even meant to investigate?

'Are you thinking it might be a forgery?' she asked him.

Gardini let slip a smile. Teresa knew it didn't denote amusement but tension, which he released with a twitch of his facial muscles.

'I'm afraid it's rather more complicated than that, Superintendent. The analysis of the drawing has thrown up unexpected and somewhat . . . disturbing results. Mr Gortan will be able to explain it better than I can.'

Teresa straightened her back. The inner scaffolding of her weary body creaked with the effort.

'Disturbing?' she echoed.

'The valuation expert was analysing the paper and the colour in order to date the work,' the dealer began to explain, 'and to determine whether or not the date marked on the painting itself conforms with the parameters of the period in which it's believed to have been created. The painting was executed with charcoal and haematite chalks. The red hue comes from haematite, a ferrous substance that produces this alluring colouring.'

'Yes, I know of it.'

'Until a few decades ago, painters used pure haematite in their work, but nowadays it's mixed with natural or synthetic waxes. By testing for the presence of these waxes, it's possible to determine whether a particular piece is recent, or older. The problem is that our expert found something else. He couldn't identify what it was, so he sent some samples to a lab for further testing.'

'And what did they find?'

It was Gardini who answered, his eyes fixed on hers, the halogen lamp throwing deep, dramatic shadows on his gaunt face.

'They found blood, Superintendent.'

It took Teresa a few moments to understand what he was getting at. She had always thought him to be a practical, sensible man, but it sounded like he'd let himself get carried away a little. She caught Marini's eye: he looked as baffled as she felt.

Teresa turned her gaze back on the deputy public prosecutor. She tried to think of a tactful combination of words for what she wanted to say, but ultimately knew she'd end up with the most straightforward one, as was in her nature.

'Prosecutor Gardini,' she began, 'there are a thousand ways in which blood might have ended up on this drawing. Perhaps the artist cut himself by accident and his blood mixed with the colour. Perhaps someone had a nosebleed. Usually, the simplest explanation is also the one that's closest to the truth.'

Gardini stayed silent, but the way he looked at her was already an answer of sorts. Teresa removed her reading glasses.

'Do you suspect someone was killed in order to make this painting?' she asked him, unable to conceal the note of incredulity in her voice.

Gardini remained impassive.

'It's not a suspicion. I am sure of it.'

Teresa looked at the portrait again, at that pale face caught in a seemingly endless exhalation. A last breath: perhaps the nymph's sleep was the eternal slumber of death.

'Why?'

Gardini leant sideways into the table and crossed his arms over his chest.

'It's not just "a few" drops of blood we're talking about,' he told her.

Teresa felt a numbness spreading across her face, as she did every time she knew she was about to hear a piece of bad news.

'How much?' she asked.

He picked up a file from the table and handed it to her, giving her a minute to leaf through it.

'The *Sleeping Nymph* is *made* out of blood, Superintendent,' he told her. 'The tests revealed traces of human cardiac tissue on the paper.'

Teresa finally understood, but it was Gardini who voiced what she was thinking.

'Alessio Andrian painted it by dipping his fingers in someone's heart.'

Cardiac tissue. Human cardiac tissue. Hands entering a ribcage and fingers dipping into a heart. The scene forming in Teresa's mind was a cameo of folly.

'Mr Gortan,' she said, turning to the art dealer. 'Are you reasonably certain that the author of the painting is Alessio Andrian?'

'I conducted further tests myself to verify the findings and I can confirm, without a shadow of a doubt, that it's authentic.'

'And how have you arrived at this conclusion?'

Gortan's lips stretched into the kind of smile reserved to the uninitiated of an art so noble that ignorance of its rules was inadmissible, to be tolerated purely out of politeness. This man, Teresa realised, considered himself nothing less than the high priest of an elite cult, and conducted himself as such. She had been wrong to think of him as a merchant.

'What makes me so sure of the attribution of the work?' Gortan retorted. 'Every single detail. The choice of paper, the colour, the handwriting for the date, but most of all the quality of the line: the pressure, the angles,' he explained, gesturing gracefully with his hands and spreading wafts of delicate perfume in the process. 'It's the overall quality of the composition, what I would call "the artist's hand". That is his true signature. It's unmistakable. This painting is Alessio Andrian's *Sleeping Nymph*.'

He certainly had no doubts. His face was flushed with genuine enthusiasm.

'I must admit I don't know the artist, nor had I ever heard of the *Sleeping Nymph* until today,' Teresa conceded.

The art dealer's clean-shaven face quivered with the passing shadow of a grimace so fleeting that Teresa wondered if she'd imagined it.

'That doesn't surprise me,' said Gortan. 'Andrian isn't a painter for the masses but for a small and, if you'll forgive me for saying it, rather *select* circle of connoisseurs. But all those who've had the rare privilege of seeing his work have remarked on its extraordinary artistic essence.'

Teresa was intrigued. Who exactly was this man? Who was Alessio Andrian?

'What do you mean by "rare privilege"?' she asked.

There was a gleam in Gortan's eyes now, something seductive in his manner – the manner of a man who knows he is the custodian of a remarkable story.

'Andrian stopped painting in 1945, Superintendent. He was only twenty-three. His works are numbered one to ten,' he explained. 'The portrait of the *Sleeping Nymph* is believed to be his last, number eleven.'

Teresa noticed that he referred to the woman in the painting as if she had really existed.

'Did he use a model to paint her?' she asked.

Gortan shook his head.

'Nobody knows.'

'Maybe he stopped painting because of what happened when he finished it,' Gardini suggested.

'I suppose you'll find that out for us, won't you?' the dealer replied.

Teresa opened her notebook.

'What's it worth?' she asked.

'Before the blood was detected, I would have said three hundred to three hundred and fifty thousand euros. But now . . . who knows? Maybe even twice as much.'

'Are you saying that this kind of morbid detail can cause an exponential increase in the value of a painting?' Marini inquired.

Gortan gave him a look of disdain, which irritated Teresa.

'No, Inspector. What I am saying is that the value of a painting, and indeed of any work of art, is linked inextricably with its history, the human element that comes with it. Alessio Andrian's story is undeniably unique and this latest piece of the puzzle can only add to the fascination.'

Teresa stopped writing.

'What story?' she asked.

'Andrian's nephew is currently abroad on a business trip but will return tonight,' Gardini interrupted. 'We're meeting him tomorrow for an informal interview. There's no one better placed than him to tell us the story.'

'Given the circumstances, I'd rather find out now,' Teresa persisted.

'Andrian was a *partigiano*, a freedom fighter during the war,'

Gortan interceded. 'He made his paintings while hiding in the mountains, in between German raids. When the war ended, his comrades couldn't find him. They thought he was dead.'

'But?' Teresa prompted.

'But he'd actually ended up in Yugoslavia. A family from Bovec sent word out to the Italians across the border that they'd found another Italian in the woods behind their home. The man was in such terrible shape that at first Tito's militias thought he was dead. It was Andrian. It had been two weeks since he'd disappeared. No one ever found out what he did during that time.'

'They didn't ask him?'

'Andrian never came to his senses to tell the story.'

'So he died?'

'No, but he went mad. And he never painted again. He never spoke again. *Ever.*'

Gortan fell silent.

'He took the secret to his grave,' Marini mused.

'Not quite,' said the prosecutor, catching Teresa's eye. 'Andrian is still alive, but he's been living in a vegetative state for almost seventy years now.'

He paused for a moment as if to give them time to prepare for what was to come.

'He isn't ill, he never has been. But he's chosen not to walk. He's chosen not to speak. For seventy years. Whatever happened to him after he painted the *Sleeping Nymph*, he chose to die a living death. He's a breathing corpse.'

3

The child hid in the woods, his chest heaving with every breath. He could still see past the edge of the forest from where he was, all the way to the meadow dotted with daisies and dandelions.

Every now and then their colours were veiled by a swift-moving shadow, but the frothy clouds were always quick to disperse.

He turned his back on the light and ventured further into the scented forest. The shouting grew more distant behind him.

The forest was silent in its welcome, a silence that slowed his steps. It was like walking into a church: the same chilly gloom, the towering vaults, the pungent smell of the resins leaking from the tree barks like wax from votive candles.

He shivered, the T-shirt under his sweatshirt soaked with perspiration. He found a recess among the roots and branches, a safe hiding place where he could shelter, and crawled inside. He rested his chin on his knees and prepared himself for a long wait.

He could hear them calling his name. His instincts urged him to respond to their calls and put an end to the cruel joke he was playing on them, but something else kept him firmly ensconced in his den: a furious sort of love.

His parents' cries echoed each other like the verses of a fearful song, interleaved with moments when the *stranger*'s voice rose above the others. He listened more closely whenever that happened and tried to interpret her tone: would he hear the indifference she'd recently reserved for him, or had his sudden disappearance reawakened her affection?

The stranger: his sister. When she'd started to change, to grow up, something between them had snapped and now she was the target of his resentment. He wanted to make her afraid of losing him. He wanted her to love him again as she used to do.

So he had decided to vanish.

He drew back deeper into his hiding place. He tore out a fern and began picking at it compulsively. He realised when he sniffed that he'd been crying again.

A churning in the fronds above his head startled him. He dried his eyes. Something was moving up there, in the depths of the emerald dome of the forest, twitching and then falling still again.

He let out a whimper when he remembered what he'd told his sister that same morning.

It's not true that vipers have their babies up in trees, he said to himself. That was a lie you made up to scare her.

He sat completely still.

But was he really sure of it? *Vipers have their babies up on tree branches so they can drop them into the world without being bitten.*

He felt something slither into his collar and scrambled to his feet with a yelp, tearing his sweatshirt off and breaking into a run.

He wanted to go back home now, back to safety. He didn't care any more about his wounded pride, his betrayed affections. He wanted his mum's kisses and his father's laugh. Even the stranger no longer seemed so hostile, so unpleasant.

But the shoots and brambles kept snatching at him and no matter how he struggled, he couldn't cut through them. They gripped his arms and curled around his legs. The forest wanted to imprison him in the wet breath of its darkness. He could feel that breath on him now.

His eyes sought out the light of the meadow, but all he could see was blackness. The trees seemed more crooked and imposing, the undergrowth more tangled.

He knew he was lost. The cold enveloped him. He realised he was only wearing a T-shirt now. His arms were ravaged with scratches, gashes on his skin from the thorns. His face was also smarting, as it would do after a day spent in the summer sun.

'Mummy,' he called out as softly as he could, so as not to wake the living creature around him.

The forest responded with a soft scrabbling sound that he hadn't noticed before.

It was moving all around him. He couldn't see it. But he could sense it.

The forest was breathing, throbbing like a single, powerful black heart, a resonant subterranean beat, to which his own heart responded by beating faster and faster.

He clenched his fists and felt pain flare up like a flame. He lifted a hand and saw a deep cut across his palm. He watched, mesmerised, as his blood dripped into the black earth.

A butterfly the same colour as the wolf's bane his mother had picked that morning came to perch on his wound. Resting on his warm flesh, it flapped its wings lazily. When he reached out to touch it, it evaded him but stayed nearby, dancing in the air. The boy decided to follow it. He hoped it would lead him to the light.

He got to where the trees started to thin out, where the sun filtered through to the undergrowth in blinding shards of light, and he was reminded of the illustrations in a book of fairy tales he used to read: Hansel and Gretel and the witch who wanted to eat them.

The butterfly came to rest on flakes of wood that time had torn away from their barks. The boy knelt and stretched a finger out to pick the butterfly up, then suddenly drew back. Those weren't flakes of wood. They were bones. Bones sticking out of the earth. Half of a skeletal hand reaching out of the soil, through moss and wild flowers.

The boy screamed and began to run, unable to shake off the image of the flailing butterfly trapped in the web of what had once been human fingers.

He was sure that he would be stuck in the forest for ever, enmeshed in its malevolent web like that butterfly, when he heard a voice calling for him. He looked up. There was a slope in the distance where the light shone a little brighter and there, he saw the gradually emerging silhouette of a familiar figure.

He responded with a desperate cry. His sister rushed to his side, her hair dishevelled, her jeans stained with mud up to her knees. She'd been crying. She fell to the ground in front of him and hugged him tighter than she had in a long time, like she used to do before they began to grow apart. The boy burst into sobs. He opened his mouth as if to rid himself of the terror he felt, but no sound came out. He turned to look back at where he'd come from, but now every part of the forest looked the same again, as if it had folded itself up.

He would never be able to find the ghost hand again. He

pressed his lips shut: nobody would believe him. He let himself be picked up and led towards the light.

He cried one final tear, for the butterfly.

Had he known that he was being watched, he would have cried for his own sake, for the silent death he had barely escaped.

For the *Tikô Wariö* can feel no pity, not even for the helpless. It must keep guard.

4

Massimo decided he wouldn't go straight back home. He wanted to go for a walk first, let himself be numbed, for once, by the city's vitality. The streets were all lit up, the chatter from the bars an enticement to stop for a glass of something cheering. The arcades around Piazza delle Erbe were swarming with the kinds of people Massimo himself had so recently belonged with. Young men in their thirties; he watched them teasing, flirting, holding in one hand a half-empty glass and in the other a cigarette – or perhaps a woman's hand. Their world was light years away from his.

He walked around aimlessly, looking at glittering shop windows without really seeing what was on display. He searched for a reflection of his own image: he saw that he had changed and he wasn't pleased with the result. He wasn't himself: he was walking when he would have liked to run; he was silent when he would have liked to scream; he was there yet far away at the same time. He kept running away and yet he ended up back where he'd started every time.

You're a coward, he thought, though he'd forgiven himself long ago for that particular flaw. He certainly had worse ones to worry about.

He fished his mobile phone out of his pocket and switched it back on, a sinking feeling in his stomach as he waited for the notifications that flashed up on his screen in quick succession.

She'd called him again. Elena never sent him any messages; she wasn't content to consign her scorn to a few lines of text on a screen. She wanted to shove her words through the phone until they exploded in his ears. She wanted the sound of her voice to strike at his heart again and again.

He was briefly tempted to linger amid the crowds and feign happiness, but then decided to veer into the silence of the quieter side streets. He turned a corner and almost crashed into a couple kissing beneath a street lamp. The woman laughed while the man pulled her closer.

Massimo felt a pang of bitterness and looked away. He used to be like that with Elena, back in a time he could no longer even remember – even though he knew on a rational level that it had only been a year, not a decade.

They had been just like that, unable to keep their hands off each other.

And then he'd left her without even offering an explanation, because that would have meant having to explain it to himself, too, when all he'd wanted was silence. She had told him she loved him and he had left her. He hadn't seen her or spoken to her again until a few weeks ago: a few hours during which he'd made love to her again, then left.

He found himself standing outside his building without quite knowing how he'd got there. He ignored the lift and made for the stairs. He didn't even have a case to work on to distract him from thoughts of her; he couldn't help but feel that it was perhaps too optimistic to think the mystery of the *Sleeping Nymph* could be solved seventy years after the fact.

He climbed up to the landing outside his flat, but stopped at the last step.

There was a woman waiting for him, sitting on a suitcase with her eyes closed and her back leaning against the door. She looked exhausted, but also like she was steeling herself for a fight. She was thinner than he remembered, even though it had only been a few weeks since the last time he'd seen her, a short span of time that seemed nevertheless to have consumed her, as if the very act of breathing had torn her slowly apart.

It has nothing to do with time.

'Elena . . . ?' he called out.

His voice came out choked, little more than a stutter, but her eyes snapped open, quick as a trap. They looked at each other without saying a word, their bodies taut and weighed down with awkwardness. Elena rose to her feet with a sigh that could have meant anything: tiredness, irritation, relief. Regret.

Massimo swallowed painfully. There were no words that could rescue him now.

'I don't know what to say,' he murmured. 'I . . . '

Elena walked up to him. Massimo thought she was going to slap him, but she just sank her face into the crook of his neck. It was like an electric shock to the senses, a wave of feeling crashing into his skin.

Massimo opened his mouth, but she covered it with her cold, trembling fingers.

'I don't know how to tell you, either, so I'm just going to say it,' she whispered. 'I'm pregnant.'

5

20 April 1945

Whatever happened that day, the mystery has been left undisturbed for more than seventy years.

Reminder: check newspapers from that era.

Tomorrow, 8.30 a.m.: meeting at the district attorney's office with

Raffaello Andrian, the painter's great-nephew.

Girl with dog standing at the corner of the gallery and the square. Blue hair. Strange feeling. Have I seen her before?

Marini: he's got a secret eating away at him.

Teresa closed her diary, her head resting against the window of the office she shared with Marini. She had watched him walk away until she'd lost sight of him in the darkness.

He's running away from something. The kid had settled into a new life, but something was stalking him. Even his body had changed over the past few weeks: it was leaner, more strained, more alert. Restless. They had something in common, Marini and her: they both had secrets to keep.

She pushed the arms of her glasses between her lips and stared out into the night, pierced here and there by street lamps and headlights. She couldn't tear her eyes away from the darkness.

She rubbed at her cheek absent-mindedly and the bangle on her wrist tinkled. It was a simple silver band with an inscription: *Your name is Teresa Battaglia.*

Her doctor's mobile phone number followed – not a husband's, nor a son's, nor a relative's. It was a message she had left for herself, she who had never needed anyone to rescue her.

She drew the curtains over the darkness outside and it was like shaking off a torpor that had weighed on her body and her mind.

Her work desk consisted of a polished surface with a computer screen and a keyboard. Over the past few months, it had changed with her, adapting itself to a world in which Teresa had had no choice but to reshape herself into a more methodical, more reflective, perhaps even a more disciplined form.

She sat down and placed her diary on the desk. She retrieved the key to the filing cabinet from under her keyboard, opened one of the drawers and looked inside.

It was like setting a box of fireflies free, dozens of numbered Post-it notes like colourful wings that fluttered to the touch and carried useful information. Yellow for work-related notes:

what her job was, how to switch a computer on, how to turn it off, how to use the telephone, how to call a taxi, the name of the person she shared an office with . . . Green for her personal life and the necessary rituals of diabetes. The message on note number one was a troubling reminder: check your bracelet.

These were her clues through a daily path that might at any moment turn unfamiliar and impenetrable.

The last few lights on the floors above were being switched off. She could hear her colleagues making their way down the stairs, their voices a distant hum moving further and further out of reach, like her dreams. She was going to miss this place.

She took a deep breath and tried to concentrate on the Alessio Andrian case and the portrait painted in blood. She was going to meet the artist's great-nephew the next day and perhaps she'd find out a few more details about the story that had brought the *Sleeping Nymph* all the way to her.

A new case was waiting to be solved, and more lies were waiting to be told. Hiding her condition meant deceiving everyone: her team, who believed in her infallibility as an article of faith; Gardini and the district attorney, who insisted on assigning all the most complex cases to her. The victims. The families of the victims.

She had to put an end to this farce before it was too late, before the illness eating away at her memory drove a wedge between her and all that she loved. Teresa had made her mind up weeks ago, but something kept holding her back. Even earlier that day she'd hesitated at the district attorney's door, until he had flung it open as if he'd expected to find her there.

'I have a case for you,' he'd said.

And so the enigma of the *Sleeping Nymph* had arrived to put off the inevitable, the only clue to a crime no one even knew where to place. As for when it had happened, the hypothesis was fairly simple: 20 April 1945, just a few days before the end of the war.

All Teresa had to work from was a beautiful and morbid portrait,

26

some unidentified blood that was bound to lead nowhere, and an old man of unsound mind who had once been a partisan and had perhaps killed someone during the war. Maybe the victim was an enemy combatant whose corpse Andrian had torn apart in the throes of madness.

He dipped his hands into the dead man's heart to draw the girl, she thought to herself. *Blood is a powerful symbol. It is life that flows through us, warm, healing, transformative.*

Despite the violence inherent in the act, Teresa couldn't see any kind of homicidal fury in it. Instead, she thought she glimpsed a more visceral urge, a passion pushed over the edge and into the arms of insanity.

She knew why Gardini had tasked her with leading the initial investigation: he trusted her instincts.

'You have an elective affinity with the dead,' he'd told her one day.

The dead always had a lot to say about the final moments of their lives, but this time there were no glassy eyes in which Teresa could search for the shadow of the killer. There were no hands that had tried to resist, to mount a last-ditch defence, tearing pieces off their aggressor in the process. The blood-soaked nymph rested in a slumber no one could ever wake her from, and her secret slept with her.

Teresa opened her diary again and leafed through it in what had now become an essential evening ritual. She scanned her own mind to work out if and when she'd lost her way.

She came across the riddle she'd been working on, though she hadn't had much time to think about it yet. Solving riddles had become a way to get through her spells of confusion. She'd found that the exercise could bring her back to the world whenever she felt something inside her slipping away. It had started as a necessity and had since become an enjoyable habit.

The police are preparing to break into a house to arrest a criminal. The only clue they have is his name: Adamo.

When they enter the house, they find a mechanic, a firefighter, a doctor and a plumber all playing cards.

Without a moment's hesitation, they arrest the mechanic.

Why?

The notebook slipped through her fingers and rustled to the floor. Teresa crouched down and stretched her hand out to retrieve it from beneath her chair.

As she straightened up, grabbing the edge of the desk for support, the notebook fell open on a page she'd filled in a few days ago. The note on the page, written in her wispy handwriting, rooted her to her chair.

Girl with blue hair and an ugly dog standing at the bus stop outside the district attorney's office. I have a feeling I've seen her before, but she left very quickly. She looked nervous.

Teresa didn't remember seeing her, nor making a note of it, but for once it wasn't this little black hole of forgetfulness that bothered her.

It was the girl with the blue hair again. Teresa had run into her at least three times now, and always in a different place.

Just a coincidence, she told herself. Or maybe someone out there had begun to follow her.

6

The forest was finally at peace. The family had left, taking that overly curious boy with them. The child was a troubled creature with a heart full of anger who had laid eyes on something he should never have seen. And yet, surprisingly, he had kept quiet about it.

It had been a long wait. The strangers had lingered until sunset, too close, too reckless. They hadn't noticed that someone was watching them.

The sun had sunk behind the purplish ring of the mountain peaks and twilight unfurled into the darkness like a nocturnal flower. Already, the light from Venus shone in the west: its name was both Lucifer – the morning star – and Vesper – the star of the evening. It appeared at this time of year in a delta of cobalt blue between two peaks.

The villages in the valley lay sleepily under its diaphanous light. The church tower with its roof of larch shingles and a weathervane instead of a cross reached towards the sky above the tapered trees.

Past the meadows, past the edge of the forest, footsteps rustled softly in the undergrowth, accompanied by the singing of a little owl. The footsteps followed a path invisible to the untrained eye, winding through white-flowered shrubs and clumps of wild mint. As the path began to slope, the steps turned into a light trot, all the way to the grave.

The night was fragrant and fell like a soft shroud over that scene of death. The bones, now exposed, gleamed with lunar whiteness against the black earth. Flowers with their petals folded against the night adorned the remains that had emerged from the recesses of the valley. A series of torrential spring showers had eroded the earth and brought to light the secret the forest had been keeping.

'*Skrit kej*,' a sweet voice whispered.

To keep a secret.

The watchful figure of the *Tikô Wariö* had returned to the forests of the valley, just like in the stories the elders used to tell around the hearth. 'He who keeps guard' had neither face nor body of its own; according to the legend, the great custodian, the fierce protector would take over the body of whoever invoked his help: a human in the shape of a boy, a woman, an old man.

And now, someone had called for him.

'*Tikô Wariö. Tikô Bronô. Te k skriwa kej,*' a singsong voice called out.

A pair of patient hands started digging, covering those other buried hands with darkness and quiet.

7

Teresa was standing at the window looking out at the world with the feeling that she wasn't really there – that she was actually at a different window, her eyes scanning a different courtyard, and that the light belonged to a day already gone by.

All night she'd wondered whether her suspicion that she was being followed might actually be a new side effect of the illness. Phobias, paranoia, manias: was this what the future held for her until Alzheimer's disease erased every last emotion and memory she had?

The district attorney's offices were still deserted. The corridors of the courthouse had just been mopped. The silence was punctuated by the dry ticking of a clock.

Teresa kept her eyes firmly on the courtyard within the walls of the late nineteenth-century complex. Marini was late and his phone was off; she had the feeling he wasn't going to turn up. She'd developed a sixth sense concerning anything to do with him, a protective instinct that was perhaps the prelude to a more obvious emotion. But she knew that it would do her no good to think of him that way: this was not a good time to get attached to anyone – she should be preparing instead to give everything up, say her goodbyes and disappear.

She closed her eyes for a moment, then opened them again: she was Superintendent Battaglia once more.

She had come to meet Alessio Andrian's great-nephew – perhaps the only person who could help her to unravel the ancient mystery concealed in the lines of that painting.

The day before, the deputy public prosecutor had described this as an informal interview, but Teresa knew that they were about to subject Raffaello Andrian to nothing less than a full interrogation – albeit one that the young man had no obligation to attend and in which he was in any case to be treated for the time being as a person of interest, not a suspect.

Raffaello had found a painting doused in human blood. Perhaps he had already known the gruesome truth about it and had hoped the results of Gortan's tests would allow him to sell it at a tidy profit. He might also have been eager to get rid of the evidence of a murder that had taken place seventy years ago. And probably he hadn't expected Gortan to do his job so thoroughly.

Teresa knew full well that hers were just the musings of a mind that was more accustomed to darkness than light: she hadn't even met Raffaello Andrian yet, but already she'd begun sketching out his possible characteristics, psychological profile and behavioural traits – all those things that would eventually help to make sense of the full picture. The more ineffable the detail, the more interested she was in it, for she knew that all crimes, no matter what kind, were always committed in the mind first.

She heard someone greet her and turned round in surprise. She hadn't noticed the deputy prosecutor enter.

'Good morning, Prosecutor Gardini,' she replied. She looked behind him, searching for the district attorney. 'Are you alone?'

The prosecutor nodded.

'Paolo isn't well. I just spoke to him. We'll have to manage without him.'

Teresa thought back to the email Ambrosini had sent her the night before – a few strained lines in which he had requested a 'consultation'. She had almost convinced herself that she *would* be capable of admitting the truth to him, but once again it seemed that life had decided to buy her a little more time.

They made their way to Gardini's office, where Raffaello Andrian had agreed to meet them.

'Worried about the case?' the deputy prosecutor asked Teresa.

'Of course I am. We both know we'll never solve it.'

Gardini stopped in his tracks, his arms cradling a jumbled pile of paperwork.

'You think it's a waste of time?' he asked.

Teresa decided not to hold anything back.

'I think it's beyond our capabilities. It's been seven *decades* – and I use that word deliberately. There's quite literally an epic dimension to this investigation. Any witnesses are probably dead by now. We don't even know where the murder took place . . .'

The courthouse had started to come to life and Gardini lowered his voice to a whisper.

'This is off the record, but just so you know, Judge Crespi has no intention of closing the case. He's worried the press will get a hold of it and should that happen, as is likely, the public will demand answers. He'll want to have at least an idea of what happened before he considers bringing the statute of limitations into play.'

'I've no doubt about that.'

The deputy prosecutor's expression relaxed.

'Let's take it one step at a time then, shall we?' he suggested. 'We can start with Andrian's nephew. Who knows, he might have something interesting to tell us.'

Teresa pulled her notebook out of her shoulder bag.

'And the painter?' she asked.

'Never mind about him. He's not a viable witness. I told you, he's basically in a vegetative state. I'd like you to deal with the nephew. Ask him any questions you deem necessary.'

A bemused-looking young man was sitting on a chair outside Gardini's office. He leapt to his feet when Gardini called his name.

Raffaello Andrian wasn't like Teresa had pictured him. He looked more like a schoolboy than a man; he was twenty-seven, but he looked not a day older than twenty. Teresa had been steeling herself for an encounter with a canny, pushy relative, but there was something faintly cherubic about him, blue eyes widened in a permanently bewildered expression and messy brown curls falling over his forehead.

They settled into the office, Gardini at his desk – more like a repository for old case files than an actual workspace – and Teresa next to the young man. She knew she intimidated him and that she had a home advantage; she sensed immediately the authority he had already ascribed her: she could see it every time Raffaello averted his timorous gaze from hers and glanced at the deputy prosecutor's benevolent face for reassurance. Teresa didn't think she was that fearsome. She hid a smile behind a grimace and put on her reading glasses, ready to take notes.

'As I explained on the phone, this is not an interrogation, Mr Andrian,' said Gardini. 'There are no suspects, nor is anyone currently being investigated. We just want to find out if you have any information that could help us to understand what happened.'

'I'd be glad to help, if I can,' he replied, but even the tone of his voice suggested that he doubted himself more than anything else in the world.

'At this stage of the investigation, and given that this is not an interrogation, there's no need for a lawyer to be present, but if you've changed your mind and would like to . . .'

'No, I've not changed my mind.'

'Are you his next of kin?' Teresa asked.

'Yes, my parents passed away and I'm an only child. I went back to live with my uncle four years ago.'

'You look after him?'

'Me and a carer who lives with us. My uncle needs round-the-clock care.'

Teresa looked at him over the top of her glasses.

'You refer to him as your uncle, but he's actually your great-uncle, isn't he? Your grandfather's brother,' she remarked.

'Yes . . . I'm sorry.'

'That's fine, I just wanted to clarify how exactly you are

related.' Teresa scribbled a few notes before posing her next question. 'Have you been advised that anything you say may be used against you in a court of law and that you have the right to remain silent?'

'Yes, they've told me.'

'I must also warn you that should you make any statement concerning the actions of a third party, you shall be considered a witness in relation to said actions.'

'I understand,' said Raffaello Andrian, just about breathing the words out.

Teresa looked into his eyes and repeated the point to make sure he was clear on the possible consequences.

'What that means is that whatever you say could also be used to incriminate your great-uncle. Do you understand?'

Raffaello Andrian nodded and Gardini handed him a piece of paper with the standard declaration he was supposed to make. Raffaello read out the oath, tripping over the words.

'Right, let's get started,' said Teresa. 'Just to be clear, Mr Andrian – please be honest. I can tell you from personal experience that lying about things or omitting the truth – even details that might seem inconsequential to you – never yields the desired outcome. Usually, things get complicated and they certainly never end well.'

Andrian looked at Gardini.

'I understand.'

'First question: did you know that the portrait had been painted in blood?'

'No.'

'Now that you do know, do you have any idea whom that blood might belong to?'

'No.'

'Has your great-uncle ever told you anything that would lead you to suspect him of having committed a crime, or broken the law in any way?'

At this, Raffaello Andrian finally looked at her directly. There was something akin to disbelief in his eyes as if Teresa had asked the wrong question, but his expression was also burdened with something that she interpreted as pity.

'I . . .' he began, reaching for the right words. 'I haven't once heard him speak, not once in twenty-seven years. No one has.'

'Never?'

'Never.'

A young man who makes the decision to confine his own body in wilful immobility, who vows to keep his lips from uttering a single word – and to do this *for ever*, no matter what. Until that moment, Teresa hadn't thought it could actually be possible.

A breathing corpse – that was how Gardini had described him.

'What's the name of his condition?' she asked.

'There isn't one. Our family has consulted a number of specialists over the years, but none of them has ever been able to make a diagnosis.'

'As far as you're aware, for how long has Alessio Andrian been like this?'

'Ever since 9 May 1945, when he was found in a forest just across the border. It was Yugoslavia back then, now it's Slovenia. That's what my father told me.'

'That's almost twenty days after he painted the *Sleeping Nymph*,' Teresa mused, 'and no one has any idea what he did in that interval. Tell me everything you know.'

'I know the story well. My father used to tell it to me like a fairy tale. He started the moment I learnt how to listen to stories and did it right up until just before he died. But I wouldn't know where to begin.'

'You can begin wherever you want. From the title of the painting, for example.'

'My father gave it that name. He swore he saw it in his uncle's room once, when he was little. It was during a rare spell when Uncle Alessio seemed to be aware of his surroundings. He was looking at the painting and my father thought he saw his lips moving, though no sound was coming out.

'After that, for as long as he lived, my father would tell people that he'd felt the name forming in his own mind in that moment. The memory of the *Sleeping Nymph* stayed with my father for ever. He used to say it had bewitched him. But the painting itself disappeared somewhere in the house and no one knew where to.'

'Where was it when you found it?'

'In an alcove up in the attic. I discovered it while shifting some old junk I wanted to get rid of.'

'So, Alessio Andrian must have left his room on at least one occasion, in order to store the drawing up there.'

'No one saw him do it.'

'Why do you think he hid it?'

'I don't know, but when he noticed that my father had been watching him, Uncle Alessio had some kind of terrible fit, howling and huffing like a wild animal. He clawed at anything he could get his hands on and flung it against the wall. He ransacked his own room and broke all the windows. My father was so upset that he never set foot inside that room again, or spent another moment alone with his uncle.

'The *Sleeping Nymph* has always hovered over our family history like a ghost. Yes, my father had caught a glimpse of it, but no one was actually sure it existed. Eventually, collectors became obsessed with it.'

'You weren't lying when you said you knew the story well,' Teresa pointed out.

Raffaello's face fell.

'Some families have epic stories of love and adventure to tell their children or to remember when they get together at Christmas. I guess the Andrian family has the *Nymph* and my uncle's madness,' he said.

Teresa decided to move on to a different topic.

'Alessio Andrian was a partisan,' she said.

'Yes, he was in the Garibaldi brigade.'

'Where was he deployed?'

'First, in the northernmost valleys of the Karst region and then, towards the end of the war, in the Canal del Ferro valley. His unit used to move around all the time – that's what his comrades told my grandfather and my father. They camped in the woods, came down to the villages to recover and then set off again.'

Teresa and Gardini exchanged a glance: perhaps they had an answer now to the question of *where* this had happened; though, admittedly, the area Raffaello had described was vast.

The Canal del Ferro – the 'iron canal' – was a rugged river valley flanked by steep mountain slopes that were covered in tangled scrubland or boulders and scree, and dropped to the valley floor like giant stage curtains. It was a millennial formation that owed its name to the trade in iron and other metals between the Roman Empire and the mines in Styria and Carinthia. The area was sparsely populated, just a few towns perched on the regional road that ran parallel to the motorway all the way to the border with Austria.

It was a start, Teresa thought. They could rule out the northern end of the valley and concentrate for the time being on where it began. Beyond those mountains was Slovenia and the little town of Bovec, where Alessio Andrian had been found. There were plenty of paths and mountain passes that could lead a man across, even on foot.

All the information they had gathered so far seemed to cohere, but at this point it was highly improbable that they would ever find a living witness who would still remember a partisan who was also a painter. They would have to rely on indirect testimony.

'What can you tell me about the day your great-uncle was found?' Teresa asked.

Raffaello swallowed audibly.

'A family in Bovec found him in the woods near their home,' he began. 'He was severely malnourished and burning up with fever. Tito's militias had recently patrolled the area, but when they saw him, they had assumed he was dead. This lumberjack

37

and his wife took him in and looked after him. For days he hovered between life and death, and eventually his fellow fighters came to retrieve him.'

Teresa felt the stirring of the instinct that had so often allowed her to home in on the singularities that could solve a case. It had responded like a physical sense, both to the way the young man's expression had suddenly darkened and to the heightened pitch of his voice. The air in the room had become saturated with the markers of reticence: Raffaello Andrian was telling them things he would have preferred not to share. Whatever they were, he was ashamed of them, though he had looked right into Teresa's eyes. That was his body's way of trying to conceal his embarrassment.

'Why did Tito's men think he was dead?' Teresa asked him.

She was watching the boy so closely that she would have noticed the slightest variation in the rhythm of his breathing. Gardini stood beside them like a statue.

'Because of the state he was in when they found him, I suppose. It was . . . bad.'

'So bad that he looked like he was dead, you said?'

'That's what the family was told.'

There it was again, that tremor in his voice. Like a crack.

'Like he'd been *killed*?' Teresa demanded.

Before the response, there was a pause.

Teresa was aware that memory was not a process of reproduction but of reconstruction. She knew that in order to remember, the mind reconstructs what it has been through, and in doing so, it sometimes unknowingly inserts elements that have nothing to do with reality. This can be a response not only to stress, but also to suggestion and to any preconceived notions a person may have formed about a given situation – all factors that can impair the recall process by causing the brain to step in and fill the gaps with false memories.

A memory is nothing more than a single clear moment recorded fortuitously by the mind and surrounded by many others, all out of focus.

It was a phenomenon that fascinated her now more than ever before in her life.

'So? Did he look like he'd been killed?' Teresa insisted.

The boy responded in a whisper.

'Yes. Yes, like he'd been killed.'

Teresa leant towards him.

'Let me ask you one more time: what condition was your great-uncle in when he was found?'

The boy lowered his eyes.

'I can't describe what I never saw,' he murmured, 'but I can tell you what his comrades told the family.'

'I'm listening.'

'The people of Bovec were scared of him.'

Teresa took her glasses off.

'Something about him disturbed them,' she deduced.

The boy looked up again. His eyes were wet.

'They were afraid of him. They called him "child of the devil". Naked and red all over, he appeared to them like a newborn demon.'

'He looked like he'd been fatally wounded, but he wasn't,' Teresa muttered. 'He was covered in blood, but it wasn't his own.'

'No, it wasn't.'

In the ensuing silence, Gardini let out a sigh that denoted a loosening of tension. They'd learnt more than they'd hoped for.

'My uncle is a good man,' Raffaello Andrian quickly added as if to make up for the truth he had just revealed.

Teresa would have wanted to reassure him but couldn't bring herself to lie. Even good people could make mistakes. Even good people could kill.

'One last question,' she said. 'Can you remember the names of any of your uncle's fellow fighters?'

The young man shook his head, but Teresa was satisfied.

'I think I'm done,' she told Gardini.

The deputy prosecutor nodded and turned to Andrian.

'If you were planning on selling the *Sleeping Nymph*, I'm afraid you're going to have to put it off. We'll have to confiscate it for a while.'

The young man's eyes flashed with sudden emotion.

'I'd never sell it!'

Teresa was surprised by his vehemence. Until that moment, he had been completely docile, a frightened child.

'Forgive me for asking,' she said, 'but why?'

Raffaello Andrian shot her a look that was like a challenge. It was as if he'd been injected with a fresh dose of courage.

'My uncle was holding it when he was found. For days he wouldn't let go of it, even though he was unconscious. I don't know what the significance of that drawing is for him, I don't know what it means, but one thing I'm sure of: I won't let go of it, either.'

You don't know it, but you have a feeling about what it might be, Teresa thought. *And she had a feeling, too.*

That drawing was the legacy of an enigma, a call from the past inviting them to remember. The *Sleeping Nymph* was the key to solving this mystery.

8

May 1945

The forest was weeping tears of ice, the occasional bloated raindrop filtering through the canopy and falling onto the foliage below in a succession of wet thuds. Down there, night dawned on night: for days there had been nothing but shadow.

Or perhaps, the man thought as he staggered onwards, *the darkness had come from elsewhere, dawning inside of him like a bleak sunrise.*

He had been dragging himself forwards for so long that he'd

lost track of time, one foot bare and the other wrapped in a boot, sinking into the undergrowth with every step he took. He was feverish, the shivers rising from his gut and through his body, making his teeth chatter to the tempo of a funeral march.

The dark resonated with rustles and anxious calls heralding the trespasser's arrival: the cries of fear told the story of an invasion – and he was the invader. The creatures of the forest huddled close to their young and watched him apprehensively from their hiding places. They could smell the blood of the innocent on him.

Blood, all over his hands. Blood, all over his face and clothes.

Water didn't cleanse it but only soaked it deeper into his body. He could picture the crimson drops infiltrating his pores and burrowing into his flesh.

His weary feet slowed until he came to a standstill. He had arrived at a bank of brambles that had threaded themselves into the cracks in the rock and clung onto its crow-black peak. He turned his face up to that living wall and closed his eyes. This was a good place to die. He slumped to the ground. His knees sank into the moss and he fell sideways onto the soil. Rolling onto his back, the man waited for his own last breath with a hand placed over his heart, its vigorous beat thundering against the night. For days he hadn't eaten and now he could feel his own bones under his skin. And yet that muscle inside his chest still wouldn't give up.

In his other hand he held a painting rolled up in a leather pouch, its fire burning his fingers. The *Sleeping Nymph* had come to the world on a last breath of life: a curse, or perhaps an anointment.

His breathing grew lighter, his tears mixed with the blood on his body. His weary bones would finally rest.

Then, when everything in the world seemed forever lost, when perfect silence had found its way inside him, the forest responded.

He could hear it, just as she had once described it to him.

A crackle echoed from branch to branch, scuttling up and through the tree barks. The trees creaked – the silence was broken.

It was an invisible energy, primordial sap glistening among the leaves. It pattered across the ground and slid under his body like a million tiny insects. It climbed over his fatigued limbs, entered him with an army of minuscule legs and claws that lifted him up, swept away at his exhaustion with the beating of powerful wings above his head. It pushed the end further and further away.

'No, no, no,' he wailed in defeat. 'Please let me die.'

The forest thrummed like a gust of wind, expanding and contracting like a dark womb.

He wasn't alone in there. He never had been. Something immense and unknown was breathing with him. He had been infected with its force and it wouldn't allow him to fade away.

Even as he yearned for death, the forest delivered his rebirth.

It sent him back into the world, but stripped him of his soul, and he was born again into that darkness with a scream that plunged every living thing into silence.

9

'How are you feeling?'

It was Elena who asked first. She was the stronger one. She always had been.

Just like when Massimo had left her. Twice. Just like when she'd reached out to him and got no answer, not even the slightest acknowledgement. Just like when she consciously decided that she would not forget him, that she wanted him back in her life.

How am I feeling? Massimo asked himself.

He knew the answer: *I feel distant. I feel alone.*

He knew the answer: *I can't do this. Whatever it is that you expect of me, I can't give it to you.*

'I'm fine,' he said instead. 'And you? Better?'

She nodded, cradling a cup of herbal tea. She'd done little more than moisten her lips with it, but nevertheless she held it pressed to her face, a buffer between them.

'The cramps are gone,' she said, bringing her hand to rest on her abdomen.

She was curled up on the sofa, barefoot, her hair dishevelled.

The night had passed, the sun had risen, but they had yet to exchange all but a handful of words. Instead, they had sat there in silence, stealing probing glances whenever they thought the other wasn't looking. They had lowered their eyes, then looked up again. They had opened their mouths, but no sound had come out. Occasionally, they had both stared at the wall. They hadn't managed to tell each other much and whatever they had been able to say had been grounded firmly in facts, not emotions.

Fatigue had eventually got the better of Elena and she'd begun to feel unwell. Massimo didn't know what to do, didn't even know if he was allowed to touch her.

'I just need a little bit of peace,' she told him.

That was the one thing Massimo couldn't promise her. Finally, he reached out and pulled her into an embrace, buried his face in her neck because he was too afraid to look into her eyes – and too afraid of what she might see in his. He was running away without moving a muscle.

He felt her relax into his arms and in that moment, he pitied her. She had given in so easily to him, to his brand of tyranny.

The sun edged past the closed shutters now, illuminating Elena. She looked different, though Massimo knew the change was not in her outer appearance, but inside. She was already living in the future, all of her attention focused on the child forming in her womb. While he still floundered, she accelerated forwards, ready to leap.

A burning itch coursed through his body. He tore his gaze

away from Elena's head and his eyes fell on his mobile phone perched on the armrest of the sofa.

He had forgotten all about his phone – which would have been unthinkable only the night before. A new day had begun and he hadn't shown up at work.

He picked up his phone and switched it on. A flurry of buzzing announced the arrival of dozens of notifications. They were all messages from his colleagues. The last one was from de Carli.

'Are you dead? You'd better be. At this rate she'll have your head on a spike anyway.'

He also had two messages telling him he had missed calls from Superintendent Battaglia. He checked the timestamp: they had come in half an hour ago.

The meeting at the district attorney's office.

'Shit . . .'

It had come out sounding more like a moan than a curse. Elena pulled away and shifted to the opposite end of the sofa.

'Trouble?' she asked.

Massimo grimaced.

'That's one way to put it,' he said brusquely before realising that his tone might hurt her.

He looked up to see that it had.

'I actually forgot to go to work,' he said, hoping he was still in time to make up for it. 'See the effect you have on me?'

She bit her lip.

'I wish I really were the cause of all this agitation,' she replied, 'but something tells me I'm not.'

He took her hand and helped her to her feet.

'You definitely are,' he murmured. It was the truth and admitting it made him feel better.

Elena's expression was a mixture of relief and confusion.

'But then *why*?' she asked.

Massimo needed more time, but the universe seemed to be conspiring to make sure he didn't have any.

'I need to sort this out first,' he said, 'if you're all right to spend a couple of hours on your own . . . ?'

'I'll be fine.'

'Are you sure?'

She nodded.

He went to his room to grab a change of clothes. He couldn't just call Teresa Battaglia and tell her he wasn't going to come to work that day: she'd be sure to give him hell for it and then she'd figure out he was hiding something, as she'd more or less suspected for weeks. And once she did, she wouldn't let go until she'd squeezed every last drop of the truth out of him. Massimo didn't want to lie to her, but he wasn't ready to talk to anyone about this yet, either. So he would have to see her, do some dissembling, then find a way to get back home as quickly as possible.

'Difficult case?' Elena asked.

'A little.'

She followed him into the bathroom.

'What's it about?' she asked.

'I don't think it's healthy to talk about this stuff.'

Massimo looked in the mirror and realised that he absolutely had to take a shower if he was to have any chance of tricking Superintendent Battaglia. His face bore all the traces of a sleepless night.

'Go on, tell me,' Elena insisted.

'It's about a painting.'

She seemed taken aback, perhaps by how quickly he'd replied, or perhaps because she had been expecting something else.

'That's it?'

Massimo took off his T-shirt.

'The painting is a portrait of a very beautiful woman. She's called the *Sleeping Nymph*,' he said.

Elena pursed her lips.

'How beautiful?'

'Stunning.'

She lowered her eyes.

'You are terrible. After the trouble you've got me into,' she said, glancing at her still-flat belly, 'you should only have eyes for me.'

That same burning itch from before gripped Massimo again, but he willed it away. He saw her expression and suddenly realised that he was naked.

'Stay,' he said as she made to leave, pulling her back. 'It's nothing you haven't seen before – considering the "trouble" I've got you into . . .'

He would have liked to tell her that his body was his own and he could do with it as he pleased. That his heart belonged to him alone and always would. He would have liked to, but he couldn't.

He got into the shower and the water washed away any lingering embarrassment and unease.

'Anyway, she's seventy,' he said after a moment, his face turned into the jet of water.

'Who is?'

'The portrait. So you've got nothing to worry about. The woman in it would be at least ninety by now.'

'Idiot. So what, did someone steal it? What is it that you're meant to investigate?'

Massimo hesitated. He trusted Elena, but he really did feel that talking about death wasn't healthy.

'Massimo?'

'It's painted in blood,' he said, quickly capitulating. If he hadn't, she would have kept asking anyway. He turned the water off, took the towel she handed him and scrubbed himself dry. 'We know who the painter is but not the *donor*. The judge wants to find out what happened, or at least try, before he closes the case.'

'God, that's awful. Who's the painter?'

'Some crazy old man. Apparently, he hasn't spoken a word in decades. He's shut himself away in a room in his nephew's house, living some kind of non-life.'

A shadow fell over Elena's face.

'How terribly sad,' she said. 'I wonder what happened to him.'

'That's what we're trying to find out.'

A few minutes later, Massimo was dressed and ready to leave. As he was about to step out through the door, he hesitated.

She had kept her eyes on him, her arms crossed over her lean chest, her teeth nibbling away at her lips. One of her incisors was ever so slightly chipped – the price paid for a perhaps too boisterous childhood game – and added an endearingly ordinary charm to her otherwise perfect smile. Massimo was amazed every time by how closely the honey brown of her freckles matched her irises and her hair. If he had to compare her to a physical sensation, it would be the feel of cinnamon powder: scented, golden, intangible.

She looked anxious now and like she didn't quite know what to do with herself. She probably felt more out of place than she ever had in her life.

Massimo fingered a lock of her hair and gently pulled her towards him.

'I'll be back as soon as I can and then we'll talk. We'll really talk,' he said, forcing his mouth into a smile. 'You stay here and unpack your things.'

'Are you sure I can stay?'

'You must.'

Her mouth tensed, too – not in an expression of happiness, but with the strain of yet another reconciliation. He saw her wavering as she waited for something that didn't arrive.

She's making compromises again, Massimo thought. *When will you decide you've had enough?*

'If you need anything, call me,' he told her. 'If you don't feel well, call me straight away.'

'All right.'

As he closed the door behind him, he watched her wave goodbye.

His phone vibrated in his breast pocket, pulling his mind back to practical matters. De Carli's name popped up on the screen: Superintendent Battaglia, he said, was meeting the coroner assigned to the case.

'Parri's found something. Battaglia is heading over to meet him. Guess whose name she's cursing to high heaven? That's right: yours! Hurry up, unless you want to end up on the autopsy table, too.'

I O

The Institute of Forensic Sciences, situated on the basement floor of Block 9 of the public hospital, was known as the morgue. For Antonio Parri, who ran it, it was much more than that.

Parri had turned the detritus of death into a vocation and that place, which most people found so oppressive, benefited from the compassionate (though often misunderstood) cheer of his presence. In his eyes, the rigid bodies shut inside the morgue's cold chambers were but manifestations of life in another form and harbingers of secret messages that he was capable of deciphering.

Teresa found Parri in his laboratory. He had his hands on his hips and was leaning over a table. On the laminate tabletop lay the *Sleeping Nymph*, lit up by a desk lamp. Antonio wasn't examining her: he was admiring her, his face rapt as if he were looking at a real woman of flesh and bone. Teresa couldn't blame him. It was hard to remain unaffected by the *Sleeping Nymph*. The brutality and mystery of her origins imbued her with a pleasantly arcane appeal. The painter's hand had been kind, infused the curves of her face with soft and gentle texture, but there was also a subtle passion running through his work, flowing down her countenance all the way to her pristine neck and the hollow of her throat. You could sense the desire throbbing beneath the surface of that stillness. It was as if the palm of Alessio Andrian's hand had claimed her skin. He had captured on paper a moment of ecstasy, of eternal release. The artist's gaze was a lover's.

Teresa cleared her throat. Antonio gathered himself, pulled his glasses down his nose and smiled.

'Come in, come in,' he welcomed her.

Parri was a small and rather skinny man. As far as Teresa knew, he always wore the same clothes: jeans, a button-up shirt and a light oversized jumper. The colours and the thickness of the fabric might change, but that was his uniform, to which he added an unbuttoned lab coat when he was working.

His eyes were such a pale blue that under the light, their colour seemed to drain into the whiteness of the cornea. His pupils were two black dots in the midst of that icy pallor and were always fixed on his interlocutor. He was a few years older than Teresa, yet he had the air of a young man. Not even his mop of straight white hair could do anything to dispel that illusion and the unruly lock that kept falling over his forehead added a touch of mischief to his appearance.

'What do you think?' she asked, walking towards him.

'She's extraordinary.'

Teresa laughed. 'Do you mean the painting or the girl?'

'Both. Surely you see it, too.'

Superintendent Battaglia stood behind him, peering over his shoulder. They were quiet for a time.

'It's just a painting,' she finally said. 'Nothing more than a few lines and some colour. And yet . . .'

'And yet it makes us feel something.'

'When did you get so emotional about evidence?' she teased him.

Antonio turned to look at her, his arms crossed over his chest.

'What if I told you it's a lot more than that?'

Teresa felt one of her eyebrows shoot up.

'Meaning?'

A polite knock on the open door interrupted their exchange.

Teresa turned round to find a worried gaze that could barely hold hers.

'Ah, Inspector Marini,' she said. 'I'd just about given up on seeing you come in today.'

'Please forgive the delay, Superintendent.'

Marini walked in, greeting Parri with a nod. His demeanour was that of a man who knows he has no excuse. Teresa had been so worried that she could have smacked him out of sheer relief.

She took a closer look at him. Even his golden tan and crisp blue shirt couldn't conceal the evidence of a sleepless night, and it obviously hadn't been some kind of amorous encounter that had kept him awake. She could tell by the lost look on his face. Massimo was afraid.

'I called you. Twice,' she snapped.

'There was a problem I had to deal with.'

'Just the one? If you go on like this, you won't have a problem, you'll *be* the problem.'

'I . . .'

'Not now, Marini.' Teresa cut him off, turning towards Parri again. 'Doctor Parri has some information he was about to share.'

The coroner looked at each of them in turn – first Teresa, then the inspector, then back to Teresa again.

'You two make a cute couple,' he chuckled.

'Go on, Antonio.'

'We've just had the results back from our initial tests on the *Nymph*. The blood doesn't match Andrian's. I know you already suspected as much, but now you can be sure. Basically, I compared the results with those his nephew provided from a recent medical check-up. All very unexciting, really, but anyway, it turns out it's two different blood types.'

She nodded.

'I'm not surprised, but it's important to have it confirmed,' she said.

'The DNA testing will take longer, but there's something I can tell you unofficially.'

The note of satisfaction in his tone told Teresa that the information would be fundamental to their investigations.

'The blood belonged to a woman.'

Teresa's eyes shifted away from the coroner's face and back to the painting.

'I think this is more than just a painting,' she heard Parri say. 'I think it's a portrait of the victim. The *Sleeping Nymph* was real and she died on 20 April 1945.'

'A compelling theory, but not one based on any facts,' Teresa muttered.

She looked into Marini's eyes: he, too, was thinking that the *Sleeping Nymph* must have really existed.

'It may be just a theory, but you wouldn't dismiss it, would you?' asked Parri.

Teresa took a deep breath.

'This changes everything,' she said.

It changed the direction of their inquiry, gave it new force, and it changed Teresa's approach to the case. Now, she had the victim's face in front of her. She could hear her last breath. She could see her in her last moments as the life ebbed out of her.

He struck her and then he painted her as she lay dying. He steeped his fingers in her heart.

She slipped on a latex glove and ran a finger over the *Nymph*, feeling a shiver along the back of her own neck.

The nymph's eyes were closed, but Teresa knew what she would have seen in them if they had been open: the heavy shadow of death over life. And she knew what those lips would have whispered to her, if paper could have turned into flesh.

Help me.

Teresa would help her.

Find me.

Teresa would find her.

She felt Marini approach from behind her.

'A wartime murder,' she remarked. 'She probably disappeared one day and the body was never found, or if it was found, her fate was blamed on some soldier. It's unlikely anyone would have reported her disappearance. All people thought about back then was how to survive and hide from the Germans.'

'Yes, I don't think it's likely we'll find any traces of old police paperwork on a case that was never opened in the first place,' he concurred. 'And even if they existed, they'd be in a museum by now. We could try looking in the newspapers from around that time.'

Teresa covered the painting with a protective sleeve and removed the glove.

'I did wonder about that,' she replied, 'but we're talking about a sparsely populated mountainous district, not a city. The Nazis were furious about the way the war was going and preparing for a bloody retreat. They were shooting at people's homes, aiming for shadows at the windows. I can't see how any journalist would have bothered writing about this. People disappeared and died every day.'

'Then why do you think Judge Crespi wants to clear this up?' Parri asked.

'Because the main suspect is still alive and a renowned painter. Because he went mad after painting a portrait out of the blood of an unknown victim – and as it happens, that portrait is his best work and his most sought-after. The press will have a field day when they find out. Crespi couldn't shelve this even if he wanted to.'

'I did wonder if that might be the case when I heard that the deputy public prosecutor had summoned you – as if it were an urgent case.'

Teresa wiped the lenses of her glasses with the hem of her T-shirt.

'You know Gardini puts a lot of stock on my instincts,' she said. 'Whenever he has a case on his hands that seems to be going nowhere, he can't think of anyone else to call.'

In truth, 'instinct' wasn't what the deputy public prosecutor called it in his private conversations with Teresa. What Gardini counted on was a kind of mysterious empathy she possessed. The dead thrummed inside Teresa's mind. They were her companions on sleepless nights. They pushed her to keep going, to find the solution to their end.

'I need to speak to the district attorney,' she told Marini. 'Now.'

'You didn't hear?' Parri exclaimed.

The look on his face sent a shiver through her.

'Paolo had a heart attack, Teresa. He was hospitalised this morning.'

I I

Teresa had exhausted every flyer and bulletin board in the waiting room of the cardiology ward. She couldn't remember a word of what she'd read, but that was the least of her worries right now.

Paolo Ambrosini wasn't just her superior in rank. He was a friend she'd almost lost, a friend who perhaps she hadn't watched over as well as she should have. She felt guilty for underestimating his illness earlier: Paolo wasn't the kind to miss an appointment without good reason. *But* – she thought contritely – *she had been so absorbed in her own problems that she hadn't even thought about it.*

By sheer luck, Ambrosini had pulled through and had already been transferred out of the intensive care unit.

'Coffee?' Marini asked.

'No.'

'Water?'

'*No.*'

'My scalp?'

Teresa finally looked at him.

'Why don't you just go away?' she demanded.

'I'm surprised. Normally you would have said "just fuck off".'

Teresa cursed him under her breath and rifled through her shoulder bag in search of a sweet. All she found were dozens of empty wrappers. She swore again.

Marini sat next to her, crossed his legs and produced a packet of fruit gums from his pocket. He waved it under her nose, but when Teresa tried to grab it, he pulled his hand away.

She closed her eyes.

'For God's sake, what do you want?' she asked.

'Your forgiveness.'

'Are you serious? I'm not your mother. How many times do I have to tell you that?'

'You didn't even ask me why I was late.'

'Marini, I haven't cared to know a thing about you since your first day.'

'Bullshit. You're always breathing down my neck.'

She stood up and grabbed the sweets off him when he wasn't looking.

'So, aren't you going to ask?' he persisted.

'Why would I do that? To put you in a position where you have to lie to your superior?'

He stayed quiet. Teresa opened the packet and popped a sweet in her mouth.

'There's something eating away at you, Inspector,' she said as she chewed on the sweet. 'It has been for weeks. It's making you nervous and evasive, making you check your phone a little too often when you're at work.'

'I've never neglected my job.'

'Except for this morning . . . I think it must be something from your past, something unresolved. It's the same thing that made you run away and hide out here, but whether you like it or not, it's always there in the background.'

Marini didn't attempt a riposte.

'So, Inspector,' Teresa goaded him, 'are you still so sure you want to talk about it?'

He leapt to his feet.

'Why don't we talk about you, Superintendent?' he snapped.

'Me?'

'Yes, you and the totally unprofessional way in which you run this entire team, as if you owned each and every one of us. Or maybe we should talk about *your* secret – or did you think I wouldn't notice?'

Teresa couldn't believe the audacity.

'And the diary? Let's talk about your compulsive note-taking in that goddamned diary. What the hell do you write in it?'

Teresa allowed him to vent. He was so tense and so furious that he looked like he was about to cry. When he fell quiet, she spoke again, calmly.

'I write about how stupid you are, Marini.'

A nurse drew their attention with a small cough.

'The patient is waiting for you, ma'am,' she said.

Teresa studied her friend as he lay on the hospital bed, his chest dotted with an array of medical sensors. He looked ashen and shrivelled. Like an old man inside a hospital gown.

She sat next to the bed and reached for his hand. He squeezed it back immediately.

'Teresa, thank God you're here. I need to talk to you . . .'

'Where else would I be? Though you could have warned me you were planning on croaking. You know I can't run very fast.'

'It's only a small thing, but these people say they want me to do months of rehab. *Months*! Can you imagine?'

'And you'll do it. Everything else can wait.'

He motioned at her to lean towards him.

'There was something I'd been meaning to tell you today,' he said. 'There's a new asset. You must meet them this afternoon. It's important.'

'An asset? What, a new agent?'

'No . . .'

'Some kind of consultant?'

'Not quite . . .'

'Paolo, I don't understand.'

'Well, it's not exactly by the book. Gardini knows; he'll fill you in.'

Teresa desisted. 'As long as it's not by the book, you can count me in,' she joked.

Ambrosini's hand pressed hers harder.

'There's something else. They've appointed my stand-in.'

She nodded.

'Santi,' she said, referring to the deputy district attorney.

'No. It's someone else.'

The way he said it, the worry in his eyes – it was alarming. And in a way, perhaps she had always known this day would come; perhaps she had been waiting for that return all her life. She felt the skin on her face tighten over her bones, her body drawing in, ready to flee.

'Who is it?' she breathed.

'I'm sorry, Teresa. It's Albert.'

12

Albert Lona.

Two words that Teresa hadn't uttered, not even inside her mind, in what felt like a lifetime.

She strode through the bowels of the hospital, feeling nauseous. She was just about conscious of Marini's presence behind her and though she would have liked to dismiss him for the day, or give him some other task to do – anything to avoid that inquisitive look of his – she might as well come to terms with the truth: she felt safer with him beside her.

She couldn't drive any more unless she was prepared to risk getting caught by a spell of confusion and causing chaos. Even navigating the city by public transport could be dangerous if she was alone and she blacked out – not only for her, but for others, too. She hated this. She hated being dependent on other people.

And now Albert was back in her life.

The nausea almost made her retch. Teresa stopped walking and took a deep breath, but the air inside the ward, saturated with disinfectant, didn't do her much good. She felt her head spin, a flash of vertigo rising through her legs.

'Superintendent . . . ?'

Marini's voice seemed distant.

Teresa closed her eyes. She opened them again.

The corridors all looked the same. She had no idea which way to turn, nor which way she'd come from. She couldn't even remember where she had wanted to go.

Slowly she spun on her axis as if she were seeing the world around her for the first time.

'Superintendent!'

Teresa lifted her arm and saw that her hand was shaking. Her silver bangle glittered on her wrist, a reminder of her name. Yes, she remembered her name. It was everything else that had lost meaning and all this while terrifyingly vivid images from her past battered her like physical blows. Beneath her thin shirt, the scar on her abdomen seemed to awaken from its slumber and began to burn as if it were fresh.

A sign for the emergency exit caught her eye. Teresa lunged towards it and pushed the door open with both hands, ending up in the park that surrounded the hospital.

The sun, the scent of the flowering linden trees and the chirping thrushes all helped her to breathe again. She rummaged in her bag for her diary and quickly rifled through it until she had found what she was looking for.

She read the note, mouthing the words over and over again like a mantra.

'I'm going to call for help,' she heard Marini say.

She placed a hand on his arm to stop him.

'The police are preparing to break into a house to arrest a

criminal,' she read out. 'The only clue they have is his name: Adamo. When they enter the house, they find a mechanic, a firefighter, a doctor and a plumber, all playing cards. Without a moment's hesitation, and without saying a word, they arrest the mechanic. Why?'

Marini stared at her as if she'd gone mad.

'If you were trying to scare me, you've succeeded,' he said.

Teresa focused on the riddle.

Calm your breathing. Be methodical. Defeat the void.

Her hand gripped Marini's arm like a vice.

'Ouch!'

'Why?' she urged him, and it was as if she were urging herself. 'Why do they go straight to him?'

Marini rolled his eyes.

'I don't know! They must have had some other clue.'

'No other clues. No information beyond what I've already told you.'

He huffed.

'Did he have an X marked on his forehead?' he asked sarcastically.

Teresa let go of his arm and took a few steps away to deliberate until finally her face broke into a relieved smile.

'Oh yes, he really did have an X all over his face. Or an XY, to be precise.'

'You do realise you're raving, don't you?'

Teresa burst out laughing.

'The mechanic was the only man at the table, Marini, that's why they knew straight away that "Adamo" had to be him.'

Marini looked taken aback.

Teresa patted his shoulder.

'You really have trouble imagining a woman being independent, don't you?'

The memory of their first meeting and the mistake he'd made still tickled her caustic sense of humour.

She sat down on a bench. Marini joined her.

'What happened in there?' he asked her eventually. He received no response. 'I gather Ambrosini's condition is serious. I'm sorry; I know you've been friends for a long time.'

Teresa straightened her back. Her friend wasn't doing too badly, actually, but if the crisis that had tripped up her mind earlier could pass as concern for her friend, then perhaps it was best to trick poor Marini into thinking that.

She nodded.

'I suppose it would be pointless to ask you for more information,' he continued.

'Let's just hope for the best,' Teresa remarked. 'There's a new district attorney now and it's not Deputy Santi.'

'Yes, I just found out. De Carli says Lona wants to see you immediately.'

Teresa let out a bitter laugh.

'So, he's already here. Of course,' she replied but stayed put. Marini studied her and finally understood.

'Oh no. *No*,' he said. 'I don't like that look.'

Teresa stood up.

'I'm afraid Lona will have to wait. We have things to do.'

'Let me get this straight: are you saying you don't intend to report to the new district attorney?'

'Not for the time being.'

'May I ask why? It's my concern too, don't you think? You're asking me to ignore a direct superior.'

Teresa scoffed.

'Good God, Marini, you're so annoying.'

He rubbed at his eyes.

'Where do you plan on going now?' he asked.

'We have a case to solve.'

'Well, we're going to need a stroke of luck, then. It's an impossible case,' he muttered in his usual melodramatic way.

In response, Teresa popped another fruit gum into her mouth.

'Maybe there was no murder,' Marini resumed. 'Maybe it was an accident.'

Teresa gave him a sideways glance.

'And Andrian, struck by sudden inspiration but tragically out of paint, thought he might as well use her blood instead. Of course! Who wouldn't do the same?' she said.

'You don't think it's possible?'

'No, Marini. I don't.' She waved a hand through the air. 'It's the blood that tells me so. Blood flowing out of a heart. Is there any symbol more powerful than that?'

'You can't possibly think we'll find the solution?' Marini persisted.

She pretended to be thinking about it.

'It sounds like a challenge, Inspector. Yes, now that you've said it, that's exactly what we'll do.'

He shook his head.

'Get up. We're going to see the only person who knows what happened on 20 April 1945.'

Marini's eyebrows shot up.

'Alessio Andrian? He can't talk.'

Teresa grimaced.

'Even the dead have much to say,' she murmured. 'And if I'm capable of intuiting what they might say, maybe I can do the same with Andrian.'

13

The Andrian home was situated outside the walls of an ancient town on a cluster of hills embroidered with rows of grapevines, where farming estates alternated with groves of fragrant acacias and centennial linden. Legend had it that the settlement had been founded by Julius Caesar, whose statue now towered over the main square. The *imperator*'s toned bronze lorica and the drapes of his paludamentum were flecked with verdigris all the way down to his thick knees and the *caligae* wrapped around his feet and heels. Archivolts, capitals and mullioned windows carved out of Istrian rock surrounded the monument, architectural vestiges of the Longobard era that had followed the Roman and now glimmered in the heavy afternoon sun as it fell sideways onto the stonework.

Teresa was craning her head out of the car window, the wind playing with the red curls around her face as the car slipped through the centre of town. Marini's driving was unhurried and he only kept one hand on the steering wheel. He was quiet, too, and looked sullen.

They had eventually reached a wordless agreement to stop trying to make each other confess whatever it was that was weighing so heavily on their minds – though Teresa did wonder how long this truce could last and how long she could keep deceiving the person she spent most of her time with.

They drove through the centre of town and across the Devil's Bridge, a stone arch stretched over a vertiginous drop that had been carved out by a river of the purest turquoise. The bridge was rumoured to have been built by Satan himself, who had claimed a soul in return for his efforts.

The car scrambled up a forested hillside as the satnav droned on in the background. The sun was still high in the sky, but even though there were some hours left until evening, the approaching twilight had already permeated the light with sunset hues. Thick shadows lurked at the edges of their field of vision, ready to unfurl further into the world by the minute.

Marini lowered the window on his side, too. It was warm outside, but every now and then there was a gust of wind that carried traces of a chill that stung the skin. At the edge of the forest, the air already smelt like night-time.

After a few more turns, the Andrian home, perched on top of a hill, finally came into view. It was an old building of typically rural appearance, built out of light, square stonework and perfectly conserved. It looked a little like a farmhouse.

A row of ancient, gnarly vine trees ran along the front of the building all the way to an arbour overhung with wisteria, sheltering a table and a few wrought-iron chairs. The wisteria's violet flowers hadn't yet bloomed, but already they had begun to spread through the air their characteristic peppery scent. A gravelled courtyard fanned out from the building and a dog lay drowsing in front of the door. It lifted one ear up when it heard their car arriving, then lowered it back down.

Once Marini had parked, they both sat there for a few moments to observe the building. Raffaello Andrian had inherited a striking property with an affectedly rustic air. The same features that had once hinted at poverty and toil had since become the stuff of real-estate fantasy.

They got out of the car and started looking around. The stillness of the countryside was punctured only by bees, golden specks buzzing tirelessly among the wild flowers swaying in the breeze.

'You can smell the nectar they're carrying,' said Marini, taking a deep breath.

'Nectar doesn't smell, Mr Poet,' said Teresa.

He shot her a sceptical look.

'What do you mean it doesn't smell?'

'Oh yes, quite an inconvenience for flowering plants, who had to find some other way to make it attractive. Their solution was quite brilliant: caffeine.'

'*Caffeine?*'

'Insects go crazy for it. It's actually caffeine they're after. And when the plant decides it's had enough, all it has to do is start emitting it in such quantities as to become toxic. It's fascinating, the perception plants have of the world.'

'Welcome.'

They turned round to find Raffaello Andrian smiling at them shyly. He stepped over the dog and came towards them, wiping his hand on his jeans before extending it in greeting.

'Sorry about this; I was working up in the attic,' he said.

'More cleaning?' Teresa asked.

'Yes, there's a lot to sort out. No one's set foot up there in decades.'

'Don't tell me you've found other paintings,' Teresa joked, though not without a note of genuine interest.

Raffaello laughed.

'No, Superintendent. No more mysterious paintings. Follow me, let's go inside.'

They walked into the shady entrance hall. Long lace curtains fluttered over the open windows, which let in the heat stored in the masonry and the scents of the natural world outside. The cherrywood floor had been polished to such a shine that it reflected the furniture – which itself looked like it must be at least a hundred years old, all made out of solid wood, its edges smoothed over with use, occasionally with a minuscule hole left on the surface by woodworm. A pair of Siamese cats lay curled on a chenille sofa, eyeing the newcomers with suspicion. They, too, looked like they belonged in another era.

Their host seemed to guess what Teresa was thinking.

'My family has lived here for generations,' he explained. 'They started off as farmers, then became merchants. My grandfather was the first to forgo farming and set up a family business. He built his office where the chicken coop used to be.'

'What kind of business was it?' Teresa inquired.

'He imported timber, especially from Slovenia and Bosnia-Herzegovina.'

'And you work in the family business, too?'

'Yes.'

'How do you like it?'

It was an instinctive question. Teresa had never been able to comprehend how people were just able to follow in someone else's footsteps when it came to a decision as personal as choosing a profession.

'It's good,' the young man replied. 'I've always pictured myself doing this, ever since I was little.'

'Then you've been lucky.'

Raffaello Andrian smiled.

'No, Superintendent. It's not luck. Uncle Alessio made sure to provide for us.'

Teresa wasn't entirely sure what he meant.

Raffaello Andrian motioned at them to follow him into a cosy sitting room. A pewter vase full of roses, two armchairs and a coffee table bearing a stack of books were arranged around the fireplace, but it was really what was hanging on the walls that caught their attention.

Andrian gestured at the paintings: six in all.

'These are the ones my father and I were able to retrieve and bring back home. We're missing four: either the prices were too high or the owners too intransigent.'

'Were they lost during the war?' Marini queried.

'No. Uncle Alessio decided to sell them to help out his brother, who was destitute and had a wife and young child – my father – to support. He was quite well known already, despite never actively having done anything to court fame. And by then he'd already withdrawn from the world.'

'How was it possible that he was well known?'

'One day an American soldier came across some drawings that Uncle Alessio's comrades had brought back with them from their mountain camps. As a civilian, this American had been a museum curator and an art expert. He wrote a piece for an industry magazine about the "partisan painter" and the legacy of madness the war had left him with. Of course, collectors and art dealers went crazy.'

Teresa was puzzled.

'You said your uncle wanted to sell his paintings to help out his family, but I had understood that Alessio Andrian had already lost his mind when he was found in the forest,' she said.

'That's correct. He didn't talk; he seemed to have gone deaf, too. He refused to eat. But my grandfather said that one day he found one of the paintings in the kitchen, wrapped in newspaper.

It looked like someone had packed it up to have it sent somewhere, but there was no address on the parcel. My grandmother said she didn't know anything about it and it couldn't have been my father, either; he was too little even to pick up the painting. It had to have been Alessio himself, but as you can imagine, it was pointless to ask him about it.'

'What did your grandfather do?'

'He unwrapped the painting and put it back.'

'Then what?'

'The next morning it was on the kitchen table again, wrapped in newspaper and string. And four more paintings with it.'

Teresa could hardly believe it.

'Alessio Andrian had packed them up overnight?' she asked.

Raffaello reached up to touch one of the paintings.

'He did much more than that, Superintendent. That night, my uncle left his room for the first time in five years to tell his family to sell the paintings and leave their poverty behind. So, you see, our fortune had nothing to do with luck. It came from an act of love: my uncle's.'

Teresa didn't know what to say. She could hear the emotion in Andrian's great-nephew's voice.

'Did they see him?' she asked, wondering whether or not she was being indelicate in addressing such an intimate family matter.

The young man nodded.

'His brother, my grandfather, saw him. He waited for him when everyone else was asleep. My grandma found him in the kitchen the next morning. He was crying, his head bowed over the wrapped-up paintings. Alessio had gone back to his room and he never left it again. My grandfather couldn't contain his tears.'

'Had he spoken to his brother?'

'No, and after that night he stayed mostly out of sight. He said he couldn't stand to show his face any more. What he saw and heard that night was so . . . unbearable that he felt it would be humiliating for his brother if he even so much as laid eyes on him again. So he said.'

Teresa couldn't help herself. 'And what had he seen? What had he heard?'

Raffaello Andrian quickly wiped his eyes dry.

'Imagine a man who hasn't walked for years, who hasn't spoken a word in years, all of his own volition,' he murmured. 'Imagine how he must have struggled, with his atrophied muscles, to stand upright, to make even the smallest of movements. How he must have groaned with frustration at having to grapple for hours with tasks that would take a normal man no more than a few minutes to complete. Imagine doing all of that for one reason only: to provide for your family.'

Teresa fell silent, touched by the young man's memories and even more so by the depth of feeling etched in his expression.

'I'll be back in a few minutes,' Andrian announced. 'Feel free to take a look at the paintings, if you wish. Then I'll take you to my uncle.'

'Thank you.'

Teresa watched him slip out into the other room – clearly needing a moment to process his emotions.

'He looked like he was about to cry,' Marini observed.

'And we'll give him the space he needs to compose himself,' she whispered back.

She walked up to the paintings. They were all fairly typical scenes, mostly landscapes, but there was also something remarkably modern in their composition, in the unorthodox use of perspective and style. The shading was so exceptionally skilled that the figures looked three-dimensional, just like the *Sleeping Nymph*. But none of these paintings had been made using haematite chalk; they had all been drawn in charcoal and depicted scenes from life in the mountains – all except the one painting which, more than the others, drew Teresa's attention.

It was a scene from war: a young man with barely the trace of a beard and two children aged about seven or eight, a boy and a girl, hiding in the undergrowth. The boy was holding a rifle, which looked like it was about to leap out of his hands as if it had just been fired. On the slope below them – the sharp incline of the valley conveyed by the use of perspective – a German soldier, identifiable from his helmet, sat teetering on a wagon cart, pulling on the horse's reins in an attempt to subdue the animal, which had been startled by the explosion of the bullet.

The expressions on each of the five subjects' faces were astonishing, so florid and tangible as to rise up from the paper: the young man's shock, the little boy's fear, the soldier's surprise and the horse's panic as it reared up on its hind legs. And the girl: standing slightly apart, her eyes wide open and her lips pressed together.

Teresa scanned the painting for clues, references to a location, or a date, or any detail that might serve to place the scene in a definite time and place, but all she found was the signature: two wispy, intersecting As.

She went from painting to painting scrutinising every line, but to no avail. She had to concede defeat: Alessio Andrian had left no trail of clues that might make their job easier. She made a note to make sure someone checked the backs of the paintings.

The gentle sound of a piano being played somewhere on the ground floor broke through the late afternoon stillness. After the first few hesitant notes, the music gradually picked up in speed and fervour until the whole house rang with its impassioned melody.

Teresa followed the piano's delicate chords as they reverberated over the wood and the upholstery of the home, letting them guide her through the corridor.

'This isn't very polite,' she heard Marini say, but she ignored him.

Eventually she reached a small room, so narrow as to fit only a grand piano and the woman whose fingers were dancing over its keys. She was around fifty years old and must have been quite tall. The curious way in which she had styled her hair – a blonde braid looped around her head and into a large bun tied up with a ribbon – suggested to Teresa that she might be from Eastern

Europe. Her outfit, though, was simple and practical: a white shirt and a pair of jeans. Her eyes were closed and her body was swaying to the rhythm of the music.

'That's Tanja,' she heard Raffaello Andrian say from somewhere behind her. 'She's been looking after my uncle for almost twenty years. We'd be lost without her.'

Teresa turned round.

'Sorry,' said Marini, looking uncomfortable. 'We didn't mean to intrude.'

'No problem. You're guests here,' Raffaello assured him.

Teresa turned to the woman again.

'I'm no expert, but she plays beautifully,' she said.

'Tanja graduated from the conservatory in Zagreb. She plays for my uncle whenever she can; she says he likes it and that it's our duty to fill this silence somehow.'

Teresa sought the young man's eyes and decided to speak plainly.

'You talk of your uncle with genuine feeling, Raffaello. And this lady here takes care to ensure there's more than just silence around him. Forgive me for being blunt, but your uncle has never reciprocated your attentions. You told me you've never once heard the sound of his voice.'

'It's true.'

'Then how can the bond between you be so strong? A relationship that's never had anything to nurture or encourage it, and yet despite all the silence and all that's missing, it survives, in fact thrives . . .'

Raffaello Andrian smiled.

'I can't explain it. I'm not able to explain it. I can only hope you might understand it yourself one day. Come, it's time for you to meet him.'

14

The room in which Alessio Andrian had spent the past seventy years of his life was nothing like Teresa had imagined it. No scent of decay, of death in waiting: instead, it was airy and bright, and so colourful that the first thing Teresa noticed wasn't Andrian but the thousands of photographs hanging on the walls. It was as if every landmark in the world had gathered there, for the eyes of an old man who wouldn't even look.

Alessio Andrian was sitting on a wheelchair with his back to them, his face turned towards a wide window that looked out at the little forest of oak and plum trees.

'I've travelled a lot,' the painter's nephew whispered. 'I took these photos myself and put them up here so that he might see the world through my eyes. But as far as I know, he's never even looked at them. Everything he wants to see is out there in those woods. Wherever he is, whether he's sitting in the chair or lying in bed, day or night, his eyes always turn towards the window. Sometimes it's as if they're cutting right through it.'

Teresa hesitated, unsure of how to approach this silent and inert man.

'Uncle, there's someone here to see you,' said Raffaello, motioning at Teresa and Marini to move closer.

Teresa took a few steps forwards.

'Mr Andrian, my name is Teresa Battaglia,' she said.

She had come to look at the suspect's face and to see what her instincts might tell her when she did so. As she walked round the wheelchair she was prepared to be faced with an empty and feeble gaze, eyes glazed over by time. What she saw instead was the exact opposite and for a moment, she was knocked off-balance.

This was not the blank look of an old man who had lost his mind: Alessio Andrian's eyes were magnetic, a pair of blazing embers embedded in the sharp bone structure of his lean face.

His expression was one of deep concentration as if he really were watching something at the edge of the forest that only he could see. It was neither a vacant stare, nor a benevolent one. It was feral.

'Mr Andrian?' she called again, a little louder this time to encourage a reaction, even the tiniest of tremors.

But the man didn't move a single muscle, not even in unconscious reflex.

Teresa studied him. Despite its gauntness, his body gave the impression of harbouring great strength. It was as if his muscles had adhered to his bones and his skin followed suit. There was no loose flesh on him, to be weighed down by gravity, but only a solid carapace.

His pyjamas hung off broad, square shoulders. His hands, lying on the armrests, were large, with long, delicate fingers. He wore a ring on his left ring finger: a plain metal loop with two intersecting As carved onto it. These were the hands of an artist — and perhaps the hands of a killer.

Alessio Andrian must have been tall and athletic. It would have been easy for him to overpower a being of ethereal grace like the *Sleeping Nymph*. The hair on his head was still thick and white, and carefully combed in a side-parting. Teresa could picture Tanja doing that for him, then slipping the old man's pale feet into his felt slippers and placing them onto the footrests of his wheelchair, while Andrian's eyes remained fixed on the woods.

Teresa crouched down wearily next to him. Marini stood at a distance, but Teresa knew that he was attuned to everything she did, as always. Every day he learnt a little more about the compassionate art of seeing into the invisible.

'We've discovered what the *Sleeping Nymph* is made of,' Teresa told Andrian. 'Her secret has been revealed. Whose blood is it?'

She wasn't expecting a reply and the silence that followed didn't surprise her. She was after something else entirely: those small signs that would show her that there was someone still in there.

'Does it belong to the girl in the drawing? It's hers, isn't it?'

Alessio Andrian blinked for the first time since Teresa had begun to observe him. A natural reflex.

'I think you killed her, Mr Andrian. Perhaps out of jealousy. Or perhaps because she resisted you. You young men would spend weeks up in the mountains. Who knows what went through your heads,' she continued.

'Superintendent, please,' Andrian's nephew protested.

But Teresa ignored him. If she was going to get a reaction out of Andrian, she couldn't afford to hesitate.

'Don't you think it might be time to relieve yourself of this burden?' she asked him.

Nothing. Not even the slightest twitch.

She produced from her bag a photograph, which she placed on the old man's lap.

'Here is your nymph,' she said.

She took one of his hands and placed it over the photograph.

'What was her name?' she asked. 'Do you even know? What must her family have thought, when she failed to return? How they must have suffered. Did she pass quickly, or was it a slow and painful death? Did you watch her die?'

Teresa tried to force herself into his line of sight.

'Did you paint this with the blood from her heart?' she asked.

'Superintendent!' Raffaello cried.

Teresa found herself staring into the old man's fathomless black eyes and felt like she was sinking. It might have seemed like Andrian was returning her stare, but that wasn't the case. Teresa could feel him looking straight through her and at the woods behind her as if she weren't even there.

'It's pointless, Superintendent. We've been trying for years. He won't respond in any way.'

There was no animosity in Raffaello Andrian's words, only a keen compassion. *He was a good man*, Teresa thought, *who felt a genuine affection for his hostile and enigmatic uncle.* She nodded as she rose to stand. Her hopes had been unfounded.

She made to take back the photograph, but something stopped her: it was Andrian.

The palm of his hand was pressing down on the picture with such force that Teresa wasn't able to wrest it free. This was the sign she had been waiting for.

She crouched down once more. She had the impression that Andrian's breathing had changed, accelerated. Hers, too, had started to race.

'You cared about her,' she whispered to him. 'The *Sleeping Nymph* was a real person and you were in love with her.'

15

Returning to the district attorney's office, Massimo thought, was like falling back into the all-consuming commotion of life. The Andrian home and its inhabitants, on the other hand, lived as if suspended in time, like those dust motes that glimmer in the light and never seem to settle on any surface.

That man had waited seventy years to do something as simple as holding on to a photograph.

Seventy years.

Alessio Andrian radiated a charisma that Massimo had rarely seen before. There was fury caged in the old man's eyes and soundless violence coursing through him.

Massimo opened the door on the passenger side. Superintendent Battaglia was still writing in her diary, as she had done throughout the drive back. Massimo, though, had been thinking about Elena. She hadn't contacted him all day and he wasn't sure whether to feel relieved or concerned. And sooner or later, he was going to have to face up to his feelings.

Teresa Battaglia clambered out of the car and looked up at the building they'd come to as if it were a living thing. Her eyes homed in on a window whose shutters were closed: the district attorney's office.

'At some point you're going to have to tell me what's going on,' Massimo told her.

She pulled at his tie as she walked past him.

'Maybe you'll figure it out yourself, Sherlock.'

They took the lift to the third floor and found de Carli and Parisi waiting for them when the doors slid open.

'Superintendent, Inspector, good evening,' they said in greeting.

'Dr Lona has been asking after you again,' de Carli added straight away.

Superintendent Battaglia didn't respond and turned instead to Parisi. 'The files from Ambrosini?' she asked.

The officer handed her a folder, but she didn't even look at it and kept walking. After a few more strides, she stopped and turned round.

'You can go home now. All of you. We'll reconvene in the morning.'

Massimo watched his colleagues take their leave but didn't move.

At her questioning look, he gestured to the door behind her and announced: 'I'll wait.'

The superintendent jabbed a finger into his chest.

'Do you actually want to be of help?' she asked. 'Then go home and sort out whatever it is that's bothering you and come back tomorrow. We'll have plenty to do and I need you focused.'

He didn't move.

Teresa Battaglia grabbed his arm.

'You really want to know who's in there? I'll tell you: a ruthless operator, an agent who's never, ever understood what it really means to be part of a team, and who'll devote every minute of every day he spends in here to testing ours. We have unfinished business, him and me, and he's come back to settle the score.' She let go of Massimo's arm. 'You must always be wary of him. Always,' she said in a low voice, 'because even when it looks like he's on your side, he's actually laying your trap.'

Massimo had never heard her sound so distressed. He thought he saw her hesitate for a moment as she stood in front of the door to the office. That wasn't like her, either. Teresa turned round to look at him one last time. Behind the forced smile on her face, Massimo glimpsed an emotion that he wasn't able to decipher but that was powerful enough to twist her features. The superintendent gave the door a single, firm knock and then, without waiting for a response, she went in.

For Teresa, crossing that threshold and breathing the same air as that man again meant letting the pain back in to finish what it had started more than thirty years before.

The room was plunged in semi-darkness, while stray rays from a copper-coloured sunset filtered through the lowered venetian blinds, standing like bulkheads against the outside world. Albert Lona was sitting behind a computer screen, his hands knotted in front of his mouth. The bluish light from the monitor accentuated his features. He hadn't changed much. The passage of decades had merely left a few streaks of white in his hair and strengthened his figure as if time had layered itself over him like armour.

He ignored her. Teresa was sure that he wasn't even going to offer her a seat. She would have to stand, exposed to his silent judgement, with her excess weight, the goodbyes from their youth still etched into her face, the fatigue from the end of her shift, the exhaustion of a body that had too often been punctured by the needle of an insulin pen, the bags under her eyes, her anger. And the scar on her abdomen pressing against her clothes as if to say: remember me?

Of course Albert remembered.

He decided that the moment had come to acknowledge her presence. He raised his eyes – nothing more. If she had allowed herself to hope even for an instant that thirty years would have been enough to cool his hatred for her, to freeze it into a

74

controlled and more muted hostility, that glance was enough to show her just how wrong she was.

Albert was here to destroy her.

'You've changed,' he said.

At the sound of his voice, she briefly, instinctively closed her eyes.

'Fire away,' she replied.

She knew he wouldn't let her go until he'd tasted at least the first few morsels of his revenge.

He surveyed her body, mortified it with his slow examination.

'I do wonder how you're still able to do this job,' he said, his hands still interlaced but now with one finger pointing at her rounded form.

Teresa didn't take the bait. This was not the time.

He stood up and walked round the desk, a cruel beast camouflaged in stylish clothes and a cultured manner.

'When I give an order,' he said slowly, in his soft cadence veined with traces of an English accent, 'I demand to be obeyed. When I tell you that I will see you, you will come running. When I tell you that you will do something, you will execute. That is what I expect.'

He leant against the desk, his manicured hands gripping the edge like claws.

She looked at his face again and realised she was no longer afraid of him. He was a reminder of excruciating pain, but that was all it was: pain.

'Do you want me to say yes, my lord?' she asked. 'Is that what you want?'

He tilted his head to one side in appraisal.

'I am beginning to realise that Dr Ambrosini has left behind a department in disarray,' he remarked. 'I sense it may be necessary to start from scratch, on firmer ground. I will have to get to know everyone here, test their proficiency and see how we might encourage fresh synergies. Set up a new system. Starting with your team.'

In the face of this odious threat, Teresa smiled. Heading for the door, she turned round.

'I'm pleased to see you haven't changed at all,' she noted.

He raised an eyebrow.

'Are you really pleased?'

'Yes. It'll make it easier to fight you.'

16

Teresa had stopped going out after dark months ago. When evening fell, her life wound down with the sunset and she withdrew into the cocoon of her home. She was scared of getting lost, of being unable to find her way back, of wandering around, confused and afraid, pleading for help from strangers.

But that night she went out.

The taxi was waiting for her outside headquarters and she climbed in, clutching a piece of paper with an address on it. She was following the instructions Ambrosini had given her from his hospital bed, but for the first time since she'd known him, she wondered if she would have been better off disregarding her friend's polite and detailed instructions.

The taxi dropped her off in a neighbourhood on the outskirts of town and close to the university, where new residential buildings and a few commercial blocks had cropped up over flat fields. She had arrived at a student dormitory.

Her footsteps echoed in a courtyard lined with racks of bicycles of all shapes and sizes, in various colours and states of disrepair. Some were missing their wheels, their rusty frames still clasped in padlocked chains no one would ever open again. From a flat on the first floor came the muted baseline of an indie rock song and the sounds of young people talking. Every now and then the door of the flat would open onto the terrace outside and the haze that muffled the sounds from inside would briefly clear.

The lift was broken. A notice signed by THE BUILDING MANAGER announced its imminent repair. It was dated three months ago. Someone had crossed out the signature and replaced it with THE DICKHEAD.

Teresa climbed the four flights of stairs to the floor she was heading for, taking as much time as she thought she needed to avoid being out of breath when she reached her destination. But it was no use. By the time she got there, she was out of breath anyway.

The whole floor was silent.

She found the apartment she was looking for and checked once more the number she'd written down. Inside her bag was a package bearing a most unusual gift. She sneaked a dubious look at it and wondered yet again whether Ambrosini had realised, when he'd tasked her with this delivery, that it could come at the expense of her career.

She knocked and almost immediately heard a rustling behind the door.

The door opened slowly, cautiously.

Standing on the other side was a girl with blue hair and the ugliest dog Teresa had ever seen. Teresa stood transfixed for a few moments longer than it was polite to be, then looked away, embarrassed by the obvious way in which she had stared at the young woman. But she quickly pulled herself together.

'Did you bring the thing?' said the girl, looking slightly intimidated and patting the dog's head as the creature eyed Teresa with suspicion.

Teresa reached for the package and the crinkling of the cellophane wrap drew their eyes – both the girl's and the dog's – to Teresa's hands. The superintendent found herself wondering which of them the gift was meant for.

Inside the package, marked with a tag that Parri had carefully erased, was a bone. A human skull.

17

Massimo couldn't sleep. As the hours of the night stretched out before him, he kept his eyes fixed on Elena's back. She was sleeping on his bed, lying on her side. He was leaning on the door, watching her.

She'd been asleep already when he'd arrived. He'd lingered in the office, letting all of his energies and thoughts unspool until he felt empty inside, all in a bid to avoid thinking of the unborn child he feared – and the woman he loved but couldn't stand to have by his side.

He'd disobeyed Superintendent Battaglia and waited for her in the office. Her expression when she'd returned from her meeting with Albert Lona had been impassive and had stayed that way during all the hours they had spent working in silence at their respective desks.

That was how she'd punished him for defying her orders.

But Massimo had caught the tremor in her lips, the falter in her step, her pallor; how could he possibly have left her alone after suddenly seeing her look so fragile and so lonely? Her past was a mystery that no one, not even De Carlo and Parisi, ever spoke about. Massimo had heard rumours of a marriage that had ended in tragedy – but what kind of tragedy? – and a life that had thereafter been devoted to solitude and work. To saving people, but never to saving herself. Clearly, the new district attorney had something to do with that past.

Elena stirred in her sleep. The way her hair fell over the white pillows reminded him of the *Sleeping Nymph*. His eyes followed the long line of her neck, traced an imaginary path from between her shoulder blades down to her buttocks, and back again.

He thought of Andrian and the mysterious girl in the painting.

Killing a woman you profess to have loved. Erasing from your life the very source of its light. It was a contradiction in terms, and yet it happened every day. Too often we romanticise stories of love turning into tragedy – and it is always the women who die. Women who were used and abused, abandoned and doomed. Women who were unable to recognise evil because it stood right next to them. How hard it was to see it clearly when it wore the face of the person who was supposed to take care of you.

Massimo remembered the story Superintendent Battaglia had told him about the first case she'd ever solved shortly after joining the police force. It had been a crime of passion, the details of which Massimo couldn't now recall. Superintendent Battaglia had interviewed the killer at length and the things he'd told her were like a sticky swamp that mired the soul. Those words had infected Massimo like toxic sludge.

'They'd been questioning him for twelve hours and he hadn't shown the slightest sign of cracking,' he'd heard her say with the absent look of someone remembering the past. 'Then I came in. I was the only woman there, barely in my twenties, new recruit. I didn't even know whether to sit or stand.'

Massimo had waited in vain for her to continue unprompted.

'And did that change anything?' he'd finally had to ask.

'It changed everything – as my boss knew it would. He'd sent me in there on purpose.'

'What happened?'

'He asked after me.'

'Who did?'

'The killer. He wanted *me*. So I spent the next few hours alone with him, listening to his story. He told me every single detail. You must be wondering why he suddenly would have decided to collaborate, after all, but that would be the wrong question. It wasn't about collaborating at all.'

She'd looked right at Massimo then, and in her eyes he had seen rage.

'It was all a sadistic game to him, another act of violence perpetrated on another. He forced me to relive with him every moment of the crime he'd committed. He described each point in such precise and morbid detail that I could have sworn I could smell the reek of blood.

'That man had stabbed his partner in the neck twelve times – one for every year of their relationship – before lying down beside her in their marital bed. He lay there as the life ebbed out of her, listened to her heartbeat slowing down until it stopped altogether, feeling the warmth of life leaving her body for ever. He waited for hours – silent hours spent in one last horrifying embrace before he finally let go of her.'

Massimo had felt a wave of nausea, which hadn't escaped Superintendent Battaglia.

'You think it can't get any worse than that?' she'd asked him as she unwrapped a sweet she then didn't eat. 'Well, it does. The worst part was the way he answered the only question I managed to ask him: why?'

The killer's answer still rattled in a low growl at the back of Massimo's mind.

Because there is no feeling more satisfying than to hold your woman in your arms as she dies. In that moment, she is truly yours. That moment is true possession, true power.

Massimo pushed the thought away in disgust. His mouth felt pasty with a sapping thirst, but he couldn't stop looking at Elena. He took a few steps towards her and stroked her neck with one finger. She turned and let out an irritated sigh in her sleep, her lips now slightly parted, but she didn't wake up.

Once again, Massimo thought of the *Sleeping Nymph*.

Why had Andrian killed her? Where had it happened? What force had led him to murder a woman who could still provoke a reaction in him, even after all this time and even in the immobility of his illness? Jealousy. Madness. An unhealthy urge for possession. Or perhaps an unequivocal rejection that had simply been impossible for him to accept.

Massimo had seen all of that before in his work. But this time there was something else going on around the edges that he still couldn't put a finger on. He had the impression that some of the cards were missing from the table and that they weren't related to the identity of the victim, but to Andrian himself. The man's eyes, always fixed on the same slice of the world outside, seemed to be looking at something that others couldn't see but that was very much present in his mind and therefore felt real to him. His gaze wasn't simply contemplative but active. Andrian was like a bloodhound, tracking something – or someone.

Elena's hand came to rest on her belly, still flat but soon bound to fill out with the life inside it, and though it was so dark that Massimo could barely see it, his dread drew a vivid picture in his mind.

The burning thirst in his throat intensified. There was a creature growing deep inside Elena, a stranger whose birth was bound to bring dangerous memories back to the surface. It was doing so already.

My throat . . . I can't breathe.

He pushed the image in his mind aside and backed away in the dark. For the first time in months, he had spent the night immersed in darkness. It wasn't something he usually did. Only Elena could give him the strength to overcome his fears, the courage to turn off the lights.

He retreated into the bathroom, turned on the tap and stuck his head under the jet of cold water. He switched on the light and looked in the mirror. His eyes were red, his pupils dilated. His face was weighed down with purple bags under his eyes. Beneath the trickles of water that ran down to his chin, he was ashen. He looked like he was about to throw up. And he would have done, had he believed it would help to flush out the past.

He washed his face once more, scrubbing at it furiously, but when he looked up at his reflection again, nothing had changed.

Same eyes. Same straight nose. Same mouth. Even his hands looked the same: large, strong.

I look like him.

He gripped the edge of the sink and stared into his reflection. 'I'm not like you,' he declared to the physical presence that weighed on him, but he knew it was a lie he'd too often tried to tell himself. The truth was that he couldn't be sure. He couldn't know whether he was really any different from his father.

18

'Smoky, sit!'

Grudgingly, the mongrel complied. He took his paws off Teresa's knees and sat in front of her, his wide ice-blue eyes – which lent him an air of gentle madness – fixed firmly upon her face. His fur half black and half a mottled grey, he looked at once comical and a little alarming, with crooked teeth sticking out of his muzzle and an awkward goatee growing on his chin. The line that split his coat in two ran straight down the middle of his nose. His ears, upright and attuned to any sound the stranger might make, were little more than twin tufts of scruffy fur. One of his shoulders was higher than the other.

'What happened to him?' asked Teresa.

The girl scratched the dog's back.

'Nothing. Smoky was born this way: lopsided. No one wanted him, so he ended up at the animal shelter. That's where we found each other. He got used to me straight away and I got used to him.'

Lopsided. The term suited the dog to perfection and Teresa liked it. She often felt lopsided, too.

The girl's eyes, too, were the colour of the sky, but a sky veiled with ethereal clouds, like pearl-white springs on her delicate face. Her brown hair fell in soft waves over her shoulders, turning blue halfway down to its tips. The absence of make-up on her face, the purity of her features, and her moonlike complexion gave her the appearance of a modern-day fantasy of the Renaissance. Teresa did wonder about the colour of her hair, though.

'Tell me about you,' she began. 'How did you get into—'

'Into sniffing about for dead people?' the girl interjected. 'That's what my father calls it.'

Teresa smiled. 'I believe, technically, it's called Human Remains Detection,' she noted.

'He knows, but he doesn't care. Lots of people feel the same way he does about it.'

'And how does he feel about it?'

The girl brought a hand up to her face, as she had done several times already since Teresa had sat down in her kitchen. She was clearly nervous.

'He says it's not a healthy hobby,' the girl replied, touching the bag with the skull inside. 'Maybe he's right.'

'I think it's wonderful.'

Blanca Zago was a revelation. Teresa thought about the unsolved case of the *Sleeping Nymph* and felt a quiver of emotion at the thought of setting this girl on the trail of the unknown woman. She knew it was only a dream, but perhaps it was not altogether far-fetched to imagine it might work.

'Anyway, technically, Smoky isn't a cadaver dog; he's more of a tracker,' Blanca explained, her voice trembling with shyness. 'Tracking human remains – human body parts – isn't the same as looking for a whole decomposing corpse. Of course, he's trained to detect the smell of blood and bones, and he's familiar with cadaverine, but those aren't the types of molecules I've focused my training on.' She touched her face again. 'Basically, if the body has been dismembered or buried, then Smoky might be able to help. Otherwise we can still give it a go, but it'll be harder for him.'

She spoke as if she were forcing the words out through her lips. For a moment, neither of them said another word – and then they both burst out laughing.

'I know, it's all very weird,' Blanca whispered, petting the dog. 'I wouldn't want to seem crazy.'

Teresa shook her head.

'Not in the least,' she said. 'How did Smoky learn? Go on, I'm not here to judge you.'

The girl bit her lip.

'We started off with some basic scents, like teabags and things like that. First, we focused on imprinting and detection. Then we moved on to more interesting molecules.' She took a deep breath. 'We used my sister's placenta.'

'What . . . ?'

'I know it sounds awful, but a placenta carries eighty per cent of human scents. It was an opportunity I couldn't pass up . . .'

Teresa didn't ask her how she'd got hold of the placenta and was glad she hadn't invited Marini to join her for this meeting. He would have made a show of outrage and ruined everything.

'I imagine it must be like a game for Smoky,' she said.

The girl clapped a hand on her knee and the dog leapt onto her lap. She squeezed him to her chest with a tenderness that moved Teresa.

'Their sense of smell is so important to them,' she explained. 'They have formidable noses and they need to use them. Scent detection can be a stimulating and fulfilling activity. We have some friends who've joined us in this adventure, so we have a good time. But it's serious work and difficult, too – though we don't expect to be paid for it.'

Teresa understood why Ambrosini had been so insistent that she include Blanca in her team. The girl was clearly very bright and – according to what the district attorney had told her – extremely professional, too, despite her age (she was only twenty) and her reserved manner. Blanca and her peers' detection abilities had already been noticed and put to good use across the border. But Blanca and Smoky were the best of the bunch.

Put her to the test and she will surprise you, Ambrosini had texted Teresa from his hospital bed.

Teresa had certainly had her misgivings on her way to this meeting, starting with the human skull, which now seemed to be staring right at them from its sheath of see-through plastic.

'Smoky practises on bits of pork,' Blanca explained. 'Sometimes we use vials of synthetic scent, chemical stuff you can order online. But molecules you get from dead people, like cadaverine and putrescine, leave a heavy environmental footprint.'

The young woman sought Teresa's hand and held it in hers. Teresa could tell she was trying to gauge her reactions.

'If you're after traces of human blood, you're going to have to use human blood,' she murmured. 'If you want to find the remains of a corpse, you're going to have to use parts from another corpse, fresh or otherwise. It may not be ethical. And it isn't legal. But there's no other way.'

It certainly wasn't legal, but it wasn't unusual, either. Ambrosini knew it and so did Parri, who'd not had any particular qualms in assisting with the theft of the skull from the forensics laboratory. After all, the skull had been evidence in a case now closed and would otherwise have been disposed of.

'Who supplies you with your . . . teaching aids?' she asked.

Blanca wrapped her slender fingers around Teresa's wrist.

'Do you really want to know?'

Teresa imagined the girl counting the beats of her heart. It was Blanca's way of identifying her interlocutors' emotions.

'Don't worry, I'm not easily shocked,' Teresa replied.

Blanca paused for a moment, then released her gentle hold on Teresa's wrist.

'We have a few friends who supply us with blood,' she explained. 'We also have a source in the hospital – you know, for any internal tissue, amputations, that kind of thing . . . And there's a guy in a funeral home who gives us cadaverine every now and then.'

'How does he do that?'

'It's nothing too complicated or invasive. All he does is put a piece of cloth under the corpse's neck in the first few hours after death. But I guess some people would be horrified even to think about it.'

'Those people should remember that one day this might help

to retrieve someone who's vanished and put their killer in prison.'

Blanca smiled gratefully.

'Yes, sometimes it works.'

Teresa watched the young woman sipping on the tea she had brewed for them both in the tidy kitchen of her humble but immaculate apartment. She was only twenty, but already she was fending for herself.

'Why have you been following me?' Teresa asked.

Blanca slowly lowered her teacup. She was obviously embarrassed.

'You noticed,' she muttered.

Teresa couldn't understand how the young woman had done it and that made her even more fascinating. For Blanca Zago was blind. Visually impaired, to be precise: her world was made of fog and shadows, and she was a tracker.

'If I hadn't, I'd probably be better off looking for another job. You had me worried for a minute there!' she said.

'I'm sorry. I just wanted to know who I'd be dealing with. I get anxious when I have to meet someone new.'

'Do you live here alone?' she asked, though she knew the answer already.

Blanca bowed her head.

'I've been looking for a flatmate to split the rent, but no one's replied to the advert yet.'

She didn't seem particularly eager to open up her unusual world to a stranger, but everything about their surroundings – the signs of wear on the few items around and the general absence of anything but the bare necessities – indicated that she had no choice. Teresa was sure that it had nothing to do with her disability but was entirely down to an objective dearth of financial resources.

'Who's the man who's always with you?' Blanca asked, her cheeks lightly flushed with embarrassment.

Teresa couldn't help but smile.

'I think you must mean Inspector Massimo Marini.'

'I call him "starchy". He always smells like fresh laundry.'

'I think so too, you know. He's such a perfectionist that I expect he sends his whole wardrobe to the dry cleaner's every week.'

'I don't like him. He seems a little . . . stiff.'

Teresa couldn't think of a more appropriate description than that.

'I always tell him he's got a broomstick up his arse,' she joked.

Blanca burst out laughing but quickly turned serious once more.

'I know people like him,' she said, drumming her fingers rhythmically on the tabletop.

Teresa studied her.

'What do people like him do?' she asked.

The girl placed a kiss on Smoky's little head, letting her lips linger more than was strictly necessary.

'They judge,' she breathed in response.

Teresa leant towards her as if she were about to make a confession.

'It's true that Marini is a bit like that,' she said gently, 'but he's not all bad. And I have a great time teasing him. I expect he'll be very jealous of you. He's only just carved out a place for himself on the team and your arrival will unsettle him. He always wants things to be just so; he'll find it difficult to adjust.'

Blanca lifted her face.

'Adjust to what?'

'To the total disregard of rules and regulations that your presence shall inevitably entail.'

The girl smiled. She looked so lovely when her expression wasn't veiled by anxiety.

'He doesn't know that Smoky practises on smuggled bones?' she asked.

'I haven't really told him anything yet. But you know what? I can't wait to do so. He'll go crazy.'

They both touched the skull. Teresa thought she could almost spy a comical expression in its slightly raised brow ridge.

'It might help to dispel its baleful aura if we give it a name,' she said.

Blanca picked it up and turned it over in her hands, stroking its skeletal dome.

'We'll call him Mr Skinny,' she announced after she'd pondered the matter for a time.

Teresa nodded. She liked the sound of 'Mr Skinny', too.

19

At dawn, the valley awoke beneath a cloak of dew. Condensation shone in glimmering droplets, softening tree barks and sliding down the plumage of birds. It was a gradual awakening that followed its own mysterious rhythms, marked by birdsong, cadenced pecking and a leisurely tiptoeing in the undergrowth.

The moisture had resurfaced the verdant scents of nature as if there were sap suspended in the very air. Even the gurgling of the river seemed sharper in the light of day.

The village was already stirring with quiet activity and the smell of coffee wafted out of a solitary cafe.

Its patrons conversed in muted tones – all except old Emmanuel: the village madman was re-enacting a dance of distant origins, but he was putting his own spin on it, his footsteps shaky with age and alcohol, and the effects of the illness that had never allowed his mind to develop into adulthood. He was so small that he looked like a child. A child with wrinkles all over his face and a smile that resembled the keys of a piano. He was holding a scrunched-up newspaper, waving it about like a messenger electrified by the news he brought. The headline declared the rediscovery of a lost painting.

'Nothing stays hidden for ever,' he croaked through a volley of coughs, the stink of almost a century's living on his breath. 'Soon enough it'll come afloat, like the skeletons in the cemetery when the River *Wöda* floods. And it'll smell just as bad.'

Nobody paid heed to his words. Almost nobody. For there was someone there who had been observing him for a long time.

Someone who carried the wrath of the *Tikô Wariö* within and who understood that old Emmanuel wasn't crazy.

Old Emmanuel *knew*.

20

The building that housed the headquarters of the police was a block of concrete arranged into sharp corners and perpendicular planes. It was as grey as stone and devoid of any decorative elements, with rows of identical windows lending it an air of efficiency and with pillars standing upright like forbidding watchmen. It was as austere as a fortress and a little depressing, too.

But the atmosphere inside its hallways was altogether different: the steady back and forth of police officers and clerks breathed life into the place and imbued it with an air of a machine at work, which was precisely what Massimo liked about it. In there he always knew what to do, how to channel his thoughts to constructive effect.

The office he shared with Superintendent Battaglia was empty. He was shocked; it was the first time since they'd met that he had arrived to find she wasn't already at work. He knocked on Parisi and de Carli's door and stuck his head inside.

'Anyone seen Battaglia?' he asked.

'Good morning to you,' said de Carli, his eyes fixed on the coffee he was stirring.

'Yes, good morning. So, have you seen her?'

'Not yet,' Parisi replied. 'I know she stayed late last night, though, so maybe she's sleeping in.'

Marini wouldn't have believed it even if he'd seen it with his own eyes. He stepped inside, closing the door behind him.

'Do you know how her meeting with Lona went?' he asked.

Usually, Parisi was up to date with everything that happened and not a word that was uttered within those walls escaped him.

His colleague drank his coffee in a single gulp.

'Didn't she tell you?' he said when he was done.

'We're talking about Battaglia here . . .'

Parisi shrugged.

'I don't know for sure, but it seems it was one–nil to her this time.'

Massimo leant on his desk.

'What do you mean?'

'That's what I heard from a colleague who was on watch duty. He heard the district attorney complaining on the phone to someone. Someone important, judging by his tone. Superintendent Battaglia must have served him one of her put-downs.'

Massimo muttered a curse.

'She just can't keep her mouth shut,' he said.

He made for the door, then changed his mind and turned round.

'What's their history?' he asked. 'Why all the hostility?'

His colleagues exchanged a look.

'We don't know. Nobody knows, but feel free to call it "hatred", because that's what it is,' said de Carli.

One glance at them both and Massimo knew they were lying. As usual, they were forming their protective barrier around her and he was back to being the new guy who mustn't be let in.

'You'll have to tell me eventually,' he said. 'You'll have to tell me what happened to her.'

'Don't you think that maybe she has a right to tell you herself?' said de Carli.

'Yes, and that's exactly why I'm going to go and look for her now.'

Parisi threw an envelope at him, which Massimo caught mid-air.

'What's this?'

'News on the case of the *Sleeping Nymph*.'

Massimo didn't open it. He would let the superintendent do it, as was her right.

'Did you find a witness?' he asked.

'No one who's still alive, though I'm not giving up yet. But meanwhile, I've found something just as good.'

'And what's that?'

'The parish priest of the town in Slovenia where Andrian was found.'

'The priest?'

'Why are you so surprised?'

'Well, what's the priest got to do with Andrian? Was he there?'

'He wasn't, but his predecessor, Father Jakob, was.'

'Is this Father Jakob still alive?'

'No, he's dead.'

'Please tell me he's left something behind.'

Parisi stretched his arms, looking pleased with himself.

'Yes, he's left something behind.'

Massimo rushed out of the office but quickly stopped in his tracks.

Albert Lona was standing in the middle of the hallway, watching him. He looked as if he had been waiting for him. When Massimo walked up to him, Lona extended a hand in greeting.

'Inspector Marini, we finally meet.'

Massimo returned the handshake. The district attorney's grip was firm but not as aggressive as Massimo had expected. He had all the appearance of a perfectly courteous man, with nothing about him to suggest otherwise. And yet Massimo's instinct was to draw his hand back as quickly as he could.

'Doctor Lona,' he replied in acknowledgment.

'I regret that we haven't yet had time to arrange a formal meeting, but as you will imagine, the circumstances of my presence here are somewhat unusual. I understand you are in Superintendent Battaglia's team and that you are working with Deputy Prosecutor Gardini on the case of the bloodied portrait.'

Massimo wasn't fond of approximations. The portrait wasn't bloodied. It had been painted with blood. There was a difference – in intent, in psychological profile, in the sequence of events that had led to the final result, and even in its aftermath. But he simply nodded.

'Very good,' said Lona, speaking slowly.

He was studying Marini and not even bothering to hide it. Then, placing a solicitous hand on Marini's arm, he led him on a walk.

'Did you know that Superintendent Battaglia and I joined the force at the same time?' he began. 'We were . . . friends. After all these years, I was astonished to find her still here, exactly where she started. I suppose one must bear in mind she has a rather difficult temper, as I expect you will have gathered already. You will concur, I am sure, that for those who fail to demonstrate the right kind of attitude, any slip can be ruinous.'

Lona stopped walking and gave him a friendly smile.

'I hope I shall find in you a more amenable interlocutor than Superintendent Battaglia. That, I think, would be to everybody's benefit.'

Massimo detected the implied threat in what appeared on the surface a mere suggestion. This man was dangerous.

'I'll keep you informed on how the investigation develops,' he replied.

Lona nodded, showing no trace of surprise.

'I'm counting on it, Inspector Marini. And is there any news yet?'

He glanced at the envelope Marini was still holding.

'No. No news.'

Lona checked the time.

'Then let me know as soon as you have any.'

He walked away. The scent of his cologne lingered in the air: the scent of a predator, a hunter whose methods were sophisticated, who knew how to conceal his true nature, how to seduce and reassure his prey before he tore it apart.

He realised he had just lied to one of his superiors. He had never imagined he could do that. He felt breathless, his heart racing. He was afraid, but not for himself: for her.

'One more thing, Inspector,' said Lona, who had walked a few steps back in the meantime. 'I have been thinking of initiating a disciplinary review of Superintendent Battaglia's work and I may require your take on things, too. The superintendent seems a little . . . "lost". Wouldn't you say?'

Lona didn't wait for Massimo to reply, which was just as well; he wouldn't have known what to say.

21

Frank Sinatra sang 'Fly Me to the Moon' while the skilful, harmonious notes of Count Basie's orchestra twirled through the air. The multicoloured shimmer of 1960s dance floors was transformed into music and sound.

Teresa opened one eye, then the other. Sunlight had flooded the room and was striking her face. She had been woken up by a persistent noise, and it certainly wasn't Frank's baritone. She sat up and pushed her blanket aside. Her body had left a hollow in the couch.

The doorbell rang again.

Teresa got up, confused. The CD kept spinning inside her stereo, the lights were still on from the night before and she had no recollection of how she'd got home. She was still drowsy and it took her a few moments to work out what time it was.

'Shit.'

She looked around. Her house keys were on the coffee table next to the sofa, her bag was hanging on its hook and there were her shoes, side by side near the door. There was a receipt from a taxi company on the shelf in the hallway. She checked the date and time on it. So that was how she'd got home.

Someone banged on the door. The doorbell rang again. Teresa tightened the belt on her kimono and opened the door.

Marini turned round, one foot already on the step that led back down to the street. With one hand in his pocket, his jacket hanging off a shoulder and wearing a silk tie, he seemed attuned to the music playing in the background. There was an old-school elegance about him.

He was looking at her now as if he were seeing her for the first time. Teresa could picture what he must be thinking, just as she could picture how she must look, with her hair in disarray and the shape of the blanket still imprinted on her face. And finally her dressing gown, which just about covered her knees.

'Never seen a kimono before, Inspector?' she queried, leaning on the door frame.

He looked away in embarrassment.

'I was concerned,' he said. 'While you were asleep—'

'Careful with that sarcasm, now.'

Massimo crossed his arms and looked up at the sky, doing anything he could to avoid looking at Teresa.

'While you were asleep,' he resumed, 'Doctor Lona came to me to make sure I knew whose side I should be on, and he wasn't too subtle about it, either. He threatened you, too: he's planning to put you under disciplinary investigation.'

Teresa remained expressionless, but beneath the surface, she was in a state of turmoil. She had been expecting an attack, but not quite so soon. Albert's ascent to the top of the hierarchical pecking order had made him more ruthless.

'What did he tell you?' she asked.

Marini finally looked at her.

'On your history with him? Nothing, if that's what you're most worried about. And I can see that it is. Aren't you going to ask me whether or not I plan to take him up on his offer?'

Teresa could feel herself smiling, even though her life had just become infinitely more complicated in a way she'd never expected to have to deal with again.

'I don't need to ask, Inspector,' she replied.

Marini's face lit up. He waved an envelope at her.

'What's this?' Teresa asked.

'News from 1945, Superintendent. Now, would you please get dressed? This is really disturbing.'

Bovec. Plezzo. Flitsch.

Three names in three different languages – Slovenian, Italian and German – all referring to the same spot ensconced in the Alps, the meeting point of three nations, where a step in any direction could lead you across a new border. The past was a heavy burden on this land and was said to have warped the very nature of those who lived on it. Too many conquering armies had been and gone for the DNA of its people not to bear the traces of ancient wounds.

Teresa saw that on the surface of things, those wounds were invisible. The astonishing beauty of the natural landscape in which the town was immersed – the Triglav reserve – had eluded any kind of change for thousands of years. The word *Triglav* meant 'three horns': the high valley was encircled to the north, east and south by majestic peaks of bare, razor-sharp rock that soared high over lush forests of shimmering green. Through it flowed the river SoĐa, believed by some to be the most charming in Europe: its turquoise-streaked waters had carved through the limestone, coiling their way into tunnel formations and emerging as iridescent waterfalls and pristine springs.

On the grassy meadows that flanked the road to Bovec, they could see homes typical to rural Slovenia, with pitched roofs, flowerpots hanging from the attic and wooden balconies.

Marini was driving with one hand on the steering wheel and the other hanging outside the window, letting the wind run through his fingers. He gestured at the houses.

'Very picturesque,' he remarked.

'They're called *zindanice*.'

'What does it say on those signs?'

'That the owners have vegetables, *slivovitz* and honey to sell. Others announce they have *sobe* to rent out to tourists – little rooms converted from attics or added as extensions to the backs of people's homes, often with rather quaint designs. During the communist era, having a *soba* at their disposal could mean for some families the difference between not having enough to eat and being able to conduct a dignified existence.'

They arrived in Bovec, a little town of no more than two thousand souls, which nevertheless seemed remarkably busy with visitors, particularly those who had come to do some trekking or white-water rafting. Marini parked outside a *gostilna*, with its traditional outdoor rotisserie already spinning on its axis. They could see the church tower a few streets down.

They climbed out of the car and Teresa stretched her back, twisting left and right. The mountains were a silent yet powerful draw for her thoughts; she asked herself where Andrian might have come from that day so long ago, what trails his feet might have stepped over, which vistas may have unfurled before his unseeing eyes.

'*Dobrodošli*. Superintendent Battaglia?'

Teresa turned round. There was a priest across the road, sitting astride a mountain bike and staring at her. He had rolled up and clipped his robe over his muscular calves. Brightly coloured tennis shoes adorned his feet and he was wearing his hair in a stylish quiff. He looked young and tanned.

'That's me,' she replied. 'Father Georg?'

The priest's face glowed with a warm smile.

'Yes. Good morning. In case you're wondering how I knew

it was you, there's quite an interesting selection of images on Google,' he said, showing them his mobile phone.

'I'm not particularly photogenic.'

'I beg to differ. Follow me; the rectory is back here.'

Inside the church it was cool and shady, and there was a smell of beeswax. Teresa could just picture some old lady from the village spending hours and hours polishing pews in that compact nave decorated with sprigs of daisies and ears of grain. A handful of ancient and rather bleak paintings hung on the walls, depicting saints and martyrs wearing melancholy expressions.

Father Georg knelt and crossed himself before the altar.

Teresa and Marini waited behind him, standing straight.

The priest remained in that position for a few moments, head bowed, then got up and motioned at them to follow him.

'This way,' he said.

They entered a room adjoining the pulpit, a storeroom with a bench, a coat rack, and several photographs of Pope John Paul II on the walls.

'He's still very popular here,' he explained, noticing Teresa's glance. 'Though the new one's got plenty of fans, too.'

Teresa smiled.

'I confess I'm not much of a believer,' she declared.

He looked at her.

'So what do you lean on, when your job brings you face to face with Evil?'

It was a terribly serious question, which Teresa hadn't been expecting.

'On compassion, Father,' she replied.

He seemed to weigh her words before nodding.

'A difficult choice,' he said. 'Compassion is a painful virtue.'

'Your Italian is very good,' Marini remarked.

'My mother was Italian and I took my vows in Italy. I served for a time in a little town in Abruzzo, near Chieti. Come, my rooms are this way.'

He opened another door and showed them into a sitting room

that reminded Teresa of her grandparents' house. The upholstery on the sofa and the chenille armchair was worn, a pair of embroidered cushions resting on opposite ends of the sofa in a perfectly symmetrical arrangement. There was a lace doily on the glass coffee table and the walnut sideboard was immaculate, with not a single speck of dust on it. Everything in there was old but smelt clean. Over the door hung a crucifix with an olive branch.

'Please, take a seat. Would you like a glass of iced tea? Or something else?'

'Iced tea would be nice, thank you.'

Father Georg vanished into what Teresa assumed must be the kitchen. She heard the clinking of crockery, and a cupboard being opened and shut.

Father Georg returned shortly thereafter bearing a tray with three glasses and a jug. He placed it on the coffee table, then disappeared once more. When he returned it was with an envelope held carefully in his hands; he sat on the armchair and placed the envelope on his lap.

'Your colleague told me on the phone about the case you're working on,' he said, pouring their drinks. 'I checked Father Jakob's journals straight away and found something there that might interest you; though I doubt it can be of much help. They're just accounts of what was happening around that time, with no attempt to investigate, nor any pretensions of completeness.'

Teresa sipped her tea, then lowered her glass and looked at him.

'I understand that, Father, but given we're looking at something that happened at the end of the Second World War and that these journals are the only source of information we've found so far, I consider myself lucky even to have a chance to take a look,' she replied.

'Good, I hope you'll find them to be of some use. It was Father Jakob's wish that the journals should be stored in the little Church of St Lenart nearby, but the church authorities wouldn't allow it because of the damp. St Lenart's is in the heart of Ravne forest, between Bovec and the fortress of Kluže. Have you ever been?'

'No.'

Teresa watched him slip on a pair of gloves he'd extracted from the envelope. They were made of white silk and looked like the kind worn by restorers and people who handled works of art and historic relics.

'The Church of St Lenart holds a special significance for the people of Bovec,' the priest explained. 'They took refuge there during the invasion of the Turks in the sixteenth century. It was St Lenart who ensured the invaders didn't find the chapel and slaughter all the helpless people who'd sheltered inside it. A miracle.

'Father Jakob asked for his journals to be placed there some day, for he'd written in its pages about a war so brutal and bloody that the only way it could have spared the people of Bovec must have been through St Lenart's renewed intercession.'

Teresa nodded. She considered herself to be agnostic but was inclined to respect those who held religious beliefs, particularly if they had managed to come through one of the darkest episodes in the history of humanity with their faith intact.

Father Georg pulled out a bundle from the envelope and carefully lifted each corner of the cloth aside until the notebook was revealed. It was covered in a thin sheet of blue wrapping paper slightly frayed around the corners. The number eight had been written on the cover in elegant handwriting and below it was a name that Teresa supposed must be the author's.

'I wasn't able to photocopy the pages you need, Superintendent, because that would require official permission from the Church and I understand you're in something of a hurry. Besides, you'd have needed a translator to read them.'

'That's all right. I'm going to take notes, if you don't mind,' Teresa replied, looking for her notebook inside her shoulder bag.

'Sure. I'll be very precise with the translation.'

'Thank you, Father.'

The priest opened the journal with solemn care. The pages had grown thick and yellow, and crackled every time he touched them.

'A few decades' worth of damp,' he explained. 'This is the eighth journal from the year 1945, the second to last one that year. Father Jakob filled twenty-three in all.'

Teresa craned her neck to get a closer look. The entries were dense but neat, chronicles of a time she and so many others knew so little about. It really was a bitter irony that the value of a memory was so often recognised when the person capable of passing it on was no longer alive to do so. She thought of her parents and her grandparents who had lived through the war and had remembered it clearly, too: they had tried to tell her about it, but she had been young and hadn't paid them much heed. The hunger for life, which could be such a potent force in youth, always tended to overshadow the misfortunes of the past. But thinking about it now, she felt poorer for not having listened then.

'The man you're looking to find out more about is mentioned in the entry dated 9 May 1945,' Father Georg continued. 'Of course, they didn't know his name then. I'll read the passage out to you now, but from the beginning, so that you may understand the true circumstances of those terrible days.'

Teresa was intrigued by this observation.

'Do you feel that the reverberations of the war could be considered a mitigating factor in the event of a homicide?' she asked.

The intensity in Father Georg's expression was of a magnitude Teresa had rarely encountered.

'I believe that death begets death, Superintendent, even in the purest hearts. Many good people killed to protect themselves, and many more would have done the same had they needed to.'

'That's not what I would have expected to hear from a man of God,' said Marini.

Father Georg brushed his fingers over the page.

'We can't even imagine what war is, Inspector,' he said. 'The kind that breaks into your home, manhandles your kids and savages your wife. I'd urge you to listen before you judge.'

Bovec, 9 May 1945

The war that has soaked the world in blood has ended on paper and in the politicians' speeches, but the final echoes of its tragic violence endure in this stretch of Yugoslavia. The bullets of Marshal Tito's 9th Corps still hiss and slice through the night, not far from here. Some of these men are no longer men but beasts thirsting for blood, as if there hadn't been enough spilled into the earth already. They seem to crave it, even their own people's, if necessary. We live in terror. They are oblivious to ideals, to responsibility, to duty. They no longer know the meaning of honour. They strut around like lords of sin, cowards hiding under the festering cloak of impunity.

War plants the seeds of mournful fruits into every human soul. The flower of the basest of evils has blossomed in theirs: the evil that preys on the meek. A woman can no longer leave the city to go into the fields unless she is accompanied by a man. Animals are not safe when they are out grazing and sometimes they're not safe in the barns, either. The elderly who live in isolation are harassed and coerced into giving up what few possessions they have. Robbery, beatings, violence: that is what the soldiers I am about to write about shall always be remembered for.

Around dawn this morning, they arrived in Bovec, a ragtag band of nine. Demons, the lot of them.

Their leader, who never divulged his rank, called himself Mika. An ancient scar cut his face in half, though I think he could not even have been forty yet.

They made all of us – even the elderly who can hardly walk and the sick – come out into the street, wearing nothing but the mantle of sleep. They combed through the town and turned it inside out. They kept barking orders. They lashed out indiscriminately at anyone who happened to linger at the door of their home, or dared to lift their eyes from the ground. They were looking for anyone who opposed Tito, shouting at the town to hand them over immediately. Needless to say, there was no opposition in town — only poor exhausted souls who had briefly harboured the illusion that they had finally found some peace again.

They searched every single home and all the stables. They ate our food, sat at our tables and took turns beating up some of the men — a couple of them little more than boys — to induce the others to speak out. They took them out into the town square and hit them with the butts of their rifles until they lost consciousness. I feared for the women, for I saw the primal thirst with which those beasts looked at them — and particularly at young Maja Belec, on whom their collective attention was soon focused. They made her scream in terror as they lifted her petticoat up to her waist, exposing her nakedness for all to see. But her tears only fuelled the fire of their wickedness. They shaved off her mother's hair, too, declaring that they suspected her of collaborating with the Nazis, only because she had dared to look at them in a way they hadn't liked.

Thank God, and surely by the grace of St Lenart, they did not go any further.

They stayed until sunset, until finally, their bellies full of our food and our fear, they moved on to resume their search of the forests, and we never saw them again.

But the passage of the soldiers of the 9th Corps was not the day's only calamity.

Zoran Pavlin, the lumberjack, found the body of a man in the woods. His wife, who came to fetch me, described him as a corpse painted in blood and still breathing.

I hurried towards their home. The Pavlins had put him in the stables. He certainly did appear to be dead — and yet he was breathing. Using a lamp to look more closely revealed the faintest movement around his ribs, which were expanding and contracting.

He was covered in blood and mud that even the rain hadn't been able to wash away. His colouring a deep red, he smelt of death.

He looked like a newborn demon, lying on the hay curled up like a foetus in the womb of the darkness that had delivered him. In one hand he gripped a leather bundle, which he refused to release, even when he lay unconscious. I tried to loosen the grip of his fingers around it, but his strength was such that I failed.

His clothes were in tatters, torn all over and soaked in blood, and at first I thought he must have received some mortal blow that had left him fighting for his life. But I was wrong.

We stripped him. The lumberjack's wife brought some warm water and clean cloths, which we used to wash him: we discovered that apart from a handful of light scrapes over his arms and thighs, the young man carried no other wounds. The blood wasn't his.

We looked at each other then, distressed by our discovery, and the thought that had come to us all in the same moment escaped our lips in the softest murmur: have we taken in a savage killer?

Father Georg paused.

'The same question you're wondering about now, seventy years later, Superintendent,' he remarked.

Teresa nodded, disturbed by the account. She and Marini exchanged a series of quick glances: Alessio Andrian had been covered in blood that wasn't his own. The sinister rumours about the day he had been found could now be confirmed.

Teresa turned to Father Georg again.

'Did Father Jakob write any more on this?' she asked him.

'He made a few more notes over the following days. Let me see if I can find those passages for you.' The priest ran his finger down the page. 'Here's one,' he said, reading aloud again.

11 May 1945

The young man remains unconscious. He is running a fever and was in a state of delirium through the night. He has drunk barely half a glass of water and I believe he must be severely dehydrated. I wonder how long it has been since he last ate. We worked out from the handkerchief that was tied around his neck that he is an Italian partisan. Zoran Pavlin says he can deliver a message to his comrades. With any luck, they will come to retrieve him soon.

His hand remains clasped around what I think may be a drawing. I haven't attempted to take it away from him again, for he gets agitated when I do, as if it were his very life I was trying to prise away. Once, for the briefest of moments that was nevertheless enough to frighten me, he looked up and stared at me with black and burning eyes, the warning not to touch the drawing like a soundless howl from his closed lips.

Teresa thought of Andrian then, of the unexpected strength the old man had displayed the day before when he'd held the drawing in place with his hand. The strength of insanity, perhaps.

'It was indeed a drawing, and one that he'd made himself,' she said, showing Father Georg the photograph of the *Sleeping Nymph*. 'It's dated 20 April 1945. I wonder what Alessio Andrian did during the weeks in between.'

The priest picked up the photograph and studied it for a time.

'He wandered around the woods,' he replied, lost in reverie. 'Nothing to eat, nothing to drink. Shivering with fever. It's certainly a vivid portrait, and masterly in its execution.'

'Andrian was probably suffering the effects of a powerful shock. The question is, what could have happened to unsettle him so deeply? What death?'

Father Georg shook his head.

'Humans are capable of killing their fellow humans and sometimes they do, but there's nothing to say they should necessarily enjoy doing so, or even have a choice in the matter,' he noted.

'Are you saying that Andrian may have been forced to kill someone in order to protect himself? He only had scratches on him. If he was merely defending himself, then his reaction was disproportionate to the offence. We believe the victim was female. Father Jakob wrote in his journal that those were dangerous times for young women . . .'

'I never heard of any acts of sexual violence committed by your partisans around here or along the border. I will not claim to know what may have happened, Superintendent. Nor can I presume to enter the mind of a man I don't even know and whom we're judging for a murder he may or may not have committed in wartime. But there's one thing I'm sure of: the young man's deteriorated state as Father Jakob describes it doesn't strike me as that of a cold-blooded killer. Rather, I can't help but sense a kind of overwhelming despair coming from the man. Wouldn't you agree?'

Teresa took back the photograph the priest had handed her.

'Andrian is a sick man, Father. His mind is not . . . healthy, and perhaps it never has been.'

'Your colleague gave me some background on the case when he got in touch. I suppose it was necessary for him to do that, so that I'd understand how important it was that I should help in any way I could. I understand this artist may have taken someone's life in order to paint this portrait.'

Teresa's fingers lingered briefly on the face of the nymph.

'Perhaps what you're describing as despair was actually a form of psychiatric disorder – serious enough to lead him to kill someone,' she said.

'That may be so, but it wasn't anyone from in and around Bovec. There are no reports of violent deaths or disappearances from around that time. If there had been, Father Jakob wouldn't have failed to record them.'

'Where do you think Andrian could have come from?'

'It's hard to say. He could have come through the western end of the valley, or along the pass further north. The line of the border isn't far from here and runs across the whole region, from the Alps to the Adriatic Sea.'

'And is that the end of Father Jakob's notes on the matter?'

The priest flicked through a couple more pages.

'I'm afraid so. There are just a few more lines to say that the young man never uttered a single word, not even so much as a sigh. The partisans collected him the next day and no one here heard anything about him ever again, never even learnt his name. That is, until yesterday.'

'All right,' said Teresa. 'Thank you.'

The priest returned the journal to its sheath.

'I wish I could have been of more assistance, Superintendent, but as you've heard, the journal holds little in the way of concrete information.'

'I can assure you it's been very useful in allowing me to form a clearer picture of the case.'

Teresa was standing up to leave, when her phone rang inside her bag.

'Excuse me, I'll have to take this.'

She stepped away before answering Parri's call.

'What is it, Antonio?'

The coroner wasted no time.

'Come to my office as soon as you can, Teresa. I have some rather interesting updates.'

'Have you received the results of the genetic testing?'

'Yes.'

Parri's reticence was unusual and puzzled Teresa. Ordinarily, he was more than happy to expound.

'Aren't you going to give me anything?' she asked.

'To tell you the truth, it's something of a long story, and not even too pertinent to the field of medical science.'

'Then what is it pertinent to?'

'Fourteen hundred years of history, more or less. Hurry up; I'm waiting for you.'

22

May 1945

The moon, rising in a wispy purple haze behind the peaks of the Kanin, was blood red that night. A bad omen, according to the lumberjack's wife.

And not the only one, either. A few days ago, a goat had given birth to a one-eyed, tar-black kid that had begun to bite its mother before it had even learnt how to breathe.

The lumberjack had arranged for someone to pray over the barn and had devoted more time to the kid than to any of the other animals, in keeping with conventional wisdom: if you light one candle to God, light another to the devil, as the saying went. It was right to fear evil, but one should know how to keep it on side, too.

Ever since that day he'd had trouble falling asleep and now the bloody moon fuelled his unease.

As he entered the forest with his wife clinging to his arm and a lantern to guide his steps, he tried to will all inauspicious thoughts away. He would rather have been in bed, sleeping the sleep of the just, but first there was something he had to do to protect his home from misfortune.

The soldiers of Tito's 9th Corps had come that morning, crossed his land all the way to the woods and back. He'd been forced to give them fresh milk and a sow. They were looking for deserters and their thirst for blood was matched only by their hunger for the food they took by force.

He overheard them speaking of a young man who had died in the woods not far from the lumberjack's fields. Those savages had just left him there, without even bothering to give him a proper Christian burial. His wife had been pestering him about it since, unable to bear the thought of that poor soul to whom absolution and paradise had both been denied. He wasn't comfortable, either, with the idea of a rotting corpse just beyond his garden. If it rained, it might contaminate his crop.

'We must bury him,' his wife had pleaded.

They had waited for nightfall before setting out with a spade, some holy water and a wooden crucifix.

They didn't have to go far. They found the corpse lying on a bed of ferns.

The lumberjack brought his lamp closer.

Blood. Blood all over. It covered the corpse from head to toe like a second skin.

The body looked so gaunt that it was as if death had been eating away at it for days, though without causing it to bloat.

'Mother of God!'

His wife crossed herself, placed the crucifix over the corpse's chest and began to pray.

The man took off his jumper and picked up the spade but was startled by a sudden cry from his wife. He quickly covered her mouth with his hand.

'Quiet!' he muttered. 'Don't let them hear you.'

Tito's men might still be lingering nearby. But something in her expression, in the tremors that shook her, unnerved him.

He lifted his hand away from her mouth and followed her eyes to the crucifix.

'It's moving,' the woman whispered.

The corpse was breathing.

23

Teresa and Marini arrived at the Institute of Forensic Sciences an hour later. Teresa strode down the hallways with a vigour in her step she was surprised to possess still. Even Marini noticed it.

'Parri's not going anywhere, you know,' he pointed out, though he could comfortably keep pace with her.

Marini didn't understand. How could he? Teresa had known the coroner for almost thirty years and on the phone she had heard in his voice that peculiar and unmistakable note of excitement that could only mean one thing: the blood had spoken to him and revealed all its secrets. Like a necromancer, Parri had made death sing to him.

By the time she reached his office, Teresa was flushed.

'So?' she said, standing at the door.

Parri didn't look up from his computer screen.

'I thought you'd get here sooner,' he said.

'We were in Bovec, interviewing the parish priest. He translated some documents for us about the day Andrian was found.'

Parri looked up at them then with newfound interest.

'Was it useful?'

Teresa sat down and began to fan herself with her diary.

'The condition they found him in could certainly have resulted from a crime of a particularly brutal sort, likely a crime of passion,' she said. 'He was covered in blood that wasn't his own and was clearly in a state of shock.'

'So you've already convicted him,' said Parri, shaking his head. 'That's not like you.'

Teresa opened her diary.

'I haven't convicted him. I'm only following the clues,' she muttered, noting down the date and time.

'But you think he's guilty,' the coroner pressed.

Teresa looked up.

'And you think he's old enough that whatever he may have done in the past no longer matters. Isn't that right?' she asked.

'You said it yourself, the man isn't even aware of his own existence.'

'You sound just like Father Georg. I got the feeling he, too, was suggesting I should let it go.'

'He's a priest. They're all about forgiveness.'

Teresa smiled.

'It's not my place to forgive, Antonio; only victims and their families can do that. And in order for them to be able to forgive, we must first give them *someone* to forgive.'

He considered this for a moment, then shrugged. 'I can't fault your logic.'

'Now, will you tell us what the news is?'

Parri opened a folder and pulled out some documents containing graphs and numerical data, the results of the tests he'd ordered. Among the papers, Teresa glimpsed a photograph of the

Sleeping Nymph. Her face seemed to follow her wherever Teresa went.

'You find her fascinating, don't you?' said Parri.

'I do,' Teresa conceded, her eyes fixed firmly on the portrait. 'I can feel how real she was and maybe that's why I can't even think of giving up. I have to keep looking for her.'

'What if I told you exactly where to look?'

His lips where curled in a half-smile, but the coroner was serious. He'd meant what he had said.

'What have you found?' Teresa asked.

Parri turned the sheet with the test results towards them and pointed at one specific entry, some sort of code that meant nothing to Teresa. She showed it to Marini.

'The DNA testing has highlighted a number of distinctive traits in the blood we extracted from the painting,' Parri began. 'Once we were able to map the genome, we noticed that it's of a most unusual kind. Unique, in fact.'

Teresa frowned.

'Did you find some kind of abnormality?' she asked.

Parri laughed.

'From a biological standpoint, it's completely normal. We're not talking about a person with genetic mutations.'

'I don't understand.'

'I'll try to keep it simple. Human genomes are subdivided into types. In Western Europe, there are three, maybe four common types. The structure of a given ethnic group's genetic scaffolding contains a wealth of information about the migrations it's undertaken over the course of the centuries, its evolution and how it's intermingled with other ethnic groups – all through the comparative study of different genomes. Forty per cent of the population falls within Haplogroup H.'

'So, are you saying that the blood belongs to a foreigner? To someone from outside of Europe?'

'Yes and no. In fact, I'd say it's quintessentially Italian and has been for at least a thousand years.'

'You're confusing me.'

'The genome we've identified is unique in the world, characteristic of a very small community based only a few miles from here but with nothing in common – genetically speaking – with the rest of the European populations around it, including Italians. I'm talking about Resians.'

It took Teresa a moment to process this information. She had heard before of the peculiarities of the inhabitants of the Resia Valley and the strange language they spoke but had never really given the matter much thought.

'So, you think that blood belongs to a Resian?' she asked.

'I'm sure of it. It's in the DNA.'

'And you're saying it's unique.'

'The Resia Valley is an almost perfectly preserved – and therefore scientifically priceless – genetic and linguistic enclave. Or at least it was perfectly preserved until a few years ago, isolated from the rest of the world by virtue of its location in a closed valley system. ROH charts of its population will reveal long runs of homozygosity, which tells us that for thousands of years, it's received hardly any genetic interference at all.

'Resians today have the same DNA as their ancestors from whom the community originates. But we know very little about where those ancestors came from. Resians themselves are still searching today for answers to key existential questions about their community: where do they come from? Who are they really? What we do know is that their DNA doesn't belong to any genetic type found in Western Europe. Their common tongue is an ancient, archaic form of Slavic. It survives to this day.'

'Well, I suppose Slovenia is only round the corner,' said Marini, handing the test results back to the coroner.

Parri winced.

'I wouldn't say that in the presence of any Resians, if I were you!' he said. 'You'd certainly cause offence. Resians are not Slovenians – neither in their blood, nor in their culture – and the Resian language is not a dialect of Slovenian. It is proto-Slavic, something infinitely more ancient, more noble and more complex than a simple dialect inherited from some neighbours across the border. It has words in common with Russian, Serbian, Croatian and Ukrainian, but it's not the same as any of these languages. In fact, it may itself be the source of all those other languages. For years, Resians have been trying to resist the destructive force of lazy assumptions. Their identity deserves to be honoured.'

'But where did they come from?' Teresa asked.

'Probably from the Caspian Sea, around the sixth century AD, in caravans following the Huns and the Avars. Indeed, there are glimmers of resemblance between the genetic profile of the inhabitants of that region and the Resian genome.' He spoke now with a glint of excitement in his eyes. 'Don't you see how remarkable it all is? Resians seem to have appeared entirely out of the blue, their DNA completely different from any other groups in their immediate vicinity. Their only known genetic links are to be found somewhere far away, east of the Caspian Sea.

'For centuries, their blood has remained pure. They carry in their veins the same traits as their ancestors who first came over and populated the valley one thousand four hundred years ago, at the end of a journey of unimaginable length. We can still trace in their blood today the genetic make-up of the four main tribes who established their key settlements in the valley.'

'You seem to know a lot about this,' said Teresa.

Parri picked out an academic journal from the bookshelf behind him and placed it on the table, leafing through it until he found the article he was looking for.

'When their genomic idiosyncrasies were pinpointed for the first time a few years ago, the discovery generated significant interest among members of the scientific community – myself included. Sadly, the story didn't gain much traction in the mass media. A pity. Very few people know the history of the Resians and yet it's endlessly fascinating.'

Teresa picked up the photograph of the *Sleeping Nymph* and placed it next to the article in the journal. Suddenly, the exotic foreignness of her countenance was imbued with new meaning. Perhaps it was just a coincidence, a random quirk of nature. Or perhaps it was the awakening of an ancient legacy.

'A Resian . . .' she whispered.

'That's right, Teresa. That's the valley you need to be looking in.'

'It's not inconsistent with our findings so far,' Marini remarked. 'The Resia Valley borders the Canal del Ferro valley. Andrian could have crossed into Bovec from there.'

Parri nodded.

'That is possible, though it wouldn't have been easy.'

Teresa stood up, still holding the photograph.

'I need to work out what my next move will be, but the simplest and most obvious thing to do is to go there.'

Parri smiled.

'What are you going to do, wander around showing people the photograph and asking if anyone recognises the woman in the painting?'

Teresa shrugged.

'And why not?' she murmured, still gazing at the *Sleeping Nymph*. 'It's not the kind of face you forget, not even after seventy years. Andrian hasn't forgotten it. I can only hope someone else might remember it, too.'

24

When the *Tikô Wariö* called out to him from the forest, old Emmanuel was in his backyard. His house was the last one before the river, situated on a sloping meadow surrounded by larch and beech trees.

He sat under the arbour as the valley exhaled its cool breeze, drinking wine from a bottle and throwing feed at his hens.

When he heard the call, the old man got to his feet, his bony knees wobbling, one hand holding the half-empty wine bottle and the other clasped around the walking stick he told everyone he had carved himself when he was a boy. It was in the shape of a serpent baring its fangs, its body twisting like that of a grass snake fleeing from the beak of an eagle.

The *Tikô Wariö* watched him make his weary way to the edge of the forest.

'Where are you?' Emmanuel called out, unsighted by the sudden shade of the forest. 'I can't see you.'

The thrust to his chest was quick and plunged effortlessly into his heart as if it had slipped into his flesh rather than cut through it.

The bottle fell from the old man's grasp and onto a tangle of roots.

The wine spread over the earth like a bloodstain. It nourished the forest, which seemed to thirst for it. Crimson drops trickled into the soil and vanished immediately, devoured perhaps by the inferno beneath his feet. The *Tikô Wariö* saw Emmanuel look at his own chest in shock. The dagger was still planted in his ribs.

A soft lament escaped the old man's lips, as weak as the southerly breeze. Emmanuel seemed to deflate as if his very life were draining from his body together with his blood. He fell to his knees. He looked up at the figure standing before him, motionless in its contemplation of Emmanuel's agony.

The *Tikô Wariö* saw the flash of understanding in the old man's eyes. Emmanuel understood why he had to die. The past had returned. There was a formidable force roaming the valley once more and it expected to remain hidden.

Emmanuel was dying to protect a secret.

25

I'm not sure why I still feel that this is the job I am meant to be doing, that I will always be doing, and how I can possibly believe that the woman I am today bears any resemblance to the woman I once was.

And yet every morning when I wake up, I am a cop. Every hour of every day. Every single minute.

My profession is what defines me, what gives meaning to every tired breath I take.

I don't know whether to call it 'hope', this habit I have of clinging to time as if I could slow its endless march. What I do know is that every farewell needs preparation and it is my duty now to leave matters in the hands of those who will take the requisite care.

I have learnt that 'survival' is a noble word.

There is no greater dignity than the dignity of those who must at all costs survive.

'Weren't we meant to be going to the valley?' said Marini.

Teresa had made him drive towards the hills on the outskirts of the city but had given him no directions other than the occasional comment on when and where to turn.

'We will,' she replied, closing her notebook. 'But first there's someone we need to visit.'

Out of the corner of her eye, she could see him glance at her again and again. She unwrapped a sweet and popped it into her mouth.

'Since you're so determined to kill yourself with all that sugar, the least you could do is offer me one,' he muttered.

'Even if I did, you'd refuse.'

'I knew you'd say that.'

'Would you like one?'

'No.'

'How predictable.'

'How *consistent*, you mean. Who are we visiting?'

Teresa knew that her gambit was bound to unleash a barrage of objections; Marini was so cautious and distrustful, so excessively prudent, so terribly conscientious. Even worse: he was conservative.

'An asset,' she replied, looking away.

'We're going to meet an asset?'

'Yes.'

'And we're meeting this asset in the countryside?'

'Do you have a problem with the countryside?'

'I won't even bother asking whether or not you've cleared this with Lona.'

'Good boy.'

Her young colleague shook his head but said nothing further in reply. Teresa gestured towards a distant spot on the hill.

'What's that?' he asked.

'What *was* it. A madhouse. That's where we're headed.'

Marini shifted gears and turned into an uphill lane overrun with weeds.

'Sounds about right,' he grumbled.

Undone by years of neglect and inclement weather, the old psychiatric hospital had been consigned, stripped bare, to the hillside. Doors and windows had morphed into wet and crumbling fissures, and anyone who stood facing the main entrance would see right through the ground floor to the meadow on the other side.

A new colony had been formed, aided and abetted by wind and rain that had swept soil and seeds onto what used to be a floor. Now, the building's hallways were teeming with vegetation, leaves and shoots jostling for room and light, like pioneers unafraid of darkness. Leafy tangles of dog rose clung to the banisters, luring bees in from a nearby hive.

Teresa found herself thinking that nature's terrifying force had performed some kind of miracle in here: it had meted out destruction at the gentle pace of a growing seedling, and with all the tender grace of a flower in full bloom. With miles and miles of slender roots it had slowly, patiently crushed the work of man and had managed to redeem even that sliver of hell on earth.

Marini joined her at the entrance. Someone had spray-painted a word onto a wall from which the plaster had long fallen off. Beneath the word was an arrow pointing the way.

'Cadaver,' he read out. 'Is this some kind of joke?'

Teresa let her gaze roam over the building.

'It's a training camp,' she said softly.

'For whom?'

The sound of pattering paws announced the arrival of their guest.

'For him,' said Teresa.

The dog ran down the stairs in leaps and bounds but stopped in its tracks when it spotted Marini.

'Hello, Smoky,' Teresa greeted him.

'Who's Smoky?'

Marini looked confused – and when he was confused, he tended to get petulant, too.

'A new friend, I hope.'

They turned round and saw a young woman leaning over the first-floor parapet.

'Is she the asset?' Marini asked in a low voice, scrutinising Blanca's blue hair, her frail build, discoloured jeans and baggy T-shirt, and most of all the blank void in her eyes.

'I have a name, you know,' said the girl.

'Blanca Zago. And this is Inspector Massimo Marini,' said Teresa by way of introduction.

Blanca made her way down the steps. Smoky hurried to her side and stood by her as she gripped the handle on his harness.

'He's just like you described him,' she told Teresa, throwing caution to the wind.

Marini looked at his boss.

'What's that supposed to mean?'

'He's the asset: Smoky,' said Teresa, changing the subject.

Marini looked him over.

'A mongrel?'

'A sniffer dog.'

'Narcotics?'

'Human remains and biological matter,' Blanca interjected, uncharacteristically emphatic.

'They're a rare breed,' remarked Teresa.

Marini held a hand out as he approached the dog. Smoky bared his teeth.

'He looks a little feral to me,' he said, pulling his hand back.

'Oh, Marini. Must you always be so detestable?'

'Me?'

She swatted his arm.

'Ambrosini had in mind a possible collaboration between our squad, and Blanca and Smoky,' she said.

Marini crossed his arms.

'Too bad he had himself a heart attack. I doubt the new district attorney would approve.'

'Let's leave him out of this,' Teresa snapped.

'Can we do that?'

'We already have.'

Massimo sighed.

'This just keeps getting better and better,' he said.

The grating of tyres over what little gravel was left in the courtyard outside heralded the arrival of the other visitors Teresa had been expecting. A few seconds later, Deputy Public Prosecutor Gardini and the chief of the forensics team both appeared at the door.

Marini looked at Teresa.

'You're actually serious about this,' he said.

Once the introductions had been made, Teresa turned to Blanca.

'So, are you ready to show them how good the two of you are?' she asked, smiling.

Blanca nodded. She rummaged in the pocket of her jeans for an object, which she handed to Marini. He took it and turned it over in his fingers, frowning.

'It's a vial. This looks like blood. Whose is it?' he asked.

'Mine,' Blanca replied.

He stared at her.

'Obviously, your dog will have no trouble finding it, if that's what you've been using to train him.'

She lifted her chin in defiance.

'Obviously, you have no idea what you're talking about,' she replied. 'A sniffer dog won't just find *one* type of blood. He'll find *any* blood. He won't go looking for *one* corpse. He'll look for *any* corpse.'

The room went utterly quiet.

'Perhaps you could talk us through the procedure, Blanca,' said Gardini eventually.

The girl nodded, keeping Smoky close as if his presence gave her the courage to face these strangers who'd come to put her to the test.

'Once you've hidden the biological matter, it's then imperative to contaminate the search area. Dogs are clever. Rather than track the target itself, they'll follow the scent left by whoever has planted it. When we're training them, we always make sure to walk around and touch things at random, maybe even sit on the floor; that's how we make sure we've left our scent everywhere.'

'All perfectly clear,' said Gardini gently. 'Is there anything else you'd like to tell us before we begin?'

'VOCs – Volatile Organic Compounds – tend to sink to the ground once they're released, so in our training, Smoky and I have mostly focused on tracing remains at ground level; after all, if there's blood on a ceiling, it's likely there will be some on the floor as well. It would be implausible for there not to be.'

'Agreed,' said the head of the forensics unit.

'Sniffer dogs will always have a harder time pinpointing targets located at a height beyond their physical reach,' Blanca continued, getting into her stride. 'Smoky's alert signal for a scent that he's found at ground level is to lie down and fix his eyes on the source. If the scent is located at medium height, he'll sit and stare at it. If it's higher than that, he'll sit and bark three times – as if to say how do you expect me to reach all the way up there?'

Gardini chuckled.

'That's fair enough.'

Blanca's hand found Teresa's, who clasped it in hers, encouraging the young woman to keep going.

'It's a similar process for buried corpses, though in that case the scent will not originate from a single point, as it would do for a drop of blood, say, or a bone, but from a broader surface area, corresponding more or less to the outline of the cadaver underground. The alert signal will also differ: Smoky will wag his tail, turn on the spot and maybe even start digging.'

Marini coughed.

'I won't even ask you how you got hold of a corpse to practise on . . .' he muttered.

'Blanca and Smoky are no amateurs,' Teresa intervened. 'They've already led several search parties across the border, and taken part in seminars in Sweden, Great Britain and Finland. Let's make sure we don't drive them away, shall we?' She pinched his cheek. 'Now, go and spread a few drops around,' she added matter-of-factly, glancing at the vial Marini was still holding. 'Then it'll be Smoky's turn to show us where they are.'

'Why me?'

'Because you're our doubting Thomas. And don't forget, you've got to muddle the search area with your own scent.'

After a moment's hesitation, and the long-suffering – or was it despairing? – look of a man indulging other people's madness, Marini disappeared into the hallways of the asylum, tailed by Gardini and by the head of the forensics squad.

'He doesn't like me,' Blanca said softly, stroking Smoky's fur.

All of a sudden, she seemed sad.

'On the contrary,' said Teresa reassuringly. 'I don't know why it is, but despite how clever and talented he is, that handsome young man has a rather low opinion of himself. He sees you as a threat because he can see how good you are.'

'Really?'

'Oh, definitely. Massimo Marini's biggest problem is Massimo Marini.'

It took Inspector Marini about twenty minutes to decide where to hide the five drops of blood. He was aided in this task by the head of the forensics team, who'd also brought along a briefcase containing a series of 'decoys' designed to disturb the dog's olfactory powers.

Teresa and Blanca waited patiently until Marini re-emerged, looking pleased with himself. He knew he had made it as tough as he could.

'Shall we proceed?' he said.

Blanca didn't need asking twice. She called for Smoky, and once he was at her feet and ready, she gave the command: 'Sniff!'

They began a kind of dance, a choreography of scent molecules and chemosensors, a performance of symbiotic, elective affinity. The girl and the dog understood each other, could detect in each other's movements signals that remained indecipherable to the rest of the world. Unlike the dog handlers Teresa had seen in the police force, Blanca's manner with Smoky wasn't imperious. They were a single unit. They could communicate without making a sound. Blanca followed Smoky's lead, knew when to coax him on, and when to sit back and let him take his time over things. She lived in a world of darkness, a world of endless confusion. Yet there she was, actually dancing, floating somewhere far above the shadows in her eyes.

Everyone else followed their progress from afar, afraid of distracting them.

'I can't picture *them* at the police academy,' Marini muttered.

Teresa looked at him in amazement.

'I had no idea you were such an arsehole,' she said.

'For expressing my perfectly justified misgivings?'

'For having a go at a girl who's barely twenty.'

'I'm not having a go at her. She's *blind*, for God's sake. Don't you see the position you've put her in? How much pressure she must be under?'

Teresa confronted him then, holding her head so high it almost touched his.

'Don't set her boundaries she doesn't feel the need for. You'd be doing her a disservice. I'm sure plenty of people have tried to do that to her before, yet here she is. She's left them all behind. She's stronger than you give her credit for and if you don't get that, then that's your problem.'

He spread his arms out, then let them fall to his side.

'I'm sorry, I just don't have that kind of faith,' he replied. 'They're never going to make it.'

'Then go and see how she's doing, St Thomas,' she said, urging him to follow the girl.

Marini took his new role of sceptical observer very seriously indeed, steadfast in his determination to adhere to a notion of protocol – even though any semblance of correct procedure had been shattered the moment Teresa had turned up to see Blanca with Mr Skinny in tow.

The girl was patient with Marini and put up with his presence, though there was a flush to her cheeks now that could have been a sign of vexation. Occasionally, she allowed herself to push him away with an outstretched arm, demanding that he give her more room and dial back his pedantic scrutiny – which also betrayed a certain fascination with her and the urge to help her in some way. It was all in the tiniest gestures, in the way Marini's hand would stretch out of its own accord to steady her in case she should need it.

Teresa watched them bumping into each other, apologising, backing away to a safe distance, moving closer and bumping into each other again. It was progress: they were sizing each other up, two pieces of a puzzle, their sharp edges just about blunted, figuring out how they might fit together.

After some initial growling in Marini's direction, Smoky seemed to forget the existence of anybody other than his own human. His senses were focused entirely on the trail he was following until suddenly a new urgency crept into his movements.

Here we go. Teresa felt a knot of anxiety in her belly. A single mistake would be sufficient to cast doubt on the dog's accuracy.

Smoky sniffed excitedly around a grate on the floor, lay down and waited for Blanca to place her hand on his back.

'Here's trace number one,' she said and with barely the whisper of a command, had the dog leap back up onto its feet.

'Correct,' the head of the forensics team confirmed.

Smoky had seen through the trick: he had detected the scent cone from the blood sample even amid all that rust, which – like blood – contained ferritin.

'Let's move on,' said Gardini.

Smoky resumed his game, happily wagging his tail even as he took careful note of Blanca's occasional instructions. This time he detected a trace of blood on the blackened floor of the old kitchen, amid the remains of a fire that had probably been lit by kids in search of adventure.

Hidden in ash, which – Teresa realised – would have got into the dog's nose and hindered his sensory faculties.

'Trace number two.'

'Correct!'

The third drop had been hidden among some rubbish inside a cupboard and the fourth in the cork of a bottle of grappa, still redolent with the heady scent of alcohol.

The test came to a close in a second-floor bathroom. Smoky sat down and barked thrice at the mouldy ceiling.

'Trace number five.'

'Correct. You've passed.'

Marini had done a decent job, but it hadn't been enough. Evidently, his precognitive qualities left much to be desired.

'They're never going to make it,' he'd said earlier. Teresa could tell from his expression now that he would really have liked to take that back. Ambrosini had not been exaggerating. This girl and her dog were invaluable assets.

Would Smoky's senses be able to detect – in the heart of an unfamiliar forest, amid millions of other scents – the presence of a body that had been buried seventy years ago?

Could he be the one to bring to the surface the bones of the *Sleeping Nymph*?

26

I'm such an idiot!

The realisation of what he'd done struck Massimo like a bolt of lightning. It came as he was driving home, his thoughts revolving around a dog with the ability to discover the presence of death in places nobody else could see, the blind girl who followed him in total, reverent silence and the mysterious designs Teresa Battaglia had in store for her team.

Elena's text had reached him a few hours earlier, but he'd only read it now, while waiting at a red light.

The light turned green, but he didn't move.

He'd forgotten about the check-up he was meant to attend with her.

He'd forgotten about his baby before it was even born.

The horror he felt was so overwhelming that he couldn't move. Only when the honking behind him became relentless, and a car trying to overtake him nearly crashed into a van coming down the other lane, did he manage to pull himself together.

He shifted into first gear and drove home, his weakness leaving a bitter taste in his mouth.

I'm such an idiot.

Massimo's throat was dry and he felt like screaming. Yet again, he'd managed to ruin everything – perhaps irreparably this time. He had hurt Elena too often to hope she might forgive him. And that reckless, pure and peerless love he'd felt for her seemed to have disappeared, as if her body had absorbed every drop of it the moment it had opened up to the new life growing inside it.

He drove around in circles for half an hour before finally turning into the lane that led to his building. He parked, then looked up at the third floor. The French windows on the terrace were open. Elena was back.

For a brief moment, he was tempted to turn round and leave, postpone the inevitable confrontation. Instead, he took out his keys and went upstairs.

Her scent was everywhere. It enveloped Massimo the moment he set foot through his front door. She had only been here a few days, and yet Elena's essence seemed to have seeped into every object and every fold of his life. It wasn't some artificial industrial concoction, an expensive fragrance to spray over one's skin and clothes. It was more complex than that: an invisible scaffolding that had been erected almost overnight, a mark of territorial possession that signalled the presence of the woman who ruled over that realm. It was a fragrance pyramid composed of the smell of the books Elena had brought with her and that he kept finding scattered across the various rooms of the house; of sprigs of lavender she had stuffed into pouches of organza and buried among her clothes. It carried traces of her favourite soap, which smelt like the sea, of the candles she lit up in the evenings as if every night were a romantic occasion, of her honey-flavoured shampoo, the only kind that didn't spoil her hair, and of the cake she'd baked the day before – Massimo's favourite. The essence of vanilla and sugar still lingered in the air.

Sometimes Elena's scent was reassuringly maternal; sometimes it was sensual and sometimes joyful. But it was, in all its forms, the element that turned those four walls into a home.

He found her lying with her eyes closed on a sunlounger on

the terrace, a glass of mint-infused water in her hand. Her other hand stroked her abdomen over and over again, caressing the unborn creature within, cradling it already.

Massimo stood at the door, trying to find the right words to break the silence without breaking the peace.

'Don't say anything,' she said, her eyes still closed. 'I'm not interested.'

He swallowed.

'How are you?' he asked.

Elena finally looked at him.

He could see in her eyes that she had been crying, but Massimo wasn't sure he was the cause of it. Her emotion seemed to have stemmed not from sadness or despair, but from an overwhelming love that had shaken her to the core and that – for the first time since he'd met her – wasn't directed at him.

Elena had been crying tears of joy.

'We're all right,' she replied. 'You?'

Massimo sat beside her. Elena put the glass down on a small table, right next to an envelope. Massimo's first thought when he saw it was that she must have left him a letter. His stomach churned.

'I don't recognise myself any more,' he whispered without looking at her. 'It's not an excuse. It's the truth.'

'I know.'

'I don't like myself, Elena. I hate the person I've become. But I can't spend my whole life pretending, either. I—'

'Don't say it,' she interjected. 'Don't say things you'll end up regretting.'

Massimo fell silent. He really had been on the verge of admitting that he didn't want the child. He had no idea why Elena was still wasting her time with him. He couldn't understand her. Even he was sickened by his own behaviour.

He realised then that the quality in her that he'd previously identified as meekness was actually a form of powerful determination: Elena wanted him by her side and she didn't mind that he was weak; instead, she would encourage him to overcome his flaws and claim the place in her life that she was saving for him. Now that she was pregnant, the strength of her will shone with every look she gave him.

'Elena . . .' he murmured.

She stood up, took a couple of steps away, then changed her mind and leant over to embrace him from behind his back.

'You're not like him, Massimo. You're not like your father,' she whispered, her warm cheek resting against his.

Massimo froze, his breath hitching.

'Who told you?' he asked, though he already knew the answer: his mother.

Elena loosened her embrace.

'The envelope's for you. Open it. Do it now.'

She left him alone and all of a sudden, the breeze seemed a little less warm.

His heart felt like a battering ram beating against his ribcage, threatening to open old wounds that had never properly healed.

So Elena knew. He was stunned by the discovery, wondered what she might be thinking, whether or not his mother had told her everything, every awful detail. Somehow, he didn't think so; surely Elena wouldn't have stayed if she'd known.

He picked up the envelope and prepared for the worst, but what he found inside wasn't the letter of farewell he had expected. As he stared at the black-and-white photos inside, he found he was having trouble formulating any kind of coherent thought. The pictures from the ultrasound fluttered in his hands like the banners of a gentle army laying siege to the wall of indifference he had constructed to shield his retreat. The commander of the invading forces was no longer than an inch and looked like a kidney bean.

It was his son.

27

Teresa finished her entry for that day and closed her notebook before switching off all the lights in her home. One by one, following the trail of her footsteps, the rooms that contained her life fell into darkness.

There were nights when in her desolation, Teresa yearned for the pain, let it overcome her, and was grateful for its presence, knowing that her grief never came unaccompanied. In the darkness, the silence, the solitude of those nights, she could almost feel the embrace of the child she had never had.

Some evenings were so desperate that Teresa felt like she was the one shattering. She had been broken one night thirty years ago in that operating theatre from which she had emerged alone. But motherhood is an irreversible condition. One day there are two of you and afterwards, no matter what happens, you can never go back to being just one.

Only when the pain was too much to bear, so terrible that she felt she might die, did her baby come to her. His nearness was inscrutable yet tangible.

Teresa would start to cry then.

She lay in bed. Her scar had stopped stinging, for her son was with her now. He was in that room, near the music box whose melody he had never had the chance to hear, near a mother who had never had the chance to cradle him. Their bond had never been severed and their love had outlasted death. Her baby had come to tell her that she was and would always be his mother.

Teresa reached out into the heavy darkness and it felt like he was right there.

'Forgive me,' she whispered.

28

Visions of the *Sleeping Nymph* and of his own unborn child raced through Massimo's mind, the city unspooling behind them like the painted backdrop of a silent film. Different, yet similar too, the two images had become his companions during sleepless nights and anxious days: on one side a dead woman and on the other a new life, which would soon force him to face his greatest fear.

The soles of his running shoes pounded the tarmac in a smooth and rapid rhythm. It wasn't even seven in the morning and he'd already run ten miles.

Neither his mind nor his body were at ease.

Elena had allowed him to sleep beside her that night, but they hadn't talked things through. He hadn't been able to find the words to ask the one question that had been plaguing him since the moment she had mentioned his father. She seemed calm; she hadn't pulled away when he'd embraced her – and that was already more than what Massimo could have legitimately hoped for. He'd felt her slipping into sleep, her breathing growing lighter. That was when he'd allowed himself to rest his hand over her stomach.

Later, he would try to work out how he'd felt in that moment but fail to come up with a clear answer. He hadn't experienced the instant revulsion he'd initially feared, but he hadn't felt the beginnings of a visceral and transcendental bond, either. If anything, it had been something of a truce, an opportunity to lay down arms and study the enemy. Except that the enemy showed no signs of aggression. It bided its time in the recesses of its mother's womb, preparing to upend the lives of those who had brought it into being. Massimo had drawn his hand back, feeling foolish.

He ran faster now, his heart beating madly in his chest.

The enemy was not the child but something that lay dormant in Massimo's very nature, ensconced inside the nucleus of every cell in his body: the DNA of a madman.

He dashed sideways, then sprinted as fast as he could. By the time he reached the gym, he could hardly breathe.

He'd been going there since he had first moved here and recently, his visits had become imbued with a greater urgency. It wasn't one of those fashionable gyms that doubled as social hubs, places where people got together to plan their next night out. There was only one commandment that mattered in there: those who entered must not be afraid of getting their hands dirty.

Massimo secretly suspected that the gym was one simple health inspection away from being shut down, but he liked the coarse and refreshingly honest feel of the place, its unwillingness to clean up just for the sake of someone's approval. More importantly, Massimo needed it, needed a place where he could satisfy an increasingly frequent urge to throw a few punches, to release all the anger he carried in his body.

The gym always opened early, well before anyone was out on the streets, and usually its lights were the last in the street to be switched off. Massimo knew that some nights the room in the back filled with the electric thrum of secretive conversation and a crowd of mysterious, skulking figures: they came for the cage fighting, bouts of mixed martial arts where very little was regulated. Massimo had refrained from asking too many questions, though he was sure they didn't have a licence.

As he walked down the corridor that led from the main entrance to the training room, he saw Lucius, the owner. Lucius was a former ballet dancer from the corps de ballet of the opera house in Tirana and he was as passionate about Greco-Roman wrestling as he was about dance. At the age of thirty, he'd concluded that a *rond de jambe en l'air* wouldn't save his life, but a clandestine crossing just might. So in 1991, he arrived in Bari aboard the *Vlora*, along with twenty thousand others who had, like him, run out of hope.

From that day on, Italy had become his home. That was what he said whenever anybody asked him about his life back in Albania, and that was what the Italian flags draped all over his gym declared. Lucius didn't like to talk about the crossing. In fact, he didn't much like talking at all. The one thing he did remember about those days was the thirst: so intense as to drive a man insane.

He was wiping the windows now, as he did every morning.

'He's waiting for you,' he said solemnly, chewing on an unlit cigar.

Massimo stood still.

'Who?'

'Challenge.'

'Challenge is waiting for me?'

It was still dark inside the training room, but someone was already in there; Massimo could tell from the creak of a cabinet door being shut. He had a hunch about who his opponent might be. Their rivalry extended beyond the realm of the physical and encompassed a whole host of different categories, not all of them obvious. The man waiting for him was Christian Neri. He was a gendarme.

Massimo had never agreed to fight him before, lest the fiery competition between them should overpower his self-control and trigger an eruption of violence he had no wish to acquaint himself with. After all, he was here to release tension, not accumulate it.

The lights came on. Christian was sitting on a bench, lacing his trainers up. He was the same age as Massimo and had a son who wasn't his, but his ex-girlfriend had left him when she returned to Romania. He was in the division of the gendarmerie that dealt with cultural artefacts.

'I hear Deputy Public Prosecutor Gardini has given you lot the Andrian case,' said Neri as he stood up and approached the boxing ring. 'We've already got bets going on how long it'll take you to fuck it up.'

131

'You just can't stand it, can you?' said Marini, laughing. 'Anyway, given your track record with solving cases, I'd say we can take it pretty easy.'

That wiped the smirk off Neri's face.

'Why don't you get over here and say that again?' Neri barked, gesturing at Marini to come closer.

Massimo turned away.

'Maybe next time,' he said, declining the invitation.

'What is it, are you scared Daddy will tell you off?'

Massimo went still. He wondered for a moment if Neri somehow knew something about his father, if he was trying to provoke him with the only thing that could rile him up. But he quickly set the thought aside: there was no way Neri could know. Yet, the damage was done: the tension that had been building inside Massimo was like a pressurised gas and now it was on the verge of exploding.

Massimo went to the ring, threw his gym bag down and climbed over the ropes.

'No gloves, no padding,' he said. 'I'll try to go easy on you.'

But his opponent moved so fast that Massimo didn't even see the hits coming. They rained down on his face like bolts of lightning: three to the right and an even stronger hit to the left. He could almost feel his bones changing shape and the walls of the gym began to whirl around his head. His nostrils filled with the smell of the rubber mat.

Massimo was swaying so badly that he had to hold on to the ropes for support.

'Don't make me come over there and get you,' Christian snarled, motioning with his hand for Massimo to return to the centre of the ring.

Massimo charged at him headfirst and grabbed his waist, but lifting him up proved harder than expected. It was like grappling with a snake. Christian used Massimo's torso for leverage and before he knew what was happening, Massimo found his opponent attached to his back and with his legs wrapped around

Massimo's neck. But somehow, he managed to break free and now it was his turn to hit. It was a scarily liberating feeling and he found it hard to stop. He had to push his opponent away before he lost control completely.

Just then, Massimo's mobile, which he'd left by the mat, began to ring.

'Pick that up and I'll break you in half,' said Christian in a menacing growl, his breathing heavy and one half of his jaw beginning to bruise.

But once he'd issued his threat, he took advantage of Massimo's distraction to lunge at him again. A flurry of kicks – one to the shins and two to the stomach – and Massimo let slip a howl. As he fell to the floor, he hit his forehead against a corner pad.

'Fuck!'

Massimo lay on the floor, dazed by the unexpected blow to the head. He rolled over onto his back and measured the damage: there was a suspicious throbbing in one of his knees.

'Get up!' yelled Lucius, watching ringside. 'Too easy!'

'Why don't you come here and say that?' Massimo snapped.

Meanwhile, the ringing hadn't stopped. Massimo caught a glimpse of the caller's name on his screen. He managed to grab his phone and took the call.

'What is it? Quick!' he said, stepping away from the corner.

'Good morning to you,' de Carli replied. 'Is this a bad time?'

Massimo ducked to evade another kick. Christian had been aiming for his face.

'It's always a bad time lately,' he replied.

'Ouch. I smell self-pity. You know, I think these bad times of yours might just be about to get a whole lot worse.'

Massimo parried a hit, but another landed on his ribs.

'Shit!' he yelped.

'You can say that again. Battaglia wants to see you. She's already here.'

'Just what I need.'

Massimo tried to squat, but one of his joints had gone stiff and his knee had begun to swell.

'It's going to take me at least an hour,' he said.

'Are you joking? You haven't got an hour.'

Massimo touched his cheek and when he pulled his hand away, he saw that his fingers were stained with blood.

'Did she say what's lit a fire under her arse?' he asked.

The sudden silence from de Carli was alarming. He heard the sound of a scuffle at the end of the line.

Then: 'I'll light a fire under *your* arse if you don't get a move on,' Battaglia roared.

A flying kick hit Massimo right in the face and knocked him out.

29

For the second time now, the local paper was running a story on the *Sleeping Nymph*. That morning's brazen headline revealed the identity of the purported killer: Alessio Andrian.

The reporter who'd penned the article must be cleverer than she was, Teresa thought, *if he was already so categorically sure of who the culprit was*. The copy was illustrated by two images: a reproduction of one of Andrian's alpine landscapes and a recent photograph of Gortan posing outside his gallery.

There's our deep throat: he just couldn't wait *to talk.*

Teresa skimmed the piece in a state of barely contained fury. The article was unsurprisingly generous on gruesome detail, and replete with inaccuracies and exaggerations, giving the impression that the recovered portrait was covered in the biological remains of an entire corpse.

Gortan had relayed the story of how the painting had been

found and played up his own role in its discovery. Evidently, the journalist had been more than happy to indulge him. The piece showered Gortan with praise while making thinly veiled remarks that suggested the killer simply had to be the mad, misanthropic painter who'd immersed himself in silence and solitude for more than half a century.

Teresa flung the paper onto her desk in disgust. This brand of aggressive, voyeuristic journalism had always irritated her, particularly when it collided with the painstaking investigations and elusive subtleties of her job – a job founded on reason and certainly not on idle talk.

'Where the hell is Marini?' she thundered.

De Carli poked his head in through the door.

'Shall I get Parisi?'

'*Marini.*'

'We haven't seen him come in yet, Superintendent. Though you'll be pleased to hear Lona's car has just pulled up.'

'Fuck.'

De Carli looked over his shoulder into the hallway.

'Um, I think Marini's just arrived,' he said.

'You think?'

'Well, what I'm actually seeing is a chap with a limp and a swollen lip.'

Teresa got up to see for herself.

Marini was indeed walking with an obvious limp and one of his lips had expanded to several times its usual size. But that wasn't even the worst of it.

'What happened?' she asked, walking up to him.

He grimaced.

'Well?' she insisted.

'I guess someone had a score to settle,' he replied.

Teresa stared at him. His hair was a mess, his face was flushed and his skin was wet with perspiration. His choice of outfit was perplexing to say the least and in other circumstances, she might have assumed it was some kind of practical joke. The shorts he was wearing were far too tight and his sports shirt was torn across the shoulder.

'Did you get yourself beaten up?' she asked in disbelief.

Inspector Marini raised a hand in a gesture that seemed to cost him significant effort.

'Not on purpose. It's a long story,' he sighed.

She grabbed his arm and ushered him into her office.

'Don't think you've got away with it,' she hissed. 'You think it's appropriate to show up at work like this?'

'I thought it was important . . .'

'What, being on time for work? Yes, I would say so.'

'I'm sorry to interrupt,' said de Carli, still standing by the door, 'but Lona's on his way.'

'Get in here,' Teresa commanded. 'And give me your jacket.'

When Albert Lona walked in, Teresa was by the window and Marini was sitting at his desk, wearing a jacket that was too small for him.

Albert graced them with what Teresa deemed a perilous smile. In her experience, it tended to be followed by a snarl befitting the jackal that he was.

'Good morning,' he greeted them. 'I suppose you will have seen the front pages today.'

'Yes, we have,' Teresa replied.

The new district attorney began pacing around the room, examining the paperwork on their desks, the expressions on their faces and even the contents of a penholder. After some deliberation, he selected a biro and used the tip to lift up the cover of a file.

'It is the last thing we needed,' he murmured as he read the contents of the file. 'Judge Crespi will not let this go until we give him a name.'

He let the cover of the file fall shut once more.

'If you are hoping people might forget about Alessio Andrian and his painting in a few weeks' time, you are mistaken; this Gortan will make sure that doesn't happen,' he remarked. 'This is all excellent free publicity for his gallery: I would not be surprised if he already had some events planned around this.'

Teresa couldn't help but agree. Albert might not be anyone's idea of a helpful boss, but he certainly knew how these things worked.

'The eyes of the public are upon us,' Albert continued. 'The media have got their stopwatches out, timing how long it takes us to make our next move. They're waiting for us to slip up so that they can crucify us, but if we can find a scrap to throw them, we will soon have them eating out of our hands.' He looked at them each in turn. 'Now, my question for you is: do we have that scrap?'

He had addressed this remark to Teresa, who was conscious of the trap that lay behind his words. He wasn't just a direct superior requesting updates on an investigation: Albert Lona was looking for a way to tear her down and take the rest of her team with her. She had to give him something, but she also had to make sure it wasn't enough to let him get too close — close in every sense of the word: Teresa didn't even want to think of how he would react if he happened to glance under the table and see Marini's comically undersized shorts.

'I have a lead,' she admitted. 'Nothing's certain yet, but I think I know where to look now.'

Albert's eyes lit up as if he'd caught a whiff of fresh prey to dig his teeth into.

'Interesting. Let's hear it,' he pressed.

'We found something in the blood that might prove to be the key to revealing where the victim was from,' Teresa explained reluctantly.

He frowned, looking suspicious.

'Can blood really do that?'

'*This* blood can. But Doctor Parri will need a few more days before he can give us a definitive response. For now, it's just a theory that needs confirming.'

Just then, the district attorney's phone started ringing, interrupting their exchange. Albert took the call, speaking in mono-syllables; it seemed there was yet another mishap he was expected to sort out. De Carli was doing a good job from the office next door . . .

Albert hung up and made for the door, and even that small distance was enough for Teresa to breathe a little easier.

'I need to go now,' he told her, 'but I will be back soon. Tell Doctor Parri that I want facts, not theories.'

Only then did he seem to notice the bruise on Marini's face. He stepped towards him.

'What happened to you?' he asked.

'An accident in training. Nothing serious.'

Teresa wondered in the ensuing silence whether or not Albert had noticed the tremor in the young officer's voice, the absolute stillness with which she and Marini were holding their breath, how her eyes had darted instinctively towards the garish running shoes sticking out from under the desk before promptly looking away.

'As you know, Superintendent Battaglia, your team is now under disciplinary review. Believe me when I say I am taking the task very seriously indeed.'

And after this last barb in her direction, Albert Lona finally turned round and left.

30

Tempus valet, volat, velat. The words keep going round and round in my head; they've earned their place among the memories I've entrusted to this journal. It's remarkable to think how pertinent they are to this investigation.

Time is valuable – it flees and it conceals.

Time is always hiding something: a secret, a memory, a broken promise, a surge of grief. It spills over thoughts and emotions, covers them in the sweet fog of oblivion – and in its measured advance, consumes them undetected.

Time conceals, too; even crimes. Buried for years, for decades, under the quivering warmth of life, death seems not so abominable, not so fearsome, after all. Its colour fades, it is stripped of feeling, until ultimately it is forgotten – and with it, its victims, too.

Tempus valet, volat, velat. The Latin maxim was emblazoned on the church tower that stood at the entrance to the Resia Valley. The church was a modern construction, a hunk of concrete and chrome that stuck out like a sore thumb in that landscape. Teresa wondered what vision had guided the architect's hand; perhaps some kind of faith in a future that had subsequently failed to materialise.

Marini was just about managing to drive, stifling groans of pain each time he had to switch gears and brushing a hand over his lap every few minutes, exasperated by the dog hair that kept attaching itself to the fabric.

'Did we have to bring *them* along?' he complained, glancing in the rear-view mirror.

Smoky growled at him from the back seat. They hadn't quite set their differences aside yet.

'Why, are you scared?' said Blanca.

'I'm not scared. I just don't enjoy having a dog wheezing onto the back of my neck.'

'Boohoo, poor baby.'

'It wouldn't be so bad if his breath didn't stink of death.'

'Stop that. We're a team now,' said Teresa. 'We must learn to get along.'

She was sure they would warm to each other eventually, but Marini was being difficult and growing increasingly aloof. Before they'd headed for the valley, they had stopped at his apartment so he could run upstairs for a change of clothes. That was when

Teresa had spotted the young woman on his balcony. Teresa had been shocked: as far as Marini's colleagues knew, there wasn't anyone he shared his life with. He'd only had one romantic entanglement since his transfer, and that hadn't lasted long. Teresa was curious to know who this mysterious guest might be and whether or not she might be the cause of his recent malaise.

The road wound its way uphill, flanked by lush woodland on one side and the Resia river on the other. The river's emerald waters glistened in the sun and turned translucent as they twisted around pale rocks and gravelly beaches and wound their way beneath the odd wooden bridge. Up on the bluffs, they could see the occasional mountain shed peeking through the vegetation, while around them the Musi, Kanin and Plauris massifs soared into the clear sky. The tallest of these peaks reached an altitude of over eight thousand two hundred feet, but today they wouldn't need to go anywhere near that height: the local settlements all hovered between the first layer of coniferous forests and the vegetable gardens slightly further up the slopes.

Bovec is somewhere over there, thought Teresa as she looked eastwards, five to ten miles through the woods, a distance Alessio Andrian would have had to cover while in a state of shock.

Who knows how many miles he travelled. He must have walked for days, going round in circles, lost.

A few hairpin turns later, the whole valley suddenly opened itself up to their gaze. It was a deep hollow, steep along the edges and lined at the base with wide expanses of forested moraines. There were very few meadows and no real plateaus. The far-flung settlements that formed the municipality of Resia consisted essentially of clusters of rooftops and church towers hidden among the trees: five towns and six hamlets for a total population of just over a thousand.

As soon as they spotted the first local road signs, Teresa understood why Parri had been so adamant that they mustn't think of the Resian language as a dialect.

It had little in common with Slovenian. In fact, it seemed to have nothing to do with any language Teresa had ever heard before.

The administrative capital, Prato di Resia, became *Ravanza*. San Giorgio was *Bilä*. Gniva was *Njïwa*, with the nearby hamlet of *Hözd*. Oseacco was *Osoanë*. The sign that indicated the Resia river said *Tavilïka Wöda*.

Marini slowed down and came to a stop at a fork in the road.

'Which way now?' he asked.

Teresa rolled the passenger window down and tried to make out what the sign said, but she had no idea how to interpret its obscure combination of vowels and consonants. More pressingly, she had no idea which way to go. So far, they hadn't run into a single human being. They weren't far from the local highway that led to the border, yet Teresa felt as if they had crossed into some distant realm.

She had experienced this same sensation before – only a few months ago, in fact, in another forest very different from this one but just as imposing. The seasons had since moved forwards, there were no frozen ravines, no piles of snow, and yet the feeling that they were being watched persisted as if there were someone there observing their every move. Nature, in her mysterious, unnerving way, seemed to be moving and breathing all around them.

'Switch off the engine,' Teresa said.

Marini complied and immediately the sounds of the forest were upon their ears like the exhalations of a massive organism playing host to their presence. Instead of the silence Teresa had expected, they heard a symphony of voices chorusing in perfect harmony, bound by a profoundly symbiotic connection: the whisper of verdant canopies, the rush of the river as it flowed over the rocks and its gentler gurgling further up the slopes, where its course was slower, a sudden rustling among the nettles, the crackle of woodland creatures slithering in the undergrowth, a tremor of wind skimming the tops of the trees, lifting and bending their branches like a cresting wave. In that universe of echoes, even the light seemed to have its own sound: a low hum that curled over Teresa's skin, skipped, luminous, across the water and warmed the shimmering pebbles.

But Teresa knew that the forest was also a place for secrets and revelations, for darkness and death, and that sometimes it hid the bones of those who had lost their way and never returned.

The scene left her in a temporary daze. In the city, one's senses grew tame and accustomed to a faded version of the world, but here, every single organism – no matter how still and inanimate it appeared to be – was saturated with vitality. The natural landscape of the valley was at once austere and majestic. What it lacked in exotic extravagances, it made up for in the unmistakable grandeur of its shapes and colours.

Teresa reluctantly ordered Marini to turn the engine back on and make for Prato, the largest settlement in the valley.

They followed the road as it twisted and turned uphill in endless sharp bends until another church tower appeared before them.

The sign at the entrance to the settlement – just a handful of homes along a main street – read *RoĐajanskë kumün*. The buildings weren't in the alpine style but looked fairly run-of-the-mill and were clearly of recent construction. Here, too, the 1976 earthquake seemed to have erased almost all traces of the past. Some of the facades were adorned with murals depicting the recent history of the local populace, images of moustachioed men wearing hats, thick suits and waistcoats, carrying what looked like chests of drawers tied to their shoulders with leather straps, a community of emigrants, knife makers, itinerant craftsmen who spent the winter months creating furniture in the dim light of their lamps and went out as soon as the snows melted to wander the world and sell their wares.

Teresa spotted an inn and gestured at Marini to park nearby. They had arrived at a street with an apparently unpronounceable name: *Ta-w Hradö*.

'This place is paradise,' said Blanca, stepping out of the car with Smoky by her side. 'The air smells amazing.'

'All I can smell is dog breath.'

'Don't be so irritating, Marini.'

'I'm only being honest.'

Teresa took Blanca's arm.

'He's just jealous,' she whispered into the girl's ear.

They crossed a bridge over the turquoise waters of a rocky stream. Some children had gathered near a cluster of enormous limestone boulders and were skipping around and laughing. When they saw Teresa leaning over the parapet, they quickly scattered, abandoning their multicoloured toy boats to the current.

The Fortune Tavern was an historic establishment, dating – according to the sign outside – to the year 1902. Its oak door opened inwards into a dimly lit interior. Inside, the air felt cool and refreshing against Teresa's overheated limbs.

'Welcome,' the innkeeper greeted them as they stepped in through the door.

The innkeeper was busy wiping vigorously at a set of tumblers and placing them in a row over the counter, so at first, they only saw her back. But when she finally turned round, they realised that she possessed an unconventional sort of beauty. She was wearing an ochre tunic that fell all the way to her feet and it was impossible to determine her age; her perfectly white hair, pulled up in a high ponytail, contrasted with the smoothness of her skin and the determined arc of her eyebrows, which she had painted black. Her eyes were a deep blue that complemented her scarlet lips and the lapis lazuli ensconced in the silver framework of the large earrings hanging from her ears. On her hands she wore fingerless lace gloves. She was tall. She was, quite simply, majestic.

So far, they had only heard their hostess say one word, but it had been enough to reveal the unusual accent that marked her speech, which sounded like she had broken each syllable into its component parts before sewing them back together in her own personal, pleasing cadence.

They returned her greeting and sat on the stools at the bar. Smoky settled calmly and quietly between Blanca's feet.

One of the other customers paid his bill and left, bidding the innkeeper farewell on his way out. Teresa thought she heard him say her name: it sounded like 'Mat'.

'What would you like?' she asked them as she placed the departing customer's money in the cash register.

They ordered soft drinks. It was past eleven in the morning now and the only other patrons were two old men sitting in a corner with their heads buried in a game of cards. The tavern was rather unusual in appearance. The walls and the ceiling were panelled in a light honey-hued wood. Long strings of garlic hung from the rafters like celebratory bunting, in a nod to the area's agrarian roots. A bulbous black cast-iron stove held a bouquet of wild flowers bound with red and blue ribbon, the same kind that had been tied around the necks of the dozens of violins hanging from the walls. Some of these must have been antiques. Even more numerous were the photographs arranged in tidy rows beneath each instrument: portraits of men and women of all ages, and across several generations. There must have been over a hundred of these all around the room.

Teresa watched the woman working behind the counter. After she'd served them their drinks, she'd gone back to wiping the tumblers, her blue nail polish standing out against the kitchen towel.

'We saw some kids playing by the river on our way here,' Teresa began. 'But I think I must have startled them. They ran away when they spotted me and their toys were swept off in the current. I'm very sorry.'

The woman laughed.

'Don't worry. They'll find them,' she said, turning round. 'There's a bend in the river a little way down the valley. We call it the gully. It's where the river deposits anything it's picked up along the way. Their toys will have washed up there already. But say, what brings you here? You're not tourists.'

There was an element of curiosity in the woman's tone, but it was tinged with something else, too, something less obvious and thus more interesting to Teresa: it wasn't suspicion, nor was it annoyance. Teresa couldn't quite put her finger on it.

'We're interested in the history of the valley. We've heard a lot about your people,' she replied evasively.

The woman smiled cautiously in response. She wasn't convinced.

Teresa studied the photographs on the walls and Mat followed her gaze.

'Portraits of our musicians, the ones who are no longer with us,' she said in answer to the unspoken question. 'This is our homage to the cultural heritage of our valley, a tribute to those who've passed on our ancient musical traditions. They've bequeathed us the art of the *cïtira* and the *bünkula*.'

'Is that what you call the violin?'

The woman briefly walked out of the room before returning with a musical instrument to show them.

'This is a *cïtira*, a modified violin. The *bünkula* is more like a cello. They're traditional Resian folk instruments. You won't find them anywhere else in the world. And the third "instrument" in our music is the tapping of the foot. Have you ever heard one of our songs?'

Teresa shook her head.

'I haven't, unfortunately. You said the instruments are modified. What exactly do you mean?'

'They're especially crafted to mimic the sound of a kind of bagpipe, the *dudy*, that used to be played in the valley before the arrival of string instruments.'

'I gather your people are rich in idiosyncrasies.'

'You'll see for yourselves if you ever come to one of our festivals. We have our own carnival, the *Püst*. Our dances are beautiful, and very old.'

'How old?'

The woman's expression now was one of delight mixed with

pride. How many times must she have explained all this to tourists before?

'Thousands of years,' she said.

'And do they persist in their original form, so to speak?'

'Entirely unaltered.'

'Where do people learn how to play the old way? Is there a school?' asked Marini.

'No school. The young learn by listening to the old. That's the way it's always been. Follow me.'

Mat took Blanca's hand as if they had known each other for a long time and led them all to the adjoining room, a small restaurant area finished in natural stone. She was wearing a bell around her ankle, which jingled with every step she took and occasionally poked out from beneath the hem of her tunic. She took them to a wooden mannequin standing in a corner of the room, wearing what Teresa guessed must have been some form of traditional attire. It looked rather strange.

'What is it?' she asked.

'It's a traditional *lipe bile maškire* from our carnival. The name means "beautiful white mask".'

The mannequin was female in form, and had been dressed in a costume composed of several layers of skirts and a fine blouse in gauze, held around the waist with a belt the same shade of red as the ribbons that festooned the hems of the dress. Little bells had been sewn into the fabric. But the standout feature was the cap, shaped like a low cylinder and decorated with paper flowers in a variety of colours.

'It's really beautiful,' Teresa remarked.

The woman didn't seem to hear. She was staring at the outfit, lost in thought.

'During the *Püst*, our white masks will dance from sunset on Shrove Tuesday to dawn on Ash Wednesday,' she said, speaking very slowly. 'And they'll light the fire in which the *Babaz* is to burn.'

Teresa felt Marini inching closer behind her but didn't turn round.

'What's the *Babaz*?' she asked.

The woman pointed at the ceiling, where Teresa saw hanging from one of the wooden beams an effigy made out of straw and rags. It was the size of an adult male and dressed like one, too, wearing an outfit similar to Teresa's grandfather's Sunday best. It even had a hat on, with human features painted onto the piece of cloth that served as its face. It was smiling, but its smile was stiff and melancholy.

Perhaps he knows he's going to end up in flames, Teresa thought to herself.

'I'm the keeper of its ashes,' the woman continued. She went up to a sideboard and ran her hand over a row of terracotta vases. 'The *Babaz* represents the old year, the cold and barren darkness of winter, the past with all its suffering and sin. My duty is to gather its remains while they're still hot.'

'I think it's the first time I've ever heard of a ritual where it's a male figure who ends up incinerated in a metaphorical pagan sacrifice.'

Their hostess threw her head back in laughter, exposing her pale throat. She must have been at least fifty years old, but time seemed to have stopped having an effect on her long ago and only the occasional ripple across her face revealed glimpses of what she should, by rights, have looked like all the time.

'We treasure our difference,' the woman replied.

Teresa caught her eye.

'Yes – more so, I gather, than people do elsewhere. Or am I wrong?' she queried.

The woman's expression turned serious.

'You're not wrong. It must be that we can feel it slipping through our fingers. But I suppose modern life is, by definition, a general bastardisation of all things – and I mean that in the best possible way. Now, they want to take our difference away from us, erase it and replace it with something that isn't ours, not in the slightest. I'll never understand it.'

'What do you mean?'

'They've introduced a new law designed to protect minorities, but in practice it'll wipe our culture out,' the woman explained, releasing a sigh that seemed to suggest it caused her physical pain even to talk about this. 'They've grouped our culture with Slovenian culture, but we're not Slovenians and never have been. I often wonder if some day in the distant past someone mixed up Slavonic with Slovenian and we're now paying for their mistake. This law will engulf our most precious inheritance.'

'Engulf it?' said Marini, echoing her words.

The woman picked up a vase and ran her hand over it.

'It places an improper label upon our history,' she muttered. 'Imagine if they told you your family had never existed, that your parents aren't the people who brought you to life. Imagine if someone suddenly erased your ancestors' past, stole it, handed it over to somebody else. They're essentially telling us that our history isn't real, that our language is a dialect. A dialect – can you believe it? Even Unesco list it as an endangered *language*.

'The Slovenians have always had designs on our lands, but we'll never allow their plans to come to fruition. We're Resians and we're Italians. In that order. We've earned the right to be Italians. We've fought in this country's every war, we've done our part in protecting its borders.'

She put the vase carefully back in its place and spoke no more. Her breathing had quickened; Teresa could hear it. This was something the woman cared deeply about, something that stole the air out of her lungs. Teresa wondered what it must be like to be so attached to one's origins as to suffer so deeply when they were questioned.

'You were saying someone had made a mistake . . .' she prompted.

'Yes, a mistake with grave consequences. There are some among us – a handful at best – who'd prefer to live under

Slovenian tutelage. And they've had their wish, thanks to an unconstitutional rule that's allowed a small minority to surrender the rest of us – a thousand people, a whole valley and our history – into the grasp of a preposterous law.

'If you go to a museum now, you'll see artefacts that had belonged to our ancestors marked as Slovenian, not Resian. Our dances and our songs, the likes of which exist nowhere else in the world, are described as being *Slovenian*. Do you see what they're doing to us? They're annihilating us. They're *erasing* us.'

Teresa nodded, although she didn't think a non-native could ever really comprehend the sheer force of the pain that the woman's words revealed.

'Forgive me, but you didn't come here just to learn about the folklore of the valley, did you?' the woman asked them.

'I'm Superintendent Battaglia,' said Teresa, introducing herself. 'And this is my team.'

'I'm Matriona, though everyone calls me Mat.'

They shook hands.

'Perhaps you've read or heard about the famous painting that was recently discovered,' Teresa resumed.

The woman nodded.

'The portrait painted in blood,' she said.

'I'm going to ask you something now, and I know it'll sound strange, but I wouldn't do it if I weren't convinced that this person really had existed.' Teresa reached into her shoulder bag to pull out the picture of the *Sleeping Nymph*. 'I believe this young woman was born here and lived here, in this valley, until she disappeared on 20 April 1945. I'm looking for someone who might remember who she was. I understand that—'

'Krisnja,' the woman whispered.

She had taken the photograph from Teresa and was staring at it now, her expression unreadable.

'*Krisnja?*'

'It means "cherry" in our language. That's her name.'

'You know this girl?' Teresa asked, glancing at Marini in amazement.

'I know who she is, but I don't understand the date . . . 1945 – that's just not possible.'

'Why?'

Matriona returned the photograph.

'Because Krisnja is alive. She's never gone missing and she can't be much older than twenty.'

31

When Teresa had revealed the true reason for their trip to the valley, Matriona's gaze had fallen upon one of the tables, where a copy of the morning paper lay in plain sight. The front page carried a story about the *Sleeping Nymph*. The expression on Matriona's face had shifted then, as if she'd suddenly grasped the importance of what she had told the police.

'I hope we may count on your discretion,' Teresa had said. 'It'll be essential, at this early stage of our investigation.'

Judge Crespi had been very clear in his instructions: no images of the portrait were to be released to the public just yet. The last thing he wanted was to encourage the pathological liars to come out of the woodwork. In a case like this, an onslaught of false reports could prove to be a severe hindrance to their search.

Matriona had given them a name and an address. From that moment on, she'd become more guarded; though the shift in her manner would have been imperceptible to most. She'd told them nothing else, only assured them that soon they would find the answers they were seeking. Or some of them, at least.

'You'll be opening some very old wounds,' she'd said. 'Make sure to do it respectfully.'

The ancient scars to which Mat referred belonged to Krisnja's family, the di Lenardos. Their home was a yellow cottage surrounded by a large and impeccably kept lawn. In the backdrop were the forest and a magnificent vista of the colossal limestone slopes of Mount Kanin.

Teresa didn't have a speech prepared and wasn't sure how to broach the subject with these people, how to probe their past for a murder they might not even know about. But she was excited at the prospect of finally finding the thread that connected the painting to that fateful day in the distant past.

'I'm going alone,' said Teresa, stepping out of the car and leaning on the open door.

Marini scowled in obvious disapproval.

'I don't want this to come across as a siege, so don't hang around here like little sentinels. Off you go, explore.'

The lane that led to the house was hedged with holly. Before she'd even had a chance to ring the doorbell, she heard a man calling out to her from a nearby hill.

'I'm coming!' he shouted.

He made his way towards her with nimble gait. Teresa thought he must be in his seventies, or perhaps a few years younger. But it was hard to know for sure: the man's deeply furrowed face contrasted with his physique, which seemed robust and not yet past its prime. He wasn't particularly tall, but nevertheless radiated an air of peaceful authority. He had a thick head of hair, still dark, with only a touch of grey around the temples. He'd rolled his checked shirt up to his elbows, revealing strong, tanned forearms.

He walked up to Teresa with a curious, surveying look.

'Can I help you?' he asked.

His tone was terse, but perhaps it was just the unpretentiousness of a man not accustomed to receiving visitors.

Teresa decided she would speak openly this time and not bother to conceal her identity. Upon hearing the word 'police', the man gave her a half-hearted handshake and let go almost immediately.

'I'm looking for Krisnja di Lenardo,' said Teresa, watching him closely for a reaction.

The man frowned.

'She's my great-niece. She lives over there,' he said, pointing at a house on the other side of the hill. 'But she's not in right now. Is there a problem?'

'No, there isn't.'

'Cops don't usually go looking for people unless there's a problem.'

Teresa smiled.

'You're right, but I'm absolutely certain that our problem doesn't concern your niece – not directly, anyway. In fact, I think you're the one who might be able to help me.'

'I'll do what I can, of course.'

Teresa caught herself examining the man's distinctive features. Francesco Di Lenardo had black eyes, small yet fiery, and slightly slanted. His flat, wide nose arced gently towards his thin lips, and high cheekbones framed the faintly exotic and perfectly symmetrical oval of his face. These were traits that seemed to belong in a distant land, yet Teresa had seen them before. She'd seen them in that portrait whose restless presence she could feel reaching out for her from inside her bag. She'd seen them a few years ago in a photography exhibition about the Hazaras, a people of Mongolian descent and with hints of Caucasian heritage. But now she was in the Resia Valley, not in some far-flung steppe of the Caucasus.

She told herself it was nothing more than a coincidence – a suggestive twist of fate.

She took out the photograph of the *Sleeping Nymph* and handed it to the man.

'I'm looking for this woman,' she said, hoping she didn't sound too crazy.

Francesco di Lenardo held the image between his fingertips. It looked like he had stopped breathing. After a long, silent pause, he sat down on the steps of the porch.

'Who told you to come here?' he said, his eyes fixed on that face that looked so like his own.

'I showed the picture to someone in town and they told me to ask for Krisnja di Lenardo. They told me she's a young woman, but the person I'm looking for must be around—'

'Ninety,' said the man, finishing her sentence. He looked at her. 'This isn't my niece, Krisnja. This is a portrait of my aunt. Her name was Aniza.'

32

'Aniza was my father's sister. She disappeared on the night of 20 April 1945 and there's been no trace of her since. All my life I've hoped she might have just run away to start a new life somewhere else and now here you are, telling me she died that very night.'

Francesco di Lenardo looked down at the empty cup he kept turning round and round in his hands. He'd shown Teresa inside for a coffee, watching her closely as he poured it out for her, his curiosity tinged with suspicion.

Teresa didn't blame him for his misgivings. She wouldn't have liked it, either, if a stranger had barged into her home to tell her of some awful tragedy that had befallen her family – and so long ago that there was nothing much she could do about it now except learn how to come to terms with death. Suddenly that tidy, cosy home had filled with grief.

There were so many books that it looked as if the walls were built out of them. On the shelves, Teresa had spotted philosophical treatises, and volumes on history, archaeology and botany. Francesco explained that his wife had been a schoolteacher and ever since she'd died, years ago, he'd found her memory in the pages of those books.

'I can't prove it yet,' Teresa told him, 'but if the blood on the painting really is Aniza's, then yes, she's undoubtedly dead. We found traces of cardiac tissue in the fibres of the paper. That blood came from someone's heart and I'm afraid that kind of wound is—'

'Fatal.'

'I'm sorry.'

'I suppose you'll need a sample of my blood for testing.'

Teresa nodded.

'You don't have to agree, but if you did, it would help us – and your family – remove all doubt.'

'Of course. I have no objections.'

'Thank you. I'll have someone get in touch about it.'

The silence that followed proved difficult to break. The ticking of a clock marked the vacuum left by their unspoken words.

'Why did you say you hoped she had run away?' Teresa eventually asked. 'What made you think that might even be a possibility?'

Francesco shrugged, his gaze still turned downwards, contemplating the young woman in the photograph of the painting. Every now and then he caressed her face with his fingers.

'Despair, I suppose,' he whispered. 'Nothing more than that.'

'Do you know anyone still alive today who knew her back then? I'd like to speak to them if so.'

The man gave her a startled look.

'I was,' he said.

'You?'

'I was eight when she vanished. I remember it clearly. She lived with us in my grandfather's home. She wasn't married. She used to call me *Franchincec*.'

Teresa hadn't been expecting that. She made a quick calculation.

'I thought you were much younger than that,' she said.

Francesco smiled forlornly. It was as if the climate of his day had assumed a whole new complexion.

'I'm almost eighty now,' he told Teresa. 'And I've got a good memory, which I suppose you'll be eager to exploit.'

'I realise this won't be easy for you, but I'd like you to tell me about Aniza. There may be something in your memories that can help me to understand what might have happened to her.'

Francesco stood up and went to the window, his eyes on the sunlit peaks of Mount Kanin.

'Where shall I start?' he asked.

'Start with the bond you shared, if you can bear it. It's been seventy years, yet you're hurting as if the wound were fresh.'

'It is. I still carry her here,' he said, laying the palm of his hand against his chest. 'We were like brother and sister, despite the age difference. Perhaps more than that: she was like a second mother to me, as kind and loving as if I'd been her own.'

'I'd like to ask you something. Let's go back to what you told me a minute ago: are you sure you don't remember anything that might hint at an argument, some kind of tension, something that would have driven her away from the family?'

'I don't remember anything like that and I was old enough to notice. An eight-year-old back then wasn't like an eight-year-old today. I was already working, helping my father to sharpen knives in winter and out in the fields with my grandfather when the weather turned warm. In those days you were never a child for long.'

'What did Aniza do?'

'Oh, she worked at the textile mill in Ravanza, not too far from here. It was a linen mill. She also did a lot of embroidery, crocheting mainly. She was very good at it and managed to sell much of her handiwork. She had the most wonderful hands.'

'Did she have a boyfriend?'

'No, but there was no shortage of suitors. My grandfather used to have to chase them away from the front door. He didn't think they were worthy.'

'What did Aniza make of that? Did it upset her?'

'Oh, no, not at all. There was nothing sinister in it. Aniza never gave my grandfather reason to think she actually liked any of those young men. She'd hide with me on the stairs to spy, and we'd eavesdrop and laugh at the lot of them.' He turned away from the window and looked at the photograph again, his eyes shining. 'She was so beautiful she could have had anyone she wanted, but it was like she was waiting for some great love to appear on the horizon. She hadn't found it yet, but already it lit up her eyes like something out of a fairy tale. That's what Aniza was like. She was life itself.'

'Perhaps there was someone who felt possessive of her beauty?'

'I've no idea, but I don't remember ever seeing her looking worried or even angry about anything of that sort. Admittedly, these are all childhood memories, but I wouldn't think they've been sweetened by time, or by her absence. I'm not saying she was perfect, but she was a normal twenty-year-old girl, happy and content. She wasn't short of friends, either; though you'll find they've all passed away by now.'

Francesco had returned to his seat across from her. He seemed calmer now.

'The village was a peaceful place, I suppose,' Teresa resumed.

'If you mean to say there weren't any psychopaths around like the kind you see everywhere today, then yes, you'd be right; though we did have the war to liven things up in the valley.'

'What do you remember of the war?'

He sat with his fingers interlinked and hovering over the picture. His hands were shaking.

'There was a famine, there were the Germans coming up from the flatlands to patrol the villages in the vale and there were the partisans sniping at them from up in the highland pastures. We were caught in the middle.'

Teresa had a hunch that she had perhaps found the missing link she had been looking for, the starting point of the thread she was hoping to follow.

'Tell me about the partisans,' she said, taking her notebook out of her pocket. 'Which division was it?'

Francesco looked uneasy. He wouldn't stop fidgeting.

'Ah, yes, the partisans,' he said as if the taste of bile had filled up his mouth. 'I don't recall ever seeing the green kerchiefs of the Osoppo brigade around here, only the red of the Garibaldi brigade, who were aligned with Tito. They came from the Natisone Valley. The word I'd immediately associate with the memory of their presence is stoicism. You could say that the Resians endured the partisans, but not that they hated them. The true aberration was the war itself.

'At the end of the day, most of the partisans were decent young men, many of them little more than boys – not even eighteen and already holding rifles. Can you imagine? They lived in the woods and up on the pastures, and came down to the villages every now and then to stock up on food.'

'You said *most* of them were decent. Were some of them not?'

'My grandfather used to say, "Give a fool a gun and you'll get yourself a fool with an ego". They certainly weren't saints, but they weren't devils, either. They never caused any trouble here in our valley. Now, we find out one of them painted Aniza's face out of blood.'

His hands shook harder than ever. He hid them under the table.

Teresa persevered.

'Do you not have even a single negative memory associated with them?'

The silence that followed her question was ominous.

'Mr di Lenardo?'

'It was 1945, towards the end of winter. Every Thursday morning one of the Germans would come up from the bottom of the valley on a horse-drawn cart. He'd head to the bakery in San Giorgio for fresh bread, whipping the horse forwards, not even bothering with an escort. He didn't need one: he was untouchable, and he knew it. If anyone tried anything, there would be hell to pay for the rest of the valley. That's the way it was with the Germans.'

'I can imagine.'

'From our villages nestled up on the moraines, we'd watch him advancing along the road that ran by the mountain and the river. That day the partisans saw him, too, but they didn't scatter into the forest. They didn't need to; they knew the German would pick up his bread as he did every week, then go straight back to his *kommandant*, without bothering anyone.'

'But not that day. That day was different,' said Teresa instinctively.

'Yes, that day was different,' he sighed.

33

Massimo was leaning on the car, observing the green canopy that swept over the mountain slopes and the valley like a vast stretch of living, interconnected tissue. He had learnt both to fear it and to respect it. He still carried inside him the echoes of what he and Teresa Battaglia and the rest of the team had been through just a few months ago in a forest not too far from this one.

Every now and then, he touched his black eye. It kept watering, sensitive to the gusts of cool, damp wind roaring through the channel the river had carved out. The wind carried the smell of wet rock and of the clumps of dripping moss that clung onto the riverbanks.

He felt the car give a slight wobble. Blanca had stepped out and now she, too, was leaning on the still warm hood of the vehicle that had brought into the valley the noxious, chemical smell of the world they had come from.

Out of the corner of his eye, he watched her cross her arms over her chest, just as he had done. Even her expression matched his: grave, but only half-heartedly so.

He couldn't help but smile.

'I'm sorry,' she said out of the blue.

Massimo turned towards her. It was clear that it had cost her considerable pride to say that.

'What for?' he asked.

Blanca turned crimson with embarrassment. It was adorable.

'I . . . I snapped at you once or twice,' she began. 'It's not like me.'

He elbowed her softly.

'I should be the one apologising,' he said. 'I've been an arsehole.'

Blanca bit her lip. Her eyes, so distinctive in their appearance, now roamed over the forest, seeing nothing. To her, it must look like the sea at night, blurry and dark.

'Do you think we'll ever be able to find her?' she asked.

Massimo fixed his gaze onto the dense expanse of life before him, this organism that didn't always return all that it swallowed.

'It depends on the forest,' he murmured, a shiver coursing through him in spite of the mild day.

'You speak of it as if it were a sentient being.'

As he stared at that vast world of shadows and cracks, he felt for a moment as if it were staring right back at him.

'Believe me, it is.'

34

'Just before the German soldier was due to pass through town, my sister, Ewa, Krisnja's grandmother, came looking for me in the meadow, where I'd taken the cows to graze,' said Francesco.

Teresa noticed that a thin sheen of sweat had formed over his face, though he was trying to appear impassive. She let him continue.

'Ewa was only a year older than me, but she'd brought a rifle.

It was meant to be for play. She'd got it from a partisan she'd made friends with. A forbidden friendship. He'd taken the bullets out and taught her how to shoot.'

'Was this a regular pastime?' she asked.

'I knew nothing about it, but I did find out later on that it had happened a few times before. He was a young lad of seventeen, that I remember. He had curly red hair and a smattering of freckles over his face. That day he took us to the field next to the road. Over on the other side, hidden in the trees, was a partisan outpost.

'We crouched down and Ewa gave me the rifle. She was giggling. I took aim and pulled the trigger, pretending to shoot – except that the rifle actually fired. The bullet smashed through the harness that secured the horse to the cart. It was bedlam. The horse bolted and dragged the soldier down the valley.

'The Germans showed up within the hour, in a spray of machine-gun fire and rifle shots ricocheting among the houses and the fields. Luckily, our terror alone was sufficient reward, else it could have been much worse. I never did find out whether that boy had really forgotten to take the bullets out, or if it had all been some kind of sadistic game.'

Teresa swallowed audibly.

'Is something wrong?' Francesco asked, seeing the look on her face.

Teresa assured him it was nothing, but that wasn't entirely true: Francesco di Lenardo had just described one of the paintings that Teresa had seen in Andrian's home. So the painter had been present at the scene, and watched as his comrade had made Francesco shoot the rifle; he had been right there, probably hiding in the partisan encampment hidden among the trees in the hill across the road, mere yards from the nephew of the woman he would eventually kill. He had watched the boy, studied his movements, like an invisible guest who had breached the tight circle of Aniza's family.

'Do you remember what the red-haired partisan was called?

He was probably a comrade of Andrian's,' said Teresa.

'No.'

'Do you remember anyone else's name?'

'I'm sorry, I don't. We didn't really socialise with them; it was too dangerous. They didn't even use their real names but called each other by their battle names instead.'

Teresa finally asked him the question they had both known was coming since the moment they'd begun their conversation.

'What happened on the night Aniza disappeared?'

Francesco's expression shifted.

'What happened changed my life,' he said. 'The evening was warm – it seemed summer was in a hurry to begin. Aniza had been in her room all day, doing her embroidery.'

'Was that unusual?'

'Not particularly. She'd spent a lot of time in there over the past several weeks. She said she had a job to finish and needed to get it done soon. Back then I spent most of my time playing outside with the other kids, so I never really noticed. I'll never forgive myself for that.'

'You didn't do anything wrong,' said Teresa, but Francesco seemed not to hear her.

'Just before dinner, Aniza said she was going to visit her friend Katerina to show her the linens she'd been embroidering for her baby. Katerina's baby was due in a few weeks. Aniza was very fond of her.'

'What did Katerina have to say about that visit?'

'Nothing. They never saw each other. Aniza never got there, though Katerina lived only a few minutes' walk from here. We asked everyone in the village, but nobody saw my aunt anywhere near her friend's house that day.

'Someone swore they saw her walking down the road that led to the forest, to the east, on the other side of town. But why would she go into the forest by herself at that time of night? I've driven myself crazy all these years, trying to find an answer to that question.'

Teresa picked her words carefully and spoke them as gently as she could.

'I don't think Aniza was alone in the forest,' she said softly. 'I think someone was waiting for her among the trees.'

Francesco looked at her.

'You think someone lured her there?' he asked.

'Not exactly. They'd already arranged it. Aniza was going to meet someone that night, but not Katerina.'

Francesco stiffened.

'Are you saying Aniza lied to her family? To me?'

Teresa smiled to soften the truth.

'Young people do that sometimes and they probably did it more often in the past, to find ways to meet up with their lovers,' she said.

'My aunt was old enough to get married. If she was in love with a boy, she had no reason to hide it from my grandfather.'

'She would have had every reason to hide it if her boyfriend happened to be one of the partisans hiding in these mountains.'

Francesco seemed speechless.

'Andrian?' he whispered.

'Yes.'

A series of conflicting emotions passed over Francesco's face: shock, resignation, distress and finally anger.

'She loved him and he killed her,' he muttered, his eyes widening in horror, his hands resting on the image of the *Sleeping Nymph* as if to draw her back into his life.

'There's still a lot we need to clarify,' Teresa pointed out.

'Why did he do this to her?'

'Francesco, all we have for now are theories. Please try to remain calm.'

He stared into empty space as if thoughts he'd never dared to think before were now taking shape before his very eyes.

'How did he kill her?' he asked.

'It's hard to know, without a body. In fact, with no body and

162

no confession, I'm afraid we're in no position even to call this a murder.'

Francesco glared at her.

'So what is it, then?' he hissed.

'The judge might even rule it a tragic accident. Aniza may have got hurt some other way. What if she fell into a crevasse? Perhaps Andrian was there but couldn't help her and the pain drove him insane.'

Francesco seemed to consider this possibility for a brief moment before immediately and decisively setting it aside.

'There was nowhere on earth Aniza would have been safer than in the woods of this valley. She was born here. She knew every crack in the rocks, every gully and every cliff edge. No, Superintendent, the valley would never kill one of its children.'

Teresa didn't think so, either, but she felt duty-bound to consider every possible lead.

'If there had been an accident, Andrian would have come to us,' said Francesco, now in a state of heightened agitation. 'He could have asked for help; he could have tried to rescue her! He could have come to us and told us where she was!'

He burst into tears, but his was a restrained sort of grief. He buried his face in his hands and sighed.

'I'm sorry,' he quickly added. 'I don't usually do this, but the strain is just . . .'

Teresa put her hand on his shoulder and gave his sturdy, suffering frame a gentle squeeze.

'There's no need to apologise, Francesco. Tell me, do you think you can keep going?'

The man nodded.

'You said Aniza left the house just before dinner. Did you see her go?'

'I did. I was out playing in the yard. She gave me a kiss. I watched her walking down the road. She was singing.'

'Then what?'

'Then nothing. She never came back. It got dark and my

grandfather was furious. There was a war on and it was never a good idea to stay out so late at night. He went looking for her at Katerina's place. He went alone. I was at home with my mother and father, who were laughing at the thought of the scolding Aniza would get from my grandfather.

'When he finally came back, he was like a different person. I will never forget the look on his face. It was as if he knew. He knew he'd never see her again.'

'What did he say to you?' Teresa asked, her voice barely a whisper.

Francesco's head was in his hands, his eyes fixed on the *Nymph.*

'He kept saying the darkness took her from me. *The darkness took her from me.* But softly, as if he'd lost his voice. It took my father a minute to work out what he was saying and then he went out – combed the village door to door looking for her.

'Lots of people went searching in the woods with torches and lanterns. I remember the night lit up with lamps and the silence interrupted by all of those people calling out her name in the dark. Aniza, Aniza. Even the animals in their coops and their stables seemed restless as if our unease had infected them, too.'

He fell silent, then gave a sigh before resuming his story.

'All that effort with nothing to show for it, not that night nor any other night thereafter. All we ever found was her embroidery bag. It was right at the edge of the forest.'

Teresa could feel a throbbing inside her chest, like something heavy tugging at her heart.

'I wish I could do something to relieve your suffering,' she managed to say.

'And that music. That damned melody,' said Francesco, his voice sounding as if he'd fallen too far into his memories now ever to come back.

'What music?'

'We could hear a violin playing in the dark, somewhere in the woods, right there on the mountain. It played almost right through the night. There was the odd pause, but then it would pick up again.'

'Who was it?'

'We never found out. We used to have a very good teacher here in the valley who was an expert on classical music. He told us he was sure he recognised the melody. It was Tartini's Violin Sonata in G Minor – better known as the 'Devil's Trill'. Whoever it was playing it that night, their execution was magnificent.'

Teresa was surprised.

'It's not my area of expertise, but I do know it's meant to be one of the most technically challenging compositions ever created for a solo violin,' she mused. 'Was there anyone in the valley who'd have been capable of playing it? Surely that level of skill wouldn't have gone unnoticed.'

'Nobody. And in case you're wondering whether or not the music was coming from one of our local musical instruments, I can tell you straight away that it wasn't. It wasn't a Resian sound. Even now it makes me shiver just to think about it.' He paused as if he were unsure of whether or not to continue. 'Do you know what Tartini used to say about it?'

Teresa shook her head.

'He said that the sonata had been inspired by a dream in which he'd made a pact with the devil. He'd dreamt that Lucifer himself had performed the piece for him with the kind of genius and precision that could only find quarter in hell. When he woke up, Tartini tried to transcribe the music he'd heard, but he swore for the rest of his life that he hadn't even come close to reproducing its brilliance. The sonata came to light exactly seventeen years after the night he had that fateful dream.'

'It's certainly an intriguing interpretation,' Teresa remarked.

'The older generation of Resians took the story very literally. They claimed the devil himself had kidnapped Aniza, snatched her away from life, taken her into the forest and into the darkness – the kind that never gives way to dawn. His trill was heard for several nights thereafter. Carried in the wind, close at first, then further away. It was like it was playing games with us. It made a mockery of our hope of finding Aniza alive.

'My grandfather used to say that all things considered, the devil had been magnanimous, for he'd never let us find her body. He left us with a sliver of hope to cling on to, if we really wished to do so.'

He fell quiet.

Teresa asked him one last question.

'I suppose you never reported her missing?'

'To whom? This was a borderland and the horrors of the war were at their peak. There was no State and the authorities had hundreds of thousands of dead to worry about. Italy was in disarray. We were alone. Aniza was alone. Lost.'

Teresa closed her notebook.

'I think that'll be sufficient for the time being,' she said. 'Thank you. This has been most useful.'

Francesco emerged from his reverie and did something Teresa hadn't expected him to do.

He asked about Andrian.

'I did read about this in the newspaper, but there was nothing in there to connect the story with Aniza. Is it true that he hasn't spoken a word since 1945?'

'Yes, it's true.'

'You think he's the one who killed her, don't you?'

'It's a possibility, but there's a lot that we still need to consider.'

There was a brief silence, in which Francesco gathered the strength he needed to say what came next.

'Do you think I could meet him?'

35

The police had come into the valley, taking care not to draw undue attention to their presence. They were following the trail of a heart that had beaten there nearly a hundred years ago and unwittingly peering into a past that should never have come back to light. Even after all this time, that old blood was still warm, kept that way by the everlasting memories of those who had loved the young woman in whose veins it had once flowed. That old blood had spoken and it had led the police here much sooner than expected.

But however discreet the officer with the red hair and the sharp eyes had been in her approach so far, someone had noticed her and her colleagues' presence in the valley. Someone was following them. Someone had watched them intrude upon an ancient mystery with every step they took and every word they uttered.

The *Tikô Wariö* carried a basket on its back. The liquid oozing through its patterned weave had the colour and consistency of crushed ripe cherries, but its scent was the metallic vital essence that filled the veins of the living.

A heart for a heart. That was the punishment for betrayal.

The police weren't the only danger lurking. Other presences were patrolling the valley like nocturnal predators.

The delicate weight inside the basket on its back was a silent, furious warning never to forget that what had happened that night in the forest seventy years ago must remain buried and hidden for ever.

It must rest in its grave. For ever inside the valley.

36

A fierce wind was blowing, heavy with moisture. The sun was covered by a frothy cloud whose shape kept changing and casting its tentacular shadow across the valley. The shadow crept along the mountain slopes and the riverbed like the hand of a giant, raking its fingers through the soil, emitting shivers of cold, stealing warmth from the rocks and sending the animals of the valley scampering back to their dens.

The air was electric, charged with the promise of a thunderstorm. Towards the east, a shard of sky ensconced among the spires of alpine peaks was a whorl of rain-dense clouds, a maelstrom of steely grey traversed with flashes of lightning, each crack followed by a clap of thunder that sounded like the voice of the mountain itself — a roar that carved through the air and exploded in a cacophony of sound.

Teresa crouched at the foot of the ancient linden tree Francesco had pointed out to her. Its branches were being tossed to and fro by gust upon gust of restless wind. It looked like they were shaking with suppressed rage.

She hadn't spoken to Marini and Blanca yet. There was still plenty of time to untangle the story she had just heard. All she wanted to do for the time being was simply to 'feel'.

The village had changed, but not as much as she had previously assumed. Teresa saw before her the same landscape she had already seen in Andrian's painting. He had captured it from exactly the spot in which Teresa stood now, observing the view and picturing the two children and the red-haired partisan watching the German soldier drive his cart over the steep, sloping road.

Andrian had stood in that spot seventy years before Teresa had. He had looked at what she was looking at now. He had breathed in the fragrance of the valley and studied its people. He had approached Aniza unbeknown to her family. He had stood within touching distance of Francesco, but Francesco had never even known he'd existed, never known about those secret urges that had, perhaps, led Andrian to kill the object of his deepest desires.

Teresa ran her hands over the roots of the linden tree. They looked like sinewy arms plunging into the earth. She thought of Andrian sitting there with his rifle and his pencils, picking up a sheet of paper and starting to draw.

Teresa needed to think. She needed to try to fathom what had happened inside the painter's mind, what those distant days might have been like. She needed to form a connection with him, feel what he had felt, capture his hopes, his heartbreak. His obsession.

This old, mad painter was all she had. Aniza was ashes and dust by now, her body no longer there.

She remembered the way Andrian had stared at the forest outside his room. As if there were something there staring right back at him.

Andrian isn't looking at the forest near his home, she reasoned. *In his world, time has stopped. What he is looking at is Aniza's tomb. Somewhere around here. He buried her where only he could see her. Where she would belong to him alone. And she's still there where he can see her.*

'Where are you?' she murmured. 'Where did he hide you?'

37

20 April 1945

The purple shadows of twilight were taking over the village. It was the hour when day and night brushed briefly against each other, the line of daylight moving up over the walls of people's homes like an obedient army retreating in tight formation, a golden front creeping back towards the roofs while the flame of the sun flickered and died like a used candle behind the castellated ridge of the mountains.

As she walked briskly down the road that led to the church, Aniza inhaled those darkening hues with every breath. She felt that something inside her had shifted over the past few weeks. The sky over her life had always shone bright, but night had fallen now. It was a night scented with wild flowers and stolen kisses, two bodies intertwined on a meadow. And promises of eternal love, the fragrance of a secret passion that stole her appetite and her sleep, lighting up her cheeks with a crimson blush that – he said – made her look even more beautiful than she already was.

But ultimately, the night was made of darkness. It extinguished reason and tore down every defence. And above all, it brought betrayal – like every time she was forced to lie to her family. Aniza was torn between the person she was, and the person this love was demanding that she become. But in fact she had already made up her mind.

Katerina's house was just across from the church, no more than a few steps away now. But Aniza turned left and took the footpath that would soon deteriorate into little more than a mule track. She glanced over her shoulder. No one must ever find out. No one would ever understand.

A trail of wild narcissi seemed to be pointing out the way, in among scatterings of acacia flowers whose whiteness matched that of her dress and clusters of dog rose. Mountain orchids bloomed darkly among rippling feather grass.

She pulled her shawl over her head and felt like a bride. The forest was the temple and nature was the god.

He was waiting for her.

38

'Aniza. So she really did exist.'

Marini spoke in a doleful sigh. Teresa couldn't blame him. She understood that feeling of helplessness, the subtle but persistent melancholy that overwhelmed them every time they realised they'd come too late to save the victim. That sickening feeling, that fury: they had experienced it all before.

They'd got to Aniza seventy years too late.

'We can still find out what happened to her.'

That was Blanca's suggestion, uttered with a note of urgency that warmed Teresa's heart. And the way Blanca had said 'we' – Teresa couldn't help but smile at that.

'We'll certainly try,' Teresa promised.

An expression of disappointment combined with concern dawned over the young woman's face.

'That's it?' she exclaimed.

Marini burst out laughing.

'You wish,' he said. 'You might not know it yet, but when this lady says "we'll try", what she means is that she'll literally have us sweating blood until we've got the killer's name and figured out a clear and unassailable motive.'

'Call me "lady" one more time and you can fuck right off. Clear?'

'Crystal, ma'am.'

Blanca shook her head.

'So what happens now?' she asked.

Teresa drew her notebook out of her shoulder bag. She found a blank page and fixed her gaze upon the village.

'Now, we dig deeper.'

Francesco di Lenardo had invited them to attend a meeting of the local society for the preservation of Resian identity. The event was to be held in Matriona's inn, where a sizeable and animated crowd had already formed. Teresa suspected the day's agenda was likely to be dominated not by the preservation of the linguistic and cultural heritage of the valley, but by the murder of the young woman who had vanished all those years ago. Everyone was talking about Aniza now. She had, in a way, come home.

Teresa was surprised again by the depths of feeling that such a distant episode had seemingly elicited in the community; though unlike Francesco's grief, the explanation that lay behind it was perhaps more mundane. Simply put, the Resia Valley had always been a world devoid of crime. The killing of Aniza – whether or not it was a killing – was probably the first time such an act had ever sullied life in the valley. And it had shuddered and clanged its way into the community's consciousness like a metal cannonball falling down a flight of stairs.

As soon as the presence of strangers was detected, dozens of pairs of eyes turned towards the door. Suddenly the room went silent, the only sound a snort from Smoky. The dog had been anxious and restless ever since they'd set foot in the valley, pacing in endless circles, sitting every now and then to howl and bark, then standing again to resume his relentless fidgeting.

'Maybe he's bored,' Blanca had suggested, though without much conviction.

'Ever since the *Nymph* came to light, things seem to be falling apart,' Marini had replied cryptically.

Teresa had shot him an angry look. She hated superstitions, and even more so those who pandered to them. Superstitions had done humanity no good whatsoever.

'I was only joking,' he'd clarified.

'I should hope so.'

Teresa returned the locals' scrutiny without even bothering to hide her interest. She was searching for a common denominator on their faces, some visible sign of their shared ancestry. She'd heard that the people who inhabited that valley all resembled each other a little. That may have been the case in the not too distant past, Teresa mused, though that unifying physical trait – assuming there had been one in the first place – seemed to have long since been blurred and diluted.

Francesco walked towards them and that seemed to lift the shackles that had temporarily stopped the passage of time: conversations, previously interrupted, were resumed and people drew closer to the newcomers, their curiosity piqued.

'Calm down, calm down,' said Francesco, trying to keep them at bay. 'Let's settle down first, then you can all ask whatever you want to ask.'

The questions were numerous and Teresa patiently answered them all. She couldn't give much away about their progress with the investigation, but she was eager to involve them all as much as she possibly could, to capture the mood of these women and these men who had never met Aniza but who'd been left wondering about the terrible fate that had wrenched her away from her family. She could feel the existence of a bond between these people that went far beyond those of mere neighbourhood.

'Was there a murderer among us, or is the killer this man Andrian?' someone asked.

Others were looking around the room as if in search of an answer, but there wasn't one – not for either of the two possibilities.

'It's too early to say with any certainty who the perpetrator is,' said Teresa.

Eventually, once every aspect of the matter had been probed, the mood began to soften and conversations in the room took other trajectories, the chatter eased by a glass or two of good wine. People switched from Italian to a language made of a gentle, mysterious clicking of consonants, its tones harmonious and appealingly exotic.

Matriona was an attentive hostess. Teresa watched her weaving between tables, refilling glasses and serving fragrant appetisers. Some other women were helping her out. Teresa had noticed them because of all the people in the room, they had been the only ones who hadn't approached her and who refrained from asking her any questions. Instead, they had stood watching her from a distance, their faces betraying no trace of emotion.

'You must try our wild garlic cream,' said Francesco, handing her a tray loaded with canapes.

The bread was still warm and the cream a vivid green. The smell, though, wasn't as pungent as Teresa had expected.

'Go on, have some,' Francesco encouraged them. 'You won't find this anywhere else.'

'Is the garlic here special, too?' Massimo queried, taking a bite.

'It's not just the human population of the valley that's been affected by its seclusion.' Francesco gestured at the strings of garlic hanging from the ceiling. 'Our variety is called *strock*. It's red in colour and produces small, sweet cloves. As with all precious things, it's not particularly fruitful.'

Teresa and Blanca tasted it, too.

'Delicious.'

The refreshments began to edge – virtually unnoticed by Teresa – into a full lunch. She tried to protest that they had to return to the city, but Matriona was the first to insist that they should stay. She'd already brought out steaming bowls of soup.

'Our famous garlic soup. You can't leave without trying some,' she said. 'There's *calcüne*, too. I gathered the plantain and bladder campion for the filling just this morning. And I bet you've never eaten wild carrot before.'

'We've never had any of the rest of it, either!' Blanca laughed.

Matriona patted her shoulder.

'Well then, it's decided,' she said, moving on to look after her other customers, too.

Teresa pointed out the other women who were helping her out.

'I haven't met them yet,' she remarked.

Francesco followed her gaze.

'They work in Mat's farming business,' he explained. 'They

grow garlic and medicinal herbs, particularly mallow. They dry it out, then they package it and sell it as herbal tea or as a pharmaceutical remedy. As far as social and economic experiments go, it's been a successful one, and a path through which many of our young women have reconnected with the land. Some who'd moved away have even come back to live in the valley.' He pointed at the ribbons tied around the peg boxes of the violins on the wall. 'Each woman has her own kind of ribbon, in her own colours. She'll use it to decorate the basket with which she goes foraging for plants and flowers. It's a way of treasuring our traditions that also allows for self-expression.'

'You all have Italian surnames,' Teresa remarked. 'Yet many of the women here have Resian first names. Not the men, though.'

Francesco nodded in agreement.

'Our language has been transmitted through the centuries in oral form alone. Only recently have we sought to codify it in writing – perhaps because we're so close to losing it for ever. Taking on Italian surnames was, I think, a natural consequence of the valley opening up to the rest of the world. I couldn't say exactly when that happened.

'Many people see me as the guardian of our collective historical memory, but I'm not sure I'm old enough to remember what truly matters and regrettably, all of our ancient knowledge has been lost for ever. We don't know where we come from.

'But our women have always preserved some part of our history. They nurture it like a sacred flame to be kept alive for ever. They're the ones passing on our traditional names through the generations and teaching the kids our language. They're the ones who bring this land back to life each spring, planting and harvesting their herbs. Well, all right, not all of them, perhaps. Some of them. But I have no doubt their numbers will only increase. Females of every species always take the utmost care of the one thing the males hardly even think about.'

'What's that?' asked Marini.

'The future. It's an innate genetic imperative.'

'In this place, the past and the future seem intertwined,' Teresa observed.

Francesco seemed to ponder her words for a moment.

'The ancients didn't ascribe linear progress to time as we do,' he said. 'For them it was a cyclical thing, like the seasons. Winter was a door into spring. Death was a passage to a new life. In this valley, too, the past is both a starting point and a place to return to.'

'Is it really true that you have no information at all about your origins?' asked Blanca.

She seemed utterly fascinated.

'None. We've lived here for almost two thousand years, but any traces of our arrival seem to have vanished altogether. The two things that speak to our provenance are both ephemeral and intangible: our language and our songs.'

'Your songs?'

'I don't suppose you've ever heard of Ella von Schultz-Adaïewsky. She was a Russian composer and musicologist who lived in Italy for some time. She specialised early on in ethnomusicology. In 1897, she published a paper entitled "La Berceuse Populaire".'

'The folk lullaby,' Teresa translated.

'She studied numerous traditional Indo–European lullabies, travelling extensively for her research. She theorised that there are soothing, sedative properties encoded in the very rhythms of the traditional ditties people sing to help children fall asleep. Also, that it's thanks to an innate ancestral wisdom that lullabies exclude all musical patterns that might prove to have stimulating properties.

'Needless to say, it's all much more technically complex than my summary suggests. Ella also pointed to the existence of sequences of notes placed on the downbeat of a bar of music, known as anacruses, which she described as having "unsettling properties unconducive to rest".'

'Forgive me,' Marini interjected. 'I'm not sure I understand what the connection is to the question of the origins of your community.'

'In this particular paper, Ella describes a Mingrelian lullaby. The Mingrelians are a people who inhabit a mountainous region on the shores of the Black Sea: the ancient kingdom of Colchis, home to Medea and possibly even the Amazons. Ella specifically visited the town of Tsaishi in the Caucasus. She described its people as "dark and fiery". She heard their traditional lullaby, a *paeon epibatus*, where the melody was accompanied by a beat tapped out with the foot.'

'Just like in your songs,' Teresa murmured, understanding what Francesco was getting at.

He nodded, watching her with a silent intensity.

'Ella wrote in her paper that she'd heard a version of that lullaby before,' he continued. 'This had been during two visits she'd made to Italy towards the end of the 1800s, in a valley she described as picturesque.'

'The Resia Valley.'

'That's right. Our home. Ella refers to it explicitly in her research and describes its traditional arias. The only difference she detected between the two lullabies is that ours is in iambic tetrameter, whereas the Mingrel version is in trochaic dimeter. But it's the kind of technical detail that won't mean anything to most people. To our ears – to most people's ears – those two lullabies sound very similar – almost identical, in fact.'

He leant forwards then and stared at them each in turn, his eyes blazing.

'This means we have the flicker of a flame to illuminate our past – and it isn't here, it isn't across these borders that surround us but much, much further East, in the Orient. And genome studies confirm it. We have science on our side now, telling us we're not the delusional fools that we've been portrayed as for so long.'

He sipped his wine. His hands were shaking a little.

'There's another difference, too,' he added, perhaps faltering a little.

'What is it?' asked Teresa.

'Our lullaby is also a funeral dirge,' he murmured. 'In our community, the end is also a new beginning. We lull our dead to sleep, cradle them as they pass away. Death is merely a journey.'

Teresa thought back to his earlier comments on the ancient understanding of the cyclical nature of time, an old form of wisdom that seemed to have survived in that valley even as it had been forgotten everywhere else.

'What exactly is your theory on the origins of the Resians?' she asked him.

Francesco took a deep breath.

'Our story most probably begins near the shores of the Aral Sea. That's where the pastoral communities from Mesopotamia came to settle. They were looking for pasture and found plenty of it there, though these steppes were ruled by brutal, oppressive clans. Eventually, the depression reached this part of the world, too: there was no more water left, nor enough grass for the herds. So the herdsmen moved north-east and ended up in the Caucasus.

'Tacitus signals their presence in his writings in what's modern-day Ukraine and he provides detailed descriptions, too: unlike the existing populations of the steppes, whose manner was coarse, and who communicated through gestures and grunts, the newcomers lived in huts and dressed in comparatively elaborate clothing, engaged in both animal husbandry and agriculture, and spoke their own language. Tacitus referred to them as *sclaves*, because they were usually exploited and subjugated by the local horseback clans.

'They were also kept divided and that separation led to slight linguistic divergences. It's believed that they once again fled north-east around the sixth century, in the wake of the armies of the Huns. Four of these tribes eventually made it into our valley, bringing four different forms of archaic Slavic with them. The renowned linguist Hamp has identified us as a linguistically autonomous Slavic clan.'

Francesco fell silent, lowering his gaze to the linen tablecloth, which he was compulsively smoothing over with his fingers. He seemed lost in his own thoughts, as if that ancient past he had just described was now a series of images projected on to the white screen of that cloth.

'The land of the Amazons,' said Blanca in quiet awe. 'What an amazing story!'

Everyone laughed at that.

'It's funny how of all the things he told us, the bit you're most interested in is the part that's a myth,' Marini teased her.

'That's what you think.'

'That's what history says, actually.'

'To tell you the truth, we've got plenty of Amazons here among us,' said Francesco. 'Our women are strong and independent – very much so.' He looked up then, his gaze becalmed. 'You're going to meet one of them soon. I think you'll be astonished when you set eyes on her.'

This was the moment Teresa had been waiting for and now that it was about to happen, her heart began to hammer in her chest. They were going to meet Krisnja, Aniza's great-niece.

They were about to see, alive before them, the face of the *Sleeping Nymph*.

39

When she wasn't busy attending classes at university, Krisnja volunteered at the valley's ethnographic museum. The museum consisted of a series of open-plan rooms housing a permanent exhibition on the ancient art of itinerant furniture-making from which – up until a few decades ago – so many generations of Resians had made a living. Adjacent to the main complex was another building constructed in a more old-fashioned rural style:

a reproduction of a typical local dwelling.

Francesco had told them Krisnja would be waiting for them there, in the annexe.

'Ready?' said Marini, with a wry look on his face designed, perhaps, to temper his own nerves.

They'd obsessed over the *Sleeping Nymph* for so long now that it seemed inevitable they would be disappointed: surely the resemblance between the two women couldn't be as pronounced as they'd been told and it was impossible that the allure of the mysterious painting could be found intact in a real living person.

'Ready or not, we're going in,' said Teresa.

The sun was enveloped in enormous whorls of grey that swirled around the mountain peaks, forming clouds that looked like dark, oppressive whirlpools. The weather had shifted again; the day had turned dark, the sky gloomy and pale; gusts of wind carried the scent of rain. In the distance, the dark space between two mountain peaks was sliced open by fierce flashes of lightning.

They left Smoky in the car, with the window rolled halfway down. Inside the annexe was a flight of wooden stairs and from behind the door that had been left ajar at the top of the staircase they could hear the voice of a woman singing in the Resian language, a gentle, languorous ballad. Teresa was reminded of the songs she would hear the farmers sing when, as a child, she would go out with her grandparents to gather hay for the beasts, or to harvest the ripe, syrupy fruit of the grapevines, when the air was still warm but the leaves were already laced with the colours of the approaching autumn. She could almost smell the scent of those days now, taste their sweetness on her tongue.

The door sprang open with the gentlest of touches and Teresa suddenly found herself immersed in the past. The place smelt of the hand-carved wooden benches that lined either side of the room, of the baskets of viburnum hanging from the walls, flanked by other handicrafts and photographs of ageing faces that stood out like statues sculpted out of time. Bunches of dried herbs hung from the rafters. There was a stove ensconced in the other wall, with an antique cauldron perched on a stool next to it.

And there she was, her profile concealed by a mane of dark hair, which cascaded over her shoulders and down her back. She was wearing a long black skirt embroidered with flowers along the hem and a white blouse tied at the waist with a sash the colour of cornflowers. She'd rolled up her sleeves all the way to her elbows and was sifting through a hamper filled with tiny white flowers, releasing the familiar honeyed fragrance of chamomile into the air – a scent made all the more intense by the process of desiccation the flowers had been put through, which would have taken the best part of a year.

Outside, there was a storm brewing, but in that room Krisnja kept singing her song of peace. It was an enchanted moment and they were loath to interrupt it. Her voice rang with calm dignity against the force of the elements pounding at the windows and seemed to nullify their fury as if it had the power to tame nature itself. Blanca gave Teresa's hand a quick squeeze; she knew exactly how Teresa felt.

The singing stopped and their breathing stopped with it.

Krisnja turned round. Teresa felt like she was looking at someone she had always known but never met before. She gripped Blanca's hand in turn as if to say: feel what I am feeling.

That's her.

The *Sleeping Nymph* stood reincarnated before them, the perfect oval of her face, her straight nose, her eyes – as black as Teresa had pictured them – ever so slightly slanted, her hair falling in waves over her breast, so similar to the way it looked in the portrait, but alive and gleaming.

Krisnja made them coffee the Resian way, in a saucepan. It was difficult not to stare at her, but she seemed not to mind.

'Francesco told me the story of the portrait,' she said as she handed them a plate of *sope* – sliced bread dipped in egg batter, fried and glazed with sugar.

Marini and Blanca tucked right in, but Teresa spared a thought for her glucose levels and decided to abstain. Krisnja joined them at the table.

'It's all been such a shock for him. He adored Aniza. When I was little, he used to tell me how much I resembled her all the time. Then one day he stopped saying it. I suppose he thought he should stop comparing me to a dead woman. But I could see it in his eyes anyway, every time he looked at me.'

She faltered for a moment, then glanced at Teresa.

'Do I really look like her?' she asked.

Teresa showed her the photograph she carried of the portrait. The young woman covered her mouth with her hand.

'So that's her,' she whispered. 'I could never bring myself to ask Francesco for his old photographs of her. They're like sacred relics to him.'

'Francesco speaks of you with great fondness,' Teresa said.

Krisnja smiled.

'I'm very fond of him, too. He's always been there for me as if I were the daughter he never had. Ewa, my grandmother, was widowed at a very young age and my father left the valley when I was little, abandoning my mother, Hanna. In some ways Francesco took his place, though I've grown up surrounded almost entirely by women.'

'I get the feeling that among your people, it's you, the women, who are more dedicated to preserving your cultural heritage,' Teresa remarked as she studied the various objects exhibited in the room.

Krisnja's expression turned sombre.

'Our community is going through a difficult time, a painful time. We're divided in ways we never have been before, not in all the many centuries of our history.' She gestured at the displays and at the many panels that illustrated the valley's past. 'That's one reason I've chosen to stay here. It's my duty to keep watch over the truth. To bring it back to light.'

*

The car rolled through the driving rain. Blanca sat in the back with a pensive look on her face, lost in reverie and holding Smoky close. Marini drove slowly, peering over the wheel as the car sliced through a wall of rain. Torrents of water on either side of the road were carrying their load of silt down the mountain.

Teresa felt exhausted, as if the day's exertions had finally caught up with her the moment she had got back into the car and shut the valley out. All emotions came with a physical weight: she knew this for a fact. They could crush your heart and your body, and they burdened your back no matter how strong your shoulders were.

Teresa was like a sponge, soaking up the mood of the world around her, making its light and its shadows her own. She had absorbed plenty of darkness so far, but somehow, she had managed to convert most of it into fire and a burning appetite for life. The darkness had sunk to the depths of her soul and she had learnt to live with it, to treat it like a poison best left undisturbed. She had let it settle as deep as it would go – but nevertheless it was still there, and every now and then she felt it rise to the surface like a toxic fume.

The ricochet of water on the windscreen was hypnotic. Teresa's eyes closed of their own accord. Images of Matriona, Francesco and Krisnja flitted across the blank screen of her mind like cards on a poker table.

The alarm on her phone went off, reminding her that she'd have to take her daily insulin injection in an hour. She made a quick calculation: she had plenty of time to get to headquarters, draft a perfunctory report and then pierce yet another hole through her own skin, which was so much more delicate than it looked and which sometimes no longer felt like hers. She had plenty of time to find that she was alone again, a little more bruised than she had been when she had woken up that morning. A little more tired.

Names and words stood out now like paths on a map she was still struggling to read.

Rain. Origins. Krisnja. Illness.

More rain. Francesco. Memories. An illness that erases memories.

She opened her eyes just enough to see. The storm was getting worse. Marini kept having to slow down to avoid dead wood and leaves that had fallen across the road. The wind whistled through the trees, in gusts strong enough to break branches. Buckets of rain lashed at the car windows.

Teresa's eyes closed again.

'Maybe we should stop here and wait it out,' she heard Blanca say.

'We're almost at the highway, just a few more turns,' Marini reassured her.

A terrifying roar ripped across the sky, a clap of thunder rattling the frame and windows of the car.

Blanca screamed.

'We've awakened a hostile god.'

Only after her lips had closed around the last word did Teresa realise that she had been the one to speak. She could still feel the words now on the tip of her tongue, heavy and unwelcome. It wasn't the kind of thing she usually said.

She opened her eyes again. All she could see before her now was a relentless, furious cascade of metallic grey cutting through the world like a guillotine, a screen of water whipped up into foaming white swirls by the ripping wind. All of a sudden, in the midst of that soaked inferno, Teresa glimpsed the dark silhouette of something else, something standing in the middle of the short stretch of straight road they were on. She focused her eyes and with each frantic swipe of the windscreen wipers, the shadow took clearer form. Until it was too late.

'Careful!' she yelled.

Instinctively, she took hold of the steering wheel and pulled it towards her.

The car swerved and smashed through the crash barrier, rolling down the edge of the road for the duration of a terrified scream before crashing to a halt against a tree trunk.

The silence that followed was very brief and bedlam soon ensued, Smoky barking non-stop and the rest of them shouting at each other to check for damage. Blanca kicking at the door to try and get out. Marini grabbing hold of the girl and dragging her out onto the grass.

Teresa was gasping for air. She wasn't in pain, but she had entered a stage of benumbed confusion that was, for her, worse than death.

'Superintendent! Can you hear me? Superintendent!'

Marini was shaking her. She was still in the front passenger seat with her seat belt on. Instead of replying to Marini, she grabbed his arm.

'Did you manage to avoid him?' she asked.

He stared at her uncomprehendingly.

'Avoid what?'

Teresa looked up towards the road, which shimmered like a mirage under the relentless rain.

'There was someone there. Didn't you see him?'

She watched the colour drain from his face. Marini quickly clambered back up to the road and disappeared from sight. Smoky led Blanca to Teresa. The young woman's unseeing eyes were wide open in terror and her blood must have frozen inside her, judging by how pale she looked. Rivulets of water ran down her face like semi-transparent veins.

'Are you all right?' she asked Teresa.

Blanca looked like she was on the verge of tears.

Teresa mumbled a yes, grabbing hold of Blanca's outstretched arm as she stepped out of the vehicle.

Marini soon returned, sliding down the embankment to save time. There was a deep cut across his forehead, but the rain kept washing the blood away.

'I didn't see anyone,' he said with an expression she was unable to decipher. 'There was no one there, Superintendent.'

The roar of the storm around them began to fade as the gale

dwindled into mere rain drumming against the carcass of their car.

Teresa looked away and her eyes fell upon the sharp cliff edge just feet away from where they had come to a stop.

What have I done?

40

Massimo prodded at the plaster on his forehead and let slip a curse. He could feel the stitches underneath pulling at his skin.

'Does it hurt?' Blanca asked.

He rubbed her arm.

'No, it doesn't,' he said soothingly. 'How are you feeling?'

She let out a long breath.

'Nervous.'

She and Smoky had been lucky to escape without a scratch, but Blanca was anxious: she'd had to leave her dog with de Carli in the waiting room of A & E. Now, she couldn't stop fidgeting and her restlessness had infected Massimo, too. He had tried to reason with her, but then he'd remembered how important Smoky was to her and realised that she wouldn't rest until they'd been reunited – like a mother with her lost child.

They were both waiting for Superintendent Battaglia to emerge from the treatment room, where she was being looked after for a sprained wrist. According to the information Massimo had gleaned from a nurse who'd just come out of that same room, the superintendent hadn't broken anything.

But it wasn't physical injuries Massimo was worried about. He had to talk to her so that he could tell her that no one blamed her for what had happened – least of all him. They'd been lucky and this was just an unfortunate accident that they'd already put behind them. Soon, the memory of it would fade altogether and he never intended to mention it again.

She had looked so mortified, so scared, so ashamed of the inexplicable impulse she had acted upon.

For a minute, Massimo had really believed he'd run someone over. He'd climbed back up to the road with a knot in his stomach, terrified and nearly throwing up at the thought that he might find a body splayed over the tarmac. But there had been nothing except a few broken branches and a blanket of wind-swept leaves. There were no words to describe the sheer relief he had felt in that moment, but that sensation had quickly morphed into concern: the Teresa Battaglia he knew would never have behaved so recklessly.

'Go home,' he told Blanca. 'There's no point in both of us waiting.'

She shook her head.

'No, I want to make sure she's all right.'

He patted her head in response but was so surprised by his own gesture that he quickly pulled his hand away.

'Of course she's all right,' he said comfortingly.

'Then why won't she come out?'

'Because she's a police superintendent who's been involved in an accident,' he lied. 'You've no idea how many forms she's going to have to fill in. It'll take for ever. Go on, go. De Carli's been waiting to drop you home.'

Her frown deepened.

'Is she going to be in trouble because of the car?'

'No. There was a branch blocking the road. I didn't see it because of the rain, so I had to swerve at the last second.'

She briefly fell silent as if she were weighing his words.

'Is that the "official" story?' she asked.

Massimo grimaced.

'If you call it "official" it sounds wrong,' he replied. 'It's just what happened, isn't it?'

She smiled.

'It is.'

'Off you go, then.'

'All right, I'll go, but please tell her I'm not upset with her.'

Massimo beckoned a nurse over to help Blanca.

'Of course,' Massimo replied.

He stared at the door of the treatment room. It was so quiet it might as well have been empty.

He held his face in his hands. How would Albert Lona react to this news? If he'd been waiting for an excuse to have a go at the superintendent, fate couldn't have handed him a better chance than this. They would have to close ranks around her, Massimo and all the others, too.

He was startled by the touch of a hand upon his back.

'Hey. It's me.'

It was Elena. She eyed the plaster on his forehead apprehensively. Massimo stood up.

'Hi. You didn't have to come,' he blurted out. 'I told you I'd grab a taxi. How are you?'

She drew back.

'You're asking me? You're the one who's almost had his head split open.'

Massimo realised how he must look to her, his clothes crumpled and stained with blood, and the plaster on his head so much bigger than the wound it covered.

He pointed at his forehead and forced a smile.

'My head's all right. Really, you shouldn't have troubled yourself.'

But instead of relaxing, her expression grew harder.

'Right. I guess there's nothing I can ever do for you,' she said.

He raised his arm as if to touch her, but then let it drop to his side.

'That's not what I meant.'

'Then what did you mean? I was worried, and with good reason, I think.'

He pulled her closer.

'I'm sorry,' he whispered, resting his forehead against hers. She felt cold to the touch, or perhaps he was the one who was frozen.

'Marini?'

Massimo turned round. It was Parri. He felt Elena slip away from his embrace and he did nothing to stop her.

'They won't let me in, Doctor Parri,' he said, unable to disguise his consternation.

The coroner flashed a smile, surveying the bruise blooming across Marini's jaw.

'Don't worry, I'll look after our Battaglia. My colleagues here have assured me she'll be just fine. Go home now, put some ice on that and try to get some sleep.'

Massimo wanted to tell him that he was worried, that it wasn't him but Teresa Battaglia who needed comforting, who needed Massimo to tell her that what had happened to her could have happened to anyone.

'I'd like to see her,' he said instead.

Parri looked at Elena then before shifting his gaze back onto Marini's face. He put his hand on Marini's shoulder and squeezed it hard.

'I'll take her home and keep her company. You don't need to worry. About *anything*,' he promised.

41

Teresa pressed her index finger against the bracelet and sent it spinning with a flick around her uninjured wrist. It was Russian roulette of a sort: the rule was that if the bracelet stopped at her name, she would flick it again; but if it stopped at the phone number, she would make the call. She would tell her doctor that the moment they'd talked about over and over again had finally arrived. She had to quit her job.

But the bracelet hadn't once landed on the phone number. Statistically speaking, it was some kind of miracle.

Sitting on the hospital bed with her legs dangling off the side, Teresa felt like she was perched on the edge of a cliff, not brave enough to jump off, not strong enough to back away. She was appalled at herself, at what she had been on the verge of causing: the untimely death of two young people. And all that – she thought in horror – for the sake of a non-existent shadow.

She had made many mistakes in her life. She had fallen down and picked herself back up again. She'd lost everything and started from scratch. She'd bid farewell to many people and met plenty more. But she had never hurt anyone.

With one crucial exception.

She spun the bracelet round again, and again it landed on her name.

Had the illness accelerated its advance? Should she get used to experiencing hallucinations too, now, in addition to the memory lapses? It was definitely possible – probable, even. Almost certainly it explained what had happened that day.

A non-existent shadow.

It hadn't just been some shimmer in the darkness, a trick of the light in the driving rain. It had seemed so much more substantial; it had looked alive.

And angry.

She shook her head as if to rid her mind of the disturbing image.

The door opened and she breathed a sigh of relief at the sight of Antonio Parri's smiling face.

He gave her a hug, saying nothing. Teresa didn't protest. She needed it. She desperately needed someone to look after her, someone to whom she might hand over – even temporarily – the reins of her own life, for she didn't feel like she could hold on to them herself for much longer.

'It's going to be OK,' she heard him whisper against her hair.

It wasn't true, but there was no harm just then in a white lie. Teresa welcomed it, but at the same time she felt compelled to explain herself, to get the weight of the truth off her chest. She looked into her old friend's eyes.

'Antonio . . .' she began.

'Shhh, don't worry; they told me everything on the phone.'

'But I need to talk about it.'

He ignored her, his arms still cradling her as if she were a little girl.

'Marini's sorted everything out and you've been discharged,' he told her. 'I've come to pick you up.'

Teresa gently pushed him away.

'What did he sort out?' she asked.

Antonio peered at her over the frame of his glasses.

'He explained about the branch that had fallen onto the road and how he had to swerve to avoid it.'

'There was no branch,' Teresa murmured.

'Parisi and de Carli cleared it away when they came to collect you all.'

Teresa stared at him.

'You know it's bullshit.'

'Of course.'

He was protecting her. Just like Marini, just like de Carli and Parisi.

She looked away, her eyes stinging.

All she could say was: 'Why?'

He draped his jacket over her shoulders.

'Because I've lost count of all the times you took my drink away when I was too drunk even to remember my own name,' he whispered into her ear.

Teresa squeezed his hand. She would have given anything to be able to explain to him why she had pulled the steering wheel and almost caused them all to meet their Maker at the bottom of a cliff.

But she couldn't do it. For the first time in her life, she couldn't confide in him.

Because what she had thought she'd glimpsed through the

lashings of rain had been a human figure, standing, fists clenched, in the middle of the road and leaning forwards as if daring her to drive past.

But she could never speak openly about what she had thought she had seen without also being willing to admit to everything else, too, including her illness – which was the only thing that could explain what had happened.

'Did you take your insulin?' said Antonio as he helped her off the bed.

'Yes.'

'Then let's go.'

Teresa nodded. 'I can't say I'm too thrilled at the prospect of sitting at home, brooding,' she muttered.

Parri took her arm.

'But I'm not taking you home. Not yet,' he said with a sly smile.

'Oh, really?'

'I've got a surprise for you. And since you've just fallen down an embankment and somehow managed to come out of it unscathed, I think now is the time to give it to you.'

'Is it edible and full of sugar?'

'No, but I bet you'll like it just the same. It's waiting for you in my lab.'

Teresa stopped in her tracks.

'Is it about the *Sleeping Nymph*?'

Antonio Parri's smile broadened in response.

'I'm good, aren't I?'

'You're the best.'

It was evening already and the hallways of the morgue were dark and deserted. Apart from the lobby and the refrigeration chambers, Parri's office was the only room with the lights still on. The security guard looked up as they walked in and nodded in greeting before returning to his newspaper.

Parri's office was bathed in the bluish light of his computer monitor, the screensaver a skull rotating on its axis. The only sound in the room was the hum of the computer. Behind Parri's desk a human skeleton beckoned her with its index finger.

'Who's he?' Teresa asked.

'The latest gift from my PhD students.'

Antonio sat down at his desk and entered the password to access his files.

'I've actually got two surprises for you. The first is a confirmation: the DNA we extracted from the portrait is a ninety-eight per cent match with Francesco di Lenardo's.'

'So it is Aniza's blood. What's the other surprise?'

'Come round,' he told her. 'I haven't had a chance to print the photographs out yet.'

'The photographs?'

'Enlargements. Look.'

The images he was showing her were enlargements of the portrait of the *Nymph*, divided into sections. Each section was overlaid with a digital grid, similar to the way the forensics team would have divided a stretch of land to examine it for evidence, or how an archaeologist would have handled a dig.

Teresa's gaze fell upon a quadrant near the lower-left border of the painting. The processing software had detected and marked out a smudge that looked, to the naked eye, like nothing more than a spot shaded a little darker than the others. Antonio clicked through to the next image, where that particular section had been enlarged and where someone had drawn a red circle around an unusual pattern detected by the software.

'Is that what I think it is?' Teresa asked.

'I think so. I was waiting for another colleague to confirm before alerting you. We have two partial fingerprints here, an index finger and a ring finger. We used an algorithm to work out the dimensions and found that their lengths are different. They must belong to an adult male.'

'Are you sure?'

'Yes. If they were a woman's, the length would be the same.

193

And I might as well answer your next question: they don't belong to Alessio Andrian. I've already run a comparison test.'

Teresa thought of what Francesco had told her about the violin playing in the forest the night Aniza disappeared. In the absence of proof, and with nothing to go on except the recollections of a man who'd been just a boy at the time, she'd set that story aside. She took a deep breath.

'So, there really was someone else around that night, as Aniza lay dying and Andrian painted her picture,' she murmured. 'Someone who touched her blood while it was still warm.'

42

That ticking sound was back again, inexorable and relentless. And that horrible, oppressive catch in his throat.

Massimo swallowed, trying to get rid of it, but it only got worse, like a razor blade, a burning that made him cough.

He couldn't figure out where he was. He couldn't remember. The forest, perhaps.

The ticking turned into an ominous pounding, counting down to the moment time inevitably ran out.

Massimo tried to get up, but he couldn't feel his arms or his legs. He was lying paralysed somewhere in that thick darkness. Only his thoughts seemed capable of motion, but they were like fish darting about in the stillness of a pond. They surfaced for brief moments, only to dive back into liquid oblivion, flashes of confusion far removed from coherent thought.

His breathing quickened with the pounding. Massimo could feel it hammering inside his chest. It was a buzzing in his ears, a pressure against his temples. It was blood roaring through his veins like the rapids of a river, cascading through his motionless body like a waterfall.

He tried to open his eyes in the night, but his eyelids seemed locked in the iron grip of exhaustion. With great effort, he managed to crack them open and in that hazy limbo, he spied a shadow, a shadow with the voice of a woman who was calling out his name.

Aniza, he thought.

The feeling that he was no longer alone became a certainty when he felt a gentle touch upon his face.

'Where are you?' he called out.

He couldn't see her. The darkness that surrounded him seemed possessed of a physical mass, just like the air, which felt as thick as concrete and hardened inside him until it took up every last furrow in his flesh. It was like solid poison. Marini pictured his helpless lungs collapsing under its steady advance, his alveoli shrivelling up like the parched branches of a dying tree.

He was aware now that he was dreaming, but he couldn't wake up. Something was keeping him anchored to the depths of that black dream, something that smelt distinctly of powdered bone.

He felt his breathing quicken until it became a silent scream. The dream had begun to show him its true face: his father's. Massimo could see him now, emerging from the darkness like a corpse floating on water. He was pale. There was no blood flowing under his bloated, transparent flesh. There was no life.

The scream died away and Massimo began to whimper, just as he used to do as a child when he saw his father approach. He was a grown man now and still he shook. Was this really all it took to shatter what he had spent almost thirty years trying to build? Nothing more than a glance from that pair of eyes so similar to his own?

In the nightmare, his father was growing, fed by Massimo's revulsion, or perhaps by his fear. His mouth, half-open, resembled an open tomb. The breath coming out of it smelt of flowers.

Massimo felt his throat tighten and the air run out. A pair of enormous hands was attacking him now, but he managed to grab them before they could grab him. He knew how to defend himself now. He just had to push back, push back hard, until he'd pushed him over . . .

He squeezed until he felt his fingers piercing the flesh of that fiendish creature his mind had produced.

The silence screamed back at him with a woman's voice.

Massimo opened his eyes. He was awake now. The wrists he was clasping belonged to Elena, so delicate they'd disappeared entirely in his grip.

He let go in horror.

She was short of breath, just as he was. They both sounded like they'd come out of a physical altercation. Elena was silent. The light from the floor lamp illuminated her eyes, the pupils dilated in fear. She was staring at him as if she could no longer recognise him. Massimo had feared this moment ever since the day he'd realised he had fallen in love with her.

'Massimo . . .'

'*No.*'

He ignored her hand reaching out to him and pushed her away. He saw her flinch: she was scared of him. Finally, his greatest fear had come true. He looked at her wrists. Her skin was red where he'd held her in his grip. He felt tears mixing with the sweat that stung at his eyes.

'It's nothing,' he heard her say through the sobs now rising in her throat, her arms instinctively cradling her abdomen as if to protect it.

She was lying, of course. It wasn't nothing; it was more than Massimo was prepared to live with.

I'm just like him. It's in my blood. I'm a monster.

He had to protect her from that monster.

'Leave,' he shouted, feeling like he was dying. 'Go! Leave now and never come back.'

43

There was once a cat that caught a mouse, but just as he was preparing to eat it, the wretched mouse pleaded with his captor:
'Cat, oh cat, will you give me a chance to escape?'
The cat, relishing the creature's plight, replied as follows:
'I shan't eat you, sweet little mouse, if and only if you can guess what it is that I shall do next . . .'

Teresa puzzled over the riddle for a while, then closed her notebook and saved the solution for another day. It was late and her eyes were too tired, though she doubted she'd be able to sleep.

'I'm like a trapped mouse,' she huffed.

Throughout her career, even in the toughest situations, she had never once felt cornered. She had always felt that she had a choice, even if some of those choices had required a certain degree of courage. But ever since the day the *Sleeping Nymph* had entered her life, she had felt like a trapped mouse, and the feeling had nothing to do with her illness.

There was a mysterious presence looming over this case, putting Teresa's senses on high alert. Teresa had felt it. And perhaps Antonio Parri had glimpsed it, too, in those fingerprints he'd found on the painting.

Whoever it was, they had probably died long ago. *So why do I feel them lurking over my shoulder?*

The neighbourhood dogs had been barking for the last few minutes. First, it was those that lived at the other end of the road, but then the barking had spread from house to house right up to her next-door neighbours', each new burst of sound signalling the approach of an unwelcome visitor. There was something out there, and it wasn't a cat. Cats didn't walk in a straight line for hundreds of yards and, more importantly, they couldn't stand the sound of dogs howling.

Teresa checked the time. It was the middle of the night. And again, there was that feeling of being watched.

She went to the window quietly and parted the curtains just enough to bring one eye to the glass and peer into the darkness.

There was an eye staring right back at her. She jumped away from the window and nearly yelped in shock. Pressing a hand to her chest as if to hold her heart in place, she opened the window.

'Have you gone mad?' she breathed.

Blanca and Smoky stood rooted to the spot like garden gnomes.

'Are you angry?' the young woman asked.

'I almost died. Why are you so obsessed with watching people in secret?'

Blanca smiled.

'I can't exactly watch people. I'm blind. I was just eavesdropping. We just wanted to see how you were doing,' she said. 'We couldn't tell from the voicemail you left us.'

'Come inside. Through the front door.'

Blanca took a step back.

'No, that's all right. You've got company. I heard voices. Was it your husband?'

Teresa turned to look at the couch, where Antonio Parri had fallen asleep with the TV remote clasped in one hand. He'd insisted on staying the night.

Teresa turned to Blanca once more. Who knew how long the girl had been waiting out there.

'He's not my husband. He's just a worried friend,' she clarified.

'I'm glad he stayed.'

Teresa leant over the railing.

'I'm sorry about today,' she said. 'I have no idea what came over me. I almost killed the two of you.'

Blanca's expression darkened as if some viscous substance had been poured over her emotions.

'Why do you always talk that way? You said you almost killed "the two of you", but you were there, too. You could have died, too,' she pointed out. 'It's like you don't care about your own life at all.'

Teresa thought about it.

'It's terribly silly, isn't it?' she remarked.

Blanca shook her head.

'It's terribly maternal,' she replied gently.

They fell quiet, but it wasn't a heavy silence: it was a moment of peace under a night sky that finally shone with stars.

44

'Fffooagh . . . I . . . I . . . don't . . . didn't . . . no.'

De Carli frowned.

'That's not Marini,' he said, referring to the message he'd just heard on Teresa's mobile phone.

'I'm telling you, it's him. It's his number,' she muttered. 'What on earth is he saying?'

'*Ffooagh*,' said de Carli.

'Very helpful, thank you.'

Teresa had woken up that morning to find this deranged message on her voicemail, followed almost immediately by a call from police headquarters relaying some shocking news. It had been a bad start to what promised to be a long and complicated day.

'Try calling him back,' she told de Carli. 'We don't have much time.'

He played the message again on speaker and just then, Parisi walked in.

'We're ready to go,' he announced, then paused when he heard the garbled voicemail. 'Is that who I think it is?' he asked in amazement.

'Who do *you* think it is?' Teresa replied.

'A drunk detective.'

Teresa banged her fist on the table.

'I knew it!' She got up and grabbed her bag. 'Let's go get that idiot.'

As she walked out of the door, she barged into Albert Lona and shuddered at the unexpected physical contact. He seemed perfectly aware of the distress his proximity was causing: he had always been able to sniff out the slightest shifts in her mood and use them to his own advantage.

He grabbed her arm.

'You look like you can hardly stand, Superintendent Battaglia,' he said.

He tightened his hold on her arm for a brief moment, then loosened his grip and let go.

No one spoke. Teresa could feel the presence of her men behind her, sense the silent fury coming from them.

'We're ready,' she declared, ignoring his taunt.

He scanned her face, the scratches the accident had left on her cheek and the darker spot where her head had bumped against the frame of the car.

'I heard about what happened yesterday. How irksome for the police to be involved in an accident of this kind.' He looked around the office. 'Where's Inspector Marini?' he asked.

'He already left. He went ahead of us,' said Teresa.

Albert smiled.

'I hope he can be trusted to do his job,' he said cryptically, then leant close to her ear. 'Though I do wonder: can you? I'm not so sure,' he murmured.

Teresa stepped away, feigning composure.

'We're an efficient team,' Parisi piped up behind her.

'And Superintendent Battaglia is the best there is, on and off the field,' added de Carli.

Lona spared them the briefest of inquisitive glances, but Teresa knew he'd seen all he needed to see: Parisi and de Carli were on the new district attorney's radar now, and they would have to be very careful.

'I do hope so, for your sake,' Lona replied courteously. 'It seems the case of the *Sleeping Nymph* has suddenly become rather more complicated.'

He walked off with an air that promised trouble. Teresa turned to her men.

'Don't challenge him,' she scolded them. 'That's exactly what he wants you to do.'

But she could tell from the look they gave her in response that nothing she said would make a difference. She'd always suspected it, but now she knew for sure: Parisi and de Carli knew about her past.

The keys were still in the lock and the front door was ajar. Marini must be home.

'I'll go in alone,' said Teresa. 'Wait in the car.'

'Please take pictures,' de Carli begged her.

'Go!'

The flat was just as Teresa had pictured it. The colour palette and the absence of all inessential items exuded a kind of masculinity and it was as neat as its owner, the tidiness like a cloak, a way of keeping life on a tight leash and controlling its shape.

'Marini?' she called out. 'Is anyone home?'

She felt uneasy walking among his possessions, in his carefully designed and yet sparsely furnished home, befitting a man who, like a soldier, seemed to feel the need to adhere to a strict notion of order. She was prying, uninvited, into his hidden world, though her gut told her that most of what she could see was pretence.

Teresa also saw the traces of something unexpected but very familiar: loneliness. It was there in certain details that would have escaped another person's notice and it was even more obvious in what was absent: there were no photographs and no souvenirs. Not a single one. Marini had erased himself. He seemed to exist wholly in the present. There was no trace even of the woman Teresa had seen on the terrace the day before. Whoever she was, she'd disappeared and left nothing in her wake.

'Marini?' she called out once more.

She walked into his bedroom. Sunlight filtered in through small eye-shaped holes in the closed shutters. Teresa noticed a pile of books on a bedside table, including several texts she had 'strongly' recommended that he should consult: volumes on criminal psychology and forensic pathology. She had never thought he'd actually read them.

A slight movement drew her attention to a dim corner of the room, where Marini was sat on the floor, his body slumped against the wall. She crouched down next to him. He reeked of alcohol.

'Jesus Christ, how much did you have to drink?'

He tilted his face up and her heart broke a little. Massimo had been crying.

'What happened?' she whispered.

He opened his eyes. A tear slipped through his lashes and slid all the way down to his chin.

'I'm finished,' he told her.

Teresa tried to pull him to his feet, but he was like a dead weight.

'If Lona finds out about this, you're definitely finished,' she snapped, but she knew that anger was merely her way of dissimulating her concern. 'He thinks you're busy cracking the case. Imagine that! He'd have a fit if he saw the state you're in . . .'

Marini pushed away the trembling hands with which she had tried in vain to pull him up, but he didn't let go. He held them tight in his own.

'Is he angry with you?' he asked her.

Teresa had expected his speech to be slurred, but he just sounded tired. She recognised that tiredness. It was the residue of despair.

'No, not yet,' she replied softly, forcing a smile.

He gripped her hands tighter before letting go.

'I'm so sorry,' he said.

Teresa looked into his eyes properly. She saw fear in them and couldn't fathom what might have reduced this bright, determined young man to this wretched state.

'What's going on with you, Marini?' she asked him softly, scared of breaking the fragile connection that had formed between them.

He put his head in his hands.

'I'm lost.'

'Tell me what happened and maybe I'll manage to find you.'

Marini looked at her and Teresa saw no trace of hope in his eyes.

'Is someone ill? Are *you* ill?' she volunteered.

He let out a quick laugh like a strangled sob.

'No one's ill, Superintendent.'

Teresa couldn't think of anything else. She'd seen him look troubled, melancholy even, but never quite so utterly hopeless. She put her hand under his chin.

'What happened when you went home for the holidays?' she asked.

He tried to look away, but Teresa wouldn't let him.

'What happened when you went home?' she repeated, more forcefully this time, feeling certain now that the home Marini had come from, perhaps even run away from, was where the source of the problem lay.

Teresa was beginning to think she wouldn't get anything out of him, when Marini finally spoke.

'I saw Elena again,' he whispered. 'We slept together.'

Teresa didn't know what to say.

'Well,' she said. 'That's not the end of the world, is it?'

'I left while she slept, and then for weeks and weeks I avoided her calls.'

Teresa was surprised.

'That's not good,' she remarked.

'Elena is pregnant.'

The words fell from his mouth in a quick exhale as if he were confessing to some torturous sin or dark passion. Marini was staring into space, his elbows resting on his knees, his shirt unbuttoned and blotched with stains.

'Aren't you going to say anything?' he said.

With a sigh, Teresa sat on the floor next to him.

'Forgive me for asking, but . . .' she began.

'Yes, the baby is mine.'

She was staring into space now, too. It wasn't hard to guess where the problem lay: he didn't want the child.

'Elena came looking for me,' he resumed, 'but again, I rejected her. She said she'll be staying in a hotel for a few more days, but then . . .'

Teresa couldn't help herself.

'Is this really who you are?' she snapped. 'If you were only looking for some casual fun—'

'It's not casual. It never was.'

He spoke with such forcefulness that she could see there must be a lot more to this story beyond what those few words revealed.

'Well, what is she to you, then?' she inquired, her tone more even now.

Her hope was that in talking things through, Marini might be able to organise his thoughts better and perhaps make sense of the emotions that seemed to be crushing him into a broken mess.

He made a vague gesture as if to say: how can I explain to you something that even I don't know how to describe?

'We've got plenty of time,' she said untruthfully, settling in beside him. The hardness of the floor was like a knife twisting into her beleaguered back. 'I'm not going anywhere.'

Marini sighed.

'I mean it, you know. I'm not going anywhere.'

'She was my first,' he said, his voice barely a whisper now. 'And still my only one.'

Teresa wasn't sure she'd heard right.

'When you say your only one . . .'

'Just her.'

'In what way?'

'In every way.'

'It's very romantic,' she said.

He rested his chin on his knees.

'It's weird. I know you're thinking it.'

She shrugged.

'I'll admit I didn't expect it of someone like you. But what about all these girls you've been going out with?'

He made a face.

'There haven't been that many. And they were dates, that's all.'

Teresa did laugh then.

'God knows what they must have thought of you,' she said.

'I can only imagine.'

Teresa gave him a gentle nudge.

'So then, what's the problem?' she asked. 'If she's the one you've chosen, why all this drama?'

She would never forget the expression on Marini's face when he looked at her then: so vulnerable, so scared. He was distraught.

'Because I can't,' he replied, his gaze sliding back into the empty distance.

Once again, they were silent. Teresa couldn't figure out what he was so terrified of. He hadn't told her everything, and certainly didn't intend to do so right then and there. But she could sense his suffering, like a chill surrounding his body, a nausea biting at his insides, a restlessness wringing his hands.

'Tell me what to do,' she heard him say.

Teresa looked up at the sky. It was hidden behind the roof, but it was like she could see it anyway.

'I can't help you,' she told him. 'You want me to tell you that you're right to give them up if you don't feel ready, but if I were you, I'd take that baby in a heartbeat,'

She was conscious of him staring at the side of her face now, his gaze suddenly more focused. She was conscious of how her voice had betrayed her and cracked as she'd spoken, of all her defences crumbling into dust.

Tell him. Tell him now and don't overthink it.

'It feels like someone else's life now, but once upon a time, I was married,' she began. 'I was thirty and a cop already. I was more than capable in the professional sphere, but I can't say the same about my private life.

'He used to beat me. Regularly. Even when I got pregnant, he didn't stop. I know now that a woman whose partner beats her when she's pregnant is twice as likely to be killed by that same man. But back then I was a shadow of myself. By the time I'd mustered the strength to leave, it was too late: he found me and beat me one last time. I lost the baby – and the ability to become a mother. For ever.'

She got to the end of her speech, out of breath and with her heart beating madly in her chest. She had never thought she would speak of that old sorrow ever again. There was too much anguish in it, too much shame.

'Superintendent—'

Teresa raised a hand to stop him.

'Not a day goes by when I don't think of how that love was betrayed, betrayed by me of all people, when it was my job to protect it. Not a day goes by when I don't think about the baby I never got to hold,' she said. 'There's nothing, *nothing* I wouldn't do to have him here with me.'

She clasped a hand over her stomach as if to cling to the scar that sliced through it and marked the fork in her life.

'You don't realise what it is you're giving up and the thing that drives me mad is that I could sit here for hours, for days, trying to convince you and still you wouldn't understand. We never understand what it's worth until it's lost.'

She dried her eyes. The silence was so thick that she could hear Marini swallow.

'Elena will move on,' she whispered. 'She'll have your baby

and she'll know happiness, never mind you, never mind the complications. You, on the other hand . . . You, Marini, will drown in your regrets. You've been invited to witness a miracle. Think about that the next time you even consider turning the invitation down.'

She stood up, smoothed her trousers down. She managed somehow to regain her composure and held out a hand to help him to his feet.

'Get yourself cleaned up now. There's been a murder in the valley of the *Sleeping Nymph*,' she told him.

She watched as the effects of this news wiped the tumult and confusion from his expression. She paused before letting the other shoe drop.

'They've found a heart. We don't know yet whose it is.'

45

What drives a man to reject his own unborn child?

What drives a man to rip the heart out of another man's breast?

To beat a woman unconscious, to paint the walls of their marriage with her blood?

What drives that woman to stay?

We can never really know ourselves or those we spend our lives with. We can try to describe ourselves somehow, but ultimately, it's what we choose to do when we are presented with a fork in the road that reveals who we truly are. Either that, or the secrets we hide.

Marini's secret, whatever it is, must be as dark and painful as the mystery that lies hidden in the heart of this valley's past.

Back in the valley, Teresa felt as if they had wandered into a maze of shadows and now it was her task to shine a light towards the way out. But that morning darkness was more than just a figure of speech. The day had dawned murky over the Resia Valley as if the night had found a way to multiply and had generated an imperfect replica of itself, bruised, bloated and seething. The clouds above their heads were like purple lungs, expanding and contracting in turn, releasing downpours so thick that they obscured the outline of the mountains. From the depths of the forest rose a sinister stench of rot, of decay accelerated by persistent moisture.

Had Teresa believed in magic – the dark kind – she would have interpreted all this as a bad omen. She didn't think this recent homicide was a coincidence; it had to be connected to the discovery of the *Sleeping Nymph* and the arrival of the police in the valley. That's what years of experience and an understanding of the laws of probability told her. But, more importantly, it was her subconscious warning her, alerting her to the presence of evil – and not some generic evil, either: it was methodical, as evolved as it was brutal, and directly hostile, too. This was no longer a cold case: the danger was imminent now.

The discovery had been made at the spot where the road to the villages turned uphill. The area had already been cordoned off. Police cars blocked the entrance, with officers stationed to direct authorised personnel and turn away those who had no business being there. But people had found other ways to get close to the scene and they stood now along the edge of the forest, bursts of motionless colour amid the foliage. Through the trees, they watched with quiet composure the early progress of the investigation.

Parri was already there, directing the crime scene search. Agents from the forensics team were combing the area for clues, personal items and any other evidence. The flash of the reflex cameras was indistinguishable from the bursts of lightning the sky periodically hurled into the forest.

'It'll be bedlam here soon,' Teresa heard him say as he urged his colleagues to locate, tag and photograph every trace before the rain erased it for ever.

Teresa and Marini walked up to him, pausing on the other side of the cordon until Parri spotted them and waved them over. They put on crime scene suits and shoe covers, then followed a path through an area already marked and thoroughly searched by the forensics team.

The coroner greeted them with a wry smile.

'Well, the plot has certainly thickened,' he remarked.

Parri's hair was heavy with the droplets of water that hung suspended over the forest. He was carrying a clipboard, on which he jotted down his observations. The paper looked lumpy, its fibres saturated with moisture. Some of Parri's notes had been reduced to smudges of blurred ink.

'Are you all right?' he asked Teresa.

She nodded, grateful for his concern. She wasn't sure she could say the same for Marini; though there was no denying the kid was tough: no one would have guessed what state he was actually in. She'd been on the fence about bringing him along, but in the end she had decided that the only way to tear him away from the destructive thoughts that tormented him was to throw him into the murky waters of this case and hope that they might awaken his survival instinct.

Parri stepped to one side for a better view of the scene, beckoning at them to join him. And it really was a spectacle – one that Teresa was sure had been set up for their benefit.

On the sign that marked the border of the district, someone had nailed a heart ripped out of an unidentified victim. The symbolism was clear; the lifeless organ carried a powerful message.

A heart for a heart, thought Teresa.

First, almost a hundred years ago, Aniza's heart and now this second nameless heart, appearing just as the girl's true fate was beginning to come to light.

Teresa took out her phone and activated the voice recorder.

'Is it a human heart?' she asked Parri.

'It is. Extracted from the thorax with a double-edged blade. The incisions are clean and precise.'

'No signs of hesitation,' Teresa muttered.

Marini brought his face up close to the dead organ, peering into its bluish surface.

'When did it happen?' he asked.

'Based on the current stage of chromatic degeneration, I'd say anywhere between twenty-four and thirty-six hours ago. But it's difficult to be more precise when the weather's this humid.' He slipped on a pair of gloves and showed them one of the incisions. 'This darker colouring that you see here will spread over the superficial venous network first before it seeps deeper into the organ. As you can see here, the inner tissue retains its crimson colouring. In mild weather, the process of discolouration ordinarily begins after twenty-four hours.'

'I expect it's too early to ask you for anything more,' said Teresa.

'Well, I can tell you now that it's not a healthy heart. The valves are worn. The victim probably suffered from mitral insufficiency. The organ is enlarged, and not from any post-mortem gaseous discharge. This wasn't a young person's heart.'

Teresa brought the microphone to her mouth.

'Check for reports of any local – presumed elderly – who hasn't been seen in at least a day or two,' she noted.

She kept staring at the blackened heart. It almost looked like it was still beating, though she knew it was just her imagination, her way of forging an emotional connection with what little remained of this latest victim.

'I'll need to take the heart to the lab for more detailed testing in order to determine whether the extraction of the organ occurred after death, or whether it was indeed the cause of death,' Parri explained. 'There appears to be a fairly deep knife wound near the right atrium. I can't yet say whether it is peri-mortem or post-mortem.'

Teresa saw a black car arrive upon the scene. Albert Lona

stepped out of the car, together with Deputy Prosecutor Gardini. Even among all the officers on guard duty, the forensics team and the local police keeping the area cordoned off, Lona spotted Teresa right away, almost as if he'd come specifically for her. Perhaps he had.

She turned back towards Parri.

'I've found no traces of diptera. No eggs, no larvae of any kind,' he was saying. He removed his gloves and threw them into a bag for medical waste. 'Whoever did this took good care of this heart before putting it on display. Our friend has made our job a little easier: we won't have to worry about catching flies and scooping out larvae.'

Teresa and Marini exchanged a knowing look. There was order here, an attention to detail that bordered on neurosis.

'We've been told you haven't found any fingerprints yet, nor any signs of the body,' said Teresa.

Parri nodded.

'Indeed. And I'm not surprised. It fits with the picture.'

'We'll let you get on with it, then, but I'll come with you to the lab, if you don't mind.'

They started to walk away and as soon as they'd slipped out from beneath the rope that marked the scene, Teresa breathed easier. She could see Gardini talking to the head of the forensics team, but there was no trace of Albert. The deputy prosecutor joined them shortly thereafter.

'So, what's the verdict for now?' Gardini asked.

'It's a warning,' she said decisively, rifling inside her bag in search of her notebook. 'It's a message for us, telling us there are borders we mustn't breach.'

'If it really is a message, the killer took a huge risk to deliver it,' Marini remarked.

Teresa pondered his comment.

'Fear can make people bold, even reckless,' she said. 'We got too close to something that was meant to stay buried for ever. It's still buried, in fact, though little by little it's coming to light.'

'Nevertheless, he appears to know what he's doing,' Gardini noted.

'Not only that, but he's intelligent, too, and extremely careful. It's a clean job.'

'How strong do you need to be to rip someone's heart out of their chest?' Marini muttered.

Probably not that strong, Teresa thought. And in fact, it wasn't the killer's physical vigour that struck her.

'You're thinking of physical strength. I'm more interested in mental fortitude,' she said. 'How strong does a person's will need to be to rip a *beating* heart out of someone's chest?'

Gardini looked at her in surprise.

'Is there evidence to suggest that's what happened?'

Teresa didn't reply, but the slight tilt of her head implied that although it might be too early to know for sure, she suspected that the victim's role in all this was central. He or she hadn't been selected at random. The symbolism of the act was too potent, too archaic, and the risk the killer had taken was too great – the message that had been sent their way was too powerful. And she had no doubt that the victim had died as horrible a death as the warning the killer had left for them to find.

One of the officers from the forensics team called out to Gardini and the deputy prosecutor took his leave.

Marini looked at the heart hanging on the threshold of the village like a death banner. A bolt of lightning illuminated the landscape with an eerie glow.

'Maybe that shape you saw in the middle of the road yesterday wasn't just a shadow,' he murmured.

Maybe it wasn't. Teresa had thought it, too.

A sudden gust of wind brought a familiar scent, which caused her stomach to cramp.

She turned round and there was Albert, standing hardly an arm's length away, watching her. She had to fight the urge to step back but, more importantly, she couldn't help but wonder whether he'd heard Marini's comment. His expression, which appeared entirely unmoved, seemed to indicate he'd heard nothing at all.

'Superintendent, Inspector,' said the district attorney, greeting them both.

'Good morning, Doctor Lona,' Marini replied.

Teresa had the feeling he had spoken first to relieve her of the effort. She merely nodded.

Despite the rain, the blood seeping into the earth mere steps from his expensive shoes and the mud that surrounded him, Albert retained his habitual elegance. He hadn't brought an umbrella, instead letting the water soak his hair and flow in thin streams down the collar of his shirt. His indifference to the elements was a sign of his animalistic nature. Alberto Lona was a beast – refined and magnificent in his savagery, perhaps, but a beast nonetheless. Teresa wondered if he still lived alone, or if there was a woman waiting for him to come home so she could wash and dry his sodden clothes – the only occupation this man would ever consider befitting her sex.

'Update me,' he told them, his casual tone masking the brusqueness of his command.

Teresa relayed the little information they'd had from Parri and took care not to give anything away about her own initial impressions.

She saw him frown, his eyes now fixed on some distant point.

'It's not enough,' he declared – as if they could have made the killer leave more traces behind by sheer force of will.

'The lab tests might tell us more,' she said, though even to her own ears, her words sounded like a feeble stopgap.

Albert shook his head.

'It's not enough,' he repeated, his voice hardening and his eyes now fixed firmly on hers. 'I want more. There are similarities with the Imset case, do you not think?'

Teresa said nothing. The mention of Imset, the ancient Egyptian funerary deity, had failed to evoke any particular memory.

'You handled that case, Superintendent – and successfully, too, to everyone's surprise,' Albert insisted, irritated by her prolonged silence.

Teresa ran the name over and over in her mind as if it were some flavour she had to sample and identify. She could sense both men's eyes on her, Albert's inquisitive, vaguely hostile stare and from Marini, a curiosity tinged with bemusement. The former left a bitter, acidic taste in her mouth; the latter something green and sour, and far too youthful.

Teresa couldn't remember. She couldn't retrieve that case and that name from among her memories, couldn't recall a single face or a sliver of conversation. It was as if she'd never had anything to do with it at all. She had simply lost a piece of her life. She tightened her grip on the notebook in her pocket.

'Every case is different,' she improvised, her heart beating in her throat and feeling as if it were about to explode with fear.

'Nonsense!' he thundered. 'Obviously, I was not suggesting there was a connection. But the act itself . . .'

Teresa could feel herself sinking deeper into a morass of panic, the toxic venom of doubt seeping into her mouth and stealing the oxygen from her lungs.

'I remember that case,' Marini volunteered. 'I studied the file when I first arrived here. The killer extracted his victims' internal organs, one organ from each corpse, four corpses in all. They were eventually found stored in ancient Canopic jars dating back four thousand years. In that case, the organs had been taken as trophies. Isn't that right, Superintendent?'

He gave her an encouraging glance and Teresa nodded.

'But this is no trophy,' she managed to say. 'It's not a totem whose glow the killer privately basks in, reliving his dreams of omnipotence. He's chosen to share it with us. It's *for us*.'

Lona seemed to ponder her words but didn't make any further comment. Later, Marini might be made to pay for having dared to question the district attorney's thinking, but this wasn't the moment for that.

Albert changed the subject.

'The canine unit will be here soon,' he told them. 'We need to find that body. The press will not be as patient as the deputy public prosecutor has been.'

Teresa and Marini looked at each other and realised they'd had the same thought. But this time it was Teresa who took the plunge.

'I would propose we deploy an asset Ambrosini was in the process of vetting before he became indisposed. The asset is external to the force but potentially—'

'Have I not made myself clear?'

Teresa didn't bother to finish her sentence. There was no point. Albert stalked off, leaving her seething with rage and burdened with a fear that left her shaking: the fear that she was disappearing, along with her mind. What was she without the cases she'd worked, the desperate investigations, the decisive breakthroughs, the compassion she'd felt for all the victims she had known – and occasionally rescued?

'I'm sorry,' she heard Marini say.

'Thank you,' she replied in a low voice.

'You're welcome. He's a dickhead.'

It was raining harder now, but the locals who'd come to watch were still there. Teresa gathered herself together, raised her hand and called out to de Carli.

'Send them away,' she ordered. 'Tell them to go home.'

He hesitated.

'They're praying, Superintendent.'

Teresa saw that beneath their hoods and their umbrellas, their heads were bowed. And then, as if called forth by Teresa's gaze, a female voice rose in song, voicing a lament whose power silenced every other human sound.

The crowd parted, revealing a woman in a long robe, her white hair wet with rain. She was singing a song as old as the history of her people. It was the proud, majestic figure of Matriona, seemingly staring straight into Teresa's eyes.

Teresa had never heard anything like it. It was an ancient

melody from a world that had long since vanished and yet remained alive. The song mixed with the sound of wood crackling in the depths of the forest.

She remembered Francesco's words.

It was the lullaby for the dead.

46

Massimo took another painkiller. The first pill hadn't even made a dent in the headache that had been tormenting him for hours. The second had made it just about bearable. He hoped the third might provide enough relief to allow him to keep his eyes open and his mind focused. He took a sip from the water he'd just bought from the vending machine and vowed for the hundredth time that day that he would never, ever touch alcohol again.

Standing outside the autopsy room at the morgue wasn't exactly helping with the nausea.

He looked at his phone. Elena still hadn't called. In fact, she hadn't been in touch at all except to send him a text with the address of the hotel she'd be staying at for a few days.

'Are you still with us, Marini?' he heard Superintendent Battaglia say from inside the autopsy room.

Massimo shook his head. That morning, in his apartment, he'd been on the verge of telling her everything. But now the superintendent was back to her normal surly and overbearing self.

He stepped into the autopsy room and prayed that his stomach might hold it together for at least another couple of hours. It's only a heart, he kept telling himself as he stared at the dark, fist-sized lump on the steel table. It was a good thing there wasn't a whole corpse there, otherwise the stench would surely have forced him into an ignominious retreat.

Parri had begun dissecting the organ already and was soon

able to confirm what he'd already surmised at the scene of the discovery: the heart had belonged to an elderly person and it wasn't in good health – not just because of its age, but also owing to a defect that had caused a weakening of the cardiac valves.

'Our colleagues are already searching the valley,' said the superintendent. 'We'll know soon enough who's unaccounted for.'

'I'm extracting tissue samples for the genetics and toxicology testing,' said Parri, fiddling with a set of slides, 'but I've already run a glycophorin test and the result is positive.'

Superintendent Battaglia's jaw tightened.

'If an organ reacts to glycophorin, we know it must have been removed when the victim was still alive,' she explained for Massimo's benefit.

'Hold on a minute,' Parri interjected. 'There's something blocking the mitral valve.'

He took a pair of pointed tongs from his tool tray and switched on the headlamp on his forehead.

A few moments later, he pulled the tongs from inside the cavity and brought out a small, dark object.

Superintendent Battaglia moved closer, pushing her reading glasses further up the bridge of her nose.

'It's a twig,' said Massimo. 'The storm must have blown it in there.'

Parri looked at him.

'It was stuck all the way inside,' he said. 'The wind doesn't have fingers.'

'Someone took good care of this heart. You said it yourself, Antonio,' the superintendent recalled. 'They kept it safe from insects and larvae. They looked after it for us so that they could present it to us; they would never have allowed any dirt to get in.'

She took the tongs from Parri and began inspecting the twig from every angle, bringing it up to her nose to sniff it.

'It's thyme,' she said, sounding surprised. 'It's a sprig of thyme woven into a ring.'

'How bizarre,' said Parri.

He glanced at the superintendent and as she returned his look, they seem to reach some kind of telepathic understanding.

Superintendent Battaglia was picking at her lips, deep in concentration.

'Thyme is a medicinal herb that's been in use since antiquity,' she noted. 'It also possesses magical properties, or so the ancients believed. The strength of its fragrance meant it was frequently employed during sacrificial cremations. My grandmother used to say that if you walked among plants of thyme at twilight, you would see the spirits of the dead.'

'So there's a ritualistic aspect here,' Massimo muttered.

'*Thymus, thymi, thymo, thymum* . . . What's the declension?' she said.

He spread his arms.

'I don't know.'

'It's Latin.'

'I guessed as much.'

Superintendent Battaglia scribbled something down, looked up as if emerging from a state of apnoea, then immediately buried her face in her notebook again.

'*Thumos, thumon.* Greek,' she went on.

'I was never good at translations,' Massimo confessed.

'Me neither,' said Parri.

Superintendent Battaglia sniffed at the twig again, turning it over in her fingers.

'These words all share a common root, one that's extremely interesting from an etymological perspective, but also unusually prolific,' she explained.

Massimo's stomach was on the verge of insubordination.

'Do you have to hold it so close to your nose? *It was inside a heart*,' he reminded her.

'In Greek, *Thuos* means sacrifice, or offering. *Thumiào* means to burn something, to immolate. And finally *Thumòs*: meaning ire, but also the emotional state of the soul, a deep-seated connection with the body, with blood and breathing,' she continued. She seemed relieved she could remember so much, and smiled slyly at him and at Parri.

'And there we have all the elements of this death,' she concluded. 'This is the killer telling us: I sacrificed something for the greater good and I did it in anger.'

She snapped her diary shut.

'He's angry and he's scared: we've got too close to something he holds sacred.'

47

Francesco di Lenardo was standing with one hand on his hip and the other shielding his eyes from the rays of the sinking sun, when he saw them coming towards him in the distance. He skipped down the flank of the mountain with astonishing agility for a man his age and soon he had reached the road that coiled through the forest, the mountain on one side and the drop to the river on the other. The road was so narrow there was barely room enough for a single car to pass through. When he reached Teresa and Marini, he wasn't even out of breath.

'I'll walk with you,' he volunteered once Teresa had explained they'd come specifically to see him.

To glimpse the face of the killer they were hunting today, they would have to dig much deeper into the past. They needed Francesco's memories again.

They walked in silence, the shadows lengthening around their footsteps. Nearing its end now, the day had become imbued with a gleaming splendour. Birds flew back and forth across the sky, whole flocks changing direction without warning. Their flight was perfectly synchronised as if they were a single organism.

Francesco stopped to watch. They had come to a halt at a

section of the road where the wall of trees in the adjacent forest was briefly interrupted, only to begin again a few yards down.

'An old firebreak,' he said, offering no further explanation.

Teresa had met people like him before, as solitary as the old larch tree that towered over the meadow a few turns down the road. She knew he needed time. If they insisted now, if they tried to rush him, he would simply retreat further into himself.

A young man emerged from a path among the trees, carrying a backpack on his shoulder and wearing a T-shirt tied around his head like a bandanna. His face looked flushed and tanned already, though it was only spring.

Francesco waved at him.

'This is Sandro, Krisnja's sweetheart,' he explained, greeting the young man with a hug.

Sandro looked down.

'Yes, well, I'm her boyfriend,' he said with a sheepish laugh.

Teresa remembered him from the community meeting they had all attended.

'Sandro wasn't born in the valley, but he might as well have been,' said Francesco. 'He's studying for his forestry diploma.'

The young man put his hands up as if to hide behind them.

'Mostly, I spend my time sampling the circumference of alder trees,' he said.

They all laughed. Sandro bid them farewell and continued on his way towards the valley. Francesco's gaze followed him until he disappeared round a bend in the road.

'Many have left,' he said quietly, 'but others have come to take their place. We could do with more young people like Sandro, for the valley and for the forest. Some day it'll be Sandro looking after these woods. Right now, he's learning that it's important not to reforest every clearing, that it's useful to leave the odd dead tree in the undergrowth for the scavengers to feast on. He understands how essential it is to leave untouched those trees that serve as meeting spots for animals preparing to mate. He's learning how to safeguard the biodiversity of this landscape.'

Teresa peered into the undergrowth, where the colours of the forest faded into hues of darker green. It was a world submerged, its rarefied light possessing an almost tangible consistency.

'It's to do with forest shade,' Francesco explained when she pointed it out. 'Not all light is able to filter through the canopy and reach the ground. What does get through corresponds to just three per cent of the spectrum, the part that's no use in photosynthesis. In fact, you'll find that in the denser forests, the shape of the undergrowth can be as stark as a desert.'

'You know this world well,' Teresa noted.

'It's my world. We're not so different from trees, after all. In fact, we're more alike than we'd like to admit. Almost every living thing upon this earth is a plant – which tells us that plants are a long-running and near-perfect genetic experiment in both conquest and survival.'

'When you put it that way, it sounds a little creepy,' Marini observed.

'It is. But fascinating, too. Plants see light through photo-receptors scattered over their surface. Hundreds of miniature eyes that, in their own strange way, look out at the world just as we do. They can tell night from day, they wake up and go to sleep, they sense the changing seasons by observing the days expand or contract. Like all living things, they rest, too: when it's dark, plants are known to droop, at times by as much as four inches.

'They're equipped with a sense of touch and smell: they can sniff out neighbouring plants they might potentially latch on to, analysing their scent to determine whether or not they'd make healthy hosts. They use their roots to share nutrients with their weaker peers and if they're attacked by parasites, they release toxins that make their leaves taste foul. They compete with each other, they fight. They have memories and a sense of balance that enables them to grow straight even on sloping ground. They communicate, too, in ways we can only partially comprehend.'

He crouched down, brushing his fingers over the earth.

'And that's just what's going on "upstairs". Underneath it all, there's a vast and boundless neural network of roots. Plants make multiple complex decisions every day.'

'So as far as senses go, they've got the full set,' said Marini.

'They say plants are deaf, actually, but I wouldn't be surprised if science eventually proved us wrong on that, too. Did you know that Darwin tried testing for that once? He'd later describe it as a moment of "madness". Darwin loved musical instruments and one day he thought he'd play the bassoon to his *Mimosa pudica* and watch for a reaction. Nothing happened, of course.' Francesco looked at the forest again, his expression serious. 'Perhaps the reason they're deaf is simply that they don't need to hear.'

He grabbed a fistful of soil.

'We know so little about all this vegetation, this organism that does our breathing for us,' he said. 'This handful of earth is home to a million microbes, bound to each other by mechanisms of interdependence so complex that they still elude our attempts to recreate them in a laboratory. That's why they die if they're isolated from their wider habitat.'

Teresa had let him talk without interruption; there had been elements in Francesco's account that had awakened some instinct within her.

Francesco stood up, shaking the dirt off his trousers.

'You think the heart they found at the turn into the valley is connected to Aniza's disappearance, don't you?' he finally asked them.

'I'm inclined to think so, yes,' Teresa replied.

Francesco turned towards the horizon. The sky was darkening. They heard a stag braying in the distance.

'Our elders used to say it's the spirit of the day calling forth the night,' he murmured. 'Now, a darkness has fallen upon this land, but this time there will be no dawn to follow it – only uncertainty and pain.'

Teresa stepped towards him.

'Someone in the valley feels threatened,' she said.

'Why are you looking at me like that?'

'You know about botany; you might also know how to read nature's more cryptic signs,' she persisted, not unkindly.

'What's *that* supposed to mean?'

'You tell me: *thymus*, for example.'

He shook his head.

'I'm not sure what you're trying to get at. You act as if you expect me to know something, but if you think I might have had anything to do with Aniza's disappearance, you're mistaken. Unless you deem an eight-year-old capable of murder.'

Teresa didn't reply. She could sense his quiet outrage at what he perceived as an ambush and she could sense, too, Marini's unease as he stood beside her.

'I think you've kept all of Aniza's personal belongings,' she said.

The expression on Francesco's face answered for him.

'I'd like to see them, please.'

48

The wooden steps creaked under Massimo's feet as he followed Superintendent Battaglia and Francesco di Lenardo up the stairs to the top floor of the house. The attic had a sloping roof, with a skylight on one side that covered the full length of the wall and offered a breathtaking view of the Musi mountain range. The pinewood panelling brought the scent of the forest into the room, of unrushed work that followed the rhythm of the changing seasons, of a world Massimo barely knew but that seemed nevertheless to strike a chord with him, like an invitation to remember what he had forgotten.

The attic wasn't the dusty, neglected storeroom Massimo had expected. It was the hidden heart of the house. In one corner a majolica stove lay in wait, ready to warm its surroundings when the next winter came. A velvet armchair had been turned to face the view, next to a pile of books that reached all the way up to the armrest. A heavy tome lay upon the padded seat.

Massimo ran his fingers over the cover. It was an anthology of old folk tales set in the woods. A dried edelweiss served as a bookmark, its furred silvery petals peeking out from between the pages. Francesco must have picked it himself when he was younger, down some perilous crag, perhaps, the kind of place where this milk-white plant – the so-called 'rock flower' – tended to thrive.

He looked at Francesco, whose profile betrayed nothing of his emotions but whose body language spoke of wounded pride – like a man being subjected to some kind of deeply insulting examination.

'Her things are all in there,' he said, pointing to a heavily carved trunk pushed up against the wall.

A master craftsman had etched floral motifs – gentian blooms – into the wood. These had then been painted a deep blue. Even after all those years, the colour still retained its shine.

Francesco sank to one knee and ran a hand over the wood.

'This was her dowry chest,' he reminisced. 'Every young woman had one. It was meant to store her trousseau and she'd take it with her on her wedding day when she left her father's house. It was considered essential to the formation of a new family. Women would inherit them from their mothers, who would, in turn, have inherited them from their own mothers. They travelled through history, passed on from female hand to female hand. This one is more than three hundred years old.'

He turned the key in the lock, then stopped as if in deference to his memories.

'I'm sorry,' he sighed. 'I don't often open this and I don't enjoy doing it.'

'Take all the time you need,' said Superintendent Battaglia.

She was being gentle with him again now as if to concede that

224

his doubtlessly sincere grief deserved a degree of sensitivity and tact even from those who barely knew him.

And this was, after all, Teresa's way. She put people to the test, probed them with her razor-sharp barbs, because she knew – better than anyone Massimo had ever met – that humans spend every day of their lives pretending: out of laziness, or habit, or for the sake of convention, for some ulterior motive, for self-preservation. Or even, quite simply, to survive.

Francesco lifted the lid of the trunk and Massimo saw a date carved into the wood: 1706. He closed his eyes briefly, wishing he could run away from this place that suddenly seemed so full of bitter echoes from his own life. At the same time he felt as if he were being led by the hand on a journey that made him think, for the first time in a long time, that there might be hope for him yet. Aniza was leading the way, her face blurring in his mind with Elena's.

When he opened his eyes again, Francesco was holding a white dress that resembled the one they had seen in Matriona's tavern. The little bells sewn onto the sash tinkled softly.

'This is one of our traditional dresses,' Francesco explained. 'My wife and I never had any children. I'd love for Krisnja to have this some day, to wear on her wedding day.' He smiled. 'Though I think young people today have different tastes. As they should, I suppose.'

He carefully folded the dress and put it on the floor. Next, his hands shaking, he took out a photograph and quickly handed it over as if he'd rather not look at it himself.

'Aniza is wearing the dress in this picture. It must have been around the time of the spring festival, not long before she disappeared. She was preparing to perform the *Kölu*, the "circle dance".'

Teresa Battaglia studied the photograph closely.

'And here's some of her needlework,' said Francesco, opening a sewing box. 'Some of these she'd just finished; others, she never got a chance to.'

The superintendent handed the photograph to Massimo and peered inside the wicker sewing box. He did the same and felt a pang.

Aniza had knitted a pair of baby shoes the colour of meadows in spring, of marigolds and cornflowers.

It was too much. Massimo walked away, far enough that the sound of the superintendent's voice and Francesco's faded into a murmur.

His grip on the photograph tightened and finally he mustered the courage to look at it.

Aniza was staring at him from the surface of the greyscale image, white as a bride in a field of long grass. Sunlight streamed through the folds in her skirt until it looked, in parts, translucent. She'd put flowers in her hair. A few strands seemed to flutter around her face, lifted by a breeze for ever crystallised in that image. The beginnings of a smile flickered on her lips. One hand hung in the air, caught perhaps on its way to tucking a loose strand of hair behind her ear.

But it was the position of her other hand, cupped over her stomach, which hit Massimo like a gut-punch.

Massimo knew that instinctively protective gesture: Elena had done it, too, the night before.

His breath caught as he thought of the baby clothes they'd seen in the trunk.

She hadn't made them for her friend.

He saw himself walk back towards Superintendent Battaglia, pull her aside, return her puzzled gaze and lean towards her – but it was as if someone else were doing it all for him.

'She was pregnant,' he whispered into her ear.

49

Aniza walked through the forest like a bride: the path in the grass was the nave that led to the altar; the trunks of the centennial oaks were the columns that lined her passage. By now, the village was no more than the glimpse of a church tower behind her, its tip just visible over the tops of the tallest trees. Over her veiled head, the branches of hazelnut trees, acacias and sessile oaks were like enormous gnarled beams, their fronds forming a tunnel into the darkness and towards a new life.

She turned round and looked at her past. The line of the sun beat a quick retreat over the sphere of the weathervane on top of the church tower and once the sphere had been swallowed completely by shadow, she dropped her knitting basket onto the grass and resumed her march into the depths of the forest.

Her footsteps were soon accompanied by the sound of a woman's voice singing in the village. The melody soared into the sky like a smoke ring, twirling and twisting in the air, and spread through the valley, the woman singing heartily in her ancestors' tongue of all the things that families did when they gathered together at dusk. It was a way of taking leave of the day and of greeting the arrival of evening, praying that it wouldn't bring with it the phantoms that emerged from the mountain fog at nightfall, but only sweet dreams and dew to quench the thirst of the villagers' fields.

From across the bridge over the river *Wöda*, another woman took up the call and their two voices chased each other in the air, carried by the wind that reared its head from the riverbed at twilight. Other voices soon followed from farther away. They were the 'mothers of the valley', those who'd given birth to the most daughters and whose daughters, in turn, had become mothers themselves.

Softly, Aniza joined the singing, her hand cradling her belly. It was still flat for now, but soon, the life it carried would grow. Her singing was matched by the primitive melody of the forest; when the wind found its way through the dry, hollow branches of fallen tree trunks, it was like hearing the sound of a flute.

Aniza looked up at the sky. She saw Venus gleaming overhead between the crowns of the trees. A silver-feathered barn owl took flight from a nearby branch, its wings flapping vigorously. It was the spirit of the night, summoned forth by the braying of the stag that ruled over the slopes of the Musi mountain range.

Aniza thanked the Mother for this good omen. She plucked the pale pink buttercups that lined her path and gathered them into a bridal bouquet.

The singing ended. People were closing their front doors now and the animals were resting in their barns. Lamps burned bright and the youngest had been put to sleep in their cots.

She got ready to wait, her heart beating faster.

He was on his way.

50

Teresa was shaking as she left Francesco's house. It was as if she'd just come wading out of some dense, sticky swamp. On its surface she had glimpsed the reflection of a life snuffed out too soon, which in itself had been painful enough, but now there was a fresh horror to deal with. If Marini was right, then there was a second victim hidden in that dark past: a baby who had never been born.

Inspector Marini looked shattered, his features taut with misery, his gaze feverish.

'She was pregnant,' she heard him say again, though perhaps it was just a trick of the wind. 'And someone killed her.'

Teresa would have liked to respond with some decisive counter-argument, but something stopped her, like a disembodied hand gripping her throat: it was her subconscious again, telling her not to look away, not to deny what she knew to be the truth, but to follow instead the path she was on until she reached the end.

At the foot of the hill they saw a familiar figure walking in the opposite direction, followed by a dog. It was Krisnja. She disappeared among the trees.

'We need to talk to her,' said Teresa.

They made their way down the slope. Krisnja turned round and smiled in recognition when Marini called out her name; though her face fell when she noticed their expressions. She glanced up at her uncle's house.

'Has something happened?' she asked, alarmed.

'Nothing new,' Teresa reassured her, 'but until we've figured out what's been going on in this valley, it's not safe for you to venture into the forest alone, especially when it's about to get dark.'

Krisnja turned towards the woods. The heart had been discovered over there, past the grove of beech trees and the bridge, after the next turn in the road. They didn't know yet to whom it had belonged, but Teresa was sure they would soon have a name and a face to look for.

The news had spread through the valley promptly, passed on from neighbour to neighbour. Everyone had offered to help. Everyone was doing their part, flinging farm doors open, checking barns and tool sheds. The police, meanwhile, continued to search the scene of the discovery, as well as the surrounding area.

Krisnja crossed her arms over her chest and turned back towards them.

'We're not used to feeling afraid around here,' she said.

Teresa could see how lost she must be feeling. An act of murder had defiled the paradise she lived in; the soil she walked on had tasted blood. Nothing would ever be the same again.

'We were just visiting your uncle,' Teresa told her, hoping to distract the girl from her thoughts. 'We went through Aniza's belongings.'

Krisnja stared at them then with those extraordinary eyes she had inherited from Aniza, from history, from a thousand-year legacy; she carried the signs of her ancestry so openly.

'He never shows them to anyone,' she told them. 'It's very painful for him.'

Teresa thought about what she could say.

'They must have had such a strong bond,' she remarked at length. 'Rarely have I seen such stubborn grief, as fresh as the day the loss was suffered.'

Krisnja turned her head to look at the mountains and the wind lifted her hair, revealing her proud profile.

'He has his own torments to contend with,' she murmured. 'Those were terrible days. No one around here has ever really managed to shake off the past.'

'Of course. The tragedy of Aniza's disappearance must have destroyed the peace and tranquillity of the whole valley,' Teresa mused.

The light in Krisnja's eyes flickered; for the briefest of moments, it had gone out.

'That wasn't the only tragedy,' she said. 'Didn't Francesco tell you?'

51

Francesco had been lying. Even as it slithered away from the valley in retreat, the war had stamped upon the Resian soil its mark of death and destruction. And the inhabitants of the valley, who had continued to live off the fruits of that soil, had been christened with the blood of innocent lives. Krisnja had told them of a horrific episode, which had left a permanent scar on those parts: an execution the invaders had intended as a warning to all Resians. An act of vengeance.

Teresa wondered why Francesco had chosen not to tell them about it when she'd asked him whether there had been any atrocities committed in connection to the partisan presence in the valley.

'Our fear alone was sufficient reward,' he'd told her, recalling how the Nazis had responded to the shot fired from the partisan rifle. Teresa had made a note of this in her diary, and not even a quick scribble: she'd taken down the sentence word for word as if she'd known even then that those words would eventually point her towards where she was meant to look.

Perhaps there was nothing there to see, but she knew from experience that there were only two reasons why people lied about seemingly minor details: it was either a pathological condition, or they had something to hide.

She decided that before she turned up at Francesco's front door again, demanding an explanation, she needed to find out more. Perhaps it was her way of lulling him into a false sense of security until he gave away more than he would have liked. Or perhaps she was overthinking things again; perhaps she had become too accustomed to expecting the worst at all times – at least where human nature was concerned.

But there was something else she wanted to do before darkness fell and brought her some respite from the toils of the day.

'Are you sure you're up for this?' she asked Marini.

He nodded.

They rang Raffaello Andrian's doorbell.

'A violin?' said the young man after he'd heard what Teresa had come to ask him. 'I don't recall anyone ever mentioning that my uncle owned a violin, nor that he'd have known how to play one.'

Teresa decided not to tell him about the unidentified fingerprint they'd found on the painting.

'Can you think of anything that might connect him to such an instrument?' she asked. 'Even a passing interest, say, or a friendship . . .'

The young man thought about this for a moment.

'The only thing I can think of is that for many decades, we Andrians have been trading in tonewood. We're probably the last supplier left in Italy. I'm certainly not aware of any other wholesalers still in business.'

'Could you elaborate on that?' Marini asked.

'It's European spruce wood. Quite rare. We're lucky enough to have a whole thousand-year-old forest of it here, over on the border with Austria and Slovenia. It's the only material that will do if you want to produce proper, good-quality stringed instruments. The trees must be at least two hundred years old, and must have grown slowly and steadily throughout that time. Can you imagine that degree of consistency in an ecosystem as inherently fragile as that of a forest? It's quite a miracle.'

'So, this kind of material is essential for guaranteeing sound quality,' Teresa remarked.

Raffaello Andrian nodded in confirmation.

'The wood is dried, first, a lengthy process during which resin crystallises along the inner walls of the plant's vascular tissue. Nature's own organ pipes, if you will. It's the wood itself that amplifies the sound. It sings for us.'

It was fascinating, but Teresa didn't think it amounted to a lead she could follow. She had to look elsewhere.

'How is your uncle?' she asked, feeling slightly guilty for not having asked sooner.

The young man's expression darkened.

'You've brought back some memories that were perhaps best left buried,' he told them with a glance at the closed door of his uncle's room at the end of the corridor. 'I've never seen him like this.'

'Is he grieving?'

'No, Superintendent. It's not grief he's feeling. It's—'

'Hatred,' she ventured.

'Yes. Hatred.'

Teresa pulled out of her bag the one keepsake that Francesco had let them take, though he'd needed some persuading. It hadn't been easy for him to relinquish it, nor had it been easy for Teresa to ask.

But really, it belongs to someone else, she'd told herself: it was Alessio Andrian's as much as it had been Aniza's.

She showed it to Raffaello, who looked at it uncomprehendingly. When Teresa explained their theory, the object's significance became suddenly clearer and Raffaello's eyes filled with tears. He stepped aside and looked towards Alessio's room, effectively giving them his blessing – and an invitation, perhaps, to do what needed to be done after seven decades of misery and solitude.

Teresa made her way down the corridor. At every step, she turned the words over in her mind in search of the most tactful way of saying what she had to say. But perhaps the right words simply didn't exist.

She walked past the painting with the two children crouching by the partisan fighter, the rifle firing at the unsuspecting enemy soldier. It seemed incredible that they had actually managed to trace that scene back to the moment in which it had occurred. And it was disturbing to think that for all these years, Francesco and Alessio had been connected by a memory they unknowingly had in common.

She studied the painting for a moment longer before moving on. At the end of the corridor, she brushed her knuckles against the door in the gentlest of knocks and stepped inside.

It was as if Andrian hadn't moved at all since she had last seen him. The way his body was positioned, the direction of his gaze, still fixed upon the forest, though it was dark now – nothing had changed. The room was bathed in soft lamplight. He was wearing a fresh set of pyjamas and there was a blanket laid carefully over his knees. Someone had picked flowers for him and put them in a vase on his bedside table. They smelt of sunlit fields, of honey, and of the life that carried on in the world outside that room. They brought light into that darkness, though Teresa was sure he hardly even noticed.

She knelt beside his wheelchair and studied his profile, those eyes that seemed to have nothing human left in them and whose expression Teresa now felt she could perhaps understand.

She didn't know yet if the man before her really was a killer, or a man with a sick mind, or simply someone who had chosen to spend every day for the rest of the life he had left upon this earth in mourning. His grief was absolute.

She observed his hands. They might never have killed anyone, but they had definitely painted a portrait of Aniza with blood. And they had touched her heart. But how? Had they struck in a violent frenzy? Or had they given it one last loving caress? He may never have played the violin, but those hands certainly belonged to an artist.

Into their grip, Teresa now pushed the object she'd been holding in her own, knowing in that moment that no words would be required.

At long last, the tiny primrose-coloured baby shoes had found their place with Alessio. Perhaps that was where they had always been destined for: the memory of a son cradled in the palm of his father's hand.

Teresa heard Raffaello crying behind her. She could imagine how he must be feeling, and Marini, too; she was struggling herself to stay in that room, to hold it together, to breathe. Because Alessio — though still immobile, as he had chosen to be — had started to cry. He hadn't even looked down at his lap and his expression hadn't changed at all. But there were tears streaming down his face.

The ring on his finger glistened with the wetness of his tears. Teresa touched his warm hand and finally understood what the two As carved upon the gold really meant: they weren't Alessio

Andrian's own initials, but those of two young people in love.
Alessio and Aniza.

It was a wedding band.

52

20 April 1945

The song of the women faded with the daylight, but traces of its
melody still lingered over the forest, thrumming low like a gale
blowing from the lungs of a god. The sound travelled through
the gorges, bouncing from cliff to cliff along the river in an endless echoing rumble. And animals all over the valley answered
the call of the 'mothers of the valley', awakened by that atavistic
bond all living creatures shared.

Afterwards, silence fell once more over the woodland, but
it was altogether different from the kind the forest had grown
accustomed to: the absence of sound and movement was so absolute that it signalled danger.

The invisible borders of the animals' dens, of the places where
they stopped to rest and that they guarded from all intruders, had
been breached by a foreign presence, leaving a trail of fear in its
wake.

It didn't snarl. It didn't howl. It didn't bare its fangs in the
night; it didn't have claws with which to tear the flesh off its
prey.

It carried a human scent, and its advance was accompanied by a
melody that was both torment and ecstasy, a tune that came from
the underworld but soared now to such heights that it seemed to
brush the very tops of the mountain peaks.

A man's fingers pressed as if possessed upon the strings of
a violin and manoeuvred the bow in a frenzied fervour. The

'Devil's Trill' rose with the moon from the mountain ridge, malignant and romantic, majestic and relentless. Legend had it that strange things would always happen whenever someone dared perform it – mysterious phenomena that were usually of little consequence but that could sometimes turn bloody.

To the violinist in the forest, the instrument was a door to hell, through which the voice of Lucifer howled at the world – as did his own voice, too.

He played for her, though she didn't even notice him.

He played for her, who waited among those trees for her love.

He played for her and her alone, his pale Venus, his blazing star, mistress of his cursed and miserable heart.

53

There's so much about this case that resonates with me. I can see in it what I once was and what I'll never be; what I've become and what I'll turn into. At every turn it forces me to confront the loss that both destroyed me and made me the person I am today – and the fear of a future that lies all too near.

Whatever the reason, I just can't seem to let go. This case and its baggage of memories and horrors is mine in every way. And I need to get it over with before my own winter comes. Autumn is creeping in already, so much earlier than it should, and with it I can feel this instinct to step back and focus the energies I have left solely on what matters most.

If I believed in karma, in fate or in magic, I would say that this case has been waiting for me.

The Sleeping Nymph *Aniza, and Alessio have been waiting for me.*

There was a clink of gravel against the window pane. Teresa didn't move from the sofa.

'Door's open!' she yelled.

Smoky came in first, his tail wagging with joy. He put his paws up on her knees in greeting; by now, he considered her a friend. Blanca followed him inside, finding her way by means of a white cane for the visually impaired. It was the first time Teresa had ever seen her use one.

'You should lock the door after dark,' the girl advised.

She ran her fingers over the door until she found what she was looking for and turned the key in the lock.

'Only an idiot would try to rob a cop,' Teresa replied, putting her book away and taking her reading glasses off. 'Now, tell me something: why don't you ever knock?'

Blanca felt for the sofa and sat down.

'I guess I never think anyone will be expecting me.'

'I was expecting you.'

'I just feel I'm less of a bother this way.'

She was used to walking into people's lives through the back door; perhaps no one had ever told her she had a right to come in the normal way. There was a naivety about her, a wildness that moved Teresa.

'So,' Blanca began. 'Tell me more about this indecent proposal you mentioned.'

Teresa settled deeper into the sofa, one arm flung across the backrest and a leg folded beneath her.

'It's a hunt for a corpse,' she said. 'Hidden in a forest. Someone's been murdered. You'll be taking on the police's own canine unit.'

'Oh.'

'They're not that good.'

Blanca leapt to her feet, then fell back onto the sofa.

'No way! They're amazing,' she exclaimed.

She was right, but Teresa knew that this was the perfect opportunity for Blanca and Smoky and their fellow human remains detection enthusiasts to showcase their skills and overcome the district attorney's diffidence.

'I told you, Smoky's not a cadaver dog,' Blanca protested. 'If it's blood you need to find, or body parts or something, that's fine. But a whole corpse, if it's not been buried – that's a different matter. It's a different kind of scent.'

'But you told me he was familiar with cadaverine,' Teresa pointed out.

'Yes, but it's not his area of expertise. What if he fails?'

'I don't think he'd mind too much. Would you?'

Blanca bowed her head.

'Maybe a little. Is that bad?'

'No, it isn't, but in any case, I don't think there's any risk of that happening.'

She really did believe that, otherwise she would never have asked the girl for help.

Blanca seemed to be weighing Teresa's words.

'If I did make a mistake, you'd be the one to pay for it, wouldn't you?'

'That's not a problem.'

'But . . .'

'I need you, and I need Smoky. I want to bring you into the team properly, but for that to happen I need everyone else to start believing in you, too. I don't want to have to recruit external help any more. I want us to have everything we need in our *own* team. I'm sorry to have to ask you to take such a big leap, but I wouldn't do it if I wasn't sure you could do it.'

'But it'll take time . . .' Blanca murmured. 'If you want us working on it, we'll need time.'

'Time will not be an issue,' Teresa assured her.

She would be the shield between Blanca and Albert. She would absorb any abuse the district attorney decided to hurl Blanca's way.

'The difference between an HRD dog and a cadaver dog is in the technique they use,' the girl explained. 'If you're looking for a corpse in a forest, you'll need a dog that's trained for a surface search, a dog that can look for miles until it finds the person you're after – even if they're dead. But human remains detection dogs are trained to search inch by inch, either from scratch or based on the indications they're given, and they're as likely to find a single, tiny drop of blood as they are to find a bigger piece off a corpse.'

'A piece as big as Mr Skinny, say?'

Blanca nodded.

'Yes, like Mr Skinny, or even a whole corpse. Detection dogs always need a lot more time to clear a search area, but once they're done, you can be sure they've not missed anything.'

'You'll have all the time you need,' Teresa promised. 'So, is that a yes?'

Blanca stroked Smoky.

'When my colleagues and I first started practising with placental matter, we hid a whole jar of it once. I suppose you could say it was the equivalent of a corpse, considering how much it stank. The dogs found it straight away; they could smell it in the air. I suppose it would be the same with a decomposing corpse.' She lifted her chin. 'Yes. It's a yes.'

Teresa smiled.

'Thank you, I'm glad to hear that.' She leant forwards to pick up a file from the coffee table. 'I haven't told you the whole story yet, though. The corpse you're going to be looking for isn't intact, though we don't know if it's been dismembered, either, or whether it's been buried or left uninterred. But there will be one thing missing from it.'

She opened the file and read it out to Blanca.

'The heart,' said Blanca softly once Teresa had finished reading.

'Yes. The heart has been removed.'

Teresa gave Blanca a test tube Parri had prepared.

'I wasn't sure what you might need, so . . .' she began.

Blanca turned the vial around in her fingers, guessing its contents instinctively.

'I've never held a piece of a heart before,' she said with a sigh. 'Smoky doesn't usually need samples to work from. He's already memorised all the scents a dead body can produce: the placenta covers roughly eighty per cent of them all, but he's also been exposed to blood in various stages of "fermentation", whether it's just been spilled or has been out for over a year, to fresh bones and old bones – and, of course, to cadaverine.'

'Well, if you don't need it . . .'

The girl hugged the tube close to her chest.

'Oh, no! I'll keep this, thank you. I'd love to try it out,' she enthused. 'So, when do we start?'

'Very soon. Just be ready.'

There was a brief silence. Then Teresa asked Blanca to make her a promise.

'Find it,' she murmured. 'Find it before the others do.'

Blanca's eyes seemed to glow.

'We'll find it.'

'You won't be alone in this.'

'Neither will you.'

54

Another night had passed and a new day had dawned. Teresa felt as if she'd risen from a bed of ashes, her body weighed down with a grimy burning exhaustion and laced with the smoky tang of age – the aftermath of an unremittingly bleak chain of events.

And Marini, standing beside her now, was certainly no ray of sunshine. He looked more like some shadowy planet set on a collision course with itself.

Teresa had almost hoped he would call her to say rules and deadlines be damned, he had more urgent things to attend to that day: he was going to get his child back. But no: he was right here.

They'd just received official confirmation from headquarters of what they had already suspected: no prints had been found in the area where the heart had been discovered, nor any traces of DNA, other than the victim's own.

'A clean job, in contrast with the recklessness, the insanity of the act itself,' Marini had remarked.

'We know he did it out of fear,' she had replied. 'Now, we need to ask ourselves why.'

'We know that already, don't we? To guard a secret.'

'Not any ordinary secret, though. A sacred one. But what secret could possibly lead a person to kill for its preservation?'

Marini had taken a moment to reply.

'Love?' he'd hazarded eventually.

Teresa wasn't entirely convinced. She suspected there might be something else involved, something fiercer. But she kept her theory to herself as they stepped into the house at the farthest edge of the Resia Valley.

They'd had news a few hours ago regarding the probable identity of the victim. His name was Emmanuel Turan. He hadn't been seen in two days and it was highly unusual for the octogenarian to abstain from the day-to-day life of the village. A relative had called the police to report that there was no sign of him at home, either. Emmanuel had left the gate of the hen-house open and a fox had sneaked in at night and wreaked havoc. Emmanuel's family insisted that such a lapse was entirely out of character: something must have happened to him before dark.

The house was as modest inside as it had appeared from the outside. Its state hinted at an isolated existence, either voluntary or imposed, and reflected a mind confused, as chaotic as the disorder it had produced around it: the mind of a child, incapable of fending for itself.

Teresa always felt an undertow of pity whenever she searched the home of a victim or of someone who'd gone missing. People who vanished tended to leave behind something of themselves suspended between the walls of their home, hanging over the table they would never eat at again, on the bed that would no longer cradle their tired body at night, spread across the objects of their daily life, and inside the clothes hanging in their wardrobes.

Teresa could always tell when a missing person had breathed their last breath; she would feel an unmistakable shiver, as if their essence had come back home, yearning for all the things it could no longer touch. She had never been wrong before.

It was the same with Emmanuel Turan: she knew immediately that he was no longer alive.

'If he really is our victim, it'll take us weeks to finish searching his house,' she heard Marini say. 'I've never seen such a mess before.'

'He's definitely our victim,' Teresa muttered as she wandered among his possessions. 'And it's not mess. It's called "disposophobia". It's a condition whose sufferers experience the uncontrollable urge to hoard things. It's often associated with Diogenes syndrome, which manifests as a tendency to varying degrees of self-neglect. And that's how you'll end up, too, if you turn your back on your child and on the woman you love.'

'Superintendent . . .'

Teresa sat on her haunches. In a corner of the kitchen, beneath a pile of stained newspapers dating back several years, an electric cable was emitting a rather alarming hum.

'Have them cut the power off,' she ordered. 'The last thing we need is a fire.'

They followed the cable to the room next door. The door was already ajar and Marini gingerly pushed it open all the way, but there was nothing living waiting for them on the other side: only a memorial to a crippling loneliness.

A Christmas tree wrapped in fairy lights stood naked against the bare wall. Not a trace of its needles remained, not even on the floor. The red ribbon at its tip had blackened through several winters' worth of stove smoke.

'It's been here for years,' Marini surmised.

Teresa barely heard him. Her attention was focused on a set of framed photographs prominently displayed on the console table, the only piece of furniture in the room that was clear of any other odds and ends.

She felt a stab of icy horror as she looked at the portraits of smiling families. Every face was different. Every smile was a sham, as fake as the product it promoted. They were cut-outs of old newspaper advertisements.

It was the family Emmanuel had never had.

Someone finally cut the power off and the twisted spectacle faded into darkness with the extinguished fairy lights as if a shroud had been laid over the old man's private torments. Suddenly, all that Teresa was left with was the anguish that overcame her every time she was made to feel she'd come too late to ward off evil.

Parisi appeared at the door, trying to catch his breath.

'We've found traces of blood,' he said, 'right at the edge of the woods.'

Blood staining the earth, spattered over shards of broken glass, acorn shells, fragrant pinecones and the shallow indentations left by tiny animal paws.

'This must be where he did it,' said Marini. 'This is where the killer struck him and took out his heart.'

Any footprints had faded in the mud, but the dark stain of blood remained.

Teresa fixed her eyes deep into the heart of the forest.

'The body can't be far. He must have hidden it nearby.'

'Emmanuel Turan's family told us he's quite slight, no taller than a ten-year-old, and shrunken with age and a weakness for alcohol. He can't have been too heavy,' Marini pointed out.

Teresa grimaced.

'But he was a dead weight, nonetheless. It's hard to say. Get the forensics team here,' she told Parisi and de Carli. 'We'll have to alert the district attorney and update Gardini.'

She couldn't take her eyes off that black stain. She could almost smell it.

'Maybe the killer was trying to hide the identity of the man who was with Alessio Andrian the night Aniza died,' she said. 'The man who left his fingerprints on the *Sleeping Nymph*, but whose name we don't know yet.'

Marini stepped towards her, his eyes also fixed on the blood-soaked earth.

'So all we need to do is find him, right?'

Teresa nodded.

'I think I know where to look. But first, there's someone else I need you to find.'

55

It was a village tavern like any other, standing in a fertile plain dotted with farms. Teresa surveyed her surroundings: plenty of fields, very few houses and no trace of anyone on the streets.

'Are you sure this source of yours can be trusted?' she asked Marini.

'Well, yes,' he replied, 'unless you're doubting Guglielmo Mori.'

'And who's that supposed to be?'

'Parisi's grandfather.'

She stared at him.

'That's your source? Your colleague's granddad?'

'Parisi says he knows all there is to know about the Second World War and what happened next. You did say you w—'

'Fine! Fine.'

'Well, anyway, Guglielmo was sure we'd find the man you're looking for here. It's basically a clubhouse; it's where this organisation has its headquarters.'

Teresa sighed. She didn't need to ask what kind of organisation Marini was referring to: she could guess. If the person Marini had promised he'd find for her really was in that tavern, this was not going to be a pleasant meeting.

Inside, everything was just as Teresa had imagined it would be: old, chipped tiles, a rather dated feel to the decor, and a bar that was at least half a century old and ran all the way across the room. Dusty neon lamps hung from the ceiling and a TV with the volume turned off was showing a game of pool.

Clusters of elderly men sat at every table, playing cards. The hum of conversation faded as Teresa and Marini walked in, and stopped altogether when they asked the innkeeper for the person they were looking for.

'Are you journalists?' the man asked in response.

His tone told Teresa that the media frenzy generated by the discovery of the *Sleeping Nymph* must have found its way here, too; though not for the same reasons that had brought Teresa here. People were intrigued by Alessio Andrian's past, imagining a bloodthirsty monster lying in wait up on the mountains.

'We're not journalists,' she replied.

'So what is it you want?'

The question had come from somewhere in the depths of the tavern, more specifically from the table right at the back of the room, underneath the television. Every man in the room was now wearing an expression of suspicion bordering on hostility – and one more so than the others.

Teresa knew she'd found the witness she'd been looking for. She made straight for the old man whose voice had rung so clear across the room.

Mariano Claut, code name Merlin. Nearly ninety years old, of stocky build and, according to the information Marini had managed to glean, the last partisan alive from Andrian's brigade. Except Andrian himself, of course; though everyone acted as if he were already dead.

Teresa walked up to him.

'Mr Claut. Can we talk?' she began.

The man placed his cards on the table.

'Well, the right to free speech is still enshrined in the Constitution, if I'm not mistaken,' he replied.

Not a bad start. Teresa had expected more resistance. She knew that men like Claut always had lots to say, and lots to explain, but that didn't mean they enjoyed doing it.

Claut's fellow card players left the table as if responding to a silent command.

'Well? Who are you?' he asked.

'Detective Superintendent Teresa Battaglia and Inspector Massimo Marini,' she replied.

'What an honour!' he said, flashing them a cherubic smile. 'If you've come here to be a pain in my arse, the door's over there.'

Teresa sat down.

'A little swearing won't put me off, you know,' she told him. 'I could beat you to it if I wanted to.'

'I can confirm this is true,' said Marini, nodding as he, too, sat down.

Claut appeared to have been caught off guard. To anyone unfamiliar with his history, he might have seemed a textbook case of all bark and no bite. But this was a man who'd killed – and more than once.

'We're here about the *Sleeping Nymph*,' Teresa told him, getting straight to the point. 'I'm sure you've heard about it.'

Claut rolled his eyes.

'Heard about it?' he scoffed. 'I'm sick of the whole thing. I've got journalists hounding me, asking about Andrian – but I won't talk.'

'I'm afraid I'm going to have to hound you, too.'

The man pressed the tip of his index finger into the table.

'This is where the Resistance began,' he said. 'Right here in these lands. You think you'll get anything out of me? I was killing Nazis when you were still playing with your dolls, Superintendent.'

Teresa leant forwards.

'I never played with dolls,' she told him. 'And I'm here to hunt evil down, not bring it back into your life.'

She could see him trying to figure her out, sniffing for lies in the air around her but finding nothing there.

'I will never reveal my comrades' secret identities. I will not speak of them,' he said. 'Some have been exposed already – like your painter, for example. But I swore that their secrets would die with me – not long to go now – as soon as the war ended and the inquest began. The inquest on *us*, who took up arms not as conquerors and oppressors, but only so that the horror might end sooner.'

Teresa could understand why he was so resistant: for seventy years people had doubted the sacrifices he and his comrades had made, implying that they were no less culpable than those who'd fought on the other side in the war.

'What are you still scared of?' Marini asked.

'I'm not scared of anything! I've lived long enough as it is. But let me tell you, I don't like this world I'm leaving behind. You're the ones who should be careful. I can see the signs of resurgent fascism, clear as day. We kept them at bay for fifty years, but then someone came along and gave them the all-clear. "There's no danger any more," they said. "They're all dead now," they said.' He laughed a bitter laugh. 'I say there's more of them around than ever before.'

'We're not here to judge anyone,' Teresa assured him.

Mariano's fierce gaze pierced into hers.

'Is that so?' he snapped. 'But you went to the Slavic priest first, didn't you? Word travels fast around here. I suppose he told you how awfully mean the partisans were.'

'I've come to hear *your* truth.'

'The truth,' he echoed, spitting the words out. 'Let me give you some facts: if you chose to join the Resistance, you had to leave everything behind and hide out in the mountains, to starve and to suffer the cold and the heat. But if you picked the fascists, you got a uniform and three meals a day, and did rather well for yourself, all things considered. So, who do you think was really fighting for love of country?

'We were penniless, we had nothing. Our pockets and our bellies were empty, but that poverty gave us freedom, ensured that everything we did was truly in our own and in everyone else's best interests. "Rebels", that's what we called ourselves,' he said, chuckling. 'But really we were just boys. We would have given anything to be home safe and sound. We were no devils.'

'For forty years now I've been following the trail of blood that violent death leaves in its wake,' Teresa replied. 'And I've never met the devil: only people. War's the real hell.'

He looked at her now with a different kind of light in his eyes.

'You ask me why I won't talk,' he said. 'Because I'm tired of being treated like a murderer. I lost a comrade to that war, hanged at the age of twenty. I watched another, sick with fever, betrayed to the fascists by spies in the village. They beat him, tied his neck to a railing. They cut his balls off and stuffed them in his mouth. Then they set him on fire.

'I watched a little girl climb a tree in her own backyard to celebrate the end of the war, finally free to play as much as she wanted to. The Nazis passed by as they beat their retreat, machine guns blazing. The little girl made it back to the ground to hug her mother; that's how she died, in her mother's arms. Now you tell me, Superintendent, knowing what you know about the workings of the human mind, how ordinary men can turn into such savage killers,' he murmured.

Teresa knew she was wading into a minefield and had to pick her words very carefully.

'After the First World War, military psychiatrists began to investigate the effects of conflict upon human behaviour. They discovered that statistically, only three out of ten soldiers were efficient killers. The best all shared similar traits: they tended to be psychopaths, they lacked discipline, they were aggressive, and their private and social lives were underdeveloped.

'They would tell interviewers that the pleasure they derived from killing was not too dissimilar from sexual orgasm. They would go through the same psychological phases as serial killers do, including the dehumanisation of their victims. Technically, they're "hidden serial killers", and there are so many more of them around than you might think. During war, when murder becomes socially acceptable behaviour, they get to hunt and kill with impunity.'

Mariano was watching her now with a different, more sorrowful expression on his face.

'We killed, too,' he murmured. 'But we didn't torture anyone. And we looked the fascists in the eye. That's the difference.'

There were always two truths, Teresa reflected: the executioner's, and the victim's. This man and his comrades had been on both sides of that divide. Teresa had felt the suffering of the local populace emanating from the pages of Father Jakob's diary and she had felt the same suffering again now in this ageing partisan's words, his voice choked with emotion. Each had told its own truth, which – like much of human experience – was never absolute.

Teresa remembered with a pang the plot of uncultivated land they had passed not far from here. Those unaware of its history would have been surprised to learn that it used to be the site of a concentration camp. Memorial plaques had been planted in the soil as a permanent reminder, but there was nothing else left except for grass: as soon as the war was over, the locals had picked the building apart and repurposed the materials to build a kindergarten in the village. And so from a slice of hell, a flower had blossomed. That was the lesson history taught. In time, nature always found a way to straighten out the perversions of the human spirit, burying them under new life.

Everyone loses in war, Teresa thought. The guilty and the innocent are often mixed up. Those like her, who'd come later, owed nothing but deferential silence to the people who'd experienced that devastation first-hand.

Teresa placed the photograph of the *Sleeping Nymph* on the table.

'I've come here for her,' she said. 'To find out how she died.'

Mariano studied the picture.

'So this is the portrait Andrian painted up on the mountains.'

'Yes. On 20 April 1945.'

The old man seemed lost in reverie.

'I wasn't around then. I was elsewhere during the last days of the war, further west.'

Teresa didn't give up.

'But you knew that group of partisans. They were your comrades. That night someone was playing a violin in the forest where this girl disappeared. The locals say it wasn't one of their own.'

Mariano didn't reply, didn't even lift his eyes off the *Nymph*.

'So?'

'So, tell me who was playing it. Which of your comrades played the violin?'

'Why do you want to know? You've all but convicted Andrian already. What better scapegoat than a red partisan? It won't make a jot of difference if you substitute his name for another's.'

Teresa shook her head.

'It'll make a difference to her family. If it's the truth you want people to know, now's the moment to speak up,' she said.

Mariano stretched his hand out and brushed his fingers gently over the portrait. He pushed the picture back towards Teresa.

'My comrades' names will die with me,' he repeated.

'Don't you realise you're protecting someone who's probably already dead by now?'

'This girl's dead already, too, and yet you keep looking.'

Teresa stood up, more abruptly, perhaps, than she had intended, but her voice was calm when she spoke.

'This is about justice,' she said. 'I thought I would find that here.'

She'd already reached the door, when Mariano spoke again.

'I won't give you a name, but I'll tell you how I'd go about finding him.'

Teresa turned round.

'We're hunters, you and I,' the old partisan murmured, with something akin to respect in his tone. 'I'll show you where to look.'

56

A foreign presence shook the undergrowth, driving the larger mammals away and forcing the smallest to take refuge in their subterranean dens.

The men from far away had come searching for traces they weren't equipped to detect. This wasn't their natural habitat. Their eyes weren't trained to *see*. Their ears were deaf to the vibrations of the earth they trod upon: they couldn't recognise the echoing emptiness of an ancient tomb, the distinctive ring of soil that had been dug out and moved about. Now, they were out looking for the site of a recent burial, but even if they succeeded, they would find little more than a handful of wretched remains.

The *Tikô Wariö*, on the other hand, knew how to discriminate. Nature could teach you how to interpret its language, but you had to spend a lifetime with it before you could truly understand it.

The arrival of the strangers was cause for fear, but it was also welcomed. It was necessary. Perhaps it would bring liberation.

For the moment, the 'fierce guardian' merely observed, trailing like a shadow the old huntress with red hair and her sidekick with the troubled eyes.

They were the real danger. The woman could see the path where others would have been lost. She, too, had a gift: she saw things that were hidden to most. She saw the darkness behind the light in every human soul.

And she never stopped. She never stopped looking.

57

'You'd think it's the devil himself leading the way.'

Marini had meant it as a joke, but it didn't quite come out that way; it was as if he'd suddenly realised, halfway through the sentence, that there might actually *be* a hostile and omnipotent hand directing the outcome of this story he was caught up in.

In spite of her ingrained scepticism, Teresa felt the same when she stood in front of the Trieste Conservatoire and saw the name spelt out across the entrance: Giuseppe Tartini, creator of the 'Devil's Trill'.

One of thirteen historic conservatoires in the country, the Trieste Conservatoire was housed in the Rittmeyer building, a majestic specimen of the architectural style of Trieste, that small, glittering Vienna on the sea. At sunset, the building would acquire a warm rosy gleam, the light bouncing in fiery arcs off its wide windows, shards of reflected sky for the seagulls gliding by. It was a structure typical of the Habsburg era, and featured a neoclassical flourish of capitals and caryatids.

Inside, the last slanting light of day illuminated a series of white marble staircases leading to several floors of galleries and balustrades held up by rows of pink columns. Teresa was overcome once more by the feeling that she was following a script already written and that reached, in that very spot, its climactic denouement.

She stopped, suddenly unable to keep going. She clenched her fists in her pockets. It was strange how her mind struggled to hold together the fragments of her present but still seemed so proficient in recalling incidents from the distant past. Perhaps this was her fate: to fall gradually further into the past until she became a little girl again, and finally disappeared altogether.

'This building was the scene of a particularly bloody incident,' she told Marini, her voice barely louder than a whisper. 'During the last war, it housed the Deutsches Soldatenheim, a clubhouse for the German army. It was targeted in a rebel operation that killed five soldiers. In response, on 23 April 1944, the Germans staged a savage reprisal.'

'Fifty-one prisoners were taken from the Coroneo and hanged along the staircase,' said a male voice, picking up where she'd left off.

They turned round to find a well-dressed young man with shoulder-length hair. His voice was devoid of any recognisable accent.

'When they ran out of banisters,' he continued, 'they hanged them from the windows, down the hallways and eventually inside wardrobes. They left them dangling like that for five days, guarded by gendarmes: a warning to the city lest they should ever think of defying them again.'

Teresa held out her hand.

'Superintendent Battaglia,' she said.

The man smiled.

'Luka Mendler. I'm the principal here. Welcome.'

Marini had already spoken to him on the phone to announce their visit, but he'd been intentionally vague about the reason they'd come all that way. Teresa was reluctant to give the press and the public anything else to speculate on, but the moment had come now to speak openly.

Mendler listened to her account with guarded interest.

'So you're here to find a violinist who was playing that night while that girl lay dying,' he said.

'Not an ordinary violinist,' Teresa replied. 'An exceptionally gifted one, so talented as to be able to execute Tartini's sonata to perfection. We were told we might find a trace of him here.'

Throughout their exchange, Mendler had maintained an impeccably regal composure. Teresa had met elite musicians before, but this kind of timeless elegance was only to be found among practitioners of classical music, who tended to combine the physical build of ballet dancers with an attachment to liturgical practice. It was a fascinating mixture.

'The conservatoire must produce plenty of musicians who'd be capable of playing that piece,' Marini posited.

Mendler demurred.

'Yes and no, Inspector. It would depend on what you mean by "playing". Tartini's Violin Sonata in G Minor is riddled with dangers. To the uninitiated, they're well hidden. On the surface, it seems an almost "friendly" composition, but I assure you it is in fact one of the most technically demanding pieces of music ever created. It's said that Tartini designed it specifically as a trap for his fellow musicians. It was his way of saying: you will never reach the heights I have reached. The Devil's Trill is a little like evil, Inspector; it's rather good at hiding its true nature.'

'The person who heard the violin that night was – if you'll forgive the expression – in the business,' said Teresa. 'A music teacher who graduated from the Venice conservatoire. He described it as a flawless and astonishingly beautiful execution.'

Mendler's eyebrow shot up.

'I should have liked to have heard that myself.'

'You don't think it's possible?'

'The word I'd use is "improbable". News of a talent of such proportions would inevitably have reached us here; yet, we know nothing of it.'

Teresa herself had wondered about this.

'The one explanation I can think of,' she told him, 'is that the war must have erased its traces. People had other things on their mind back then; chiefly, survival.'

'That seems plausible,' the principal concurred. 'That said, I do think it would have left some kind of trail. In writing.'

Teresa's eyes lit up and Mendler smiled at her eagerness.

'The conservatoire only moved to this building in 1954, but our library holds all the old archives, too, brought here from previous sites. You will surely find what you're looking for there – assuming this violinist protégé of Lucifer's really did exist.'

Teresa's enthusiasm waned when the doors of the Levi library swung open before her. It wasn't the opulence of the room that struck her, nor the vastness of the musicology section, nor even the ancient artefacts Mendler was now talking them through.

The old archives were, in one word, enormous.

'We're still working on indexing everything,' the principal explained.

The conservatoire's trove of documents hadn't yet been digitalised. That could only mean one thing: she would have to call Albert and beg for more resources to be funnelled into their search. And he would never agree.

Teresa stood still. Marini turned round and caught her eye, and she could see that he shared her misgivings.

The sun sank into the Adriatic Sea and a cold shadow fell over the room.

Their hunt, for now, would have to stop there.

58

20 April 1945

The music of the forest changed. The sound of a violin floated among the beech and spruce trees, over the ridge and all the way to her.

Aniza shivered, and not from the evening chill, but from the feeling that she was being watched.

She had never liked him. The way he looked at her made her uncomfortable, as if he believed she belonged to him, and her heart wasn't already entirely Alessio's.

The melody seemed to walk on human legs, moving east to west like the wind, sometimes almost fading into nothingness before returning with even greater force.

Aniza pictured the violinist playing his instrument as he wandered the forest he'd come to know so well. She pictured him thinking about her. Under the enchanted moon, he yearned for her, and she knew it, and was repulsed.

Her hand dropped to her belly, cradling it in a gentle embrace. Her lips whispered sweet words of comfort to her baby while her eyes scanned the line of trees for signs of Alessio. More than ever before, each beat of her weary heart seemed to count down the moments until she would see him again.

The music stopped. The silence that followed was unusual. It was as if the forest itself had stopped breathing.

There was a shaking among the branches, and it wasn't because of the wind.

Aniza hadn't expected his face to emerge from among the trees. She looked past him, concerned that Alessio might soon also appear and that their secret would thus be revealed, but there was no trace of him yet. So she smiled and held out her hand.

'Why are you here?' she asked in the language of her ancestors.

The embrace with which he replied was so strong that it took her breath away. So strong that it hurt.

59

Teresa Battaglia had no choice but to lay down arms for a day. It wasn't something she enjoyed. She never liked to let a headwind slow her progress.

Massimo had watched her frustration pull at the corners of her mouth, her back straightening in a burst of defiance that collided with Albert Lona's brusque denial. It had been too short a phone call; Massimo was sure the district attorney hadn't even let her finish before refusing her. He wasn't interested in facts, or in the progress of their investigation. All he seemed to want was to see her fail.

Once again, Massimo found himself wondering what unfortunate history they could possibly have shared and yet again, he failed to come up with an answer – though there was a theory now slowly taking root in his mind. But he quickly pushed it away as he climbed up the stairs to his apartment.

For Massimo, too, it was never easy to go back home when there was still a case to be solved, to act as if there wasn't a heart sitting in a fridge in the morgue, waiting to be reunited with the body it had been torn from. To pretend that the characters of this dark fairy tale from the past had never actually existed – although they were, of course, perfectly real.

Besides, ever since Elena had come back into his life only to vanish again, he had found it harder to return to an empty home every day. Even exhaustion wasn't enough to dull the sense of melancholy.

The landing outside his front door was dark. He made a mental note to change the light bulb the next day, but that thought was quickly drowned out by the crackle of shattered glass under the soles of his shoes.

He realised straight away that someone must have broken the lamp on the ceiling.

It wouldn't have been too big a deal had his door not been the only one on this floor.

It still wouldn't have been too big a deal had someone not nailed a human heart just yesterday to the sign at the turn in the road that led to the very village in which Massimo had been conducting a police investigation.

He backed away until he reached the top of the stairs, faintly illuminated by the light from the floor below. He took out his phone and put it on torch mode. Ignoring the urge to draw his gun from its holster, he pointed the flashlight into the darkness and surveyed the gloom.

There was no one there, but still Massimo's heartbeat sped up.

The dark surface of his front door shimmered as if it had turned into liquid and it seemed to be oozing down the sides.

He walked up to it cautiously, glass creaking beneath his feet again.

'Shit.'

It was covered in a dark red substance dripping to the floor, congealing into thin streams on its way down. It was odourless, or perhaps Massimo's senses had frozen. There were partial footprints across the floor all the way to the lift.

He searched instinctively for Elena's number in his phonebook. It took him two attempts before his fingers got the sequence right.

'Are you OK?' he blurted out the moment she picked up.

There was a second's hesitation at the other end of the line.

'What do you think?'

Massimo twitched with worry.

'I mean has anything strange happened, anything that might have scared you?' he added hastily. 'Has anyone been bothering you, for example?'

There was another silence.

'No one's been bothering me,' Elena replied laconically. 'And your son's fine, too, in case you were wondering.'

She hung up without further word. Massimo stood there with the phone at his ear for a moment longer, then swore.

Lately, he seemed to do everything wrong. It had become so difficult to pick the right words to say and sometimes they were impossible to speak aloud.

Of course he'd been thinking about his son. He thought about his son every time he breathed.

Of course he loved him. That was why he couldn't keep him close.

Another shiver coursed through him: the feeling that danger was near.

60

The glucose meter gave its reading, like a modern-day sibyl divining the future through blood, and the insulin pen's microscopic needle injected the medicine into the layer of fat beneath her skin.

Teresa stared down at her thighs, which for over a decade now had been the battleground she carried with her every day. Thousands of invisible perforations had turned the skin there into living armour.

Every wound is a severing of the flesh, but when the laceration heals, the skin over it grows thicker and harder than it was before. The biology of regeneration always includes an initial stage of inflammation followed by a remodelling. Over time, Teresa's body had changed with her: it had become heavier and denser, and wider, too, settling like an anchor with every step she took. It might have looked awkward, but to her it was perfectly congenial, the physical manifestation of her continued existence in the world and an affirmation of survival.

But not all wounds were the same. The tissues of the heart, of *her* heart, remained frayed. The cells of her soul hadn't been able to seal the chasm there. So she had come out of her past changed but not healed.

Now, though, something had shifted. A fresh breeze was blowing through the breach and somehow, after everything, she felt she was being born anew.

The change in her life had a name she rarely used: she preferred to call him Marini, like a teacher addressing her pupil.

It hadn't been easy to share her past with him, but in a way, the decision had freed her: for once, she had seen herself through someone else's eyes and she had felt compassion. Perhaps she would never forgive herself, but the guilt, at least, had become more bearable.

Her grandfather had taught her that a tree in the last summer of its life, sensing the end, will produce more fruit than usual in a final effort to guarantee the survival of the species. Like that tree, Teresa, too, was ready, before she disappeared, to give her young team everything she had in her, every last crumb of knowledge she had laboriously and passionately gathered over the course of her long career.

Teresa got ready for her solitary evening ritual: she chose the music, she dimmed the lights. When she'd walked in an hour ago, the house had seemed unfamiliar: she had felt an inexplicable sense of disorientation as if the co-ordinates of her life had been altered without warning, knocking her off-balance. But the feeling had soon passed and she had been grateful for the return to normality.

She poured herself a glass of wine. It was a deep ruby red, with notes of blackberry, though Teresa had yet to find any bottle that could match for fragrance the wine her grandfather used to make in his own vineyard in the countryside. Or perhaps it was the sweetness of the memories she associated with that wine that couldn't be matched.

She swirled the contents of the glass around and breathed in the aromas they released. Leaning against the kitchen counter, she took a sip and pondered what to make for dinner.

Every utensil on the kitchen counter and in the cupboards now bore its own name tag, as did the ingredients in her pantry. A piece of paper stuck to the fridge listed all the things she needed to do before she went to bed. Checking she'd turned the gas off was top of the list.

They were all points on a map designed for Teresa's mind, marking out a clear path so that she wouldn't lose her way – or at least defer that moment for as long as possible.

'All you can do is resist,' she muttered to herself without a trace of self-pity.

Her gaze fell on the immaculate dining table. Its white lacquered surface gleamed without a single scratch to mar it. Teresa couldn't even remember the last time she'd eaten a meal on it. Usually, she used the low table in front of the living-room sofa. So she knew immediately that something was wrong.

A hair, black and bristly, and roughly ten inches in length, lay lengthways across the middle of the polished surface, curling slightly, nervously inwards.

It wasn't supposed to be there: it wasn't Teresa's, nor had she had any guests over to whom it could conceivably belong – unless she'd forgotten. More importantly, it seemed to have been placed there intentionally.

Teresa didn't touch it.

She remembered the feeling she'd had when she had first walked in: the air inside had been different, carried an unusual scent. Beyond the smell of her belongings, of the plants that kept her company, of books, of the fabric of her clothes, there had been something *else* pooling underneath, a foreign, vaguely subterranean odour. Her subconscious had picked up on it.

Someone had invaded her territory while she was out. And perhaps they were still here.

She thought apprehensively of her service pistol. Had she locked it away in her desk drawer, or was it still in its holster, hanging from the coat rack, where anyone might reach it?

She couldn't remember.

She put her glass down. It clinked on the counter, and that was the only sound inside the house. That was when she realised: the music had stopped.

She went to the living room, her steps heavy with fear. She thought perhaps it was her illness making her paranoid; then she saw the hi-fi was switched on but the CD player had been put on pause, its red LED blinking at her like a warning.

For a moment, she almost hoped the early symptoms of her Alzheimer's had suddenly quickened and that the intruder who'd left its mark in the place where she felt safest might actually be her.

Her gun holster, dangling from the hook by the door, was empty.

Teresa peered into the darkness of the adjacent room: her study. There was her desk, her bag with her mobile phone inside and – possibly – her gun.

It's got to be in there, she told herself, but it was hard to remember the specifics of such a routine gesture, one she'd repeated daily for decades now. Had she really put the gun safely inside its drawer when she'd got in not even an hour ago? Or was she remembering something she'd done the day before – or the one before that?

She ran through the gestures she'd need to make to locate and turn on the light switch. She would have to stretch her arm inside the dark room, not too far and just off to the right, and her fingers were sure to find their mark, but those few moments would be sufficient to make her vulnerable.

She lifted her arm but stopped halfway.

She turned round.

Now, she was sure she wasn't alone. She had heard the intruder – not inside her study but hiding somewhere else in the house.

'I'm not afraid of you,' she yelled.

There was a reply.

It was only a rustle, but it rang crisply in the otherwise total silence, as clear as a shadow upon a sunlit wall.

'Show yourself,' Teresa challenged it.

Slowly, she pulled the door to her study shut, locked it and pocketed the key.

In the corridor, the intruder replied again with the dull thud of a soft object hitting a hard surface.

It didn't reveal itself, but neither did it flee. It stayed with her. It wanted this contact; that was why it had come.

Teresa took a few steps forwards and finally saw something, little more than a slightly darker spot on the floor, an absence of light upon the parquet tiles. She could picture the intruder inside her spare bathroom, standing motionless in the glare of the street lamps filtering through the window, a dark, indecipherable mass blocking the light.

I'm not afraid, Teresa repeated, though only to herself this time.

'Show yourself,' she called out.

She would let it make the next move; she wanted to find out if her instincts were right. Something told her that it wasn't here to hurt her, otherwise it would have done so already.

The shadow shifted and in that moment, the doorbell rang. Teresa started, and so did the intruder, knocking things over as it fled.

Teresa entered the bathroom and saw that it was empty, the window flung open. She looked outside and saw Marini running towards her.

'I saw him!' he shouted. 'Are you all right?'

She gave him a quick nod and he disappeared round the back of the house.

Teresa cursed her body, which wouldn't allow her to climb through the window and be what she still so desperately wanted to be: a real cop.

She hurried to the front door and stepped out into the garden, then ran towards the wall, covered in ivy, which faced the road. Nothing moved, save for a dog howling at the end of the street. There was no trace of the intruder, or of Marini. The thought of him giving chase – alone – to a possible killer made her anxious.

You don't know that he's actually the killer.

But she was lying to herself. She knew it was him. She could feel it.

Then someone leapt over the low wall and narrowly missed crashing into her. Teresa nearly screamed. It was Marini.

'I lost him,' he told her, straightening his jacket and shaking off twigs and leaves. He was out of breath and looked furious. 'I made it over the wall just in time to see the car go. I couldn't get a proper look at it. I lost sight of it after the turn.'

Teresa pulled herself together.

'Why are *you* here?' she asked him.

'Someone came by my place, too.'

'If it was the killer,' Teresa replied, 'his purpose was to pit his ego against ours. Come in, I need to show you something.'

Marini followed her inside and frowned when she pointed out the hair laid out on the table.

'It's staging. I'm sure of it,' she said before he could protest. 'He put that there to send me a message, though I'm not sure what. I know it might seem a bold claim, and I know I have no evidence to prove it, but I promise you that hair did not get there by accident.'

He looked at her.

'You don't need to convince me,' he said. 'I know. I'll call headquarters.'

Teresa nodded. She had to write all of this down. They had turned a corner in their investigation: the killer had tried to communicate with them, which meant he had a story to tell, and one that must mean a great deal to him.

But the fact that things had taken a drastically unexpected turn was confirmed a few minutes later, when she realised there was no trace of her diary anywhere. All that she found in her bag was the last page she'd written on, a brief note in which she'd tried to sketch out a basic profile of the killer.

It was as if the page had been left there to make a mockery of her attempts: *you have no idea*, it whispered to her, *and yet it's so obvious*.

Teresa scrunched it up in her fist. She understood now what the thud she'd heard earlier had been: the sound of a notebook being slammed shut.

'He took my diary,' she said.

Marini paused in the middle of a sentence and covered his phone with the palm of his hand.

'What did you say?'

'He took my diary.'

264

Marini's expression hardened. A few short remarks later, he ended his phone call.

'We'll get it back. Don't worry.'

Teresa didn't doubt it, but she thought by then it might be too late: too late to rescue her memories and preserve the secret of what was happening to her. It gave her another reason to hunt this killer, but now he was equipped with a powerful weapon to use against her. He might even think he'd dealt her a fatal blow. Whoever had taken her diary hadn't done so by accident; they knew exactly how important it was to Teresa. Which could only mean one thing: they had been watching her all along.

Marini took out his car keys.

'They're sending a team over to gather evidence,' he told her, 'but we can't sit around doing nothing. We need to go back to the conservatoire to do some research and we need support. Parisi and de Carli are on their way.'

Teresa frowned. Parisi and de Carli had only just come off their shifts – as had Teresa and Marini. Marini guessed what she was thinking.

'Don't tell them to go back home. They won't. And no, I didn't run it by the district attorney.' He gave her a reassuring smile. 'They're coming because of you. *I* am here because of you.'

61

The night was fading into a perfectly clear dawn. The creamy marble facades of Trieste shone like mother of pearl under the gleaming sky. A couple of squawking seagulls were out already, gliding over the unruffled surface of the water. A ship swayed on the horizon; behind it, the blurred silhouettes of oil tankers rose like mirages on a backdrop of cobalt blue.

The library of the conservatoire was already filled with light and the section that housed the old archives was abuzz with activity, the rustle of paper like a laboured breathing rising from the piles of ancient tomes. The smell of paper, of expensive wood and of the silk that covered the walls mixed with the everyday scent of coffee from the vending machine in the corridor.

Luka Mendler had brought in his most zealous students for a rather special treasure hunt. Which of the institute's former pupils had possessed a talent as prodigious as Giuseppe Tartini's? Which name, out of hundreds, belonged to the only man capable of producing that unparalleled execution of the 'Devil's Trill'?

The answer lay buried somewhere among those thousands of pages.

Marini, de Carli and Parisi, too, were sitting with the students and poring over piles of books. Teresa glanced at them every now and then, and felt deeply indebted. She knew they were here for her, and not just because Marini had told her so: she could see it in their eyes, feel it in the rage coursing through their bodies. They were there because they wanted to protect her.

They had just heard from headquarters: the intruder had left no trace at all in her house. He had been prudent. Even in his escape, he had made sure not to step outside the paving stones. He hadn't left a single mark.

Except for the hair. Parri was already having it tested, but this would take time and Teresa sensed they didn't have much of that left.

The killer had also splashed a bucket of paint the colour of blood over Marini's front door.

It was a perplexingly incongruous detail.

You don't rip a man's heart out of his chest but then use paint to try to scare the people who are hunting you down.

They seemed like the actions of two entirely separate personalities, the former altogether brutal, the latter only superficially cruel. But what were the chances that the murder, the blood on

Marini's door and the stranger's visit to her home were unconnected incidents?

'I think I've found him!' someone yelled, and the cry spread through the room like the burst of excitement that had generated it.

The young woman who'd spoken up was now beckoning Mendler over. Teresa joined the principal and together they read through the page the woman was pointing at.

It recorded a date and the details of a special function: 29 July 1943, concert for the fascist authorities. It was the date of Mussolini's sixtieth birthday and this was the way the local mayor, who'd been appointed by the regime, had seen fit to celebrate the occasion. A student of the conservatoire had performed a solo: Tartini's Violin Sonata in G Minor.

A shiver ran down the back of Teresa's neck as she read the student's name: Carlo Alberto Morandini, born in 1928. He would have been seventeen when Aniza disappeared.

Later, someone had crossed his name off the page in an act of *damnatio memoriae*, though this hadn't erased his existence entirely. A note in the margin of the page explained what had happened: in September that same year, Carlo Alberto Morandini had joined the partisan resistance.

62

Carlo Alberto Morandini, code name 'Cam' – Cam, or Kam, another name for Ham, son of Noah, who cursed his son and all of his descendants. Cam had been dead for fifteen years.

Teresa had anticipated this, but still it felt like crossing the finish line too early. All that she could hope to gather now were the memories of those who had known him best.

But the woman she had come to see, huddled before her in a

matted woollen sweater, put a swift end to her hopes.

'I barely knew the man,' she muttered distractedly, folding and unfolding the edge of her sleeve over her forearm. 'He was a stranger who came home occasionally and sometimes remembered to look at me. But it wasn't often he did that.'

Teresa pitied her.

'He was still your father,' she said.

Maddalena's eyes darted up to hers, signalling anger – not at Teresa, but rather at that missing parent, the absence of his love clearly still a heavy cross to bear.

'I can tell you what the back of his head looked like better than I can describe his face. I can hardly remember the sound of his voice,' the woman continued. 'Even on his deathbed, he wasn't interested in seeing me. My son was with him, though: the male descendant, the only person he seemed to care about.' She lit a cigarette, her hands shaking. 'He used to take him away for days on end.'

'Where to?'

'He was obsessed with the mountains. They were his greatest passion, right up until the end. They used to go on treks together.'

'I'd like to talk to your son.'

The woman burst into bitter laughter.

'So would I. I haven't heard from him in two years. The last time I tried to call him, I got an automated message saying his number was no longer in use. Of course, my son had forgotten to inform me.'

'I'm sorry.'

The woman shrugged.

'He doesn't hate me. There's never been a problem. It's just . . . he's like his grandfather. Other people are nothing but shadows in their lives. Just shadows passing by.'

Teresa glanced at Marini. His expression was strained.

'Did your father ever talk to you or your mother about the war?' she asked the woman.

Maddalena stubbed her cigarette out in an ashtray and lit

another.

'Only when he wanted to remind us of our insignificance. We could never understand, that's what he used to say. Unlike him, we'd never had to fight for our freedom.'

'What happened to his violin?'

'I've no idea. It wasn't among his possessions when he died.'

Teresa asked her if she had any pictures of her father to show them. The woman looked up and exhaled a cloud of cigarette smoke, wishing perhaps she could just as easily expel the rancour that was still eating away at her.

'I removed all traces of him from this house,' she replied. 'I put them in a box in the attic for years, locked away with all of my resentment until I could finally bring myself to get rid of it. The only photo I didn't destroy is the one you'll find in the cemetery.'

Teresa did go to the cemetery. She saw the tomb overrun with weeds. She saw the bare, desolate flower vase. Finally, she saw Cam.

And she recognised him.

63

Francesco was in his woodshed, stacking logs with the energy and vigour of a much younger man. He didn't turn round as Teresa approached, though somehow, he seemed to know who it was, walking up to him.

'The forest is overrun with your people,' he said, using a handkerchief to wipe the sweat off his neck. 'They've been out looking for Emmanuel from dawn till dusk, but still they haven't found him.'

Teresa watched him moving blocks of wood about, his gestures seemingly effortless. She hadn't been able to tell from his tone whether or not the presence of the police displeased him. He didn't seem surprised by the temporary impasse in which the investigation was currently languishing. It just meant that the forest – with its crevasses, its muddy plateaus, and its screes that could collapse into landslides at a moment's notice and drag you hundreds of feet from where you had just been standing – was doing its job: protecting what was concealed inside it, like a single giant trap guarding everything that dwelt inside it.

'You lied to me,' said Teresa, sitting on a bench carved from the trunk of a pine tree.

At that, Francesco finally turned round, one hand on his side and the other clasping his handkerchief. His gaze flitted between Teresa and Marini, but he never looked down. He pulled out his axe from a stump and sat down.

'It's not very courteous to turn up at someone's house and accuse him of being a liar,' he said without acrimony.

'I don't pay courtesy visits when I'm working,' Teresa replied in similarly mild fashion. 'Besides, I was simply making an observation. Am I wrong?'

Francesco didn't reply.

Teresa showed him a printout of a photograph of a middle-aged man with hair still as thick and curly as it would have been in his youth. It was a portrait of Cam, the likeness she'd found on his tomb.

'He didn't change much, did he?' she remarked.

The expression on Francesco's face shifted. He looked alarmed, as if he'd come face to face with a man who'd returned from the dead to drag him down to hell.

'His name was Carlo Alberto Morandini,' Teresa continued. 'You might not have known that, but you do know that he was a partisan and that he was somewhere in these mountains during the dying days of the war. He was the one who gave you the rifle you fired at the German soldier's cart that day.'

Francesco made no attempt to take the printout Teresa was showing him.

'How did you figure it out?' he whispered.

'I recognised him. Alessio Andrian painted him. He painted the whole scene. He was watching you that day. It was Cam who gave you the rifle, wasn't it?'

Francesco nodded, his elbows resting on his knees and his hands clasped together in front of his mouth. Teresa gave Marini a knowing look.

'Why did you lie to me about what the Germans did? Why didn't you tell me that they executed a Resian man?' she asked Francesco.

Francesco bowed his head.

'Because I was ashamed,' he confessed. 'It's been seventy years and still the shame won't go away. They carried out the execution to punish us for the shot I fired at the German soldier, though nobody knew that at the time. My sister Ewa and I never told anyone what had really happened and an innocent boy died without even knowing why. They butchered him, right there in front of us, and we never said a word.'

'You made a pact,' Teresa suggested.

Francesco looked away, and right into the past.

'Yes,' he murmured. 'We made a pact. A terrible pact.'

64

March 1945

The arrival of the Germans was announced by the roar of the engines that powered their trucks up the hairpin turns. The exhaust fumes rose through the gorge and reached the first village, heralding an event that would for ever alter the landscape of that little world that had so far escaped the war unscathed.

Francesco saw them rounding the last turn, but he didn't yet know why they had come. They seemed different from the soldier who drove the cart up the valley every Thursday to fetch bread from the bakery. These soldiers looked angry.

His sister, Ewa, grabbed his arm and pushed him towards their house, but before they could go inside and hide behind the door, the trucks had already surrounded the village. One by one, the soldiers stepped out from beneath the tents on the backs of the trucks, moving as swiftly as a pack of hungry wolves. They were armed, and they were looking at the villagers as if they saw them as something less than human.

The war, Francesco thought, *was a strange thing indeed*. An imaginary line drawn by a stranger somewhere far away now marked the boundary between brotherhood and hate. Friends and enemies were made on the basis of which side of that border they happened to be born on.

He realised that these soldiers had come because of the shot he had fired. They would tell him off now and his father would be angry with him. He looked at Ewa and trembled, but his sister gripped his hand harder and placed a single finger on his lips.

You swore, *Franchincec*, she was telling him. They had sworn they would keep quiet.

The soldiers searched every home and gathered everybody – men, women, children and the elderly – in the main square. Their weapons were pointed at the villagers' heaving chests. Their leader – *so striking*, Francesco thought, *in his uniform* – barked a series of orders at the mayor, Gilberto Turan. Gilberto wasn't entirely unacquainted with the soldier's dry, jagged language and replied in a mixture of fear, unfamiliar words and pleas in Italian.

Nobody was hiding any weapons, he said. Nobody had fired any shots at any Germans.

Francesco lowered his eyes, which had now begun to sting with tears. And even when it all began, he kept his gaze firmly on the place where his fingers intertwined with Ewa's, the seal of a pact that must never be broken.

The foreign wolves surrounded the lambs and selected the one they would sacrifice. Gwén had only just turned fifteen and in a few days he was due to take the few cows they still had left up to the highlands for pasture. He would return to the valley at the end of the summer. He had never touched a rifle in his life.

Francesco looked up and spotted Aniza in the crowd. She was peering into the forest, her face a mask of anguished expectation as if she thought someone would turn up at any moment and save them all.

The children of the valley had never known what war was really like, not until that moment.

Francesco discovered that day that it had a very specific smell – of blood, of metal forged into weapons, of beatings that sliced people's flesh open. Of the foreign scent of the invaders, of leather boots so heavy they crushed the flowers they trod upon.

The war sounded like the rattle of machine-gun fire, like a strange snarling language, like empty cartridges crackling against stone. It sounded like the hysterical sobs of a mother, the quiet weeping of a father, a boy crumpling to the floor onto a bed of crushed crocuses. It sounded like the last tremor in his limbs as he lay cradled in the arms of a woman who had no air left in her lungs to cry. It sounded, too, like the teardrop falling to the ground from Gwén's red-stained face: Francesco heard it clearly, or maybe what he heard was the sound of the innocence being ripped out of his soul to mix with the blood that soaked the earth.

The first shots fired from the forest startled the wolves. Suddenly, the partisans erupted from the trees, spraying bullets everywhere. The village descended into chaos.

Amid all the noise and the shouting, Francesco felt himself being lifted into the air. Aniza had picked him up, Ewa clinging to her skirts. There was a man with Aniza whom Francesco had never seen before, and would never see again. He had a red bandana tied around his neck and his fingers, wrapped around his rifle, were stained with paint. He was protecting them as they fled, ushering them far away from there, to a place where they could hide. He didn't stop shooting until they were safe.

Inside the granary, Aniza watched through a gap in the planks as silence once again fell upon the village, while Francesco, his vision blurred with tears and the salty tang of his runny nose upon his tongue, watched Ewa. He saw her pursing her lips and the subtle gesture with which she tucked under her skirt the treasure they'd stolen from the German soldier.

That treasure was filthy now, soaked with blood and human life.

65

Massimo listened to Francesco's account with his heart throbbing in his throat, lodged there like a bullet refusing to budge.

The old man seemed to be seeing the echoes of a painful past flash before his eyes.

'I think I remember now,' he whispered. 'One of the partisans helped us to escape the crossfire that day. He came straight for Aniza. For us. It must have been him. It must have been Andrian.'

He covered his face with his hands.

'I will never forgive myself for not speaking up. What happened to Gwèn will haunt me for the rest of my life,' he said, sounding angry now. He looked down at his upturned palms. 'His blood is on my hands; I can feel it there. But I swear that rifle wasn't supposed to be loaded. It was meant to be a game. I was aiming at the German soldier as a game.

'Ewa and I spent a lot of time in the fields outside the village. That's how we met that partisan. He let us play with his rifle whenever he'd had a few glasses of grappa and was in a good mood. But he was never reckless. He always took the bullets out.'

'But not that day,' Superintendent Battaglia urged him.

Francesco looked at each of them in turn.

'I still can't remember whether or not I saw him do it that day,' he said. 'But the rifle did fire a shot and the shot grazed the German soldier. And then Gwèn was slaughtered. Because of a scratch. Because of a *game*.'

Massimo could almost feel the crushing weight of the man's guilt. And he could also feel that something about this tale still remained hidden, buried so deep that it was little more than the dark outline of a shape he couldn't yet make out.

'That partisan called himself Cam,' said Superintendent Battaglia. 'Did you know that?'

'No. We weren't close. It wasn't really a friendship. We were. . . a diversion, to him.'

'Did you know that he was an exceptional violinist and that he had performed the 'Devil's Trill' for the mayor of Trieste?'

The horrified look on Francesco's face answered for him.

'So *he* was the one in the woods that night,' he whispered.

'We still need to determine whether or not he was involved in Aniza's disappearance,' the superintendent replied. 'But we're sure he was somewhere in the forest: the partisan camp wasn't far off, anyway. He must have been the one playing the violin that night. But it remains to be seen whether or not he was also the one who murdered Aniza and hid her body. What might have been his motive? Obsession? Sexual compulsion? Perhaps he assaulted her and when she tried to resist him, he lost control.'

Francesco closed his eyes.

'If he was the one who hurt Aniza, then my silence killed two people.'

His hands were shaking in his lap and Massimo could feel that tremor boring its way into his own gut, infecting him, too, with its pain.

He understood how Francesco felt. He knew.

He looked away in search of some kind of relief, a way to forget about the superintendent for a moment, and that old man who was still trapped in his own past. If only he could lose himself in the wild scents of the forest. He had to find a different perspective, or else he would go mad. It was as if he had reached a point of no return – regarding Elena, regarding his life. It was the kind of moment when you realise that nothing will ever be the way it used to be. The rift Massimo had created was like death: irreversible.

It was imperative that he should banish Elena from his heart, push her far from the reach of his violent hands. But instead there was a chain that bound them together – a chain made out of his own DNA. The child's umbilical cord was like a knot that tied them both together.

He closed his eyes for a moment. He took a step back, then another and another until his slow retreat turned into flight.

66

When she looked up to find Marini gone, Teresa was stunned. She saw him turn round to glance at her one last time before getting into the car. Then he turned on the engine and fled as if his very survival depended on making his escape.

She kept looking even after he was long gone, vanished out of sight behind a turn in the road. She thought of the expression on his face, which was enough to convince her that there was no more time left to lose. She had to find out what it was that had been eating away at him. She had to figure out how to save him.

The explanation she was looking for wasn't in his file, which she had been sent before his transfer to the team. She hadn't been surprised at the information she'd found there: she had expected the flawless CV, the high marks and the immaculate disciplinary record, all the glittering trophies of a man destined for a stellar career. Massimo Marini's success so far was the result of a hard-fought campaign for personal redemption.

The sparkle had begun to fade as Teresa had read further down the page. She hadn't been prepared for what she'd found there: the sanitised description, couched in legal terminology, of a tragic event that had likely affected every single moment of Marini's life thereafter.

And yet Teresa had the feeling that something was missing. There had to be more to this than what she had read in his file, something unresolved: not just grief, but anguish, too. Guilt.

She scrolled through the contacts in her phone until she found the number she was looking for and made the call, grumbling to herself as she waited. She had never enjoyed calling in favours, knocking on people's doors and telling them 'I've come to you because you owe me.'

But she would do it for Massimo.

'It's a big ask,' said the voice at the other end of the line once she'd explained what she needed.

'So it can't be done?' Teresa replied, meaning something else altogether.

She heard a sigh.

'It can't be done, and I shouldn't do it. But I will.'

She hung up and clambered back down to the village, where the search teams were still scouring the forest for traces of an elusive corpse that was missing its heart. The time had come to throw Blanca and Smoky into the mix.

Inevitably, she had to call headquarters and explain to an appalled de Carli that Marini had decided to run away, so someone had to come and fetch her. She knew – she was certain, in fact – that Officer de Carli wouldn't breathe a word of this to anyone except Parisi. That was how their circle worked: a circle of trust, of honour, of shared values best described as a form of 'belonging'. She smiled, in spite of everything, at the thought that these were the same values that had governed the lives of medieval knights. And it was her responsibility to lead her young, strong, zealous knights (even when they were as troubled as Marini was), never mind the fact that she could hardly speed up her walking pace without running out of breath.

She checked the time on her mobile phone while all around her the hunt continued in a flurry of men exchanging tired commands, walkie-talkies croaking out truncated words, excited dogs relieving their weary colleagues and maps laid out over car bonnets, their corners curling up in the wet wind brought by another change in the weather. One of the maps broke free of the hands that had held it down and fluttered into the air before falling at Teresa's feet. She picked it up and studied the grid someone had drawn upon it with a red marker.

She gave it back to its owner and watched him return to his colleagues' side, his boots caked all the way to his knees with mud.

'Teresa.'

She turned round.

'Doctor Lona,' she replied.

Albert was huddled in his expensive coat, his neck wrapped in a scarf the same colour as his eyes: like the surface of a lake on a rainy day.

She wasn't surprised to see him there. He relished the power his position gave him over people. And he became incensed when confronted with people who, like Teresa, seemed immune to those effects.

'They've not made any progress,' he said, looking past her.

Teresa followed his gaze.

'These woods are vast,' she said. 'Where one forest ends, another begins. The body could be anywhere.'

'Listen to yourself. You're saying they won't find it.'

'They will find it. Eventually.'

'You act like it isn't your problem. I can assure you it is.'

Teresa put up no resistance to his calm fury: it would have been like asking a viper not to bite, or a boa constrictor not to suffocate. This was his nature.

'I have a solution,' she said instead. 'I have someone who can speed up the search.'

'And who might that be?'

'An external asset.'

'Not this again. I have given you my answer already. No.'

'But this is different . . .'

Albert whipped his head round to look at her.

'*No*. No civilians. It will be *my* men who find that damned body and solve this case.'

She let out a sigh and then the unthinkable happened. Albert brought his hand up to her face and gently cupped her cheek.

'How many more battles will you lose before you realise you can't do it alone?' she heard him say.

Teresa contemplated her existence from another's point of view and for the first time in her life, she saw that there wasn't just emptiness around her.

She had a team of young men to oversee – and to look after.

She had Blanca now, and her noble companion with his peerless nose.

She had all the victims she'd seen in her forty-year career, and cherished with a mother's love. A love that powerful was bound to leave a trace, even when the victims couldn't be saved. She could feel them, at night, all around her. She could feel them all, protecting her.

She had the victims' families, which in time had become her own.

She had friends, like Parri and Ambrosini.

But most importantly, she had herself.

She gripped his wrist. She squeezed it hard, then pushed his hand away.

'I am not alone,' she said.

Albert's expression changed like a snake shedding its skin.

'Then I will raze everything around you to the ground,' he vowed as if he were promising her eternal love.

Teresa couldn't help but smile.

'Go ahead,' she told him, 'but I still won't be yours.'

He stared at her for a few silent moments, then turned his back and walked away.

Only then did Teresa notice that de Carli had already arrived and was waiting for her by the car.

She walked up to him, knowing he'd seen far too much. The officer rushed to open the door for her.

'I won't ask what happened, Superintendent, but—'

'Good. Don't,' she said, throwing her bag onto the back seat.

'Jesus, really . . . ?'

'Be quiet.'

'I won't tell anyone,' he promised as he walked over to the other side of the car.

He jumped in and turned the engine on.

'You'd better not,' said Teresa, putting her glasses on to look at a parcel he had handed her.

It had her name on it.

'Morandini's daughter brought it over to headquarters,' he explained.

Teresa tore it open to reveal a series of landscape shots of mountain views, some really rather beautiful. There was also a handwritten note:

These are my father's photographs, the only things from among his personal belongings that I neglected to destroy.

Your visit has reopened some very deep wounds. Do not contact me again.

Teresa pulled out a tissue and sifted through the photographs, trying as much as possible to avoid touching them. She had recognised the Resia Valley and its villages immediately.

So Cam had never ventured too far from those lands. But what was it that had so engrossed him?

She grabbed her phone and called headquarters, asking for Parisi.

'We're going to need some urgent tests on the photographs Morandini's daughter handed in. Tell the forensics team I'm bringing them over now,' she instructed. 'They'll need to look for fingerprints to compare with the one we found on the painting. And call the deputy prosecutor: we'll need a warrant to search Carlo Alberto Morandini's belongings.'

She hung up, her heart thumping in her chest. Instinctively, she plunged a hand inside her shoulder bag before her brain caught up and reminded her that what she was looking for was no longer there.

Her diary was in the murderer's hands. She was sure of it. Teresa could feel him leafing through her, through page after page of her life. The killer was reading her. Getting to know her. Crawling into her personal inferno.

And that, she knew, was where they would eventually meet.

67

The wind ripped the older leaves off the ancient poplar tree before their time, making room for the younger shoots and clearing the plant of all the dead weight it had gathered. It tore through the foliage like a comb, sowing freedom in its wake.

When the occasional gust descended upon the meadow, blades of grass and stems of flowers bent obediently under the force of that cool wave, following its sudden changes in direction in a choreographed dance reminiscent of flocks of swifts. And so the sky was mirrored in the earth.

The wind ruffled the pages of the diary as if to sweep away the anguish and the sorrow lodged inside.

The *Tikô Wariö* had journeyed through the suffering enshrined in Teresa Battaglia's notes, written down in words that were as wild as her spirit. So the forthright red-haired cop wasn't as hard-hearted as she seemed – nor was she as unbreakable as she pretended to be.

She carried inside an elaborate emotional universe.

She had a secret, and she was afraid. There was someone she cared for more than she cared about herself: that young man she never let out of her sight as if it were her duty to protect him, to guard him from the self-destructive streak that threatened to destroy him.

She wasn't unbreakable, but she was strong. She was smart. She knew how to use her intuition to go where reason alone could never reach. She could see clearly where others saw only darkness.

Teresa Battaglia was a deadly huntress. But now she was on the other side.' Now, her heart had been laid bare. And it was vulnerable.

68

Massimo realised he had no idea where he was going. He had simply been driving, moved by the uncontrollable urge to get away from Francesco and his guilt, away from Superintendent Battaglia and that inquisitive gaze of hers that always seemed to be upon him, now more than ever before.

He couldn't understand why she was still chasing after his secret. Surely it was right there for her to see, spelt out in his personal file, which she *had* to have read. Massimo had been waiting for her to confront him about it since the day he'd joined her team, but so far, she'd never once mentioned it.

Recent events had conspired to take over his life and tear it to pieces: Elena and the child they were expecting, but not just that. It was as if the *Sleeping Nymph*, too, had been waiting for him, just like Superintendent Battaglia, with a baby who had never been born.

And Carlo Alberto Morandini's daughter, too: her angst over a father who'd never loved her had rattled Massimo. It had been like peering into his own future and seeing himself in the guise of the villain.

And finally, Francesco, still agonising over a death he had unwittingly caused.

He felt a wave of nausea and had to pull over. He let go of the clutch and the engine died with a shudder as other cars drove past him, horns blaring.

He rested his forehead against the steering wheel, his skin cold and clammy with panic.

He glanced at his mobile phone on the passenger seat, blinking with notifications from endless messages and missed calls. He already knew who they were from, but he couldn't let her look inside him again and see the person he truly was. Teresa Battaglia was a rope that fate had thrown his way when there had been nothing but emptiness all around. He'd clung on to it with all the strength he had, but he wouldn't allow himself to drag her down with him.

He picked up the phone and dialled the number of the only person who knew his secret. Speaking to her was never easy. He had abandoned his roots in order to make a clear break from his past – but that was the same past she was still drowning in. He wondered how she must feel whenever she looked at him and was reminded of the day Massimo had stopped being a child and became something else.

When she picked up, he didn't immediately recognise her voice. She seemed more distant than usual.

'Mum,' he said.

There was a moment's hesitation.

'Is something wrong?' she asked fearfully.

One choked word out of him had been enough to throw her into a state of alarm.

There were a thousand words Massimo could have chosen to explain what had happened, but they weren't necessary. She would understand.

'I'm going to be a father, and there's nothing I can do about it,' he whispered.

A gasp coursed through the low hiss of the telephone. His mother started crying, and they weren't tears of joy. She knew the demon that haunted her son. She'd looked it right in the eyes.

'I'm scared,' Massimo murmured into that distant weeping. 'I'm scared.'

As he turned the word over and over in his mind, he felt anger growing inside him like a sudden hunger. He needed that rage to get rid of the pain.

Finally, he knew where to go.

69

Teresa woke with a start. She was sure she'd screamed, her lips pressed against the imitation leather upholstery of the couch, whose bitter taste now filled her mouth. She was in the meeting room of the police headquarters. Someone had covered her with a plaid blanket. She shrugged it off and pushed herself upright.

The clock told her she'd slept for just over a couple of hours.

The door opened slowly and Parisi stuck his head inside.

'I'm up,' she told him.

He came in and put a file on the coffee table in front of her.

'This came in for you. But I'll need a little more time to find what you asked me for. Coffee?'

'No, thanks. Have you figured out where Marini's gone?'

'No, but we've had some news on the partial footprints found on the landing outside his flat: men's trainers, size forty-three. Soon we'll know the brand, too.'

Teresa nodded, stretching her back.

'Have you and de Carli had any sleep?' she asked.

The officer smiled.

'In instalments, like you. Oh, and by the way, the district attorney's out of the office until tomorrow.'

'Excellent news.'

'We've got him off our arses for a few hours at least, Superintendent.'

'Good God, Parisi, you've started talking like me now.'

'It's a proud moment.'

'I'm touched.' Teresa put on her glasses. 'Now, get out of here.'

Alone again, Teresa picked up the file. The sealed envelope had come with a typewritten note:

I know you'll make good use of this. We're even now.

The message was unsigned, but if it hadn't been anonymous, it would have carried the signature of the Guardian – as the keeper of the archives of the juvenile court was known. He was the only official who was authorised to access the database on 'atypical' homicides – cases involving what some cops rather morbidly referred to as 'evil in nappies'. The information in these archives was so strictly classified that none of the files mentioned full names. These tribunals followed different procedures – faster ones designed to leave no long-term trace. Sometimes they were carried out in total secrecy, for those cases no one must ever know about. And always, the imperative was to forget quickly.

Teresa broke the seal and opened the file containing the declassified portion of the court records concerning the case of a child named Massimo Marini.

There were words in there she would never have wished to read and photographs it was physically painful to look at.

When she thought she'd finally made it through to the very end of the file, she turned the page and suffered the worst blow yet. She had to read the words again and again. Her mind seemed to refuse to accept the truth. She'd been ready for anything, but not for *this*.

Finally, she understood. And now that little boy's suffering was her own, too.

She studied all the reports and the witness transcripts, checked the photographs and compared them to the coroner's findings. Everything matched, but Teresa didn't give up – she went back to the start, over and over again. She had to find something, anything – a mistake she could show that little boy so that she could tell him: 'You're free, now.'

But I can't find it. I can't find it.

Her arms fell to her sides. She couldn't help him. All she had to give him were words of comfort, which would make no difference at all.

Then, a new thought wove its way into her head. Perhaps it wasn't the truth she needed to hunt for.

She looked at her phone and picked it up.

If I make this call, there's no going back.

Parri answered on the second ring.

'I need your help and I can't give you any context,' she told him.

Her friend's laugh flooded her with relief.

'Just tell me what you need.'

Shortly thereafter, Parisi came in bringing the material she'd requested from Parri. Teresa closed the file and quickly wiped a hand over her eyes, though she wasn't sure she'd been fast enough for it to escape his notice. But Parisi didn't say anything. There was no time for jokes now. Wordlessly, he handed her a note bearing the name of a woman and the address of a hotel.

'We've found Marini, Superintendent.'

70

Practising mixed martial arts was one of the many escape routes Massimo had devised over the years. Shut inside that cage, surrounded by a circle of raging, boisterous men inciting him and his opponent to hit harder, to hurt each other more, he felt liberated, free to act as nature commanded. And so he hit out, again and again, with every fibre of his being.

Christian Neri's body was a tangle of tendons, of thick bones and hardened muscles, a body that wouldn't be overpowered but would return with interest each and every blow Massimo managed to land.

The rivalry they'd always had in the gym had finally found its outlet, but when he looked at his opponent, it wasn't Neri's eyes that Massimo saw. The true target of his anger had never been Neri. It had always been his own father who Massimo was trying to destroy – or perhaps it was himself.

Visions of Elena, of an unborn child, of his own lonely future, of his suffering mother who would never forgive him – all flashed through his mind and clouded his judgement.

But then, for the briefest moment, his eyes drifted towards the cheering crowd as if drawn there by a silent powerful call. When he spotted Teresa Battaglia's furious face in the audience, Massimo froze.

He felt something he couldn't quite name. Shame: that was the first word that came floating into his field of vision, like a punch about to smash into his face. Relief: that was the next word. She had come to save him.

The punch to his face eventually came through, though this time it was real. It was a knockout blow.

Massimo felt his head bounce against the mat, while fireworks exploded in his eyes and a hissing in his ears shut out the rest of the world. His brain seemed to be spinning inside his skull.

Someone did a countdown, which was followed by cheers for the winner. All that was left for Massimo was the coldness of the rubber mat beneath his cheek and the sting of sweat on his scratches.

Lucius, the ballet dancer turned fighter, was soon beside him, pressing a towel against his face and talking rapidly in his mother tongue. They didn't sound like words of comfort. The odour of haemostatic cream was followed by the feel of hands prodding at his face as if in search of broken bones that might need immediate setting. Massimo tasted blood on his lips: it tasted like freedom, and peace. He had managed to punish himself.

Another pair of hands was holding his head now, but the touch was gentle this time, in sharp contrast to the voice lashing out at him.

'What the hell do you think you're doing?'

It was her. It was Superintendent Battaglia, who'd climbed into the ring to help, or perhaps to smash that malfunctioning head of his.

Her voice was different than usual, a tangle of anger and affectionate concern. The strands of feeling were woven into it so thick that it was impossible to see where they began and ended. They were a single unified whole.

It was the voice of a mother grieving for her son.

71

'I could have this place shut down, you know.'

Marini opened one eye. The other was covered with an ice pack. They'd made him lie down on a bench in the changing rooms.

'Please, Superintendent . . .' he said, his voice croaky.

Teresa sat fuming beside him, keeping one of his legs elevated.

'You're a fucking idiot,' she declared. 'Have I told you that already?'

'Three times.'

She shoved him aside and leapt to her feet. She could have eaten him alive.

'Ouch!'

'Do you realise you're throwing everything away?' she yelled. 'You're throwing your future down the drain.'

She saw him lower his eyes, then look up again. He was trying to smile, to go back into hiding.

'You sound like my mother,' he said in an affectedly playful tone.

Teresa doubted it. His mother wasn't there because his mother was part of the problem. She realised then that she couldn't go back into hiding, either.

'I know your secret,' she told him.

Marini's face was like a cold, rigid mask.

'There's no secret,' he said blankly. 'It's always been in my file, very clearly spelt out.'

'Not completely,' she corrected him.

Marini slowly sat up. The ice pack fell to the floor. His hands gripped the edge of the bench. His chest was heaving. Teresa pictured his heart, struck by a fatal blow yet beating still, thumping against his ribs until it hurt. She would have given anything to soothe that pain, but first she had to carve his chest open and rip out the monster that was feeding on him. She had to make Marini look it in the eye, so he could see how easy it could be to banish the ghost that haunted him. All he had to do was forgive himself.

She watched him shrug his shoulders.

'A man beating his wife and child isn't exactly news, Superintendent,' he told her. 'He wasn't the first and he won't be the last. You know the statistics better than I do.'

Teresa hazarded a step towards him.

'You didn't kill him,' she said.

She saw him gasp, watched him flinch as if he'd been struck again.

'You're out of line.'

Teresa took another step, inching closer to the child he had once been.

'You didn't kill him,' she repeated, louder this time.

Massimo shook his head.

'Enough,' he said.

Teresa said it again.

'Enough!' he said, shouting now, one hand raised as if to stop her, as if to implore her not to break the fragile balance he was trying so desperately to hold on to.

'You were only a child, Massimo. You're not at fault.'

He shook with a powerful shiver. Something inside him seemed about to erupt.

'I pushed him,' he hissed. 'It was me.'

'*No*. It was him. You were a ten-year-old boy against a forty-year-old man. He was so drunk he could barely stand.'

'I said *enough*!'

Teresa took some papers from her bag: photocopies of old autopsy reports.

'Your father had a fracture in his head that pre-dated his death,' she pushed on, showing him some notes on an image of the back of a skull. Clearly visible in a spot somewhere just above the inferior nuchal line was a partially calcified crack. 'That fall wouldn't have killed anyone, but your father's skull was as fragile as a clay pot: it was that pre-existing fracture that killed him. It would have killed him even if someone happened to slap him on the back of his head.'

He lifted his eyes to look at her. She could see how desperately he wanted to believe her. But the past was putting up a fight.

'How did you get hold of this?'

Teresa dodged the question.

'They should have made this clear both to you and to your

mother,' she said, 'but perhaps they thought it wasn't relevant; you weren't guilty anyway.'

He opened and closed his mouth twice before he managed to speak.

'Not relevant?' he stammered.

'Blame it on the incompetence, the inexperience or the apathy of those who were supposed to investigate the case. But whatever it was, it wasn't a homicide.'

She knelt in front of him. 'It's the truth,' she whispered. 'You didn't kill him.' She spread her arms wide. 'You're not a killer, Massimo. You were only trying to defend yourself. It was a tragedy.'

'Go away!'

Teresa thought again of the photographs in his file, that little boy's back, skinny and covered in bruises. She thought of that mother who'd been unable to protect her son, just as Teresa herself had failed to do. She thought of all the barbed comments with which she'd tormented him over the past few months to try to figure out what had pushed him to seek shelter in some small provincial town, and of the formidable self-control he'd displayed when they'd worked together on a case involving the abuse of minors.

She pushed the photocopied images right up to his face and forced him to look.

'Stop being a traumatised kid, start acting like a cop and tell me what you see!'

His face was a picture of despair as he studied the greyscale images before him, but soon a kind of relief began to spread over it until it finally crumpled in an outburst of liberating tears.

Teresa cast aside the autopsy report from an old case that had nothing to do with the father of the young man before her and with it, she also cast aside a portion of her professional integrity.

But it if helped to save Marini, then no matter. She had made the conscious decision not to write any of this down in her new diary. She had discovered, in fact, that her illness granted her a kind of freedom that her sense of ethics had previously always denied her: the freedom to fabricate evidence without any adverse effects on her conscience. Soon, she would forget about this episode and it would be as if it had never happened.

She hugged him, hard. She held him as he tried to wriggle free, to push her away, even as his face turned towards her, leant into her shoulder. His struggle soon turned into a helpless clinging. Teresa made his suffering her own, absorbed it like venom. It would course through her veins in its diluted, no longer lethal form until the day her heart stopped beating.

They were quiet for a long time, sitting next to each other, Marini's head resting on Teresa's shoulder. If anyone who knew them had come across them now, they would have thought the scene bizarre, to say the least.

Teresa waited patiently until Marini was ready to talk.

'I've spent all of my life thinking I carried part of him inside of me. Like some kind of sickness,' she heard him say.

Teresa saw herself from the outside. How tiny she looked, and yet she was the one holding this young man together.

'You still think that,' she said.

'The evil gene. I read about it in some articles on psychiatry.'

'A fascinating theory, to be sure, but one that has yet to be proven true. You'll have read about that too, I expect.'

'So you don't believe in it?'

'I believe it's reassuring to blame evil on factors beyond our control, and even better if it's some sort of genetic flaw. But that's not the case with you, Marini.'

'So we're back to surnames now?'

'It's true that particularly serious cases of psychosis can lead to heinous crimes, but to speak of an actual "evil gene" strikes me as fantasy. Experiences are crucial, environments are crucial and so are dozens of other variables. You know that.'

'I guess I felt like evil must have infected me.'

'It did infect you. It infects anyone who's ever been subjected to violence.'

'Including you.'

'Including me. But we're stronger. And you're exceptionally resilient.'

Marini looked up at her.

'I think that's the first time you've ever called me anything nice.'

'Really? I'd better fix that, then: you're also a terrible fighter. How many times did he get you?'

He laughed, cradling his ribs.

'I did a pretty good job on him, too.'

'Is that a joke? He could probably go out and run a marathon now, if he wanted to.'

They fell silent.

'If there really were something wrong with you, Marini, if there were even the tiniest shadow of a doubt about that, you wouldn't be here. They'd never have let you be a cop,' she told him.

'My mother never forgave me,' he confessed. 'She still loved him, despite everything. After that day, she couldn't even bring herself to look at me any more.'

Teresa took hold of his chin and made him look at her.

'You're wrong. She can't look at you because she's over whelmed with guilt. The fear of standing up to him made her complicit in his actions until you had no choice but to fend for yourself.' When he made as if to protest, she squeezed his chin harder. 'She can't look you in the eyes because she's ashamed.'

She watched as a new glimmer of hope relaxed his features.

'Have I ever fed you any bullshit?' she asked him.

'Never.'

'Then I think you can trust me on this one, too.'

Teresa saw in the flutter of his eyelids the last traces of doubt finally leaving him.

'I know it's not my place to say this, but I think it's really unfair that life hasn't given you a child,' he said eventually.

'I do have a child,' Teresa sighed. 'He was never born, but he is mine. And I have you lot to worry about, too. I think I spend more time mothering you all than I do being a detective.' She got up and pointed to the showers. 'Now, go and get yourself cleaned up. We've got a case waiting to be solved. If you're up to it, you might as well come and give us your usual worthless input.'

Marini laughed.

'Yes, Superintendent.'

She gave him a curt nod.

'Parisi will drop you back home. Do me a favour and try to be on time tomorrow morning.'

'Tomorrow? Why tomorrow?'

Teresa turned round, one hand already on the door.

'You've got something more important to do now. You've got to free her, too.'

She saw him swallow.

'What?' he said.

'Tell her you forgive her. That's all she needs to start living again. And I know this for a fact.'

He got back to his feet.

'There's something I need to ask you, Superintendent. Was your ex-husband Albert Lona?'

Teresa was surprised by the question, but even more surprised by his courage. Had the circumstances been different, had he chosen the wrong moment, she would have torn him to shreds.

'No, he's not my ex-husband.'

She saw him hesitate, another question on the tip of his tongue. She was tempted to put him off with some withering remark, but she found that she couldn't – and perhaps she would never be able to again, not after what they had shared with each other.

'Albert Lona was a colleague. We were the same age, but our personalities and our values couldn't have been more different,' she told him. 'He realised what was happening to me, noticed the bruises under my make-up, the fear in my eyes, even my pregnancy. He offered me what he considered to be a way out. I rejected his offer and that same night I lost my child because I wasn't able to protect him.'

In the silence that followed, Teresa could almost hear her heart and Marini's beating out of synch.

'So Lona offered to arrest him?' Marini exhaled.

She gave him a bitter smile.

'No. He told me he loved me.'

72

Killing had come easy to the *Tikô Wariö*. Fear had guided the swift glide of its blade towards Emmanuel's withered chest, where the knife had lodged itself in flesh to the tune of a thrush singing in the trees and a squirrel rustling for acorns among the leaves. The old man had fallen like the hollow trunk of a long-dead tree, emitting a sigh that could have been mistaken for the low whistle of the wind blowing through gnarled blueberry shrubs.

Taking the man's heart was natural and logical, it was attack as the best form of defence, an act at once savage and entirely innocent.

But although it had been easy enough to kill, there had been consequences which, in the heat of the moment, the *Tikô Wariö* had failed to foresee.

An act whose purpose had been to protect something had resulted in a secret being revealed.

Or – perhaps – it had been the *Tikô Wariö*'s yearning for deliverance that had guided its hand and set in motion a terrifying yet inevitable chain of events.

There were certain roots that burrowed so deep that they became harmful. They turned carnivorous, they fed on life. And there were certain ties that not only meant everything, but also brought death. Ties that nourished even as they smothered.

The blade, still stained with blood, shone in the torchlight. With the soil brushed away, the skeletal hand surfaced in the darkness of the silent forest, so that the knife could be laid across the worn phalanges of what had once been its fingers.

Evil is hereditary. The true sin was love. And love had caused death.

Everything else was only devotion and sacrifice.

73

So perhaps evil didn't have to be passed on from father to son. For the first time ever, Massimo allowed himself to hope it might be true, clinging to Teresa Battaglia's words to find his way out, once and for all, from the fear that imprisoned him. She had guided him along a path she had signalled with her own suffering: she had shown him the past she still carried with her. Considering who she was, the way she was and her position, that couldn't have been easy. And he would always be grateful to her for it.

He had just arrived to meet the superintendent at an address she'd texted him, but just as the sun was rising, and before climbing up the stairs to the apartment she'd indicated, he followed her advice.

When his mother picked up, Massimo didn't even wait for her to say hello.

'I know that what I'm about to say will be painful for you to hear,' he began. He pictured her sitting down on the chair by the console table, holding the phone, no rings on her fingers. Her hands shaking.

'When it happened . . . when he died,' he continued, 'I

thought I had saved you. We were free at last. I didn't understand the silence. I didn't understand why you couldn't even look at me any more. I felt like a monster.'

His voice cracked over that last word and he heard a muffled sob at the other end of the line.

'And do you realise now why I was like that?'

'Yes, I think so.'

'Say it, Massimo. Please.'

'I forgive you, Mum.'

'I wasn't able to protect you,' she said once she'd calmed down, 'but you're different: you're not like me, you're not like him. You'll be a strong father, a good father. This is your chance to be happy.'

Massimo didn't tell her that he'd already paid far too steep a price for his new beginning, that Elena had left the day before.

He'd spent all night outside her hotel, sitting on the pavement, staring at the black sky between the street lamps. He'd fought the urge to run to the train station as if there was a chance he'd find her waiting there, like a character in a fairy tale with a happy ending.

Elena hadn't answered his calls. Their roles had been reversed. But the only reason Massimo hadn't got in his car and driven for as long as it took to find her was that there was a killer on the loose. His front door had been smeared with blood-red paint in some kind of cryptic act of intimidation. She wouldn't be safe with him, not yet – though not for the reasons he had previously imagined.

He couldn't bring her back to his place and he couldn't abandon Superintendent Battaglia, either.

The pink-hued rays of the sun warmed his face as he bid his mother farewell, promising to visit her soon, and he climbed the stairs to the apartment where Superintendent Battaglia was waiting for him. But it was Blanca who opened the door.

'Hello,' he said, injecting a genuine smile into his greeting.

'Hello,' she replied.

Massimo was fascinated by her ability to find his eyes with her own simply by following the trail of his voice. All she needed was a single word to sketch out a mental map of her interlocutor's face and find where his or her gaze lay – though it was probably something she did to put people at ease rather than for her own benefit.

She showed him inside. Hers was a humble, spartan home and Massimo's stomach dropped at the memory of how unpleasant he'd been with her when they'd first met. She was a fighter, and he would have to show her a great deal more consideration and respect than he had done so far.

Smoky was watching him from the couch, his head poking dejectedly from between his paws. Massimo had never seen him look so depressed.

'What's up with him?' he asked.

'He's in detention. He's been naughty.'

Massimo sniffed the air. It smelt of broth.

'I brought breakfast,' he said, handing her a bag of warm croissants. 'But it smells like you're already making lunch.'

Blanca was startled by the sound of a cough coming from the kitchen.

The bag fell to the floor and they both bent down to pick it up.

'I'll get it,' Massimo offered.

Blanca was blushing now and looking uncomfortable. He helped her back up.

'Are you all right?' he asked her.

Superintendent Battaglia walked out of the kitchen.

'She's all right,' she said, brushing him off. 'Why don't you take a seat here in the living room?'

Massimo looked at the couch. It was the only thing there was to sit on and currently it was occupied by a dog that had never been particularly well disposed towards him. He looked at the superintendent again.

'I think I'd prefer the kitchen.'

'The kitchen's not allowed.'

Just then, the sound of something breaking in the bedroom: there was somebody else in the house. Teresa and Blanca disappeared, leaving the kitchen unguarded. They'd looked worried, which surprised Massimo. Was one of Blanca's relatives visiting? But that wouldn't explain why the superintendent was involved.

Left on his own, he turned to Smoky, who looked almost pathetic, all sad eyes and droopy ears.

Massimo edged closer and reached out as if to pet him but almost immediately had to snatch his hand back to evade – in the nick of time – the lightning-fast attack of Smoky's jaws, which snapped shut on thin air.

'I knew it!' Massimo exclaimed. 'You're really creepy, you know that, right?'

But poor Smoky had already returned to his previous state of catatonic misery.

On the stove in the kitchen, meanwhile, a pot had begun to gurgle wrathfully, its metal lid banging like a pair of cymbals gone crazy. Water leaked out and sputtered over the gas flame, extinguishing it. Massimo put the bag of croissants on the table and hurried over to turn the gas off. The stove was covered in some kind of sticky, smelly broth.

'Well, that's lunch gone,' he muttered, lifting the lid with a towel.

He yelped and tripped backwards into a bunch of chairs. Smoky had already rushed to the scene, barking his head off.

'Jesus Christ!'

Smoky lunged for his calf but missed, grabbing hold of his trousers instead and pulling furiously at the fabric until it tore. But the dog was the least of Massimo's worries; inside that pot, partly submerged in its own broth, was a human skull, staring up at him with a look of bewilderment.

'Superintendent!' he yelled as he tried to hold Smoky at bay.

Superintendent Battaglia calmly walked over, pulled the dog aside and put the lid back on the pot.

'Do you ever just mind your own fucking business, Marini?' she muttered.

'There's a human skull in there,' he said, his tone very deliberate.

But Superintendent Battaglia seemed entirely unmoved by his outrage.

'I know, Marini.'

'And you're OK with that?' he spluttered.

'I had to sterilise it,' explained Blanca, who'd joined them in the meantime, wearing a look of consternation. 'Smoky stole it. He was using it as a toy. He contaminated it with his scent. We had to do something, otherwise we'd never have been able to use it for training again.' She wrung her hands sheepishly. 'Which would have been a pity, right?'

Massimo was speechless. He looked at Superintendent Battaglia and threw his hands in the air.

'I don't even want to know,' he said, backing away. 'You two are crazy,' he said, pointing at them both. 'That must be why you get along so well.'

He turned round and stopped in his tracks. Elena was standing in front of him. She looked as if she'd just woken up; she was still in her pyjamas and her hair was all mussed.

'What are you doing here?' he said once he'd regained his bearings.

His heart was racing. He realised he'd asked the wrong question when he saw her raise a single eyebrow.

'Teresa was worried about me,' she replied curtly. 'And Blanca has been kind enough to let me stay. She needed a flatmate and I couldn't stay in a hotel for ever.'

He swallowed. He was such a fool.

'How are you both doing?' he asked.

She brushed a hand over her stomach.

'Fine, but the nausea is killing me.'

'I'm not surprised with this stink,' he said.

She frowned.

'What stink?'

Massimo remembered the bag he'd brought. He picked it up and handed it to her.

'I got some breakfast,' he said.

For them.

But Elena didn't smile as he'd hoped. Instead, she covered her mouth, all the colour draining from her face, and bent over.

Pregnancy really was a magical thing, casting a spell so potent that it made the smell of human bones seem normal, and that of vanilla and sugar revolting.

Elena had just thrown up on his shoes.

74

Teresa was back at the painter's house, staring at Alessio and Aniza's past, at the painting where Francesco, still a child, spelt the end of his own innocence, holding a rifle too big for his little boy's hands.

Once again, she admired Alessio Andrian's masterful depiction of the emotions in his subjects' faces, of the resemblance between Francesco and his sister – whose eyes, unlike her brother's, were the colour of ice from a faraway land – and of the powerful, living energy they carried in their bodies. It was such a physical painting, almost corporeal; you could feel the weight of its subjects. But there was something else, too, some element that bothered Teresa all the way to the depths of her subconscious. She wasn't sure yet what to call it.

'I haven't had a chance to thank you yet. I'll always be indebted to you.'

She turned to Marini. The plaster on his forehead, the cut on his lip and a light bruise on one of his cheekbones were the last traces left of a war he had finally won.

'Has Elena forgiven you?' she asked him.

'No.'

Teresa took off her glasses and wiped them on her sleeve.

'Then don't thank me yet – you never know, she might well replace you.'

He smiled.

'And I'd deserve it, Superintendent.'

'I agree.'

Raffaello Andrian called them from the hallway. His uncle was ready for visitors.

Alessio Andrian was lying in bed, but he wasn't asleep. The pillows supporting his back propped him far enough up that he could still see the forest he was so obsessed with.

Teresa looked at him now through the eyes of the past, picturing him as a young man trying to get through a war neither he nor his companions had wanted or understood.

To Aniza, he had been a romantic hero. When the invaders had attacked, he'd risked his life to protect her. Teresa imagined their clandestine meetings, their stolen night-time kisses, with the forest as their only witness.

The *Sleeping Nymph* wasn't some twisted, deathly creation; it was the portrait of a love for ever lost, a desperate attempt to make something that would preserve that love somehow.

She took from Marini the photographs she hadn't yet added to the case file.

They'd had confirmation an hour ago that the fingerprint found on the *Sleeping Nymph* belonged to Carlo Alberto Morandini. The match with the fingerprints they had found on the photographs his daughter had kept left no room for doubt. So the violin-playing partisan had definitely been there when Andrian was painting his portrait. Perhaps he'd touched it while trying to talk the painter out of his madness, or perhaps he had

302

wished to claim that last memory of her, too, and steal her away from the man who loved her.

She placed the photographs on the bed near Alessio's hands. They were pictures of Cam aged seventeen, taken not too long before he'd dropped out of the conservatoire to join the partisans hiding in the forests.

Teresa sat beside Alessio.

'We know Cam was with you and Aniza the night she died,' she said. 'He's the one you see when you look at the forest, right?'

Alessio's gaze moved away from the woods – the first time that had happened since Teresa had met him – and came to rest upon that face from his past.

With great effort, his fingers, weighed down by years of immobility, crept towards the photographs and crushed them slowly in their grip.

Raffaello hurried over.

'Uncle, please,' he said, but Teresa motioned at him to let it go.

She leant towards Andrian's face.

'Was it Cam who killed her? How did he do it?' she asked him.

But Andrian had turned into a statue again. Teresa tried again and again to connect with him, but he had gone back to his world of memories and silence, shutting the door firmly behind him. Teresa rose to her feet with a sigh and was heading towards the door, when a framed photograph fell from the bedside table. She turned round and put it back. But as she made for the door again, the photograph fell once more.

Teresa glanced at Marini and saw that they were thinking the same thing: Andrian himself had nudged it to the floor.

It was a photograph of his nephew, Raffaello.

75

All eyes were on Blanca and Smoky as they stepped out of the police car Parisi had driven them in. They'd come to the scene of Emmanuel Turan's murder on a delicate mission: to locate the body, and prove to all the doubters that this scruffy mutt and the girl who handled him were as exceptional as they were rumoured to be. Teresa had tried to be circumspect about their talents, but there had only been so much she could do. The police's own search teams, meanwhile, had been infuriatingly complacent about Blanca's involvement, as if they were certain they had already won what they saw as Teresa's eccentric little game.

'We've already combed through half the forest. If we haven't found it, it means it isn't there,' the leader of the search team had just been telling her.

Teresa was sure he was wrong, but she didn't say anything; to contradict him now would mean telling him that he had failed, and so had his team. And she would rather set them straight with the facts.

The derisory chatter died down when Blanca placed the tip of her white cane on the ground. Her footsteps echoed in a silence that screamed 'people like you don't belong here'. But the clicking of the cane, fast and sure, seemed to speak for her. And it brooked no argument.

'They'll eat her alive,' said Marini. He sounded worried.

'She won't let them,' Teresa replied. 'Anyway, we're here now.'

The head of the search team walked up to them. He looked furious.

'Is this a joke?' he snapped.

'Everyone knows I have no sense of humour,' Teresa replied without even looking at him.

'The girl is blind!'

'Don't worry, my dog can see just fine,' Blanca replied from behind him.

Teresa couldn't help but smile. It can't have been easy for Blanca to muster up the courage to say that.

The man turned round, looking sheepish, all the belligerence draining away from him at the sight of her small, unthreatening figure.

'I don't mean to be rude, young lady, but—'

'Then don't be.'

He looked at Teresa and with a nod that could have signified anything – a last-minute concession, or resignation in the face of folly – the officer walked back to join the rest of his men.

The search team's German shepherd dogs had begun to show signs of restlessness, which turned into full-blown howls of rage when Smoky began to urinate right in front of their noses. That was his way of sending a message.

Teresa pulled Blanca and Marini aside.

'How are you feeling?' she asked the girl.

'Ready.'

Teresa tenderly clasped her arm.

'Take all the time you need,' she told her. 'And don't worry about anyone else.'

The girl nodded.

'We don't know what the killer might have done with the body,' Teresa resumed, 'but I'm reasonably sure that it's here somewhere. It wouldn't have made sense to take it anywhere else: it would have been too risky and used up too much energy.'

Blanca lifted her face to the sky, as if she were sniffing for wind. She seemed to be scanning the air for the trail of scents that would guide Smoky to the hidden tomb. Her clouded irises lit up with the glare of the forest, that particular mix of shadow and light that Francesco had termed 'forest shade'.

'There are wild boars all over these woods: if a corpse isn't

305

retrieved promptly, or if it's left unburied, there won't be too much of it left to find,' she mused.

'Where do you want to start?' Marini asked her.

She thought about his question as she zipped her sweater and put up her hood. The wind had picked up now, blowing strands of her hair around her face in blue waves that smelt of flowers.

'From the riverbank, or wherever there's any water,' she replied firmly. 'Wild animals tend to take their food to where they can also drink at the same time. Does anyone have a map? Could you check, please?'

The men sprang into action like gentleman courtiers. Teresa smiled.

'We'll have to divide the area into squares measuring ten by ten,' Blanca continued. 'The dogs must cover every inch of it, down to the smallest nooks and crannies. The surface of a burial site will look different from its immediate surroundings. The soil will be darker, softer, more uneven, with plants ripped out or torn. If the vegetation has already grown back, it'll be thicker than it is elsewhere, even if it's just grass.'

They marked out the zone of interest on a map, measuring approximately half a mile square, and stretching from the spot where Emmanuel Turan had been killed all the way to the bed of the river *Wöda*. That was where they would start.

'How long do we have before Lona gets here?' Marini asked quietly.

'Not long enough,' Teresa replied. 'We should prepare for the worst.'

'The wind's died down,' said Blanca.

She asked for her backpack and pulled out a vial. Marini leant towards Teresa.

'Is that *talcum powder*?' he whispered.

'Shush. Let her be.'

The girl tipped a little of the fine powder onto the palm of her hand and let it trickle through her fingers. It was so light that it caught even the slightest whiff of a breeze.

'Which way is it blowing?' she asked.

'North-east,' Marini replied.

She nodded and crouched beside Smoky. That dog was so much more than a companion who made the day-to-day difficulties of Blanca's life a little easier to bear; he was a living extension of her being, an extra sense with which to experience the world – and an inseparable part of her beating heart.

'Moving against the wind makes the job of a search dog easier,' Blanca explained, straightening up. 'They'll follow the "scent cone" all the way to its source. We might detect molecules coming from quite a distance, if we're lucky.'

She folded up her collapsible cane and stuck it in the back pocket of her jeans. Teresa tried to imagine what it must be like to walk about in total darkness along the rough floor of a forest, with the constant fear of losing your foothold and the unsettling feeling of never knowing who or what might be behind the next step – the edge of a cliff, or some treacherous obstacle. Flanked by Smoky and surrounded by all those officers, Blanca wasn't in any danger, but maybe that was the hardest part of it all: to trust others enough to place your fate in their hands.

Teresa had a theory about why Blanca put her cane away during searches: she wanted to dig into the seething universe around her with all of her other senses – go in so deep that she could feel its presence with the desperate clarity of someone drowning. One night when they were having one of their chats, Blanca had given her a rather illuminating example.

'Have you ever looked for something using just your hands, without being able to see?' she'd asked Teresa. 'Your keys inside your handbag, your handkerchief. You know they're there, but you could look for hours and never find them. Your fingers rake through dozens of different objects all cluttered in that tiny space and you can hardly tell what's what.'

Teresa had nodded. It happened quite frequently, in fact, especially when she was in a rush.

'But take just one quick glance inside and within seconds,

you'll find what you've been looking for. Your senses will have taken down the co-ordinates and plotted a new map. And do you know why that happens?' she'd asked. 'It's because you think you know what's around you, but actually all you have is a likeness, and not even a very accurate one at that.

'You don't know much about shape, about proportions, weight and surface area. You only find out about these things when the image goes dark and your eyesight deserts you. I had to learn to see with my hands, with my ears and with my nose. By using my other senses, I'm able to see things that are beyond most people's reach.'

She watched Blanca now feeling for the straps on Smoky's harness and following him into the depths of the forest, along the imaginary border of the grid they had drawn on the map. To give her something solid to hold on to, the squad had roped string between the trees, dividing the search zone into sections. But death followed no borders and all they could do was hope that the dogs would be able to catch its scent wherever it might be, even on the back of the quickest of breezes.

'Look how thick the forest is, all these brambles and hollows and crumbling slopes . . . They'll have to be better than everyone else if they're going to find the corpse here,' muttered Marini.

'They *are* better than everyone else,' Teresa replied.

'What if we're looking in the wrong place?'

'I'm sure it's the right place. The victim was elderly and small, his body shrunken with time, but still, he was an adult male. The killer couldn't have carried him too far and I don't think he'd have taken him out of the forest, either. Why would he? It's the perfect hiding place.'

'There's no doubt about that, considering how badly the search has gone so far. But maybe it's just a matter of time.'

'Time is just about the only thing we don't have right now.'

Teresa turned round to look at the road. She was concerned that Albert might turn up at any moment and throw all of their plans into disarray.

Marini seemed to read her mind.

'So Lona's like that because you rejected him.'

Teresa shook her head without looking at him.

'He's like that because it's his nature. I paid a heavy price for my freedom. He was offering me a shortcut, which would have only brought me back to where I'd started and was so desperate to get away from. He was just another man obsessed with control. He still is. The psychological abuse he inflicts is no less repugnant than physical violence.'

She closed her eyes; the forest had become a blur. Maybe it was the weight of her memories; maybe it was her illness. She opened her eyes again, but she still couldn't see clearly. She had to lean on the car. Marini rushed to her side.

'What's going on?'

'I'm dizzy.'

He eased her to the ground and knelt beside her.

'Could be a drop in your blood pressure,' he said, holding her wrist.

'It's nothing.'

'Your heartbeat has sped up.'

Teresa drew her arm back.

'For God's sake, it's nothing.'

'Have you taken your insulin shot today?'

Teresa didn't reply.

'Superintendent?'

I can't remember. I have no idea.

Whatever was happening to her seemed to be getting worse. She was burning with thirst.

She grabbed her phone: on the screen were various reminders she had ignored. She hadn't heard the alarms go off and now the time for her injection had long since passed.

'Shit,' she muttered, fighting a wave of nausea.

She rummaged for the insulin pen at the bottom of her bag, praying it was the kind that worked quickly.

'Let me help you.'

Marini found it eventually, but Teresa snatched it from his hands.

'I can manage,' she said, but then she dropped the pen.

'Just shut up, will you?'

Teresa fell quiet. She would have loved to give him a piece of her mind, but she hadn't the strength. She felt exhausted.

'Come on, just tell me what to do.'

Marini's tone was both firm and controlled. Teresa basked in its comforting calmness and succumbed to the facts: she needed help. She needed him.

She told him what to do, her face turned the other way and her eyes on anything but him. The hill on which Andrian had painted the image with Francesco as a boy wasn't far from here. She could glimpse its peak, where the crown of a linden tree swayed in a gentle breeze.

'No one's looking,' said Marini.

As if that was the problem.

'You have eyes, don't you?' she snapped.

Marini laughed quietly, lifting the hem of her sweater while she pushed down the waistband of her trousers.

'And you'd love to carve them out of my head right now, wouldn't you?' he replied. 'Well, there's things you know about me that I would have rather kept secret. *Do ut des*. Seems like a fair exchange to me.'

'What, staring at my arse?'

'If this is your arse, Superintendent, then you really are in trouble.'

Even she had to smile at that. Maybe it was a reflex, an instinctive reaction to the fact her ageing flesh was being exposed to his gaze in this way, the rolls of fat around her belly no doubt appearing even more grotesque to the eyes of a fit young man. Teresa had never felt so naked, so fragile.

The pen did its job and he pulled the curtains shut again over Teresa's body.

'You know, they have these digital devices now that could

make your life a whole lot easier,' he told her.

Teresa knew that, but recently she had been so preoccupied with holding on to her memories that diabetes, microneedles and everything else that came with the territory had been demoted to the lowest rung in her list of priorities.

'Thanks,' she huffed. She was angry at herself.

'It's nothing. Shall I drop you home?'

Teresa carefully got to her feet.

'Absolutely not.'

'Where on earth are you going?'

'Where I belong, which isn't here in the background.'

They were approached by Parisi.

'Francesco di Lenardo called, Superintendent. He asked for you. He said he needs to talk to you.'

Teresa looked at Marini and then back at Parisi again.

'Did he say why?'

'No, but it sounded urgent. He was anxious. All he said was that he couldn't wait any longer.'

76

The Andrian home stood next to a flat woodland whose appearance made for an unassuming counterpart to the spectacular forests that grew slightly further north. Separated geographically from Italy by the alpine border and stretching into the drainage basin of the Black Sea, those lands were so near and yet so distant, too, in more ways than one.

Flatland forests were gentle beasts, and not particularly wild. It was like the difference between the silky hair of a house cat and the coarse, oleaginous fur of a lynx: they might look similar to the casual observer, but in fact they were profoundly different.

Nevertheless, even these woods were dense enough to hide

the shadow that was watching the ageing painter. For a long time now, the *Tikô Wariö* had been patiently observing the august and hostile mask of Andrian's face. The painter was like an old stag ruling over a long-lost realm, slowly greying under the weight of its crown of antlers – which, given the opportunity, he wouldn't hesitate to plunge into his enemy's heart. Andrian's dark gaze was a declaration of war – one that he'd been making every day for decades now.

The *Tikô Wariö* emerged from the forest and began to walk towards Andrian. With every step it took, the *Tikô Wariö* saw the painter's expression change imperceptibly, like the springtime sky above their heads – so volatile in its moods, so violent in its reactions.

The *Tikô Wariö* walked up to the window, its eyes now staring into Andrian's. In his gaunt face, as white as a marble tomb, the old man's pupils dilated.

Andrian opened his mouth in a silent scream, and the *Tikô Wariö* copied him.

77

I don't feel so comfortable with this new diary. It's like trying to replace someone you've lost; how could you? You'll keep looking for them, even if it drives you crazy, even if it makes you sweat blood. Their very absence will ensure they remain a constant tangible presence. The void they've left behind will be a reminder of their importance, a vessel filled to the brim – and beyond – with tears. It's like rain falling backwards: from the earth up to the sky.

I wonder what the killer must be thinking, reading between the lines, reading about himself. I wonder if his mind, mired in psychosis, will recognise himself and feel pity.

Perhaps I'll be able to look him in the eyes one day and find out.

Francesco had opened the door and showed them inside without a word. He seemed resigned. He sat with his back hunched over, suddenly showing his age.

That's guilt, Teresa thought, *guilt weighing down on him.*

She got straight to the point; she had decided that she wasn't going to leave that house until she'd claimed what she had come for: the truth.

'Now is the time to get it all off your chest,' she told him.

He nodded.

'That's why I called you here. I'm ready.'

'There was a secret in that pact you made as children, isn't that right? A secret that bound you for life.'

Francesco let out a long sigh.

'That day,' he began, 'after we fired at the German soldier, we went to check whether he was dead – just me and Ewa, hand in hand and shaking like leaves. The partisan stayed hiding among the trees. He told us not to go, that there might be others around. He already knew the terrible vengeance the German commanders would wreak.'

He paused, but Teresa wasn't going to let him hide again.

'What did you see?' she asked instinctively.

'Blood, but not as much as I'd expected. I remember thinking how little there was, for a dead man. Later, I realised I was right: the soldier wasn't dead, he'd merely fainted. He'd knocked his head when he'd fallen and had a graze on his arm from where the ricocheting bullet had scratched him. I found out when he came back with his comrades to have his revenge. But revenge wasn't all he was after.'

That got Teresa's attention.

'What do you mean?' she asked.

Francesco held her stare, though clearly with some difficulty.

'We'd stolen from him,' he confessed, his voice shaking. 'We stole from a man we thought was dead.'

Teresa felt a pang of pity for him: all that agony for a childhood misdemeanour.

'You were kids,' she told him. 'You didn't understand war or death.'

He shrugged, his eyes shining with tears.

'Did the German soldier find what had been taken from him?' Marini asked.

'No. He never got round to it, what with the partisans arriving and all the shooting . . . He vanished along with the rest of his unit and they never came up to the village again. The war was almost over by then; everybody knew that. The Germans dismantled their base a few days later. And in any case, he couldn't really have exposed us, either, because we'd stolen from a thief.'

Teresa leant forwards, nodding in encouragement.

'He was carrying an icon, wrapped up in cloth and strapped to his chest with a belt,' Francesco resumed. 'It was a depiction of the Virgin. He must have stolen it from some church. It was so beautiful, it shimmered. I remember how delicate her features were, the silver and gold inlays glimmering in the sun as if we were holding a star. And the wings of the adoring angels at her feet – my God! We'd never seen anything like it in the valley. We'd never seen such beauty before. We were bewitched.'

'What happened next?'

'Ewa took it and ran away. Emmanuel and I followed her.'

Teresa and Marini exchanged a surprised glance.

'Emmanuel Turan? The man who's just been murdered? Was he with you?' she asked.

Francesco nodded.

'He was always following us around. Sometimes we let him, sometimes we shooed him away. He had always been odd, a little different. And children can be cruel.'

'Did you go back to Cam?'

'Oh, no! He was calling out to us, but we ignored him and hid in the forest. He'd seen us, he knew what we'd done, and he

314

wanted the icon. For days he harassed us about it. He'd secretly follow us. We'd see him watching us from among the trees. We were scared. He was terrifying.

'At night, he'd throw stones at our bedroom window. But Ewa refused to hand it over. "We can't leave the Holy Virgin in his filthy hands," she'd say. "It wouldn't be right." So there was only one thing left to do.'

'And what was that?' said Marini, urging him on.

Francesco looked up at him.

'We threw the icon into the river, right in front of him. He jumped into the water to look for it, but by then it was gone, lost in the current. We left him like that, alone and desolate in the freezing *Wöda*. I never saw him again.'

Carlo Alberto Morandini might never again have made his presence known to the children, but that didn't necessarily mean that he'd left. Maybe his obsession with the icon had never left him.

Teresa asked Francesco what had happened to the object.

'It was lost in the current, for ever,' he replied. 'All those gemstones, all that silver and gold, they're part of this valley now.'

Just like Aniza, Teresa thought.

Marini went off to answer a phone call and was soon beckoning at her to join him.

'We have a problem,' he announced gravely.

Teresa felt faint.

'Is it Blanca?' she asked.

'Yes. She thinks she's found the remains . . . But they're not human, Superintendent.'

78

'Glory to thee, Holy Virgin, Gate of Heaven. The day is ending and night approaches. Soon, the sun will set and the stars will rise. And so begins the sacred Evening ritual, to end the day of light.'

A soft flame illuminated the darkness.

'With this match I shall light the fire upon your altar, oh blessed one. The nightly incense will shed its golden tears and prepare my soul to receive your mystery.'

The resin released a plume of fragrant grey smoke.

The icon glimmered in the reflected light of the sacred flame, its gold and silver detailing shining like stars fallen from the sky. The Madonna's face was just visible beneath the black veil that covered it, a blur that seemed to follow the gaze of whoever set eyes upon her. Her beauty contained the universe.

'I carry inside me the *Tikô Wariö*. I am the guardian. And I carry inside me the *Tikô Bronô*. I am your protector. I offer you the magical texts inscribed in the Pyramid of Unas, the words of history's greatest mystics, the honeyed songs of Pindar and Apuleius.'

The *Tikô Wariö* clasped its hands together and bowed its head in deference.

'I call to thee with many names, o Mother, o Maker of the First. Queen of spirits. Compassionate ruler of the wretched deserts of Hell. She who seals the door to the Underworld at night. Great sorceress and healer of sickness. *Regina caeli*.'

Its knees folded. Its forehead touched the ground.

'Heaven honours you and Hell respects you. The stars, the seasons, the elements heed your will. You set the planets in their orbits and illuminate the Void. O Gentle One, o Secret One. Hent. Heqet.'

Its lips kissed the dirt.

'I bow to thee, *Mater Dei*, as your most faithful servant.'

79

Teresa pushed her way through the small crowd that had gathered at the scene; the news that the police had found something in the woods had already spread. Unfortunately, what they'd found wasn't what Teresa had hoped for.

She crossed the tape that marked the area forbidden to civilians and ventured deeper into the forest. She could feel Marini's hand on her elbow with every step she took. She bit her tongue and let him do it; she wasn't going to risk falling over in front of a bunch of truculent men who would leap at the chance to ridicule her. Now more than ever, it was imperative that her authority should remain unchallenged, so that it could shield the people who relied on her.

'Shit!' exclaimed Marini.

Teresa had rarely heard him swear before, but when she looked up, she realised he had good reason to. Blanca was standing in the middle of one of the many sectors into which the search area had been divided. She stood face to face with the head of the police search unit and the animal welfare expert attached to the canine unit. Parisi and de Carli stood between them, trying to keep the two sides apart and prevent what appeared to be an imminent conflagration. Or perhaps the conflagration had already begun. Voices were already being raised. Blanca's face was flushed and tense. She looked like she was about to burst into tears of rage.

There was another figure standing a few feet away from it all. As if he could somehow hear her thoughts, Albert Lona turned round and looked at Teresa, his expression both furious and faintly smug, relishing this opportunity to make her pay for daring to defy him.

Teresa readied herself for battle, sharpening her mental weapons and praying to whatever god might be watching that her illness wouldn't choose that very moment to manifest itself. She could picture herself reduced to a stammering mess, an imbecile, her eyes devoid of all expression. *Not now, please not now.*

'You stay right where you are,' she ordered Marini. 'Do *not* get involved.'

Teresa would deal with Albert first. She marched past Blanca, giving her a gentle squeeze as she walked by. She knew the touch wouldn't be lost on Blanca.

But the district attorney stopped her in her tracks.

'Don't say a word,' he commanded with that deceptively calm voice he employed when he wanted to obliterate his interlocutor.

The volley of complaints being fired at Teresa from all directions was relentless until eventually she had to shout to restore order.

'Show me,' she barked.

The pit was right there, a hollow that looked like a natural formation and could have easily held a curled-up corpse but that instead contained a pair of long, branching antlers.

'An older stag, judging by the shape of the horns and the pattern of dental deterioration,' explained the canine unit's animal expert. 'The enamel sheathing is absent and the dentin is exposed. I'd say the creature died of natural causes.'

The carcass was half covered in dirt and fallen leaves.

'The soil around it looks loose,' Teresa noted.

'Only because it was dumped there by the recent rains.'

Teresa looked at Blanca. She was clearly struggling, shaking as she held on to Smoky's harness. There was nothing Teresa could do. Smoky was agitated, pacing in circles over and over again to signal the presence of a corpse that just wasn't there.

The head of the search team was thoughtful enough to pull Teresa aside.

'These dogs are trained to ignore animal carcasses. Or at least they *ought* to be,' he clarified. 'This one clearly isn't reliable.'

'No!' Blanca exclaimed.

They turned to look at her.

'I'm sorry, young lady. I'm afraid it's a false positive,' he insisted.

Blanca held her hands out as if in exhortation and Teresa quickly grasped them in her own.

'There's a body buried here,' Blanca insisted. 'Smoky is never wrong. I believe him.'

Teresa tried to soothe her and meanwhile wondered frantically what Albert – who was still standing there, watching her – might do next. Whatever it was, would Teresa be able to respond with the same unshakeable faith Blanca displayed?

Teresa glanced at the pit, at the long antlers weathered by time and by the elements, like the horns of a long-forgotten god. Then she looked again at the restless, howling dog.

Is he sensing a human corpse – a scent so strong it can't be ignored?

Albert walked up to them.

'Get the girl and her dog out of here,' he ordered.

Teresa stood between Blanca and the men, with Marini by her side.

'Let's talk about this,' she ventured.

Albert looked at her as if she had uttered a profanity.

'You will follow my orders, Superintendent, and step aside. Your involvement in this investigation is now at risk.'

Teresa swore – and rather loudly, too.

'If I'm wrong, I'll go straight away,' she said, throwing the district attorney some bait. 'But if we want to find out, we're going to have to remove this carcass and keep digging.'

She watched him weighing his options – her head against a cubic metre of earth – and she knew that he wouldn't be able to resist the opportunity to witness her public humiliation.

And just as she had predicted, Albert nodded, signalling to the men that they should resume digging.

Marini picked up a shovel and joined in.

Teresa went to stand next to Blanca, making sure the girl could feel her presence while also taking care not to make their familiarity too obvious to Albert.

'It's there,' she heard Blanca whisper.

Smoky had calmed down, too: as far as he was concerned, his job was done.

The sun began to set behind a bank of inky clouds and as the shadows advanced, death emerged from beneath the veil hiding it: when the shovelling suddenly stopped, Teresa knew that something else had emerged from the earth.

'Superintendent!' Marini called out.

She hurried over. Inside the dark, wet hole, ensconced in a tangle of roots, lay the frail corpse of an old man.

It was Emmanuel Turan.

Teresa crouched at the edge of the tomb.

The body lay in the foetal position, with the arms crossed protectively, but Teresa could still clearly see its slashed chest, where in place of the heart someone had placed a flower as pale and withered as the corpse itself: wood anemone.

'A fresh corpse buried beneath an old animal carcass,' she murmured.

It was a momentous discovery and it gave them unprecedented insight into the killer's mind.

'He nearly managed to sabotage the search altogether,' remarked an incredulous Marini.

Teresa had never seen anything like this in her whole career.

'He used a natural dip in the terrain, then covered it up,' she said, gesturing at the hole.

'He knows the landscape well.'

Teresa caught a glimpse of Albert muttering under his breath, but soon he'd vanished from the scene.

She got back to her feet and tapped the chief of the search team on the shoulder. He looked a lot less sure of himself than he had been earlier.

'The girl might be blind,' Teresa remarked, throwing his own words back at him. 'But it looks like she can see better than all of you put together.'

She walked up to Blanca and took her hand.

'You've left them all speechless,' Teresa told her. 'Even I've never managed that before.'

She saw Blanca smile and finally relax.

'Men always have more trouble believing,' Blanca remarked.

How true.

Teresa peered into the edge of the forest, where more people had gathered in the meantime. She couldn't make out their faces, but she was sure there were many familiar figures there, and she was also sure the killer was among them, too. He had always been there, always one step ahead.

He's watching us. He's never stopped watching us. Even now his gaze is upon us.

Smoky was suddenly restless again. Teresa saw Blanca frown.

'What's going on?' she asked.

'He wants to go again. He's caught another scent.'

80

Marini led the way, clearing errant roots and branches that might have scratched Blanca or tripped her up. Teresa and the forensics team followed a few steps behind. Teresa watched Blanca closely, saw how she gave Smoky the time he needed to map out the smells of the unfamiliar landscape he'd been thrown into, how she waited patiently for him to retrieve the trail of the scent when it seemed to have faded. And they all held their collective breaths until he picked it up again and pushed on.

'I read him and he reads me,' Blanca had once told Teresa.

Further back, officers from the local police station, the human remains search team and, trailing behind, the environmental protection agency wound their way along the path in a silent procession, looking strained. No one dared oppose Teresa now and certainly no one questioned where the girl and her dog were leading them.

They didn't know what they would find at the end of that invisible path yet, but the scent they were following was that of human blood. Any time Smoky detected the slightest trace of haemoglobin, he would stop and let out a short bark.

It was an unsettling sound to human ears, for its rhythm had been set by the killer himself: he had sprinkled the forest floor with tiny droplets of blood, as if in a dark and terrible fairy tale. He had used what had once been Emmanuel's lifeblood to show them which way to go.

Despite their misgivings, the forensics team had agreed, at Teresa's insistence, to share their initial impressions.

'Our blood pattern analysis suggests these are passive stains caused by drops falling to the ground under gravitational pull,' the forensics expert had explained with some reluctance.

Form is key. It tells us where something began and how it developed. It also shows us its strength. And it reveals the intention behind it.

These weren't accidental splashes sprayed randomly over the surrounding vegetation; these were perfectly symmetrical drops, which had fallen perpendicular to the ground, and right along the centre of the path.

Teresa had no doubt that the perpetrator had meant it that way. He had proven himself too methodical, too clever and organised a killer to leave them there by mistake. Every time Smoky sat down to signal he'd found something, the officers in their white overalls would crouch over that part of the forest to gather and catalogue the samples to be added to the case file. Five droplets of blood had been found so far.

'What are you thinking?' Marini asked, falling back to walk beside her.

Teresa didn't immediately reply. She was searching for the

right way to put her instinctive response into words without losing her grip on reason altogether. But she couldn't find one. Her subconscious pressed upon her, clamouring to be heard.

She looked up at the ceiling of leafy branches and listened to the distant hooting of an owl, the sound carried on the wind until it reached them where they stood. Smoky's howls floated in the air like a summons. She thought again of the black heart displayed at the entrance of an old and mysterious realm, and of the droplets of blood scattered over the ground.

Five little crimson pebbles our Little Thumbling left along the way . . .

'In his own way, he's telling us a fairy tale,' she murmured.

'Fairy tales usually have a happy ending,' Marini remarked.

'That's why we're here: to give him that happy ending. And just like in every proper fairy tale, someone had to die and someone else had to suffer.'

'The trail stops here,' said Blanca, interrupting their musings. She was kneeling next to Smoky, stroking his fur. 'He can't smell anything else.'

'Well, it looks like the fairy tale . . .' Marini began, but he never completed his sentence.

His expression changed as he pointed at something he'd spotted in the vegetation, a sharp, crooked shadow rising from the earth.

'There's something there,' he said.

Teresa followed his gaze. It was a roof.

'It looks like the fairy tale continues in a little house at the edge of the forest,' she said, finishing Marini's sentence for him.

The ruin was a dilapidated homestead that hadn't been used in decades and had been entirely subsumed into the forest, which was slowly smothering it in tangles of ivy and honeysuckle. Those parts of the walls that still stood upright showed the outline of three ground-floor rooms, with a passageway of black rotting wood connecting them to what remained of the floor above.

Half of the roof had caved in and wooden beams stuck out of gaps that had once been windows.

The front door still stood, however, and the faded plaster on the architrave bore a tremulous inscription: C + M + B.

'What does it mean?' asked Marini.

Teresa ran a gloved hand over the washed-out wood of the door. She knew there was nothing sinister in those letters; she remembered them from her childhood.

'*Christus mansionem benedicat,*' she said. 'A Christian tradition in many agrarian communities, though in actual fact it is pagan in its origins. It's considered a powerful talisman against the forces of darkness. The head of the household would write these letters on the front door and on the door to the stables on the night of the Epiphany, to protect his family and his livestock. And they'd anoint the buildings with incense.'

She let her hand fall back to her side. The memories felt like fragments from someone else's life.

'I'll go in first,' said Marini.

She pulled him back and stepped across the threshold before he could.

There was little left inside that could still be considered human – or *entirely* so, at any rate. All traces of human presence were slowly being erased. What was left of the walls were flagstones on the verge of crumbling for ever into dust. The fireplace, where the family would have gathered in the evenings, had become a repository for debris. It was a sad sight, but there was also something remarkable about it all. It was a demonstration that life always survived, even if in a different form – quieter, more subtle, and yet still powerful.

Teresa opened her mouth to speak, but the words got stuck in her throat like dry seeds.

In a little nook between two stones, someone had tucked a piece of paper, its rectangular shape as familiar to Teresa as her own limbs.

Her handwriting was on it. It was a page from her diary.

The blood in her veins seemed to freeze. She stood perfectly still. That piece of paper, and the notes it bore, were evidence.

If I leave it there, everyone will be able to read it. It could be something trivial — or it could reveal my illness.

If I take it and hide it away, I'll be safe, but my personal and professional integrity will be damaged irreparably.

'Take it. Now!' said Marini, glancing over his shoulder. 'Take it and hide it.'

Teresa didn't move. She would never forgive herself if she did that.

In the end, Marini did it for her. Quickly, he took the piece of paper from the wall before anyone else could see it, folded it in half and put it away in his pocket without looking.

It was only then that Teresa came to her senses. She grabbed his arm.

'What the hell are you doing?' she snarled.

He put his hand over hers and gently pushed it away.

'I'll figure out a way to get this tested without anyone knowing it's yours,' he told her. 'Even I will never find out what it says.'

So he knew where the note came from.

Teresa swallowed her pride.

'Why are you doing this?' she managed to ask.

Marini shrugged as if it were no big deal.

'Because I owe it to you. Because it's the right thing to do.'

Teresa swayed on her feet. She felt exposed and vulnerable. She couldn't stay there, so she left, pushing her way, head down, through the throng of officers waiting outside.

Faced with a new black storm gathering on the horizon, and the looming, inscrutable presence of nature all around her, her distress transformed itself into a fiery rage.

'I won't let you intimidate me!' she shouted at the woods.

Whoever it was who had stolen her paper memories, they were out there somewhere, listening.

81

Massimo had tried calling Elena a number of times, but she wasn't picking up. He gave up and sent her a message instead:

I wish I could be there with you both.

She'd read it over an hour ago, but still hadn't responded.

It hadn't cost him anything to admit what he'd written and he wasn't trying to play games. It was the truth. But he was still stuck in that ruin of a house in the middle of the woods, feeling more tired and more filthy by the minute as he waited for the forensics team to give them the all-clear. Superintendent Battaglia was on the phone to headquarters, though he could tell from the lack of emotion in her voice that there was no news.

When the phone vibrated in his hand and he saw Elena's name come up on the screen, he reached out instinctively to lean on what was left of the wall before he opened her message.

What is it?

He quickly typed a response:

I just wanted to check that you were all right.

Tell me what you're thinking, Massimo. Stop running away.

I miss you.

She didn't reply, so he wrote again.

We need to talk.

No. Tell me what you're thinking!

He took a deep breath.

I needed to forgive myself. I've done that now. I don't want to lose you.

Her response came swiftly.

Help Teresa first. We'll be waiting for you.

Massimo could feel a smile forming on his face. He retrieved the diary page from his pocket and slipped it inside an envelope he'd pilfered earlier from someone's forensics kit. Having sealed the envelope and signed his name across the flap, he called de Carli over and gave it to him.

'This needs to get to the lab as soon as possible,' he told him. 'I've already let Colle know. Make sure you hand it to him directly, and tell him to hurry up and ask no questions.'

De Carli turned the envelope over in his hands.

'I don't suppose you'll tell me what's inside,' he said.

Massimo put the lid back on his pen and looked around for Superintendent Battaglia.

'I can tell you that what you're doing is illegal, immoral and might even cost you your job. But it's for a good cause. Anything else you need to know?' he replied.

De Carli didn't bat an eyelid.

'I'd say that's more than enough to go on. Right then, I'm off.'

Now that the torn diary entry was safe, and once he'd made sure there weren't any other pages lying around, Massimo left the forensics team to it. He sat next to Superintendent Battaglia on the worn doorstep of the ruined homestead and nudged her with his elbow. He had no clue why that notebook mattered to her so much, but the sight of her stricken face had filled him with

327

rage and protectiveness of a kind he'd rarely felt before.

'It's under control,' he told her.

She nodded but didn't speak.

'That's worrying, Superintendent; you should be telling me I've never got *anything* under control.'

She seemed on the verge of a smile, but soon looked grave again.

'I used to think you were obsessive about this sort of thing, but clearly I was wrong,' she said, her hands deep in her pockets and her eyes staring into the distance. 'What you did was crazy, and brash, and could potentially spell the end of your career.'

'Why do I get the feeling you like me more whenever I do something stupid?'

'Because I know all the stupid stuff comes from the heart.'

Massimo offered her a sweet. The superintendent took it, watching him with a shocked expression as he unwrapped his own.

'To hell with restraint,' he told her.

'To hell with restraint.'

They sat there chewing quietly on their sweets, strange tokens of a new beginning.

'What now?' Massimo said eventually.

The superintendent paused to think.

'We're getting closer. I can feel it,' she murmured. 'But not close enough yet to see his face. And I still can't figure out what it all means, what it is, deep down, that moves him.'

'You don't think we're dealing with an ordinary motive here.'

Superintendent Battaglia shook her magma-red bob vigorously from side to side.

'It's anything but ordinary, Marini. There are layers and layers of malaise lurking here, buried as deep as the skeletons hidden in this forest. Just think of the force of the symbolism he's employed.'

'Like the heart.'

'What's the first thing you thought of when you saw it? Go on, just tell me the first thing that popped into your head.'

'Some kind of ritual.'

She nodded.

'Rancour, jealousy, money: these are all things that can drive someone to commit murder. But not to rip someone's heart out.'

'What if there's more than one perpetrator?' asked Massimo.

'Are you thinking of a cult?'

'Yes.'

She seemed to be considering this for a moment.

'In the nineties, there was a sect in the United States that performed ritual sacrifices. Its devotees would eat the hearts of their victims. When they were discovered, it turned out they were all upstanding members of society, entirely beyond suspicion in the light of day. Some of them paid for their crimes, but many others were never heard of again; they probably went underground.' She stood up and brushed the dust off her trousers. 'But I don't think that's the kind of thing we're dealing with here, Inspector Marini. Our killer isn't secretive: he wants to communicate with us.'

Massimo stood up, too.

'To challenge us and to affirm his sense of self? Or to atone for a sin?' he asked her.

'I don't know yet, though the first option doesn't seem likely. He's got so much more to say than "Look at me, look how clever I am". But let's set aside the killer's profile for a moment. What do we actually have in hand, Inspector? What have we discovered?'

'A girl who disappeared seventy years ago, whose sweetheart painted her portrait by sticking his fingers in her heart and then lost his mind. And a devotional icon stolen by the Nazis, thrown into the river and never seen again.'

'Keep going.'

'A violin-playing partisan who was obsessed with this valley and presumably witnessed the murder of the girl. He and Andrian knew each other. Maybe he kept coming back to look for the icon.'

With every word he uttered, he could see the picture becoming clearer and clearer. The connections were obvious. It was like joining together bright spots in an unlit sky.

She motioned at him to continue.

'Three children who make a pact and whose shooting of the German soldier who stole the icon triggers the wrath of the Nazis,' he continued. 'Only one of them is still alive: Francesco. Emmanuel Turan was killed two days ago, his heart nailed to the entrance of the village.'

Superintendent Battaglia abruptly stopped chewing on her sweet: she'd had an intuition.

'How did Francesco's sister, Ewa, die?' she asked.

Massimo felt his heart start beating faster. They had a new lead to follow.

82

'Is this really necessary?' asked Marini, staring at the gravestone.

Teresa was adamant. She'd obtained Ewa di Lenardo's death certificate from five years ago. Ewa had died of natural causes. What Teresa wanted to know was what exactly had happened before Ewa took her last breath. Assuming anything *had* happened. Judge Crespi had agreed and he'd given her his blessing to go ahead before she'd even put in a formal request.

Of the three children who had made that pact, only one was still alive. That was the fact she kept coming back to.

Emmanuel Turan was killed and his heart was nailed to the entrance of the village, just as we were getting closer to discovering the secret that bound him to the other two.

'We can't just trust what people say any more,' she said, watching as the burial site was uncovered.

The di Lenardo family tomb stood on a hill outside the

perimeter of the local cemetery. It wasn't alone: the same steep slope housed several other vaults belonging to the valley's oldest families – simple whitewashed, rounded structures set deep into the earth. They protruded from the hill, facing eastwards, like ancient mausoleums.

The crypt of the di Lenardos was surrounded by flowers of a periwinkle blue, their countless lustrous petals like a crown adorning that resting place for the dead.

Teresa picked one of the flowers. It had no smell.

'Usually, these will only blossom between May and July, but our spring this year seems to think it's summer,' said a voice behind her.

It was Krisnja.

Teresa smiled at the girl, her soul heavy with guilt as it always was whenever she had to force anyone to go through as dehumanising an experience as seeing a loved one exhumed.

'I'm sorry,' was all she managed to say; as usual, the sight of the young woman's face had left her at a loss for words.

The girl seemed not to notice Teresa's regret. She crouched down and picked a flower herself, spinning it round in her fingers.

'Butterworts are carnivorous plants. It's strange, isn't it, finding them in this kind of place?' she murmured, her voice tinged with sorrow. 'They get their nutrients from ingesting other living beings.' She fixed her gaze on Teresa's. Her eyes were rimmed with red. 'That's what your killers do, isn't it? They feed on life.'

Teresa felt her heart contract. Marini stiffened beside her.

'Some of them do, yes,' she conceded. 'They need it, just like the rest of us need air.'

Krisnja looked away into the distance, where the wind was blasting against the mountain peaks and whipping up the clouds like dust. A bolt of lightning lit the bare rocks with a ghostly glare.

'So you think someone hurt Aniza and then my grandma, Ewa . . .'

'I don't have any evidence yet.'

'But we're here so you can find some.'

'That's right.'

The girl's eyes, reflecting the flashing sky, filled with tears.

'If it's true, then it must mean there's someone out there who wants to erase my bloodline,' she said. 'Will it be my turn next?'

Teresa looked behind Krisnja and saw that Francesco was watching them. It was hard to tell what he was thinking. They'd hardly spoken. Something had broken – his trust, or perhaps the mask behind which he'd hidden his grief for nearly a lifetime.

The gravestone slipped from the undertakers' grasp and shattered with a deafening clang. The coffin was extracted from the sepulchre and the seals were broken.

Teresa and Marini exchanged a glance, and he went to stand beside Krisnja.

Teresa walked up to the black hole they'd opened like a portal into the past. She studied the photograph on the gravestone: Ewa's gaze was magnetic ice-blue. She seemed different from her brother, and from her granddaughter.

Teresa looked down at the coffin, an instinctive shiver warning her of what they were about to discover.

The coffin was empty.

83

'I can only reiterate what I put on her death certificate: the cause of death was illness, and quite a brutal one at that. By the time she came to me, it was already too late. It had already spread through her body. Ewa was a shadow of herself.'

The doctor who'd received Teresa in his clinic had been the one to sign Ewa di Lenardo's death papers.

'Her ordeal started two years before that,' he resumed. 'She had an operation for a knee replacement. It wasn't successful and the corrective surgery only made matters worse. From then on Ewa was in terrible pain. She didn't live for much longer anyway: three months later she was diagnosed with advanced pancreatic cancer. There was nothing to be done.

'I tried to talk to her about pain relief. I told her about deep sedation. She wouldn't hear of it. She continued to live her life as if nothing had changed for as long as she could and she managed to go on for much longer than I would have thought possible: nearly ten months. I wouldn't have given her more than two. Ewa died in her own home, in her own bed. She wouldn't have had it any other way.'

Dusk had fallen over the valley by then and the clinic was illuminated with neon lighting, which seemed to throw the doctor's words into even starker relief.

'You said she was a shadow of herself. Are you certain that the body you examined was Ewa's?' Teresa asked.

He seemed to hesitate, though perhaps it was the strangeness of her question that had left him momentarily speechless.

'Yes, Superintendent. I am absolutely certain that the body I examined was Ewa di Lenardo's.'

Teresa thanked him and took her leave, but she walked out into the night with the distinct feeling that she was missing something. She looked up at the sky: it had finally cleared, revealing the brilliant orb of a full moon.

'You're not satisfied,' Marini stated.

She grimaced.

'The story of the *Sleeping Nymph* has proven to be much more complicated than I would ever have expected,' she grumbled.

'At least the district attorney won't be able to accuse you of insubordination again. If we hadn't opened that tomb, we'd never have found out that the body was stolen. Too bad none of it makes sense.'

'There *has* to be some meaning to it, even if we can't see it yet.' Teresa checked the time. 'Well, I guess our audience must have gone home by now. So, ready for the dirty work?'

'What dirty work?'

333

'I don't like cemeteries, Superintendent. Least of all at night.'

'No one alive likes cemeteries, Marini.'

'Couldn't we let the forensics team handle it?'

'In the morning. But first I want to see it with my own eyes. Put that torch up.'

The pale blue light fell upon Ewa di Lenardo's black-and-white face.

'I don't like that photo, either,' said Marini. 'It's like she's looking at us. And she's definitely not enjoying our visit.'

'Are you worried about spirits?'

'I'm just . . . *careful*. What exactly are we looking for, anyway?'

'Signs.'

'Of trespass?'

'Yes, and something else, too.'

Marini shone the torch in her face.

'Are you thinking someone exhumed the body and took it away?' he asked her, his voice a little too loud.

Teresa batted his arm away.

'Well, it's either that, Inspector, or Ewa walked out of here on her own two feet. What do you think is the likelier explanation?'

'Maybe this was never her tomb.'

'Maybe.'

'*Once you eliminate the impossible, whatever remains, no matter how improbable, must be the truth.*'

Teresa grabbed the torch off him.

'Thank you, Sherlock. Though that line's from the movie, you know.'

'Why do I always feel I'm on probation with you?'

'Because you are, obviously. Now, give me that scrubber. I'm going to scrape off this mould.'

Teresa carefully rubbed at the black patina that had formed over the opening of the crypt and when she was satisfied she'd done enough, she pointed the torch at the marble, running her fingers over it.

'Look at these scratches,' she said. 'They could be marks left by the crowbar used to push the lid off.'

Marini leant forwards to take a closer look.

'So the tomb wasn't opened recently,' he said. 'It was long before we first came to the valley.'

Teresa nodded.

'At least a year before, judging by the layer of moss and mould.'

She shone the light into the crypt. Inside the chamber of roughly levelled concrete they saw the skeletal remains of the wreaths that must have been interred with the coffin. The whole place smelt of death. But something else caught Teresa's eye.

She stuck her arm out, leaning as far inside as she could, but her body got in the way.

'Get in there,' she told Marini. 'There's something at the bottom I need to look at.'

'There's no way I'm going in.'

She gave him a look.

'Oh for God's sake, Marini! There aren't any dead people in there and we're all that's alive around here. What's your problem?'

He seemed to consider this for a moment as if trying to come up with an adequate response, or perhaps just gathering his courage. At long last, he took his jacket off and set it aside.

'Do you realise how unhygienic this is?' he snapped as he crawled into the crypt.

She gave him the torch.

'You've got gloves on,' she told him. 'It's all the way at the end.'

'*I know.*'

'Can you see it?'

'What exactly am I looking for? There's nothing here but dead flowers.'

'A rat.'

'Shit!'

'Relax, I was joking.'

'You're not normal . . . Wait, is this it?'

He slipped back out of the hole and opened his fingers.

'It looks like an old nest,' he said.

In the palm of his hand was a tangle of twigs braided with hair and feathers. Whatever it was, it didn't look like an accidental arrangement.

Teresa picked it up and sniffed it. Even though it had probably been inside that tomb for five years, it still smelt very faintly of thyme.

'What do you think it is?' asked Marini.

'A seal to ward off evil spirits,' Teresa said.

'So some kind of witchcraft?'

Teresa thought of the valley they stood in, a cradle that had preserved the purity of distant dynasties and the timeless culture and traditions of its people, bringing them all the way to the present day, intact. She thought of its isolation from the rest of the world, of the memory of its ancient origins.

'It's not witchcraft,' she replied. She looked around. The community's dead ancestors looked right back at her, a fierce pride in their eyes. 'We need to open another tomb.'

84

Hanna: another name that had left its mark on Teresa's soul, as light as a petal and yet impossible to ignore.

Hanna, daughter of Ewa, mother of Krisnja. She, too, descended from the *Sleeping Nymph*. She, too – Teresa now knew – had died a tragic death.

Her body, which Teresa had arranged to be exhumed, now lay upon a bed in the morgue. Parri was wheeling it into the room where Teresa waited with Marini. The coroner had just concluded his preliminary autopsy on the remains. He pushed the autopsy bed all the way to where Teresa stood.

Hanna's remains bore little resemblance to a human figure. It was like looking at a chrysalis, light enough that Teresa could have carried it in her arms but destined never to transform into a butterfly. The fire that had caused her death thirteen years ago had consumed her body, along with the barn she'd been in that night.

When Parri lowered the sheet that covered what was left of Hanna, Teresa felt no revulsion – only the urge to lift the sheet back up and protect her from the horror of those who would never be able to think of her as a human being again.

'Her remains are unusually well-preserved,' the coroner remarked. 'I've already begun the routine tests.'

Parri had folded the shroud in which the woman had been buried and put it in a transparent box by the bed. Teresa had seen it when the tomb had first been opened and in that moment, she'd had the fleeting impression of having been transported to a different place and a different time.

On the light cotton fabric of the shroud was a portrait. It was as if whoever had drawn it had wanted to give a face again to the woman buried inside it. Her eyes, her nose, her mouth, the way her hair fell, and all of her most essential features, painted in red ochre, an ideal of timeless femininity recreated upon the texture of that cloth.

Red ochre, a pigment derived from haematite. Haematite again: just like with the Nymph.

So they'd found another recurring element in this tale.

Parri noticed her look.

'We found paper flowers in the grave,' he told her, drawing her attention to a bag full of contaminated evidence. 'They'd been arranged around her face, but it's difficult to make out what they're supposed to be; they must have been damaged by the decomposition process.'

The shroud was ruined, too, marred with stains that seemed to pull down the edges of the portrait's mouth, even depriving Hanna of that last smile.

Krisnja's mother had died in a fire that had broken out in the barn next to the home she shared with her mother and her daughter. Krisnja had been eight at the time; she'd been at home with her grandmother, sleeping. Hanna's husband had left her when she was pregnant with Krisnja. The men in that family always seemed to be absent, or – like Francesco – relegated to a background role.

'I'll be able to give you a more definitive cause of death once the test results are back,' said Parri. 'But I can tell you unofficially that I've found traces of carbonised wood in the body.'

Teresa thought she must have misheard.

'*In* the body?' she repeated.

The coroner nodded.

'There was a stake embedded in her ribcage before the fire devoured her. The wood didn't burn away completely, though: there are traces of it still visible under a microscope,' he explained, gesturing at a part of the corpse that must have corresponded to where the woman's chest used to be.

'Are you telling me she was killed?'

'I'm inclined to think she was already dead by the time the fire got to her. But yes, that's what I'm saying: I think she was killed, unless we decide to believe she happened to fall onto a sharp object.'

'So we're dealing with a killer who appears to act through time, and always with the same unabated frenzy,' Marini concluded.

'I'm not sure "frenzy" is the right word,' Teresa murmured.

'It can't be the same person over the course of seventy years,' Parri protested.

Teresa thought of what Francesco had said.

'Unless we think a eight-year-old capable of murder,' she said, avoiding Marini's look. 'Could he be?'

They all knew that the answer was yes.

338

85

Francesco di Lenardo's shadow, joined to the valley's own, had loomed over this tale since the very beginning.

He was there when Aniza walked through the village for the last time, and he was there when Emmanuel's heart was found. He was there now that the tomb of his sister, Ewa, had been opened to reveal a disturbing absence. He was there in the concern of his niece, Krisnja, and in Andrian's paintings.

Now, Teresa had summoned him to the police headquarters. Before she confronted him, she wanted to isolate him from his natural habitat, separate him from what he knew – his mountains, his forests, his valley – and take away his bearings, those landmarks that gave him strength and compelled him to hide behind unspoken truths.

Teresa knew from experience that his earlier confession didn't necessarily mean he was innocent. She had seen many killers collaborate with the authorities before they got caught.

Francesco had lied to her before: it must never happen again.

Teresa had no proof against him, but every time her inquiring gaze lifted another layer of dust off the truth, his name seemed to come up one way or another, like a sting in her eye.

'Here's the file you were waiting for, Superintendent.'

'Thank you.'

Teresa took the report Parisi had handed her, the file still warm from the printer. It was the unofficial summary she had managed – after much effort – to extract from the forensics team. The DNA analysis they had performed on the hair she had found in her apartment was an almost perfect match for Francesco's. The percentages left no room for doubt: a first-degree blood relative. A sister.

Ewa.

Whoever had broken into her home and stolen her diary knew where Ewa's remains were hidden.

Either that, or Ewa wasn't dead at all.

She tried to push that last thought away, as it simply seemed too divorced from that sense of reality she was trying desperately to cling on to, even when the world conspired to steal it away from her.

She found Marini in the office they shared and beckoned him over.

'Let's get started,' she told him.

They went to the room where Francesco had been made to wait for at least half an hour without anyone bothering to explain why. Teresa hoped to find him with his patience wearing thin and gearing up for a confrontation. She wanted to make him lose control and see how far he was prepared to go when he felt threatened.

But instead, she found a man showing no trace of emotion and who seemed determined to resist all attempts to rattle him. Was he trying to hide a crime he'd committed? Or was he simply trying to preserve what was left of his peace of mind?

Teresa sat down opposite him.

'You've been lying to me,' she said, getting straight to the point. 'If you do it again, I'm going to have to do something about it.'

'Like a teacher with a naughty child?' he said sardonically.

'No. Like a police officer with a recalcitrant witness.'

She saw him stiffen in his chair.

'So, you've decided to condemn me now?' he asked her.

'You're present in every single frame of this story,' said Teresa, evading his question.

'You're making a criminal of me?'

A suspect, Teresa thought, but she kept that to herself. He had no motive, after all. Or at least not one that she could discern.

'How was your relationship with your sister, Ewa?' she asked him.

'It was affectionate, naturally.'

'Are you aware of the continued existence of certain practices, certain beliefs still being cultivated in this valley?'

'Excuse me?'

Teresa brought out the bag containing the third piece of evidence they had found inside Hanna's tomb: she could see now that the braided thyme was actually an ouroboros, that ancient archetypal representation of the cyclical nature of time.

'The eternal return,' she murmured, placing the object where he could see it and finally allowing herself to say out loud the words that had been whirling around her mind for some time now. 'Shamanism. Female shamanism.'

Francesco didn't reply. He seemed unable to tear his eyes from the object Teresa had pulled out of her bag.

'Do you know what this is?' Teresa asked him.

'No.'

'But you can guess.'

He said nothing.

'It's a very old symbol that seems to have survived through the ages, appearing in identical form across a number of cultures and civilisations,' Teresa resumed. 'A circle with no beginning or end, a serpent or a dragon eating its own tail. A representation of primordial androgyny, and of immortality.'

At last, he looked up.

'And is there anything wrong with that?'

'Not really, except that we found it in the tomb of a woman who was stabbed through the heart with a stake and then burned, and also in the tomb of another woman whose corpse was stolen.'

Teresa wished there had been some other way to tell him, but she knew she needed to provoke him into some kind of reaction.

'Hanna was killed?' he asked, his voice as flat as the blade of a knife.

'Yes.'

'And you brought me here because you think I'm the killer.'

'I brought you here so that you can tell me what happened

that night when your sister's daughter burned in a fire in the barn a couple of hundred yards from your house.'

Francesco blinked.

'I can't tell you what happened, because I was asleep. How boring, right? How horrifying, even: while Hanna died, I was dreaming.'

It was a chilling moment. His poise was at once impressive and disturbing. Then again, the mechanisms of the human mind are never as simple as they appear, and even Francesco had faltered. A casual observer would have missed the way his body language contrasted with what he was saying – the tiny, uncontrollable movements of his head that reflected the non-verbal denial issuing from his subconscious. The irrational side of him seemed not to agree with him. An untrained ear wouldn't have noticed the occasional upwards lilt of his voice, as if he were having trouble controlling it, as if his words weren't really answers but questions: am I saying the right thing?

Maybe he knew more than he was willing to admit to, or maybe he was just shielding himself from the remorse he might be feeling for not having been there when he had been needed.

Teresa knew that you had to tread very carefully when it came to exploring the landscape of the human soul.

Evil deceives, she reminded herself. But it could no longer surprise her. She had seen its every manifestation and there was no new flourish it could produce. That, at least, was something.

She leant towards him.

'Maybe you were asleep that night,' she told him. 'Maybe you didn't have anything to do with her death. Maybe. But one thing is for sure: you have an opportunity now to help me find out what really happened.'

He, too, leant forwards now, echoing her tone.

'I let you into my home. I told you about my people and I revisited my worst memories to answer your questions, and now you treat me like a criminal. Is it the truth you want? Ask the person who was there that night. There have always been rumours about Matriona. She was there the night Hanna died. Didn't you know? I'm sure I've told you.'

Teresa felt the blow.

Did he tell me? Is he lying? Have I forgotten? Maybe I wrote it down in my diary, or maybe it never happened.

Francesco looked at her as if he wanted to see right into her soul.

'You seem confused, Superintendent,' he remarked as if he knew about the disease that stalked her mind.

Did he have her diary? Or were the symptoms of her illness beginning to show even when she was convinced she was keeping them at bay? Maybe it was just her paranoia making her suspicious of everyone she encountered. Or maybe he was an excellent actor.

Marini came up to her and showed her a message he'd just received on his phone, confirming that there were no fingerprints other than Teresa's on the diary page they had retrieved from the ruins of the cottage in the woods.

She looked at Francesco, but he remained impassive.

She could feel a sense of unease gripping her tight enough to break her bones.

It's like hunting a ghost, she thought to herself, but soon her frustration turned into fresh determination. She had Matriona, and she had a ghost – and ghosts usually never left the place where they had died.

86

Krisnja huddled in her jumper and walked faster towards the woods. From the kitchen window, she had seen her cat trot along the path and disappear among the trees. It wasn't safe:

there had been a fox sniffing around the field next to the house for the past few days.

The day's dawn sprinkled dewdrops over the world, throwing a gleaming cloak of pink and violet like a layer of ash over the valley and all the way up to the tips of the mountains. The forest was a colourless limbo, mist rising from the undergrowth. Krisnja was surprised by that pillowy silence. Though the night had ended, the forest still seemed to be asleep, locked in an unnatural slumber.

She saw what looked like the tip of a tail slipping away behind a bush just ahead of her.

'Orpheus!' she called out, running after him. Her voice echoed in the fog.

A pair of crows flew across the path, low over the ground, and she let out a frightened scream.

Silence fell over the forest again, broken only by the heavy sound of Krisnja's breathing, in time with the sense of foreboding rising within her, and the thoughts hammering away in her head.

She felt like she was being watched. What had begun as a vague feeling of unease had now assumed the contours of a hidden presence.

For the first time in her life, she was scared of the place where she had grown up. Dark spots in the fog now began to swirl and re-form into familiar silhouettes: the grave faces of Ewa, of Krisnja's mother, Hanna, and of Aniza, billowing in the mist.

Krisnja rubbed at her eyes. When she opened them again, the faces had disappeared.

She looked back in the direction she'd come from, but the path seemed to have dissolved in a wall of smoke. But there was something there, not far from where she stood. It was walking – but no, not really. What it was doing – the *way* it was doing it – could never be described in human terms. Krisnja could hear the sound of its bones breaking as it approached her. She could hear the bubbling of its bodily humours, the clicking of its tendons. She could smell its scent.

The sound of her own keening wail reached her ears and she began to run without knowing which direction she was heading in. She had been plunged into a dark and hostile realm now, and from its recesses rose a savage roar.

Krisnja fell into a tangle of brambles, its army of tiny hooks tearing at her clothes and slicing open the skin on her face and arms. She tried desperately to break free, but her struggling merely tightened the grip of the prickly vines on her body. She realised then, and far too late, that the monstrous creature had led her exactly where it had wanted her to go: into a trap.

Her breathing now was accompanied by another's. Her terrified sobs were echoed by a guttural laugh.

Krisnja was like a butterfly trapped in a spiderweb: she could only move her eyes. When she finally worked up the courage to open them, what she saw took her breath away.

Standing before her was the *Warvar*, the keeper, the creature her grandmother, Ewa, used to tell her about.

It had two names, reflecting its dual nature.

Tikô Wariö: he who guards.

Tikô Bronô: he who protects.

The 'fierce guardian' the legends spoke of had curling horns and blood-red eyes. And the face of a woman.

87

In the barn where Hanna had died, time had stopped. The signs of the destruction that had taken place that night were still present, crystallised into black charcoal, preserved in the building's ravaged wooden beams, in its foundations laid bare under the floor.

No one had bothered to restore the barn, or perhaps they had preferred not to. It still stood on a hill that overlooked the village and Teresa wondered if it survived now as a monument to something she couldn't quite put her finger on.

She hadn't had a chance to speak with Krisnja yet about the night her mother had died. She had called round to see her, but the young woman hadn't been home.

All that Francesco had told her was that Krisnja had witnessed the fire that night. Her grandmother had been holding her in her arms when she had run to try to stop the fire, but there had been nothing she could do. Ewa's screams had woken up the whole village.

The barn was an annexe to the house in which Krisnja had lived with her mother and grandmother, the same house she still lived in, alone, and that Teresa was observing now from the adjacent meadow. A colossal oak tree stood between the two buildings, a swing made of rope and timber hanging abandoned from one of its branches. It was rocking in the wind, as if some invisible presence were pushing it lazily about while observing the flurry of activity currently taking place in the barn.

Krisnja wasn't the only person Teresa wanted to speak to. She had dispatched Parisi and de Carli to keep an eye on Matriona's house, too, which was at the back of her tavern. Teresa would pay her a visit herself soon enough, but before she confronted her, she needed to find evidence of the murder that had taken place in that barn.

Death, she reflected, *always leaves its mark on the world of the living.*

It moves on human limbs, it touches the material realm with human fingertips and prints, it leaves flecks of warm spit in its wake. Like a ghost, it haunts and never leaves the place of its last farewell. The inspection of the barn had been going on for over an hour now and Teresa was sure that the presence of death would soon be revealed. She knew what they needed to look for and she had issued the forensics team with very specific instructions.

'What are you thinking about?' Marini asked her.

Teresa chewed on the frame of her glasses.

'Fire,' she replied.

'You don't think the fire was an accident.'

'I don't, and what's more, I don't think it was started just to destroy the evidence of the murder.'

'So it was significant in some way?'

'In more ways than one, in fact. Most people overlook the fact that death by fire is the most devastating and violent fantasy a killer's mind could possibly conjure up. Flames consume the body, reduce it to ash. It is total, complete annihilation. Pyromania is often considered an indicator of borderline personality disorder.'

An officer from the forensics team called out to them from the other side of the building. As they walked up to him, he looked at Teresa as if she were a clairvoyant.

'You were right,' he said in amazement. 'It's exactly like you said.'

He showed them a section of the floor where the debris from the fire had just been cleared, revealing a series of raised stains, which the forensics team had tagged as evidence.

Teresa and Marini crouched down.

Teresa ran a gloved finger over the stains. The forensics officer had rubbed the ash off them, revealing the redness beneath.

'It's wax,' Marini murmured incredulously.

A semicircle of flickering red candles, thought Teresa.

Those were the marks she had been looking for. Ten years later, they were still there.

The traces of a fire ritual.

88

'Something's going on at Matriona's place, Superintendent. There have been women from the village turning up at her door since dawn,' said de Carli.

One after the other, the women of the community co-operative had been converging on Matriona's home in a silent, brisk parade. The only male present was a young man Teresa had never seen before and who seemed to be keeping a watchful eye over the procession of women, like an apprehensive guardian. When he saw Teresa and Marini approaching, he slipped away inside the building. Matriona emerged shortly thereafter and marched up to them with a flinty look in her eye.

'This is not a good time,' she told them.

'What were you doing in the barn?' said Teresa, forgoing pleasantries. 'What were you and Hanna doing there before the fire broke out?'

She saw Matriona flinch.

'It's taken ten years for this village to stop whispering behind my back, Superintendent,' she replied. 'And ten years to gain Krisnja's trust after she watched her mother die that night. I don't intend to revisit those horrors now.'

'Tell me what happened,' Teresa repeated, unmoved.

Matriona gave her a sad smile, but her expression was steely.

'I'll show you instead,' she said, taking off her fingerless gloves and dropping them to the floor.

Underneath, her hands were wrapped in bandages. She peeled those off, too, and showed the backs of her hands to Teresa. The skin there looked as if it had liquefied, then curdled. She turned her palms upwards: they were covered in sores deep enough to expose her flesh.

'I've tried everything, but they just won't heal. Sometimes they seem to be getting better, but then they'll open again. The pain has become part of my life now; it's been like this ever since that night.'

Matriona picked up her gloves and put them back on, her eyes fixed on Teresa's.

'There is nothing to say, except that I was too late to save Hanna and the fire had already started by the time I got there. As you can see, I tried to get through to her anyway, but at some point, I had to decide whether to save my own life or die with her. By the time Ewa had run to the barn, with Krisnja sobbing in her arms, there was nothing more that could be done. Nothing.'

'Was Hanna expecting you?' Teresa asked.

'No, but I knew I'd find her there.'

'Why?'

Matriona didn't reply, so Teresa decided to do it for her.

'Our investigation has brought to light traces of melted candle wax in the ruins of the barn. The remains of a magic circle, perhaps. I think the two of you got involved in something you couldn't quite control and the game got out of hand. I think you were practising a form of shamanism.'

'It's not a game, Detective.'

'That almost sounds like a threat. Should I be worried?'

'Not if you come in peace.'

'There won't be any peace until we've done right by the dead. Hanna was murdered – but perhaps you knew that already.'

She saw Matriona clench her jaw, the suspicion on her face shifting to determination.

'And you think I did it?'

'You were there.'

'I was there because for months, Hanna had been acting strange. She was becoming more and more distant, and she was clearly upset about something. I wanted to be with her. I wanted to be *there* for her. But I was too late to save her – too late in every way. I'll have to live with that for the rest of my life. And if someone really did kill her, then I suppose the thing that had been suffocating her all that time was fear.'

Teresa eyed her wordlessly.

'Don't leave the village. We may need to interview you again soon,' she said.

'Now you're the one making threats.'

'Not at all. You'd benefit, too, from having this matter cleared up once and for all – isn't that right?'

'I need to talk to Krisnja,' the woman replied, taking a step back to increase the physical distance between them. 'I will not let ghosts come between us again.'

Teresa took a step forwards and went further still, her stance now an open challenge.

'Do not approach the girl,' she said, her voice calm. 'And I would really suggest you follow my advice, given the circumstances.'

'It was Francesco who told you, wasn't it? It was him, trying to throw suspicion on me again.' Matriona was fuming. 'He was always jealous of the family who surrounded Ewa; they were all women, and he was excluded.'

But she was interrupted then by the sound of a woman's scream coming from the house, a roar of anguish and fury combined. Almost like a signal, it released a chorus of female chanting, their voices accompanied by an obsessive and increasingly fierce drumbeat.

'What's going on in there?' asked an alarmed Marini.

Matriona, back now to her calm and imperious self, looked at each of them in turn.

'You'll need a warrant to find out,' she replied, then turned round and walked away.

Teresa heard distinctly the sound of the key turning twice in the lock.

There was another scream, more muffled this time, but no less painful to hear.

Marini felt for his holster under his jacket, but Teresa stopped him.

'Superintendent?'

She motioned at him to remain calm.

'There's an ancient name for women like her,' she murmured, surprised at herself for remembering. '*Doula*. They deal with life, but also death. They've been assisting births and conducting abortions in villages since time immemorial. Listen: there's nothing on earth more magical than what's happening in there right now.'

In that house, in that very moment, surrounded by an infinite circle of female arms seething with unfathomable energy, a child was being born.

89

'We should really get that warrant.'

Driving back to the city, Massimo had felt the need to break the silence somehow. Superintendent Battaglia had barely spoken over the past few hours. It was as if the encounter with Matriona and the sounds of the ancient ritual they'd stumbled upon had cast her into a different dimension. Not even Blanca had managed to get her attention. They had gone to pick her and Smoky up from the search area, which had meanwhile expanded like oil on water. There was another body to look for now – Ewa's – but no one had any idea where to begin. Blanca and Smoky had been contributing valiantly to the massive search operation, which promised to be long and arduous.

'Superintendent?' said Massimo when Teresa didn't reply.

'Hmm?'

'Don't you have anything to say?'

'Let her be,' said Blanca through a yawn, curled up in the back seat with her dog.

'We don't have time just to let people be,' he groused.

Superintendent Battaglia finally tore her eyes away from the view outside the window.

'If we want Judge Crespi to issue a warrant, we're going to have to give him something more than a hunch,' she drawled. 'You can't just go into people's homes because you have a feeling they might be hiding something.'

'But that woman *is* hiding something.'

'And who isn't?'

'So you've already changed your mind about her?'

'No, but there was an investigation conducted at the time on Hanna's death and the fire, and Matriona wasn't even considered to be a suspect. Crespi won't want to revisit a closed case and cast doubt on his colleagues' judgement without valid reason – unless there's "compelling and unequivocal new evidence", as they say.'

'How could they not have noticed that she was killed?' Blanca asked.

'Because there was no autopsy. The evidence seemed clear: the fire was started by the candles the family used to illuminate the inside of the barn. There was no electricity. There was nothing to suggest there had been a homicide.'

'But now there is,' said Massimo. 'Judge Crespi will have to take that into consideration.'

They reached Blanca's place.

'Are you coming up?' she asked them.

'I am,' Superintendent Battaglia replied. She turned to Massimo. 'You?'

Massimo looked up at the window, where the lights were on.

'Maybe,' he said, gripping the steering wheel harder.

'Come on; she's not going to eat you.'

'Are you sure?'

Elena didn't look like she wanted to bite his head off. When she opened the door and saw him standing there, he thought she looked almost relieved, as if until that moment she hadn't quite let herself believe what he'd written in his text messages.

Superintendent Battaglia and Blanca promptly came up with some embarrassingly terrible excuse to leave the two of them alone.

Massimo had rarely felt so nervous. It was like starting from scratch, like a first date, a first kiss.

'Hey,' he said, mentally kicking himself.

'Hey.'

She was so beautiful in her leggings and the plain T-shirt stretched tight over her stomach. He pointed at it.

'It's already growing,' he said in wonderment.

She followed his gaze and quickly crossed her arms over her belly.

'I feel so bloated. Food seems to be the only thing that works on the nausea. It's torture . . .'

'I'm sorry. Anyway, I didn't mean to say that you've put on weight.'

'*Put on weight?*'

'And so what if you had? You look amazing anyway.'

'Anyway meaning . . . ?'

'Just a little . . . rounder, I guess?'

In the silence that followed, he felt a tingle on the back of his neck, an itch he didn't dare scratch: she was staring at him as if she were about to tear into his jugular vein.

'Elena?'

'You're such an arsehole.'

Massimo grabbed her hand before she could walk away.

'Look, I was clearly out of my mind before, but I want you in my life – both of you,' he blurted out.

'*I'm* not so sure I want *you* any more.'

'Then allow me to spend the rest of my life trying to change your mind.'

'How?'

Massimo fell to his knees and put his hands around her hips. Elena blushed.

'Your boss might see you,' she whispered.

'Oh yes, I'm sure she's watching.'

'Massimo . . .'

He rested his head on her belly, then took her hand and ran his thumb over her ring finger.

He closed his eyes. For the first time he could feel, finally, that primordial, transcendental bond with the baby growing in Elena's womb and the powerful protective urge that came with it.

Elena was preparing to become a conduit for a new human life to enter the world. She was handing her body over to the most brutal and momentous of experiences; to Massimo, who was merely a man, after all, it seemed nothing short of superhuman.

He thought of the valley where the force of the sacred feminine was an ancient wisdom preserved and passed on through generations. The Female had always survived there, and so had the notion of the Goddess within her. The women of the valley still carried the force of the sacred feminine inside them, just like Aniza and the portrait of the *Sleeping Nymph* – and even that icon of the Virgin Mother that had come through death into the hands of the children of the valley. And those children, who lived every day with the presence of that esoteric female force – what must they have thought when they saw the shining face of the Queen of Heaven?

Massimo opened his eyes. He clasped Elena's hand in his own and held back on the proposal he had been about to make. He got back to his feet.

'I'd take you both with me if I could,' he said, kissing her lips. 'But it's not safe.'

Reluctantly, he took a step back.

'Where are you going?' Elena asked, bewildered.

He smiled.

'To look for the beginning of a story, so that we can figure out how it ends.'

*

354

'I can't believe you didn't ask her!'

Massimo shook his head.

'I knew you were eavesdropping,' he replied.

'Why on earth would you get on your knees and *not* propose? That's ridiculous!'

'I wanted it to be a perfect moment.'

Battaglia swore.

'There are no perfect moments – only unforgettable ones. This could have been one of those.'

'It could have been, if it had just been the two of us without you spying through the keyhole.'

'You should thank your lucky stars I didn't come in there and kick your arse. I would have, you know. And then you came out with that line like something out of *Murder, She Wrote*. Jesus Christ! You were still thinking about the case! Unbelievable.'

'I was thinking about us, about our child. There's a killer out there who came all the way to my front door. I'm sure you'll understand if I feel I should probably sort that out before I bring Elena back into my life. Anyway, we're here.'

Battaglia swore again.

'Is this some kind of joke?' she said as they pulled up in front of the headquarters of the regional gendarmerie.

'I wish. Can you imagine the look on Lona's face if he caught us fraternising with the enemy?'

'Shit. Is that what we're doing?'

'No, no. We're just using them.'

'That sounds a lot better.'

Christian Neri greeted them at the door and made straight for Superintendent Battaglia.

'Detective Battaglia, it's an honour to finally meet you,' he said, shaking her hand. 'I'm Lieutenant Neri.'

She looked him up and down.

'I think I've seen you before,' she told him. 'Standing half-naked in a boxing ring, in fact.'

Christian smiled.

'Yes, well. I do hope you won't hold it against me,' he replied.

'No, Lieutenant. I have every respect for the occasional act of rule-breaking.'

'Oh, really?' Massimo interjected. 'That's news to me.'

'This way, please,' said Neri. 'And allow me to extend a warm welcome on behalf of the entire cultural artefacts unit here. We focus mostly on retrieving stolen artworks, among other things.'

Massimo watched them walking together down the hallway, thick as thieves.

'Cultural artefacts unit . . . What's with the fancy name?' he sniped, but neither of them bothered to reply.

Christian showed them to his office.

'In all honesty, the case of the *Sleeping Nymph* should have been assigned to our unit,' he was saying. 'But I can understand Deputy Prosecutor Gardini's decision. There's no one better at cracking a difficult case than you, Superintendent.'

Superintendent Battaglia returned his smile.

'Well, I'm lucky to be working with an excellent team,' she said.

'And now we're lucky to be collaborating with you.'

Massimo couldn't bear it any longer.

'I'm not sure collaborating is the right word,' he interjected. 'As I told you on the phone, this meeting isn't happening.'

Christian spared him a glance.

'And as I told *you*, I will be happy to assist Superintendent Battaglia.'

'Boys, I can't say I'm not flattered by all this testosterone you're expending on my account, but please remember, I'm sixty years old and it's not quite as exciting as it used to be . . . I'd be grateful if we could please get to the point. Thank you.'

Christian burst out laughing.

'Now, tell me, please: why am I here?' the superintendent resumed.

'To consult our database of stolen cultural artefacts,' Christian replied. 'It's the only database of its kind and we've made it

356

accessible to law enforcement agencies all over the world. We're really rather proud of it. Its catalogue includes more than six million artworks, each with its own unique code, which we call *Object-ID*.'

'I told Lieutenant Neri about the icon stolen by the Nazis and lost in the river,' Massimo explained.

Neri typed something into his keyboard.

'Sadly, it's nothing we haven't seen before. During the Second World War, the Germans stole millions of works of art from Italian soil and only a fraction have been recovered. Hermann Göring himself, Hitler's right hand, came up with the idea of stripping occupied territories of their national cultural heritage. Take Poland, for example; in 1939, the Nazis smuggled the country's entire artistic patrimony out. And the year after, it was Göring again, who appropriated a third of the works stolen from the Louvre for his own private collection.'

'That's a huge amount of art,' the superintendent remarked.

'Yes, it's quite extraordinary. But I think I've managed to find what you're looking for somewhere in this sea of paintings and statues.'

Christian paused as if to give them time to register the import of his words.

'In February 1945, the Germans broke into the church of the Sanctuary of Castelmonte, which isn't too far from your valley, and stole the altarpiece: a triptych in book form, screen-printed and with gold, silver and gemstone inlays. It's thought to have predated the late Byzantine era – a priceless specimen of paleo-christian art.

'It makes an appearance in the logs that were seized from the Nazi base at the entrance to the Resia Valley. The altarpiece was dismantled and its three panels were separated. According to those logs, your icon was put on a train to Vienna. But it never got there.'

'The soldier who was shot that day must have stolen it,' said Teresa.

Christian nodded.

'In those days, with the war essentially lost, it wasn't unusual for German soldiers to steal smaller works of art from right under their commanders' noses. Which makes it that much harder to trace their whereabouts today.'

Massimo and Superintendent Battaglia exchanged a glance. Another piece had just been added to the puzzle.

'Thank you,' she said, getting to her feet. 'Your help will not be forgotten.'

Christian Neri gave them a bewildered look.

'But don't you want to see it?'

He turned his screen around and the image they saw there left them both speechless.

90

'It's a *Virgen Nigra* – a black Madonna,' said Anastasiu Constantin, his eyes lighting up as he studied the image Christian Neri had printed off for Teresa.

Lieutenant Neri himself had referred them to Constantin, an expert antiquarian his unit frequently consulted when they needed to determine the authenticity of recovered artworks. When Teresa had arrived at his shop, stacked with baroque angels carved in ebony and candlesticks made of solid silver, she'd had to look down to meet his eyes; Constantin was a dwarf.

'The *Virgen Nigra* appears in many cultures across the world,' Constantin resumed, smoothing the cashmere scarf he'd placed around his neck like a ruff. 'But only a select few carry – shall we say – a rather special secret.'

The icon had originally been photographed in black and white, but when it was entered into the *Object-ID* database, the image had been enhanced with colour, using the recollections of those who had seen the object first-hand and the descriptions that appeared in the historical record.

'What secret?' Teresa asked.

Constantin didn't respond. He used a step stool to climb onto a high chair and placed the photograph onto his work table, pointing his desk lamp at the Madonna's face. It was hidden behind a black veil, just transparent enough to hint at exotic features and a pair of brown eyes that seemed to follow the viewers' movements. But the skin on her neck and her hands was clearly dark, and so was the figure of the baby Jesus feeding at her breast.

'Very few *Virgen Nigra* are authentic examples of black Madonnas,' Constantin explained. 'In most cases, the pigmentation is caused by the smoke of votive candles, which can, over the course of several centuries, attach itself semi-permanently to paintings and other decorative devotional objects.

'We've also seen instances in which a darker coat of paint appears to have been applied at a later date, perhaps to conceal particularly valuable ornamental elements. And sometimes the colouring is intended as a homage to the geographical provenance of the Virgin Mary. But the specimen whose photograph we have here doesn't fall into any of the categories I've just described.'

'You mentioned a secret earlier. Is this what you meant?'

'Precisely. You see, it's only in extremely rare cases – so rare, in fact, you could count them on the fingers of one hand – that the dark skin of a *Virgen Nigra* is indicative of her true nature. The image we have here is nothing less than the physical embodiment of blasphemy.

'Observe the positioning of the hand: her fingers are raised to indicate the number three, which stands for the Holy Trinity. This woman is telling us she *belongs* in that Trinity – she, a woman. She wears a crimson robe, as does the Christ; however, in this case the red isn't representative of the blood of Christ on the Cross, but of the blood that women pledge every month to Mother Earth. And she wears a blue cloak, the colour of the heavens from which she descends. It's iconography reminiscent of the Christ Pantocrator of the Byzantine era.'

Teresa was beginning to glimpse the occult message hidden beneath the surface of the painting.

'And see the halo here, so perfectly circular: does it not remind you of the sun? And these angels with wings like falcons – are they not the strangest you've ever seen? Not to mention the depiction of baby Jesus at her breast: its features look like a baby girl's.' He looked at them with a satisfied expression on his face. 'Do you understand now? This image is telling us that God is a woman.'

'A goddess who begets goddesses,' Teresa murmured.

'And not an ordinary goddess, either: Isis, the Great Mother, goddess of fertility and of maternity, and queen of the Night. Sometimes known as *Heqet*: the Great Sorceress. Her animal was the falcon. The cult of Isis is a mystical practice, imbued with esoteric elements. Hence the dark skin. This isn't Mary; this is Isis. Look at her: she's a teenager carrying inside her the greatest power the world has ever known.'

'Paganism disguised as Christianity,' Teresa murmured. 'For centuries, the faithful who came to the sanctuary to pray thought they were kneeling before the Virgin Mary, when in fact they were worshipping Isis.'

'Why the black veil over her face? A sign of mourning, perhaps?' Marini asked.

'Oh, no. Plutarch, the great philosopher and biographer, answers that question in *De Iside et Osiride*, when he tells us about the writing discovered in a temple in Memphis dedicated to the goddess. At the foot of a statue they found the following inscription: *Ego sum omne quod fuit, quod est, quod futurum est. Velum meum nemo mortalium rilevavit.* "I am all that was, all that is, and all that will be, and no mortal being has dared lift my veil." Some translate *velum* as tunic and interpret this as a reference to the goddess's virginity. But in fact to lift the veil of Isis means to gain access to knowledge.'

Teresa studied the photograph of the icon once more, noticing the rich symbolism of its colours.

Red: the life-giving cycle.
White: the first light of life.
Blue: the connection to the divine.
Black: death and regeneration – the cult of ancestors.
And finally, the background – green: the knowledge of plant life.

These were the colours of female shamans.

91

'They want to erase my bloodline,' Krisnja had said.

Teresa couldn't stop thinking about the words the girl had uttered as she'd stood before the tomb of her grandmother, Ewa. Now that Teresa knew the secret symbology of the lost icon, those words seemed even more ominous than before. Some kind of occult force was sweeping through the valley. People were often ready to die for what they believed to be holy. And usually they were also prepared to kill.

'She's still here,' Teresa muttered as she looked around the forest where Blanca, Smoky and the rest of the search team were scouring the riverbank for signs of Ewa's remains.

Once they'd cleared that area, they would move further into the woods.

'Who's still here?' Marini asked.

'The image of Isis. The icon was never lost.'

'You think Francesco lied to us again?'

Teresa shook her head.

'No, he told us the truth. He told us what he remembers. But I think someone else must have found it and has been worshipping it ever since – right here in the valley.'

'Cam?'

'Perhaps. But he's dead now.'

'Maybe so, but there are too many missing bodies in this case already. Will we have to open his tomb up, too?'

Teresa very much hoped it wouldn't come to that.

'But why kill?' Marini continued. 'The cult of Isis is predicated on peace and fraternity.'

'So is Christianity.'

'I'm still not seeing the connection to Emmanuel Turan's killer.'

'Emmanuel *is* the connection. He's the link between Aniza's death all those years ago and the present day. He must have witnessed something he wasn't supposed to see. A secret.'

Marini's phone vibrated.

'It's de Carli,' he announced.

He put the phone to his ear and as he listened, his face fell.

'Francesco's reported Krisnja missing,' he told her after he'd hung up.

Like her great-aunt Aniza, Krisnja had walked into the forest and never returned.

But this time we're here to look for her. And we're going to find her.

That was the promise Teresa had made to herself as she had summoned all the personnel who'd been searching the forest to the spot where Krisnja had last been seen.

'I saw her from my bedroom window,' a rattled Francesco kept saying. 'The sun wasn't up yet. Krisnja took the usual path. She was only wearing a jumper over her pyjamas. And trainers. And then she disappeared into the trees.'

'Didn't you call for her?' Marini asked him.

'No. She goes out after her cat sometimes; he's always disappearing and she worries. She keeps a close eye on him. There are foxes here and sometimes they come all the way up to people's homes. Given what she was wearing, I was sure she'd only be gone for a few minutes.'

'But?'

'But then half an hour ago, I went over to see her and the front door was wide open. She'd left the gas on and there was a pot of coffee burning on the stove. She must never have come back. Something's happened to her.'

His panic seemed real enough.

Parisi and Blanca were walking towards them, Smoky leading the way with his tail wagging merrily. As they approached, Blanca reached out and called Teresa's name.

'I'm here,' Teresa replied, clasping the girl's hand.

She pulled Blanca closer, so that they could speak without being overheard.

'Krisnja's disappeared,' she told her. 'I need you to help me find her.'

Blanca leant closer.

'You know it's blood we track,' she whispered. *Did Teresa think Krisnja was already dead?*

'Help me find whatever's left of her,' Teresa replied through gritted teeth.

Blanca nodded and called Smoky to her side.

'Take me to where she was last seen,' she said.

Marini took her hand and placed it on his arm, and together they climbed down the slope towards the path into the forest, taking Francesco with them.

'This is where I last saw her,' he was telling them through shaky breaths. 'When I figured out she wasn't home, I ran here, then kept going for another three hundred feet or so.' He paused. 'But then I realised I'd never find her. So I went back and called you. It's like the night Aniza disappeared,' he murmured.

Teresa couldn't help but feel sorry for him.

'I'll manage on my own from here,' said Blanca, letting go of Marini's arm.

'Be careful.'

Marini watched her closely, keeping an eye over every step she took.

Smoky went off immediately in a different direction from the one Francesco had initially suggested.

'She can't have gone that way,' he protested. 'Krisnja would never have ventured in alone – not at that time of day, and not dressed like that.'

'Maybe she was following the cat, like you said,' Teresa pointed out.

Francesco shook his head.

'That critter's got more of a survival instinct than I do. He'd never have gone so deep into the woods. There's wild boar, there are foxes. I've seen owls with wingspans over three foot long: they would snatch him away in the blink of an eye.'

'She went this way,' Blanca insisted not unkindly.

'We'll follow you,' said Teresa encouragingly.

Krisnja, it seemed, had soon left the path and gone deeper into the forest. They reached the edge of a cliff smothered in vegetation, where Smoky stopped in his tracks. He seemed agitated. Blanca tried to calm him down, but he wriggled away from her and threw himself further into the woods.

Blanca seemed perplexed and perhaps even a little scared.

'He's never done that before. He's never left my side,' she said.

They could hear him yowling now, just further down the slope.

Teresa called Parisi over.

'You stay here with her,' she told him, indicating Blanca.

Climbing down was tricky. Several times, Teresa tripped and almost fell over, but there was no way she was going to stand around and wait for Marini to go down there first. For his part, he made sure not to rush her, pausing so she could catch up and so that he could help her to get through the steepest parts.

Teresa could feel that Krisnja was down there somewhere – but more than that, she could sense that the case was about to take a turn that would alter its course for ever.

The yowling was closer now. Teresa took the hand Marini offered her and clambered past a boulder attached to the cliff.

Smoky was standing a few feet ahead, staring anxiously at a spot among the trees.

It was a grisly scene.

Caught in a thicket of brambles, her face disfigured, her clothes torn to shreds, Krisnja seemed to be suspended in mid-air, her limbs laid out like the figure of Christ on the Cross. She was motionless and didn't seem to be breathing. There was so much blood that it was difficult to distinguish her face.

Marini swore, then took off his jacket and wrapped it around his arm. He tried to push his way through the tangle of thorns, but the thick, sturdy branches seemed to form an impenetrable barrier that resisted every attempt he made to breach it.

He was forced to concede defeat.

'I'll go and get help. We're going to need a hedge cutter.'

Teresa walked closer to the trap nature had laid. There were traces of blood all over the thorny branches wrapped around the girl's body and her head. She couldn't have fallen into it; the cliff was at the opposite edge of the clearing and the trees around were all more than seventy foot tall.

Krisnja had walked into that hell herself.

But what could have scared her so much that she had felt compelled to try to wrestle her way through that tangle of barbed knots just to escape it?

A shiver coursed through the bloodied face before her and its eyes snapped open.

Krisnja was staring at her, pupils dilated, as if she could hear Teresa's thoughts.

'The devil . . .' she whispered.

And then, as if she could still see it, right there in front of her, she screamed.

Inside the forest, the shadows had come alive. They had a scent, and a sound: a low growl.

Marini returned to find Teresa rooted to the spot, petrified, her eyes fixed on a point in the woods where a dark figure had retreated. It was still there, staring right back at her.

Her expression must have spoken for her. Marini went to check and when he turned round to look at her, Teresa realised there was nothing there – nothing but a figment of her own imagination.

It must have been a situational hallucination. She was surprised to find that in the circumstances, her illness was almost a comfort; the alternative was simply unthinkable.

92

'You can tell me now. What did you see in the woods?' Marini whispered.

They were standing in the hallway of the emergency ward, a few feet from the room where Krisnja was being treated.

Teresa looked up to find him staring at her, far too intently.

'You looked scared, Superintendent. Tell me what you saw.'

Teresa really had been terrified. For a moment she'd thought she had come face to face with hell – when really, it had been herself she'd seen, ravaged by her illness. Her doctor had confirmed as much when they'd spoken on the phone half an hour ago.

'Visual and auditory hallucinations are all part of the process,' she'd said. 'You might find that your perception of reality is altered. You might look in the mirror one day and not recognise yourself, or forget that you've aged. You might glance at the shadow of a curtain and think it's a person.'

'Like a ghost?' Teresa had asked.

'Possibly. Hallucinations are often accompanied by paranoid delusions: fears, phobias, a persecution complex.'

'What can I do?'

'It usually helps to talk about it. I always advise my patients' families to help them reason through things, so that they can see for themselves that what they thought they experienced was merely an erroneous interpretation of reality. It's important to keep the mind as nimble as possible.'

Teresa's next question had been painful to utter.

'What if there's no one I can talk to?'

'Then you've got to do whatever you can to cling to reason. Try to be even more methodical in your day-to-day life. Turn to logic. Question everything and dissect every event. You'll have to save yourself.'

Nothing new there; I'm used to doing that, Teresa had thought.

'I saw a shadow,' she told Marini. 'Nothing more. Was I scared? Of course I was. Anyone would have been scared down there on their own.'

Antonio Parri walked briskly to their side. He'd rushed to the hospital as soon as Teresa had told him what had happened and he'd quickly obtained the latest on Krisnja's condition from his colleagues. She was conscious, though in shock. Teresa hadn't had the chance to speak to her yet.

'Her eyes are fine, thank goodness,' he told them.

'And her face?'

'Ravaged. There will be scars.'

Teresa had to look away.

'We've found significant levels of scopolamine and atropine in her blood,' Parri continued. 'Alkaloid hallucinogens.'

'What's their source?' Teresa asked.

'Biological. They can be extracted from the seeds and leaves of a common weed, the *Datura stramonium,* more widely known as the devil's snare and often associated with witchcraft.'

Teresa and Marini exchanged a glance.

'It's a plant with psychotropic properties, like opium, mandrake and the blue lotus. Historically, it's often been used for its medicinal properties; it can relieve the symptoms of bronchial asthma, for example. But an overdose can cause paralysis of the respiratory organs and a slow, terrible death by suffocation.'

'Someone drugged the girl. That's what was causing her hallucinations,' Teresa remarked.

'She's been saying that someone wanted to erase her face,' Parri reported. 'And she keeps talking about an evil presence of some sort. She really is convinced she saw the devil. Anyway, the doctors want her to rest for a few hours. I told them you'd be fine with that.'

Teresa nodded, feeling wearier than she would have liked to admit.

They were just hallucinations. Yours and hers. There was no evil presence.

'The dosage at which the effects of alkaloid hallucinogens are triggered is actually very close to the toxic level,' Parri noted. 'So whoever it was who drugged her certainly knew what they were doing.'

'Or they wanted to kill her,' Teresa murmured.

She thought of female wisdom, of the art of using plants and herbs to save a life. Or to end it.

93

The search warrants had finally come through. Teresa never enjoyed marching into people's homes and prying into their lives, having officers pull out drawers and fling open cupboard doors to reveal a private world that would be for ever altered by the intrusion. It was how you sniffed out evil, lured it out of whatever hole it had crawled into. But it was also a singularly invasive act – like a form of particularly aggressive surgery.

And sometimes, it was a mistake. You prised open a person's life like a knife sliding into the shell of an oyster and cutting right through the muscle, only to find no trace of a black pearl inside.

Teresa felt like she was holding that blade now and severing what little was left of her connection with Francesco.

Ever since they'd turned up at his house bearing the judge's orders, Francesco hadn't uttered a single word. He'd stepped aside and allowed them to invade his habitat, huddled up on a chair at his kitchen table, his body curling inwards as if to take up as little space as possible. But his eyes burned with anger.

Teresa walked up to him, looking into his eyes. He hadn't stopped watching her since she'd arrived.

'I should be in hospital,' he said. 'With Krisnja.'

'We won't be long,' she reassured him. 'I just wanted to say that if I could have avoided all this, I would have. But Krisnja was poisoned, and we need to figure out how and when.'

'Then search her place.'

'We already are.'

'You won't find anything here.'

I hope so, Teresa thought to herself. She needed to believe in this man, in the innocence his way of life projected. She needed to believe that the anguish he radiated wasn't an act.

Perhaps he was a little prickly – but so was she.

Perhaps there were parts of his life he preferred to conceal – but so did she.

They weren't so different, after all.

Marini pulled her aside.

'Our men are at Matriona's door and ready to go in, but there's no sign of her. She's been unreachable for hours, though her lawyer's been in touch. He's been looking for her, too,' he told her. 'Do you want to go ahead anyway?'

Teresa had no doubts.

'Have it put on record that it was urgent and that we made our best efforts to reach her. We're looking for hallucinogenic substances. Herbal or otherwise – those are drugs. That in itself justifies a raid. Call the deputy prosecutor and let him know. And tell her lawyer he has half an hour to get there, if he wishes to be present. We're going ahead.'

After nearly forty years conducting searches, Teresa believed that every potential crime scene fell into one of two categories. There were those that told stories more powerfully than words ever could, stories made of bricks and of human lives left stranded, and held together by the mortar of emotions and hopes.

Then there were those that kept her awake at night because they appeared to be sentient, and seemed to peer and probe into her soul.

Matriona's house fell in the latter category. Everything inside it seemed to have come straight from the past, as if she'd acquired it over the course of a lifetime that stretched far back into the centuries. Painted porcelain, copper basins, bronze cauldrons and heavy marquetry furnishings, spread few and far between. The scent of the herbs she picked and grew issued from various baskets and cotton sacks.

It all looked so harmless. And yet . . .

Inside that home, the semblance of normality was punctuated by a low thrum that quickly enveloped Teresa. The house seemed alive – and unhappy with their trespass.

Think clearly.

But instead, some mysterious force was urging her to abandon all the trappings of reason and go deeper. When she followed its lead, the hostility she'd sensed in her surroundings faded away like the last gusts of a tired wind.

It was her subconscious, clamouring to lead the way.

Teresa broke off from the rest of the team, seeking silence and solitude. Sounds became indistinct and soon she lost sight of her colleagues methodically working their way through every room.

At the back of the house was a room that looked like an old apothecary shop, lined with majolica jars full of dried herbs and powders. One of those could have contained the seeds of *Datura stramonium*, but Teresa didn't linger for long. There was something else she was looking for, something that she knew, deep inside, she was bound to find.

She had heard it in the ancient hymn Matriona had sung while the heart nailed to the entrance of the valley was still dripping with fresh blood. It had felt like a ritual, with Matriona the priestess.

She had seen it in the urns filled with the ashes of the *Babaz* kept in Matriona's inn: the remains of bonfires in which the past was exorcised and male effigies were burned.

She kept hearing it from old Emmanuel, the ghost that haunted her thoughts, with that hole in his chest and the face of a man burdened with a secret.

Behind a work surface bearing a few severed stems of unknown plants, and a pestle and mortar, a door beckoned to Teresa. She pushed it open, into darkness.

Inside, the air was saturated with indecipherable smells. Teresa's heart began to beat like the drums they'd overheard earlier, coming from the birthing ceremony.

She saw a sliver of blue light behind her. Marini had caught up.

'Close the door. Let no one else in for the time being,' she told him.

There was no light switch, but all along the walls, which were coated with dark paint, there were niches carved in the rough plaster, each holding a bowl of wax.

As if she had been there before, Teresa brought out a match and lit each wick, and soon a trembling glow spread through the room like a red dawn.

The walls and the ceiling had been painted with red ochre. There were no windows, save for some air vents on one side of the room, which reminded Teresa of the kind she had seen in ancient cave houses and early Christian mountain churches.

'A little claustrophobic,' muttered Marini.

To Teresa, it brought to mind a womb, red, dark and warm.

She saw the drums, resting silently on mats laid out over the floor. She crouched down to examine one.

'Drumbeats and chanting,' she murmured, a theory now

371

beginning to take shape in her mind as she uttered the words. 'They were methods used in antiquity to trigger trance-like states during ritual ceremonies.'

'How eerie.'

'Research has shown that they can stimulate the brain to enter into what is known as a theta rhythm, which occurs during the early stages of REM sleep. Electrical activity in the neural tissue of the brain becomes "synchronised" and stimulates a state of deepened consciousness. We know, for example, that the ancient priestesses of Denderah would beat on their drums when pregnant women went into labour.'

'What does this deepened consciousness do?'

'It connects us to the spirit world. Theta waves can even induce hypnagogic episodes – religious ecstasies, in other words.'

'You don't believe any of this, do you?'

'The Church feared their possible effects so much that they banned them.'

Marini spun on his heels.

'What the hell is this room?' he asked.

Teresa was quite certain now.

'The holiest of places – that is before the great monotheistic religions came along and handed power over to men, snuffing out the sacred feminine,' she replied in a low murmur, getting back to her feet. 'It's an ancient birth chamber.'

'So you're saying this is a war of the sexes now?'

'Idiot. You'll understand when you have a daughter.'

'Understand what?'

'The need to protect her.'

She pointed out a series of drawings on a wall. They were stylised human figures, lightly sketched with superabundant buttocks and swollen breasts. A series of white dots lined their spines all the way to their heads.

'Matriona sure takes her shamanism seriously,' Marini remarked. 'These look like ancient cave paintings.'

Teresa put on her glasses and shone her torch on the images.

'They're speaking to us,' she murmured.

'All right, surprise me: what are they saying?'

'See those white dots? They're found in countless examples of prehistoric art across different cultures, even far apart in time and space. They represent phosphenes.'

'What's a phosphene?'

'I'll show you.'

Teresa pressed her thumb into one of his eyes.

'*Are you crazy?*'

'Did you see any flashes of white?'

'*Yes.*'

'There you go. Those were phosphenes: a visual phenomenon involving the perception of sparks or luminous dots even in the absence of light.'

He rubbed his eye.

'I can't see.'

'They can be caused by pressure on the eye, hyperventilation, physical strain and deep meditation. Or by the ingestion of entheogens. Get it, Inspector?'

'So you're saying that Matriona and the women who follow her practise shamanic rituals that involve the use of hallucinogenic plants?'

'Well done.'

'But you said just now that this is a birth chamber.'

'And is there any act more shamanistic than that of a woman giving birth to a child? She, more than anyone else, lies suspended between life and death. Through that most feral of natural processes, she becomes a portal through which a soul passes from an unknown realm into ours. She puts her own body and her own life at the service of the species.'

Teresa sensed the turbulence coursing through that young man who was preparing to become a father. She could tell that his thoughts had gone straight to his partner and to the life she was about to gift him through her own.

Teresa began to study the numerous other objects that had

373

been laid out over the mats and the wooden shelves in the chamber. Others were hanging from the walls. She saw a small terracotta statue depicting a young woman weaving a thread with one hand and holding a warrior's shield in the other.

'She's weaving the thread of life, but she's also protecting it,' Teresa noted, surprised. 'It's the symbol of the midwife. Midwives were often herbalists or bonesetters, too.'

Marini was inspecting the other end of the room.

'These aren't the sort of objects you can just find in a shop,' he said.

Once more, Teresa felt that strange energy that had coursed through her when she'd first walked into the house: her subconscious again, clamouring to speak in her stead.

'These are no ordinary objects,' she said.

She needed a moment to regroup. Inside that room, the air itself seemed to have hands and carried the scent of a world that had long been presumed vanished but had instead survived in there.

The swirls and spirals painted on the terracotta sculptures weren't the abstract decorations she'd initially assumed they were, but instead symbolised the sacred waters so intimately linked to a woman's womb and the life it generated. She understood, now, what the distorted statues really were: steatopygian Venuses, female deities, in this case roughly carved or perhaps just eroded by the passage of time. There were dozens, perhaps hundreds of them.

Old Europe.

Teresa didn't realise she'd spoken the words aloud until she heard Marini ask her what she was talking about.

'Old Europe is a term that's been used by anthropologists in recent years to refer to a civilisation that's deemed to have prospered in the Balkans, along the shores of the Danube, throughout Anatolia and all the way to the Caspian Sea. A matriarchal society in which women were at the centre of the community's spiritual, social, political and artistic life, whose settlements were devoid of fortifications and weapons, and from whom we've inherited thousands of intact Neolithic-era figurines of the Great Mother.'

'Like these replicas here?'

Teresa didn't think they were replicas.

Carefully, almost tenderly, she took from his hands a long, ancient-looking staff, rounded at either end. She could hardly believe what she was seeing.

'Thirteen notches,' she said, running a finger over the marks carved into its surface. 'Thirteen, like the yearly menstrual cycles experienced by women of reproductive age.'

'What does it mean?'

'That contrary to what we've always been taught, in primitive tribes it wasn't the men, the hunters, who wielded the staff of authority, but the midwives,' she explained, putting the object back into the cabinet in which Marini had found it. 'And what's more, the staff wasn't really about power, either, as we've always thought. What you're looking at here, Inspector, is a lunar calendar, designed to predict births and keep track of ceremonial occasions.'

Marini's expression slowly shifted.

'You think these are original artefacts?' he asked, amazed.

She looked around the whole room. The candles burned in their niches, shadow and light flickering across the faces of the female deities and on their protuberant bellies decorated with spirals.

'Can you not smell it – the smell of centuries, of millennia of history?' she asked him. 'The motive for Emmanuel's murder is right here, all around us: a sense of belonging so powerful and so absolute that someone was willing to kill in order to preserve it.'

They fell silent, both feeling a little overwhelmed.

'So we've found the killer,' said Marini. 'Now, we need to figure out the connection between Matriona and the death of the *Sleeping Nymph*. I bet they've already found some devil's snare in the next room.'

'It's one thing to find some seeds in a jar; it's quite another to prove they're from the same batch as those that cropped up in Krisnja's system,' Teresa replied distractedly.

A sound from her mobile phone had just alerted her to the arrival of a new message: an update on the results of the inquiry she'd ordered on the estate of the violin-playing partisan, Carlo Alberto Morandini.

After she'd read through the report, she couldn't help but close her eyes for a moment.

'Everything OK, Superintendent?'

Everything was definitely not OK.

'The tables have just turned on us, Inspector,' she replied.

94

Some lives are tainted from the start. They carry inside a seed that will grow and grow until it will eclipse the soul of its host, generate dreams and fears that are another's dreams and fears.

Slowly, inexorably, the seed will take hold, like a degenerative disease, a quiet calamity.

Some lives aren't lives at all: merely the blurred, distorted mirror images of other lives altogether.

Alessandro loved the mountains so much that he'd chosen to spend his whole life around them, to study them, to train as a forest ranger so that he could devote his life to their conservation.

Alessandro loved the mountains, or maybe he didn't. Maybe even he wasn't sure.

When she had first met him, on that day Francesco had told her about all the mysterious ways in which the forest was connected, Teresa had later thought how refreshing it had been to come across such a gentle, timid young man who was willing to clamber up and down endless sun-baked mountain slopes purely to measure the circumference of hundreds of tree trunks. It had almost seemed a fairy tale, a story of genuine passion.

What she hadn't known then was that the young man she had just met was Carlo Alberto Morandini's grandson. Krisnja's boyfriend was a direct descendant of Cam, the violin-playing partisan who had somehow either witnessed, or indeed carried out – it still wasn't clear which – the murder of Krisnja's great-aunt.

Alessandro had severed any connection he'd had with his mother and given himself over, body and soul, to his grandfather's mission, whatever that might be.

'He's been here all along,' said Marini, staring in amazement at Alessandro's house at the entrance to the valley, the place he'd inherited upon his grandfather's passing.

'He couldn't leave,' Teresa replied. 'His sense of duty and loyalty would never have allowed it.'

'I just don't understand that.'

'That's because you've never been conditioned like he was. A child's mind is putty in an adult's hands and the adult can easily mould it in his or her own image, or in accordance with his or her own needs.

'Day after day, Cam shaped Alessandro, constantly undermining his mother's influence on him; perhaps by this point he saw her as an obstacle to his plans, a threat, even. It makes little difference that Alessandro is an intelligent, well-educated young man: it won't be an easy task to break down the cage his grandfather has erected around his mind. I would go so far as to say we're dealing with a case of brainwashing.'

The house was a typical mountain dwelling and like the clearing around it, it showed signs of neglect. The shutters needed a fresh coat of paint and the gutters were clogged with dead leaves, which must have been there since the winter. Weeds had begun to grow over what had probably once been flower beds but had since deteriorated into the odd rock sticking out of a clump of bushes.

This is not a place he loves, yet he keeps trying. It's a daily struggle.

They walked up the steps to the patio.

'He's not home,' Parisi informed them, 'though his car's in the back.'

Teresa pictured him trudging down some forest path, searching, perhaps, for a little bit of peace.

'So we'll wait,' she replied. 'In the meantime, we can take a look at what's outside.'

'There's a pair of boots over there,' Marini pointed out.

They walked up to the woodshed, where he put on his gloves and picked up the boots. He turned the soles towards Teresa.

'Size 43, like the prints we found at my place.'

She nodded silently. Assuming Alessandro was indeed the person responsible for the intimidating message left at Marini's home, his actions seemed to Teresa a desperate, irrational and clumsy attempt at protecting himself and the memory of his grandfather.

But to carve a man's heart out – that's something else.

In the profile she had sketched of the killer, paint and blood simply couldn't co-exist. It would be like comparing the actions of a misbehaving child to the clinical violence of Jack the Ripper.

At this point, her theory, which she had yet to share with the rest of the team, was that the person who'd splattered paint over Marini's front door wasn't the same person who'd broken into her home and stolen her diary – and not the person who'd murdered Emmanuel Turan, either. The killer was hiding in other people's shadows – unless she'd made a mistake and underestimated the extent to which Alessandro's will had been erased and rewired.

'We'll need to confiscate clothes and shoes and compare the patterns on the soles with any footprints we've found so far,' she said. 'If we're lucky, we might even find traces of paint.'

And if I'm wrong, we'll find my diary, too.

She let them get on with their work while she walked towards the house. It was as if spring had halted its course a few feet from the door, giving way to a persistent winter that manifested itself in gloomy colours and in the putrefying remains of dead vegetation that had yet to be absorbed into the earth. The way the house was positioned, in a north-facing clearing that backed into a rock wall, ensured the sun rarely shone on it.

The shutters had been left open and Teresa took the chance to sneak a look, her hands shielding her eyes so that she could see better. What she saw inside confirmed her suspicions.

The living room was covered in moss-green wallpaper and hunting trophies, and among these were photographs of the valley interspersed with close-ups of Krisnja. It didn't look like she had posed for any of them; rather, they seemed to be candid shots.

He's always been with her, Teresa thought. Not Alessandro: his grandfather, Cam.

Inside a glass cabinet next to the blackened fireplace were a violin and its bow, proudly on display like a relic in a monstrance. Teresa was sure it was the same instrument that had played the 'Devil's Trill' as Aniza lay dying in Alessio's arms.

She felt an excruciating sadness come over her and was forced to take a step back.

How much of his obsession had the grandfather passed on to the grandson? Had Alessandro, too, been searching for the lost icon, and how far was he prepared to go in order to find it?

Maybe he's found it already and now he's guarding it.

Teresa walked away towards the forest, her shoulders hunched. She didn't even notice the shadow moving amid the vegetation until she heard a twig snap, when she looked up.

At that same moment, Alessandro saw her, too – and sprinted off into the trees.

Teresa tried to keep up with him as best she could. Her pursuit was instinctive, powered by the urge to get to the truth before the others did, to look that young man in the eye and see whether or not he really did have the face of a killer.

'Stop!' she yelled, shoving off the branches that kept getting in her way.

She was tired, she was angry, she was sweaty, she was out of breath. She hated the burden that her flesh had become – another obstacle to deal with among so many others, both physical and psychological, that stood in her way.

Her progress became slower and more gruelling with every stride until eventually she had no choice but to stop and lean against a tree, struggling for air, her ears ringing with the roar of her heart and the heavy sound of her breathing.

She realised she was alone.

Slowly, she was taken over by a sensation she'd grown accustomed to by now: the feeling that she was losing her bearings. The void was coming.

I need to go back. Back to safety.

She turned round and found herself face to face with the young man she'd seen running away into the woods. He looked pale and sweaty, despite the slight chill in the air.

He walked up to her, so close his chest touched her body.

'I'm not a killer,' he hissed, so agitated he seemed to want to bite the air as he spoke.

'Why would you be?' she replied after a moment's hesitation.

He shook his head uncomprehendingly.

'You're all over me for something I didn't even do,' he yelled, right in her face.

Teresa could almost feel the sharpness of his teeth in her flesh, see them snapping at her like the metal spikes of a trap.

The young man brought his shaking hands all the way up to her neck.

'My grandfather spent his whole damn life looking for that Madonna, but he's not the one who killed Aniza,' he said.

He looked like he was about to burst into tears.

'He wanted me to find it, he wouldn't stop going on about it – but I let him down.'

She didn't know how to respond.

'The Madonna?' she stammered.

She had no idea what he was talking about. She had no idea who he even was.

The young man squeezed his hands tighter.

'We're not murderers. Neither of us. He didn't kill her,' he repeated.

'*Kill* her?'

She tried to push his hands away, but he was too strong.

'When my grandfather got there, the girl was already dying and that painter had lost his mind. He was using her blood to paint her portrait . . . My grandfather said he tried to grab the painting off him and get him away from there, but it didn't work. He looked possessed.'

'Who was it? Who was it who hurt the girl?' Teresa managed to ask.

The tale turned frantic, interspersed with sobs and furious expletives.

'Wait!' she pleaded as she finally managed to push him away.

She rummaged in her pocket for a pen but realised she didn't even have a piece of paper at hand: in her hurry to catch him, she'd dropped her bag.

'I know this is going to sound crazy to you,' she said, rolling up one of her sleeves all the way to the elbow, 'but would you mind writing down on my arm what you've just told me?'

He stared at her, wide-eyed.

'Are you crazy? You need to tell the others that it wasn't me!'

Teresa wanted to scream. She didn't have the words to explain to him how reality suddenly seemed to have disappeared from beneath her feet. But there was one thing she was sure of: whatever happened to her in this interlude of darkness, she had to make sure she left clues behind – clues she could later follow herself.

'I'm Teresa Battaglia. I'm Teresa Battaglia,' she said over and over again, but only because it was written on her bracelet.

'Superintendent!'

They turned round to see a man approaching them. The boy began to run, but he'd not gone a few yards before the earth crumbled under his feet and his escape turned into a plunge over the edge of the cliff. She watched him tumble down among a cascade of falling rocks, falling faster and faster, his arms folding into unnatural angles, one of his legs stretched out so high it almost reached his head. He was like a puppet, his limbs at the mercy of the landslide. When it was all over, he lay broken at the foot of the ridge.

Teresa felt faint. She fell to the ground, still holding her pen. She knew she didn't have much time before it all vanished from her mind. The names had already been lost in the breeze. All that was left was the story itself.

Quickly, she wrote it all down on her skin.

The air ambulance took off, its rotor blades and engine rumbling into life.

Teresa watched its flight, feeling as groggy as if she'd come back from the dead, headbutting her way out of her own coffin.

'Do you think he was telling the truth?' Marini asked her.

Teresa had no idea. She had managed to tell Marini that the kid's last words had been to reiterate his – and his grandfather's – total innocence, but she was still finding it difficult to string sentences together and call things by their actual names. She was even struggling to remember Marini.

So even if it made her sound like she was obsessed, she had made him go over the twists and turns of the investigation several times, made him repeat people's names and run through their roles in the case over and over again.

But what he assumed was her way of reviewing all the evidence they'd collected so far was, to her, a vital learning exercise.

'Can you trust a person who's used to lying every day of their life?' she said at one point.

She was referring not just to Alessandro, but also to herself.

He looked at her, his gaze veiled with a burning tenderness that brought a vague memory to the surface of her mind of the secret this man had carried – and that she had brought into the open.

'Maybe not,' Marini replied. 'But sometimes it's worth a try. It's worth trying to understand the other person's suffering.'

Trust. Sometimes it's worth a try.

Teresa pulled up her coat sleeve and stretched out her arm.

'Don't ask me why or how,' she murmured. 'And whatever you do, don't get too shocked.'

95

Deputy Prosecutor Gardini had arrived in the valley and delivered an official statement to the press, but even after the cameras had finished rolling, the questions kept coming. Up until that moment, the police and the local community had erected a wall around the case to keep the media at bay, but now secrecy was no longer viable. Teresa herself had pushed for the statement to be made, steering its tone and contents. The words Gardini had spoken hadn't really been meant for the assembled journalists; they were intended for the killer.

'I won't ask you anything,' said Marini, one hand still holding her forearm, 'but you've got to tell me what drugs you're on. Whatever it is, it must be pretty good stuff.'

Teresa held back a smile and allowed him to keep thinking that she'd been drugged into her current state of stupor – when in truth, the mind-altering substance that occasionally transformed her into a stranger had a medical name and a clear clinical trajectory. But she agreed with him in principle: someone should make it illegal and find a way to flush it out of her brain.

The arm she held aloft under Inspector Marini's bewildered gaze bore a series of esoteric symbols inscribed inside a primitive circle.

Teresa was fascinated by it: her mind had somehow figured out a way to translate a story that must, in that moment, have been unintelligible to her, into this mysterious language now laid out over her arm. Her brain had fallen back on symbols buried deep in her subconscious, under layers of past experiences and more recent discoveries. Meanwhile, what few words she *had* written down seemed to say nothing at all.

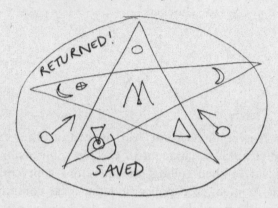

Marini took a few photographs.

'This is really quite disturbing,' he said.

'Hmm.'

'It would help if we knew what you and Alessandro were talking about . . .'

I can't remember, Marini, and if you still haven't figured that out by now, then you're in even more of a state than I am.

'About his role in Emmanuel's murder.' *I think.* 'And his grandfather's role in Aniza's disappearance.' *Probably.*

He rubbed at his eyes.

'The pentacle is a symbol often used in occult practices.'

'It is.'

'Has the devil got anything to do with this?'

'No. He would if the symbol were upside down, but this one isn't. What we're dealing with here is an ancient force. A feminine force.'

Teresa ran a hand over the diagram.

'A pentagram inscribed in a circle carries a specific set of meanings,' she explained, 'which in this case have been partly modified. It's a depiction of the female Trinity, connected to the phases of the moon. Waxing moon: the Holy Virgin. Full moon: the Nymph. Waning moon: the Elder.'

'The Nymph,' Marini echoed in a low murmur. 'And what about the two triangles?'

'Alchemical symbols, pointing upwards for fire and pointing downwards for water.'

'There's a spiral attached to the water symbol. I've seen that before, in Matriona's birth chamber.'

'Yes, on the jugs and the holy chalices. I've written "saved" next to the water; saved from what?'

'Well, we have the fire: Hanna died in a fire. Perhaps water stands for someone else's salvation.'

'Perhaps. These two identical symbols here, mirroring each other, are astronomical symbols for Mars,' Teresa continued. 'They represent the masculine. Shield and arrow for the god of fire and war. It's one of the modifications I was referring to earlier. In place of these symbols you'd usually find two snakes facing each other: man and woman.'

'But instead we have two men . . .' Marini remarked.

'Look at the arrow.'

'It's pointing upwards.'

'It's pointing towards the full moon,' she corrected him. 'Towards the Nymph.'

Marini looked up.

'Can you see who the characters are in this tale?' Teresa asked him.

'Three women. Krisnja, Aniza and Ewa. Or Hanna, Aniza and Ewa.'

'It's definitely Hanna. The fire symbol under the waxing moon points to her: she died in a fire. And we know that the Elder has "returned". That's Ewa.'

'Returned? What for?'

'I've no idea.'

'Considering that her body is missing, the idea that she might have returned is really quite alarming. What's the meaning of the cross inside the circle next to the waning moon?'

'It's the only symbol I don't recognise, but it's definitely connected to Ewa.'

'But you must recognise it. You're the one who drew it.'

Teresa shook her head. She didn't recall ever seeing it before.

'There's an M in the middle. Matriona?' Marini suggested.

'It could be.'

'This message of yours says a lot and nothing at all.'

Teresa studied the drawing for a moment.

'Why didn't I just write down what he was telling me?' she said, voicing her frustration.

You did write it down. You knew you were running out of time, but you've got the whole complicated story right here. Just read it.

'Matriona's the only one who wasn't present at the time of the events,' she said, lifting her arm to take a closer look at the lines she'd drawn.

'But she could be the killer we're looking for today,' Marini protested. 'And the spiral symbol is connected with her.'

'Yes, it's possible.'

Teresa ran the tip of her finger over the lines she'd traced on her skin.

'In the beginning there was a woman, the first point of the pentacle: Aniza. Then there were two more, her descendants: Ewa and Hanna. The phases of the moon depicted in their respective sections of the diagram indicate their age and their position. At some point, Ewa came back. We don't know where, how or why, but the water symbol is crucial here. From a stream springs salvation.

'Hanna's fate, on the other hand, is depicted in the section of the pentagram underneath her crescent moon: fire, all-consuming. There are two men competing for the Nymph, but they're not squaring up to each other; they're looking at her. One of them gets there too late: that's Cam, who leaves a fingerprint on the portrait Alessio paints with her blood.'

'Not squaring up to each other,' Marini repeated.

'I don't think it was Cam who killed Aniza. By the time he arrived on the scene, it was all over.'

'So who did it?'

Teresa stared at him wordlessly. The riddle remained unsolved.

As if on cue, a journalist began reporting live on national TV that the police had found new evidence and that they were close to solving the case of the *Sleeping Nymph*.

Teresa herself had pushed for the news to be made public.

'We took a bit of a gamble there,' Marini remarked.

Teresa was worried about that, too, but she also felt that the time had come to take a risk.

'The killer first acted because he felt threatened,' she replied. 'So we need to make him afraid.'

'He might try to kill again.'

'And this time we'll be ready.'

They were interrupted by Parisi.

'We've had a tip-off, Superintendent. A woman called head-quarters after she saw the news. Says her son told her he found a skeleton hand in the woods. The family made a trip to the valley a few days ago and the kid got lost.'

'Any other details?'

'Nothing yet, but the mother says she believes the kid: he's been having nightmares ever since. He must have seen *something*.'

Teresa was looking for someone in the crowd.

'Bring them here so they can show us where,' she commanded. 'Where's Blanca?'

She spotted her among the TV crews, news reporters and police officers milling about outside Alessandro Morandini's house. She was sitting slightly apart from everyone else, her hands buried in the pockets of her sweatshirt and Smoky's head resting on her knee.

Teresa looked up at the sky and cursed the passage of time: it was getting dark already, but she needed one last favour.

She walked up to Blanca, calling out her name. Blanca turned her face towards the sound of Teresa's voice and smiled. There was a streak of mud across her chin and she had a scratch on her cheek.

Teresa brushed her fingers over it.

'Parisi!' she barked. 'What happened to keeping her safe?'

'It's my fault,' said Blanca. 'I get carried away sometimes. I just wanted to finish before evening.'

Teresa sighed.

'I need to ask you to—' she began.

'I know,' Blanca intervened. 'I heard. I'll be ready when the boy is.'

'It's getting dark,' said Marini.

Blanca stood up.

'It's always dark for me,' she assured them. 'It won't make any difference.'

Teresa took her hand.

'We're getting closer to the truth,' she said. 'We can't stop now.'

'Superintendent . . .'

Marini's tone was so unnerving that Teresa instinctively turned round to see what he was looking at. Her hand let go of Blanca's, her feet began to move, faster and faster until she was running to the woman walking towards them on Francesco's arm.

It was Krisnja, looking at her from between her bandages, her eyes full of tears and fear.

Teresa took her coat off and used it to cover Krisnja's head, and Marini did the same, holding it up in front of her face, just in time before the cameras started flashing all around them.

Teresa caught Parisi and de Carli's eyes and motioned at them to get rid of the journalists while they led Krisnja towards the road.

'What the hell do you think you're doing?' Teresa snarled at Francesco.

388

'I asked him to bring me here,' Krisnja interceded, her voice hoarse. 'I just wanted to go home. I signed the discharge forms myself.'

'We heard on the radio about Sandro's accident,' Francesco added. 'We had to come.'

Teresa didn't tell them that Alessandro Morandini's fall hadn't been an accident. He had tried to run away from a police officer, he had indirectly admitted his involvement in the bloody tale of the *Sleeping Nymph*. And he had told this girl, who now stood crying in front of Teresa, a wicked, twisted lie.

She took the girl aside, away from her uncle. Krisnja looked past Teresa.

'Where's Alessandro?' she asked. 'I want to see him.'

Teresa held her back.

'He's just been taken to hospital, which is really where you should be.'

Krisnja shook her head.

'I'm fine,' she protested. 'They're just scratches.'

Scratches that may well leave your face scarred for ever. Teresa bit her tongue, but there was one question she knew she simply had to ask.

'Did Alessandro ever talk to you about an old devotional icon?'

She frowned.

'No. But Francesco did.'

Teresa and Marini glanced at each other.

'What did he tell you?'

'I was a little girl. He'd tell me about a treasure hidden in the valley: an icon made of gold and gemstones that no one had ever managed to find, not even him. He said it was guarded by owls and foxes and the spirit of the old stag. It was a fairy tale.'

'We think it wasn't a fairy tale and that Alessandro was looking for it, too.'

Krisnja's expression shifted: she understood now.

'You don't think *he's* the killer?'

Teresa didn't reply; though she still had her reservations, she couldn't deny that the killer might be Alessandro, just as she couldn't deny it might be Francesco, or indeed Matriona, who was still unreachable. She asked Krisnja if she knew where Matriona might have gone.

'She's not run away,' Krisnja replied gravely as if to allay Teresa's suspicions. 'She'd never do that. Sometimes she spends the whole day in the woods or up in the plateaus, gathering her herbs. She must have gone out at dawn. She's bound to be back before dark.'

'Herbs like *Datura stramonium*?' Teresa pointed out.

She felt sorry for the girl; one day someone would open her eyes to the truth about the web of lies that surrounded her.

Krisnja didn't reply.

'Did you know about the rituals Matriona performs?' Teresa insisted.

The girl seemed surprised.

'Matriona's a midwife,' she said. 'She's helped many babies from this valley into the world. Everyone knows that.'

Teresa didn't probe further.

'I'll get someone to escort you home,' she said, leading her back to Francesco.

The old man seemed genuinely fond of Krisnja, his expression filled with the kind of protective concern Teresa had only ever seen fathers wear. But fathers, too, could turn out to be the embodiment of evil.

'Stay with her,' she ordered Marini. 'Don't let her meet with anyone, not even Francesco.'

'Where are you going?'

'To Emmanuel's house, back to the only connection we have between the present and the past. That man was executed for some kind of betrayal. There must be something we've missed.'

96

Emmanuel Turan's house was just as Teresa's heart remembered it, the air inside reverberating with absence, an emptiness hidden beneath layer upon layer of objects piled up in towering heaps, like tombs that marked where happiness was buried.

The power was still cut off and would likely be cut off for ever. The bluish light from her torch roamed like a spectre over the remains of a carcass: the house itself seemed to have died with its owner.

Had the old man even been aware of the pain his life consisted of? Had he ever wished for better? *Probably not,* Teresa thought; after all, it was the only existence he'd ever known. But when her eyes fell once more upon the newspaper clippings he had framed, she felt ashamed of her own thoughtlessness: that poor man had known exactly what love was and he'd displayed his yearning for it in the very heart of his home.

She resumed her search. In recent months, she had become even more methodical and thorough than before; the fear of forgetting had made her look at the world with more attentive eyes.

It was as if the empty space left by her fading memory had been filled by a secret, omniscient awareness. Teresa *felt* things, now. Her body remembered what her mind could not. When something was different from what she had seen before, she experienced a sense of unease triggered by the discrepancy between what she was seeing and the co-ordinates of the map her subconscious had previously drawn.

And now it was happening inside this house. She'd had to break the police seal on the door to go back inside, so everything had to be exactly as she had previously left it. And yet it was different. Or was it just that it was dark?

'The photographs,' she told de Carli.

He handed her a tablet with the snapshots from their previous search of the house. Teresa swiped through them as she paced among the detritus of the old man's life.

But when she compared the photographs to the scene around her, she found nothing to justify her uneasiness.

She sat on a stool in the only spot that was clear of debris, placed her torch on her lap and set about reluctantly summarising the latest developments on a notepad that had so far failed to fill the void left by her stolen diary: it was a struggle, and it was dull, and often she didn't even finish the sentence she'd begun writing.

'You're only hurting yourself this way,' she mumbled to herself as she put on her glasses.

Her pen fell to the floor and rolled all the way to the edge of the carpet nearby.

Teresa started looking for it in the torchlight and when she found it, she stopped and stared.

'De Carli!' she called out, making no move to pick up the pen. 'The floor's sloping.'

De Carli came over to examine the worn floorboards.

'It's an old mountain cottage, Superintendent,' he remarked. 'It's made of wood, it's normal for it to sag here and there. There's a cellar underneath. We've already searched it.'

'The carpet. It's been moved.'

He went to stand behind her and looked at the photograph she had pulled up on the tablet.

'I don't think so.'

'I'm telling you it has.' Teresa stood up. 'Not by much, but it's definitely been moved.'

She took a step forwards but stopped when the floor creaked. 'Let's lift it up.'

They each grabbed a corner and pulled the carpet aside.

'Holy shit!' de Carli exclaimed.

Someone had removed the floorboards under the carpet, sawing them off haphazardly. They could see the network of beams beneath and underneath those, just darkness.

A trap. Another few steps and Teresa could have hurt herself on the sharp edges of the sawn wood – or even fallen through the gap.

'Light, please.'

Their torches lit up a tiny realm of chaos created by decades of mental illness.

'We need to get down there,' she said.

'The entrance is outside.'

When she pulled herself upright, Teresa felt her head spin.

You just need some sleep, she thought to herself. But as they walked out of the front door, she froze. It looked like they were leaving, but shouldn't they be going the other way? Hadn't they come to search the house? She put her hand on the doorknob and pushed the door back open.

'Where are you going, Superintendent?'

'Do we have the photographs from the scene?' she asked.

De Carli seemed to struggle for a response.

'You've got them . . .'

Teresa flicked the light switch over and over.

'The power's off,' she muttered, but she went in anyway, striding confidently through the house.

'Superintendent!'

The sudden feeling of emptiness beneath her feet ran like a shiver through her gut – that second brain equipped with its own extensive neural network. But it all happened strictly inside Teresa's mind; her body remained inert and by the time she'd lifted her arms to reach for something to hold on to, she'd already landed on the floor below, straight into a pile of old rags and cardboard boxes.

'Superintendent, are you all right?'

She emerged from the rubble feeling groggy. Gravity seemed to have become twice as powerful as usual. She looked up and was blinded by the beam from de Carli's torch.

'I'm fine,' she replied.

'I'm coming.'

'All right, but do go round the normal way,' she sighed, picking her own torch up in the meantime.

Its beam shone onto the wall in front of her.

There was a piece of paper stuck to the wall. Teresa walked up to it with a feeling of déjà vu. She had seen those words before, heard them in her mind. She was their author.

I'm developing a sixth sense concerning anything to do with him, like a mother with her son. A mother who not only wants to protect him, but also needs him to grow up fast, before she has to leave him for ever.

It does me no good to think of him that way – it makes me fragile; it leaves my heart exposed. It's not healthy to get so attached to someone now when I should really be preparing to say goodbye. And I also wonder . . . If I were ever put in the awful position of having to choose between saving him and saving an innocent person, what would I do? Having these feelings makes me vulnerable to manipulation and undermines my professional integrity.

It was a page ripped out from her diary, a profanation of her private world, marred by a message written in a stranger's hand. *Who will you choose?*

The stranger had drawn an almost perfect circle around Marini's name. Teresa had sent him away from the frontline of their investigation in a bid to keep him safe. He was about to become a father and Teresa didn't want him anywhere near the killer. But her orders had ended up isolating him from the rest of the squad.

Teresa felt dizzy. She had tried to lay a trap, but she had become caught up in one herself – and it certainly wasn't the hole in the floor she had just fallen through.

I came close to taking away the thing he holds most dear and now he wants to take the same thing away from me.

Teresa realised with dawning horror that she was dealing with a mind capable of predicting what she would do next, a mind that had, up until that moment, moved like a ghost that leaves no trace of its passage but had suddenly altered its modus operandi to leave her a written message. It could only mean one thing: it wasn't afraid of her, because it had nothing to lose.

Marini was in danger.

97

The coffee was boiling hot and far too sweet, but Massimo barely noticed as he drank it all up in two quick gulps, his eyes fixed on a spot beyond his own reflection on the windowpane. It was going to be a long night.

Krisnja's house faced the forest, which looked like a black silhouette swaying in the wind. Just then the moon rose from behind the crest of the mountain range and illuminated the clearing. The charred remains of the barn nearby surfaced in the night like the skeleton of some long-deceased pachyderm. Behind it, he could see the lights of the girl's uncle's house twinkling softly in the darkness.

Massimo looked closer. There was a shadow next to the swing hanging halfway between the two houses. Even at that distance, he recognised the shape: it was Francesco. He was standing there in the middle of the night, motionless, and seemed to be staring right back at Massimo.

Massimo cast a surreptitious glance towards Krisnja: she seemed oblivious to his unease and engrossed in tracing mysterious shapes on the surface of the table with the tip of her finger.

He turned again towards the clearing: it was deserted. He tried to find Francesco among the shadows moving in the wind, but he seemed to have dissolved into the darkness.

Or maybe he's moved closer.

'We'd better close these shutters, too,' he said, barricading the only access route he hadn't yet blocked.

Krisnja didn't reply. Her silence was unnerving. She seemed to be waiting for something inevitable to happen, her hands – stained red with scars and disinfectant medication – resting on the table in helpless surrender. Her face was no longer the *Sleeping Nymph*'s but a map of suffering. When she'd stood in front of the mirror and peeled off her bandages, Massimo had wanted to stop her but found that he couldn't move. He'd been petrified, not by what had emerged from beneath the plasters, but by the sight of that wounded creature, whose appearance had reminded him of a hunted animal.

'I didn't mean to scare you,' he told her. 'Nothing's going to happen.'

Krisnja closed her eyes for a moment before replying.

'Yet you're here. To protect me from someone.'

Massimo tried to smile, thinking he must look a little like a fool, and a little like a liar.

'If he'd wanted to kill you, he'd have done it back in the forest, when you were easy prey,' he replied.

'So what does he want? Why is he doing all this?'

Massimo threw his hands in the air.

'Fear, first and foremost. An unhealthy obsession with something he felt was being stolen from him and that he had to guard.'

'At any cost?'

'Yes, even at the cost of a human life.'

Krisnja lowered her eyes. The light from the ceiling lamp threw the shadows of her long eyelashes onto her cheeks.

'You sound like your superintendent,' she told him. 'Like someone who feels pity for the killer.'

Massimo wasn't sure whether 'pity' was the right word, and he wasn't sure it was compassion, either. Perhaps it was more a kind of identification: he needed to understand the killer because he had been one himself, once. And he still was.

You never stop being a killer. It's like a baptism.

'But by doing this, he's exposed himself,' Krisnja resumed, drawing Massimo's attention.

He put his empty cup on the table. His hands were shaking, though his voice was firm.

'I don't think it's possible to make that kind of calculation when you're so blinded by instinct that you're capable of cutting into someone's chest,' he replied.

Krisnja's eyes snapped up to meet his as if in response to some primal call.

'I wonder sometimes if it's possible to feel the beat of a heart, hear its dying tremors, through the blade of a knife pushing against it,' she said. 'Maybe that's how it was for Aniza, and for Emmanuel, too.'

Suddenly, she turned towards the hallway.

'Did you hear that?' she said.

'What?'

'There it is again!'

Krisnja stood up, knocking her chair over.

'Calm down,' said Massimo, walking up to her. 'I didn't hear anything.'

She placed a finger against her lips. Her pupils were dilated.

'There's someone here,' she whispered, her voice transformed by terror.

Massimo heard it too, now: a hoarse scrabbling.

Like a fingernail scratching away at something.

He motioned at her to stay where she was.

He followed the sound, which had now morphed into limping footsteps. It was coming from the room at the end of the corridor, Ewa's room, but Massimo had already been inside and checked it as thoroughly as he'd done all the others. There was no one in this house except for him and Krisnja.

He moved up to the closed door and put his ear against it.

A sudden bang against the door frame almost made him yelp.

There really was someone there – and now they were whispering something, a series of unintelligible words that seemed to be floating out of the keyhole. A rustling sound traversed the length of the door as if someone on the other side were running their hand over it in a gentle caress.

Massimo took his gun out of its holster and unlocked the safety catch. His breathing had sped up and he could feel the blood pumping in his temples. His mind ran through everything he'd ever learnt about tactical entry methods, lines of fire and, of course, cover – which he didn't have. He thought of Krisnja, who might end up caught in the crossfire if this escalated into a gunfight – a situation Massimo definitely wanted to avoid but that might become inevitable.

He should have called for reinforcements, but then a familiar voice he never thought he would hear again erased every other thought from his mind.

The light around him seemed to shimmer and Massimo flung the door open.

The bedroom was plain and sparsely furnished: a bed, a chest of drawers and a commode, all antiques. There seemed to be no one there, but Massimo had heard him clearly.

The shadows swirled in a circle around him, and then expanded and shaped themselves into the silhouette of a man. In his face made of smoke, a mouth took shape and opened like a vortex to utter Massimo's name once more.

Massimo knew now: he had crossed the threshold of hell, and that was where this man came from.

He heard the doorbell ring, but the sound seemed to belong in a different dimension. Even if he'd tried, he wouldn't have had the strength of will to shout at Krisnja not to open the door no matter who was on the other side, because the figure in front of him now was no longer human: it had long horns growing from its head and it called out to him in his father's voice.

98

The floodlights had come on. Blanca heard the click of the switches and felt a sudden warmth on her face. Nothing else, save for the blackness she saw turning to grey.

On the edge of the forest, the sound of a boy crying rose up from among the police and environmental protection agency vehicles as if in response to the sudden artificial brightness, to those electric moons creating pools of light in the darkness where Blanca and Smoky were meant to search.

The search area had been established on the basis of three co-ordinates: the place where the boy had last been seen before he'd got lost, the place where he'd been found and the place where the family had been camping. A circle had then been drawn around the resulting triangle, and that was the search area. It had been days since the family's trip and it was possible that the rains might have covered once again what had momentarily resurfaced, but the zone of interest was small and if there were any buried human remains there, Smoky was sure to find them.

'He's terrified,' said Parisi about their young witness. 'He won't go anywhere near the trees.'

'I'd like to talk to him,' said Blanca. 'Alone, please.'

She followed the sound of the boy's crying, Smoky's warm, soft body pressing against her leg with every step she took, the clicking of her cane following the rhythm of her heart. Having reached the source of the terrified sobbing, she sat down next to him, feeling her way with her hands.

'They told me you're the one who found the skeleton,' she said while Parisi spoke to the boy's parents. 'That was lucky!'

The boy sniffled.

'Aren't you scared of skeletons?' he asked her.

'Not really. They're already dead anyway. And they're funny.'

'Really?'

He didn't seem convinced. She could tell from his voice.

'I live with one, you know. He's called Mr Skinny.'

She heard him laugh in delight and horror combined.

'Why have you got a skeleton at home?' he asked her.

'Well, actually, it's only a skull. But he helps me to find others like him.'

She heard the boy gasp in amazement.

'Can he talk?' he asked her.

'Of course he can – in a way. You've got to listen very carefully if you want to hear what he's saying.'

Blanca leant towards the boy.

'They just want to be found, you know,' she confided. 'Sometimes they've got lost and never found their way home. Sometimes someone's hurt them and hidden them away so no one will ever find out.'

'Are they sad?'

'Very.'

'So maybe that skeleton hand was just trying to wave at me.'

'I'm sure it was. And it was happy you found it.'

'It scared me, though.'

Blanca felt a warm tear land on her hand with a soft splash.

'That's normal. I was scared too, at first,' she said reassuringly.

'And then what happened?'

Blanca had never told anyone what had compelled her one day to start 'searching' – searching for bodies, that is. But surely if there was someone she could tell, it was this little boy crying beside her.

'Is anyone listening to us?' she asked him.

'No. They're talking to each other.'

'I've been looking for someone I really care about,' she whispered into his ear. 'She's out there somewhere, waiting for me.'

'Do you love her?'

'I always will.'

'Who is it?'

'It's my mum.'

'I suppose your mummy can't scare you,' said the boy after a moment's pause.

His voice was stronger now and almost clear of any traces of fear.

'No, she can't. And neither can the others – not when they're all so dried out and crumbly!'

The boy laughed again and Blanca knew then that he wouldn't ever cry again about what he'd seen in the woods. Now, it was his turn to whisper in her ear.

'Are you sure?' she replied, surprised.

'Yes!'

'Ready?' Parisi asked her warmly, putting his hand on her shoulder.

Now that the air had been cleared of the child's terror, she was.

'We've had the ropes laid out and I'll always be by your side,' he told her. 'But tell me if I get in your way.'

Blanca stood up and felt for Smoky's leash. His tail kept whipping back and forth against her leg. He was excited; he couldn't wait for his favourite game to begin.

'I've just got one more request,' she murmured, unsure if it was all right for her to make it.

'Whatever you need.'

'I'd like to take the boy with me.'

Blanca's world wasn't just the dark, obstacle-ridden bubble everyone imagined it to be. The space around her spoke to her in the language of matter, made of shapes and proportions, density and emptiness, distances and patterns. Its breath, warm or cool, wrote messages on her skin made out of shivers or beads of sweat. Keeping her balance meant engaging in a perpetual dance with sudden inclines and sloping surfaces.

To anyone else, a road was either straight or curved. To her, it was thousands of things besides that: slanted, undulating, coarse if she got too close to the edge of the lane, soft and sticky if the asphalt was fresh or the heat too unforgiving. Her feet could feel the change when she stepped onto a painted zebra crossing, each stripe like the key of a piano playing a tune her mind could hear. It made sense, given black and white were the only colours she could still remember.

Her nose could smell the difference between a downtown alley and a suburban road, and – whenever she happened to walk past a bakery – the difference between a wood oven and an electric one: it was a question of ingredients, of temperatures and materials.

The forest was an infinitely more complex system, alive and pulsating.

'This is where I saw my sister,' Luca was telling her now.

Blanca stretched out her hand and her palm cradled the ticklish softness of leaves.

'I can't remember which direction I came from,' the boy told her. 'I was running.'

Blanca turned her face upwards to catch a current of cooler air that seemed to be flowing from the soil up, carrying moisture. She had felt the ground slide almost imperceptibly lower beneath her feet.

'We're coming up to a hollow, an incline of some sort,' she said.

The map on which Parisi had made various notes on the surrounding terrain crackled in his hands.

'We are,' he confirmed. 'It's about ten steps ahead of us.'

'You said you fell,' Blanca said to Luca. 'Maybe that's where it happened.'

'We're about halfway to where he disappeared,' Parisi calculated.

Blanca nodded.

'We're close to the site now,' she said.

She could feel it from the energy emanating from Smoky.

The boy pressed himself closer to her.

'Don't go there,' he whispered. 'It's dark.'

402

She stroked his cheek and loosened his grip on her waist.

'I live in the dark,' she replied.

'What are you doing? Stop,' said Parisi, holding her back. 'I'll go first.'

'We need to let Smoky get on with it.'

'I am going first.'

Parisi summoned two colleagues and told them to look after the boy.

'You wait for us right here,' he told him, his sternness leavened with a smile.

Blanca was struggling to hold Smoky back. She could feel him quivering with excitement and restlessness. The wolf still nestled inside him seemed suddenly desperate to leap out, awakened by a powerful spell.

The sound of Parisi's footsteps drew further away. Blanca could hear him climbing down into the hollow.

The wind picked up again and brought with it a new smell. Smoky growled and barked, then growled again. Blanca took a deep breath. The smell reminded her of something familiar.

Metal. Rust. A forest.

Smoky's howls confirmed that whatever it was, it wasn't good.

Metal. Rust. A forest.

About a year ago, they had been contacted by the family of a man who'd been missing for months, lost in the mountains. His family were desperate and hoped at least to be able to give him a proper burial.

Blanca had agreed to help. She'd found the man's body, or what remained of it, still caught in the trap he'd been setting up. A poacher.

Metal. Rust. Death.

'Stop!' she yelled to Parisi.

But then she put her foot in the wrong place and up became down, then up again, as she tumbled to the ground in a cloud of dirt, twigs and rocks.

She came to a stop at the bottom of the slope, buried in a pile of earth, Smoky barking in anguish.

Parisi was by her side immediately, brushing the rocks off her legs.

'Are you hurt?' he asked.

His voice was no longer brusque, nor reassuring, nor friendly. It was terrified.

'Traps,' was all she managed to say, still disoriented.

'There aren't any traps,' he said.

But when he flung one of the rocks away, the forest suddenly echoed with the sound of a metal trap snapping shut.

'Fuck!'

'A poacher,' said Blanca, feeling her legs. She wasn't in pain, but her whole body was shaking. 'He must have laid more.'

She got back to her feet and felt Parisi's hand clasping her elbow.

'I'm sure you're right, but it wasn't a poacher. Whoever it was, they didn't want us going any further. We must be close.'

Smoky emitted a howl that made a shiver run through Blanca's spine.

'I don't know what's wrong with him,' she said by way of apology.

He'd never behaved this way before, not when they were practising, and not during any of their past searches, either. He kept pushing his nose into her hand, lifting it up again and again.

'I know what it is,' said Parisi. 'Don't move. There's a skull staring up at me from between your feet.'

99

Outside Krisnja's house, there was no evidence of any kind of trouble. It was a calm evening and the crickets were chirping already. The car Marini had arrived in was parked reassuringly on the side of the road.

But all of the shutters were closed, suffusing the building with an aura of darkness and a sense of deafening loneliness. Like some remote outpost, the house was closed off to the world.

Was this the beginning of a siege? Or was it the deathly quiet that followed one? All of a sudden, Teresa was afraid.

She'd told the officers to park their cars further away and they had all approached the house on foot. Now, they stood observing it from across the road.

You have to go inside. That's the only way you'll know what awaits you across the threshold.

But she stayed where she was and tried Marini's phone again. After a brief silence, she heard it ring – not just out of her mobile, but also in the space that separated her from the building.

Marini was in there and he couldn't answer his phone.

'The district attorney and Gardini are on their way,' de Carli informed her.

This was of little comfort to Teresa. There wasn't anything they could do that she couldn't do herself.

Except, perhaps, make the right decisions.

'I'm going in,' she said, the words tumbling out of her of their own volition.

'They told us to wait, Superintendent.'

They told us to wait, Teresa thought tetchily. *Impossible.*

They heard the sound of an engine rumbling and turned round. It was an environmental protection agency jeep, from which Parisi soon emerged, helping Blanca down with him.

'We found Ewa's remains,' they said almost in unison.

Teresa hadn't expected such swift results.

'Are you sure it's her?'

'There were signs of knee replacement surgery in the left leg,' Parisi replied. 'And we found something else, too.'

He handed her a silver necklace, covered in dirt and with some of the links in its chain bent out of shape. The pendant was rather unusual, to say the least: it was a bullet shell, roughly two inches long. The steel casing still bore traces of its original green colouring. The base was flat and inscribed with the unique code that signalled its origins. At the bottom of the circle, the letter B, pointing to the firearms factory in Bologna, followed by two digits denoting the year of production: 1942.

'A 6.5mm Mannlicher Carcano,' said Parisi.

It was standard-issue ammunition for the Italian army during both world wars and all the way through to the sixties, but to Teresa, right now, it was much more than that: it was a clue, an insight into the mind of the person who had held on to it until death and beyond.

'It was still around Ewa's neck,' said Blanca, voicing Teresa's thoughts.

That necklace was an amulet, a totem Ewa had kept for ever close to her heart. Teresa thought of the rifle in Francesco's hands spitting that shell out after it fired the shot that hit the German soldier and she saw Ewa retrieve it, hold on to it like a relic, because after all, that bullet had changed her life: it had introduced her to the *Virgen Nigra*. Teresa finally understood what it was about Andrian's painting of the two children that had always subconsciously disturbed her. It was the expression on the little girl's face: not one of fear, as she had previously thought, but of *excitement*. Of evil. The mean, spiteful look of a young witch who had already understood what she needed to do in order to preserve her faith.

Teresa knew now what the sign drawn next to Ewa's symbol on her arm meant. A cross inside a circle: the ballistic symbol used by NATO to denote ammunition used by its member countries. It was absent from the shell she now held in her hands because there had been no NATO yet at the time that bullet was fired, but Teresa had used it anyway to send herself a very clear message: in practice, it had been Ewa who had fired the shot that day, not Francesco. It was the only explanation for what Teresa had drawn on her skin. Ewa knew that the rifle was loaded – and she didn't tell her brother.

Cam – tormented, perhaps, by the same remorse that had devoured Francesco – had told his grandson, Alessandro, about it.

And finally, Teresa remembered what Alessandro had told her.

On that day seventy years ago, Ewa had tasted the feeling of omnipotence that comes with taking a human life. It was the same taste she had savoured the night on which Aniza had disappeared.

100

20 April 1945

The violin had stopped playing, but the oppressive aura with which it had shrouded the forest still lingered in the silence.

Aniza hadn't expected that face to emerge from among the trees. She looked around, concerned that Alessio might soon also appear and that their secret would thus be revealed, but there was no trace of him yet. So she smiled and held out her hand.

'Why are you here?' she asked in the language of her ancestors.

The embrace was so strong that it took her breath away. So strong that it hurt.

There was something strange about the way Ewa had flung herself into Aniza's arms. Almost as if she'd wanted to knock her over. Some instinct in Aniza warned her that something was wrong and she pushed Ewa away.

'You shouldn't come to the forest at night,' she told her.

'Neither should you!' the girl replied, her manner unabashedly cocksure.

When she saw the surprise in Aniza's face, she burst out laughing.

'Why did you come here?' Aniza asked her.

Ewa spun on her heels, holding her skirt in the air.

'I'm here to meet someone. Just like you,' she replied.

Aniza grabbed her arm to stop her from spinning.

'What did you say? Who are you meeting so late at night?'

The sound of the violin crept over the forest once more, but closer this time. Aniza understood and felt her blood run cold. She gripped Ewa harder.

'You're mad!' she hissed, but the girl pulled away and scratched at her face.

'I know you've been secretly meeting up with the partisan!' she jeered. 'I'm going to tell Grandpa!'

'Hush!'

Aniza tried to pacify her, but Ewa wriggled away, laughing. She hid behind a tree trunk, running her dirty fingernails over the sharp edge of a broken branch.

Aniza approached her, holding out a hand, which Ewa took. The girl began to dance; her aunt mirrored her steps.

'I know you want to be friends with him, Ewa, but that young man has only brought misfortune to this valley,' she explained gently. 'Because of him, Francesco will be damned for all eternity for causing the death of an innocent boy. I've heard the two of you talking, I know how guilty he feels. He'll never forgive himself for firing that shot. I know your secret.'

Ewa stopped moving. She was still smiling, but there was a coldness in her eyes now.

Aniza finally understood.

'It was you,' she whispered in horror. 'Tell me it wasn't your fault!'

The girl pushed her, hard, and Aniza fell backwards.

It didn't even hurt. It was just that she couldn't get back up. It was as if something had sliced through the invisible threads that governed her gestures. So she remained slumped against the trunk of the tree, the tip of the broken branch sticking out of her chest.

She looked up, her lips moving soundlessly.

Had she been able to speak, she would have said that their dance earlier had been one of death, designed to make her fall exactly in that spot.

Then there was cold, and silence, and the shiver in her soul as it prepared to make its journey into the unknown.

Aniza felt a tear sliding down her cheek.

She saw Alessio. She didn't hear his scream.

She saw the boy with the violin appear behind him and little Emmanuel emerge from the forest.

She saw Ewa's smile.

But by then, Aniza was nearly gone.

IOI

'Stay here,' Teresa ordered, ignoring their protests.

Parisi and de Carli tried to hold her back, but they were so in awe of her that inevitably their attempts were half-hearted. Only Blanca dared to stand in her way, with Smoky echoing his human's agitation by bouncing up and down around her legs.

Teresa held the girl's face in her hands.

'I'll be back soon,' she promised.

'That's not true, you can't know that!'

She rested her forehead against Blanca's.

'I need to get him back,' she said.

'But can't you smell that?' Blanca sobbed. 'Can't you smell it?'

None of them had noticed anything. They had to go all the

way up to the door before they caught the scent.

There was no doubt about it: it was petrol. It was oozing through the door, promising destruction.

'Call the fire brigade,' said Teresa, her voice strained. 'And make sure they turn their sirens off.'

'It'll take time for them to get here, Superintendent.'

De Carli had spoken aloud what they were all thinking and Teresa knew it was true; but they didn't have time, and that was why she needed them to step aside and let her through.

'There must be fire extinguishers in the village school and in the town hall,' Parisi reasoned. 'And in all the shops, too.'

'Go and get them, then!' she said, handing a reluctant Blanca over to their care.

As she stood facing the house, Teresa saw on the ground next to the door, just lying there – like something accidentally left behind, or that had never really been that important and had eventually become superfluous – a basket decorated with Matriona's ribbons and filled with freshly picked herbs, their stems and leaves still thick with moisture. There were flowers, too, among the harvest. Teresa recognised them: they were butterworts.

A flower that fed on life: an appropriate metaphor, Teresa thought, *for a woman whose actions had led to so much innocent blood being spilled in that valley.*

Teresa was shaking so hard she could hear her own teeth chattering.

She looked over her shoulder. The car carrying Parisi, de Carli and Blanca had already pulled away and was soon out of sight, but this brought little relief to Teresa, because shortly thereafter, as if on cue, more vehicles turned up, their emergency lights flashing. An unmarked car pulled up ahead of all the others and out stepped Albert Lona, now striding swiftly towards her.

'What the hell do you think you're doing?' she heard him call out.

Teresa went towards him, hands raised as if to keep him at bay, or perhaps to implore him just to let her get on with what she needed to do, when every minute that went by could be crucial and when there was only one thing she could think of doing in that moment, even if it might kill her.

'I need to go inside,' she told him.

'No one is going anywhere. You have clear orders!'

'Marini's in there.'

Albert's expression turned flinty.

'Marini's in there because you sent him there. I am not putting my men's lives at risk.'

'I think the person responsible for Emmanuel Turan's death is inside that house and I also think I know what they want. If I can just get through to them, I know I can bring everyone out of there safely.'

Albert swore.

'Can you hear yourself? You can't even bear to say the word killer. You are pathetic. You have been defying my orders since the day I arrived, but that ends now. I will not tolerate any more of your insubordination.'

Teresa took a deep breath. Everything was clear now.

'You're right. It ends now,' she said, removing her holster and handing him her service pistol. 'I don't report to you any more.'

His expression turned flat. Anger, zeal, haste and hatred returned to their places along the taut edges of his features. In a moment, Albert had gone back to being the cold, inscrutable creature Teresa was used to.

'You are on your own,' he said after a brief silence.

He took her gun and returned to his men without once looking back as he went.

From the house, Teresa heard a scream, so chilling it almost didn't seem human. It was Marini.

'I'm going alone!' Teresa called out.

Though even she didn't know whether she meant it as a warning to Albert and the other officers watching from across the road, or as a message to the killer waiting for her behind that door.

Earlier, she had been frantically trying to work out the most appropriate strategy for breaking into the house. She'd counted the men she had at her disposal and tried to picture the layout of the rooms. As a rule, you needed at least four officers to clear a room safely and three to neutralise a suspect. But now those calculations were no longer relevant.

Teresa doubled back towards the house, feeling Albert's eyes boring into her back like voodoo pins in a ritual devoted to her annihilation.

She walked up the steps to the porch and slowly pushed the door open. There was a candle on the floor next to the door frame.

Very carefully, Teresa walked in and extinguished the candle, then flung it as far away as she could onto the meadow outside. Inside, the stench of petrol was even stronger, the fumes raking the inside of her throat and making her cough.

The house was plunged in semi-darkness, weakly illuminated by a quivering reddish haze coming from one of the rooms. Teresa went towards it as if in a trance.

The thought that this might be where her life was destined to end didn't scare her. Neither did the prospect of pain. What she couldn't bear was the idea of losing *him*.

She walked slowly, resisting the urge to run and measuring every step. She knew she had walked into a trap.

As she passed the hallway and the living room, she felt like she was being watched by the photographs lined up on every surface like toy soldiers. The pictures were all of the same three women: Ewa, Hanna and Krisnja. Ewa's and Hanna's appearance changed across the various portraits; Ewa grew older, while Hanna seemed to wilt. Krisnja, meanwhile, grew up. There were no pictures from after the fire. In that story composed of images, life had stopped thirteen years ago.

One photo in particular caught Teresa's attention. It was similar to all the others, but also disconcertingly different. Ewa was standing in the middle, her expression proud and stern. In front of her stood Krisnja, staring at the camera lens and holding a doll. Her mother, Hanna, stood apart. She was the only one not looking straight ahead. Instead, she was looking at Ewa. There were dark circles under her eyes and a slant to her mouth that denoted concern.

No, not concern: fear. *Not for herself. But for whom?*

Teresa reached the dimly lit room, her eyes stinging from the fumes in the air and the nervous sweat dripping down her forehead.

What she saw inside hit her like a physical blow to the chest.

Marini was on the floor, hog-tied like a beast to be sent for slaughter. He was writhing and calling for his father, his pupils dilated, his body soaked in sweat and pale as a corpse – and wracked by uncontrollable spasms. He had been drugged, but still he recognised her.

'Tell him to go away! Tell him to go away!' he pleaded, his eyes fixed on an empty corner of the room.

A few feet from where he lay, Krisnja was just coming to. There was blood on her temple and her hands were tied behind her back.

'Don't move!' Teresa warned.

They were surrounded by dozens of candles. The whole room was full of them, radiating wave upon wave of heat. As they melted, their wax slowly trickled towards the petrol-covered floor. In the middle of it all was Teresa's diary. She almost lunged towards it and the urge could have proven fatal if she hadn't managed to control it; all it would take was for a single drop of incandescent wax to touch the floor.

She leant towards them, stretching her arms out past the circle of fire that surrounded them, but she quickly lowered them back to her side.

It was hopeless. She would never make it. There wasn't enough time. There wasn't enough time to save them both.

But I have to.

She started extinguishing the candles by hand, one wick after

413

another, but some of them lit back up and others burned her fingers. The melting wax was beginning to look translucent and it was burning hot.

'Get away from this place, Superintendent,' she heard Marini say in a moment of clarity. 'You can't put them all out.'

Teresa stopped. She was on her knees, the tips of her fingers stripped to the flesh, her throat burning, her eyes aflame.

This isn't what I'm supposed to do, she thought to herself. *I'm supposed to choose.* 'Who will you save?' That was the question she'd been asked.

She heard a dull thud coming from another room.

Matriona.

'It's over,' Krisnja breathed out, resting her forehead on her knees.

I know what I need to do. I know.

Teresa turned the words over in her mind but didn't move.

I know what I need to do.

But she couldn't remember. She'd had a clear plan when she'd walked in. Now, that plan had vanished. Even the names of the people lying on the floor before her seemed to have evaporated in the heat from the candles.

Recently, Teresa had often thought about her own death. But she had never pictured *this*. There was a cruel irony in being unable to remember the very thing that could have saved her.

A fire about to break out, victims waiting to be rescued, yet there she was, motionless. After a lifetime spent as a warrior, she was going to die a disappointment, her arms hanging at her sides, her armour gone. She was going to die feeling helpless and inept.

A warrior? A police officer, just about. A sixty-year-old woman, and a sick one at that, trying to play the hero when she can no longer even remember what things are called.

Her mind had deserted her in the moment when she needed it most. The confusion in her head only added to the absurdity of the situation as she stood there before those terrified, pleading

414

eyes, watching her do the only thing she was capable of doing in that moment: nothing at all.

But perhaps she could try to guess. Lately, that was all she'd been able to do to survive.

Guess which direction to go in and where to look, what to say, which shadows to be wary of.

Guess her own name, even – or the name of the killer, who might be right in front of her, or elsewhere, in another room.

Which of the sacrificial victims was innocent, and which of them possessed the savage strength to rip the beating heart out of a man's chest?

Who do I save?

And there was *him*, who was looking at her like the son she'd never had. He was the only one she seemed to remember, though his name was nothing more than the trace of a whisper on her lips. But their connection was visceral. She could feel it in her gut, in the burn of her scar, in the red liquid rippling through her veins.

The walls of the house had begun to crackle now, like the voices that had been haunting her for days, turning from whispers into screams: all her greatest fears coming to the surface.

The name of the killer. The name of the killer . . .

She was in hell, face to face with death, yet all Teresa could think of was a riddle – heard who knows where and when.

The man screamed. The sound wasn't human and it shook her from the petrified torpor that had imprisoned her. Then he suddenly fell quiet.

'We have found it,' she heard him say, whispering as if to save the words for the two of them alone. His pupils were dilated. 'We have found Evil. It is here. It has been waiting for us.'

The words trickled and dripped out of him like the beads of a diabolical rosary. He lifted his index finger through the ropes that bound him and pointed towards a corner of the room, where the darkness seemed to expand and contract in time with their terrified breaths.

'We have found it. *It's not human.*'

He screamed again and something shattered inside Teresa, destroyed the hall of mirrors in which she'd lost her way.

She remembered his name. She remembered the strength of her love. But once again, fate had decided to test her.

The time had come for her to find out how far she was willing to go to save the life of an innocent.

The time had come to find out if she was willing to sacrifice Massimo Marini, the man who looked at her like the son she had never had, the man who was trembling now as if he had seen the devil himself over there, dancing in the darkness.

Reason and logic demanded that she rescue the person who was likelier to survive – and it wasn't Marini.

Teresa turned to the heavens in desperation. She wasn't sure she had the strength to do it. She spotted a painting of the Madonna, whose expression seemed to mirror her own, but the detail that struck Teresa was the monogram embroidered on the Virgin's chest: *Mater*. She'd seen it before; she'd seen it on her own skin. She pulled her sleeve up and there it was, right in the middle of the pentacle: not M for Matriona, as she'd first thought, but for the Mother.

Mater Dei. The Great Mother. Isis.

The icon was at the centre of everything and it had changed the course of all three women's lives.

Teresa realised now what had so unnerved her about that photograph she had seen earlier.

It was the little girl's pose. A hand was wrapped around Krisnja's delicate neck, almost completely hidden in her hair. Ewa's hand. That was the detail that had disturbed Teresa: that large, inelegant hand seemed to be holding the girl on a leash, and away from her own mother. It wasn't a protective gesture. Ewa wasn't holding her niece's hand, showing her the way. She was clasping her neck. It was an act of domination. And Krisnja was holding on to her doll in exactly the same way.

Love and hate. Devotion and servitude.

Teresa conserved hazy memories of the words she'd heard spoken over the course of the past few frenetic days, images that came to her now with snatches of conversation. Matriona admitting to her concern for her friend, Hanna, who had seemed ever more distant, ever more preoccupied, before her death. Francesco, disturbed by the symbiotic relationships between the women of his family, that bond they shared that excluded him from little Krisnja's day-to-day life.

Teresa went quickly over the lines of the pentacle again. She read out the words she had written down on the left-hand side, the section 'dominated' by the waning moon: Ewa.

Ewa. Ewa returning. The triangle that represented water. A vortex.

'Saved,' Teresa muttered.

Marini's whimpering stopped. Krisnja lifted her head.

Ewa. Water. A vortex.

'Ewa went back,' Teresa said, her voice firmer now.

The icon of Isis hadn't been destroyed. The little girl had never intended to give it up. And she had saved it from the river. The vortex spouting from the tip of the triangle didn't represent the relics they'd found in the midwife's home; it stood for the gully, that bend in the waters of the Wöda, where all objects lost in the river eventually washed up. Ewa must have known about it. The destruction of the *Virgen Nigra* had been staged.

She'd already fallen under her spell before she even knew her name or where she came from. She recognised her instinctively. She worshipped her immediately.

And she had forced her every female descendant to do the same. It was either that, or death.

Ewa had been willing to kill to protect her sacred secret. She had killed before, as Alessio Andrian had tried to tell Teresa in the only way he could: by knocking Raffaello's photograph to the floor on the day of their last meeting. Nephew. *Niece.* That was what he'd been trying to tell her: Aniza had been killed by her niece, Ewa.

417

Teresa had to break the chain of death that the *Virgen Nigra* had brought into the valley. She thought again of the riddle that had been spinning around in her head.

There was once a cat that caught a mouse, but just as he was preparing to eat it, the wretched mouse pleaded with his captor:
    'Cat, oh cat, will you give me a chance to escape?'
    The cat, relishing the creature's plight, replied as follows:
    'I shan't eat you, sweet little mouse, if and only if you can guess what it is that I shall do next . . .'

'And the mouse replied: you'll eat me,' Teresa said aloud.

There it was, the only possible solution: a paradox that put everything on hold.

Whoever had led her all the way into that room hadn't done so to allow her to avert the fire and save everyone.

They had done it to force her to face herself and the beliefs she had always believed she had carried.

Whoever it was would never allow her to evade that test. Their hands – the same hands that had already killed before – were ready at any moment to mete out fire and death.

And they were the only hands that could choose to spare them all.

The only way to get out of there alive was to let the killer make that choice for them.

Despite her illness, despite her exhaustion and the mistakes she had made so far, Teresa had to trust in her ability to understand the human mind and find a way to reach out to the killer's broken soul.

She reached out over the candles to touch Krisnja, her fingers brushing against the blood on her temple, there despite the absence of any wound.

She felt the girl stiffen beneath her touch. Teresa inched forwards on her knees, gradually closing the gap that stood between her and the line of candles.

'It's time you forgave yourself,' she whispered. 'There was nothing you could have done for your mother.'

Ewa had consumed her daughter Hanna's life with fear, and she had consumed Krisnja's life, too, locking her into a perennial struggle between love and guilt that had ultimately made her capable of killing the one person who could have revealed the secret of the *Virgen*. A secret that had turned into an obsession.

A cult, in other words, erecting psychological walls as solid as those of a prison.

But the girl's desperate song was also a cry for help. She was at once high priestess and traitor, constantly caught between the need to protect the secret of her faith and the urge to destroy it. And now she wished to be finally freed.

She was begging for it with the blood she had shed, with the scene of fire and sacrifice she had set up.

Who will you choose?

Krisnja desperately needed for someone to answer that question with her name.

Teresa's fingers swept up the girl's arm until they reached her shoulder.

'There was nothing you could have done for her,' she said again, but she wasn't sure whether or not Krisnja, with her mind so warped, could truly understand.

She had conducted a secret existence all of her life. She had watched her own mother die, probably killed by her grandmother for turning away from the cult, or for being too close to the child Ewa had wanted for herself, to raise as the perfect devotee that Hanna had never managed to be.

'I choose you, Krisnja,' Teresa whispered. 'But please let me save them, too.'

She let her go. The girl looked up. Tears fell down her wounded face. Her hands broke free of the false knots loosely binding them together.

With a sigh, Krisnja relaxed, her arms falling open, her eyes closed, her head lowered as if in a final act of surrender.

It happened in an instant: a drop of wax touched the floor and erupted into flames. Just in time, Teresa managed to push the girl away and to throw herself onto Marini.

The fire was licking at her shoes and consuming oxygen. The heat was already unbearable, singeing her skin. The flames had quickly crawled across the room, forming a ring around them.

'Go!' she shouted at Krisnja, but the girl didn't move.

'Forgive me,' Teresa thought she heard her say.

There was a loud thump and a gust of fresh air burst into the room. The flames crackled furiously, ingesting the new oxygen suddenly at their disposal. They grew and swallowed another part of the room. The window shattered.

'Lean on the wall!' Teresa shouted. 'We need to stay on our feet.'

She was pressed against Marini, trying to help him keep his balance. The smoke was thick and toxic, and gathered near the floor. Breathing it in would mean succumbing to certain death.

What difference does it make, at this point? It's better than burning alive.

Teresa closed her eyes against the heat and the caustic fumes from the fire. She opened them again when she felt someone grab her. The men who'd suddenly appeared in the room moved quickly, using fire extinguishers to clear a path to safety. She recognised some of her team, but there were also people there she'd never seen before.

'There's a woman in the other room!' she yelled, handing Marini over to the rescue team.

When she saw her diary among the flames, Teresa lunged towards it, but Albert pulled her back.

'We have to go!' he shouted.

Teresa threw one last glance at her burning notebook and gave up. She allowed herself to be led away and saw Parisi running out with Krisnja in his arms, as the people of the valley came by to help keep the flames down enough to allow them to flee.

It was over. They were safe.

Her paper memory, though, had turned into ash.

102

The flames had destroyed the house, reduced it to black fire-ravaged embers. Smoke rose in swirling fumes into the night sky, while white-hot ash rained onto the ground, mixing with the petals the wind had ripped from the trees in bloom.

Teresa was sitting in the back of an ambulance, with the doors open. The paramedics were dealing with a few cases of mild smoke inhalation among the people who'd come from around the valley to help beat the fire and it was down to her to keep an eye on Marini.

The young officer seemed to have mostly recovered from the hallucinogenic effects of whatever substance Krisnja had used on him, but traces of its effects still lingered, manifesting as the occasional nightmare that shook him as he rested: stretched out on the ambulance bed, he would look like he was sound asleep, but then he would sit up all of a sudden, and start raving and screaming. Teresa would have to calm him down and push him back onto the bed, and also make sure that the needle of the IV drip that was cleansing his blood drop by drop was still properly attached to his arm.

'Another minute and we'll be off,' one of the emergency medical team told her. 'Everything OK?'

Teresa nodded, though she wasn't particularly sure. Once she'd been left alone again, she looked up towards the starry sky, her lungs full of the smell of a bonfire that tasted of magic and salvation, but also of damnation.

She couldn't help but think of Krisnja, who had already been taken away by her colleagues – of the brainwashed little girl she had been, of her mother from whom she had been torn away by the person who had then raised her and so heavily conditioned her mind: Ewa, grandmother and executioner, who seemed to have cursed her own bloodline, who kept coming back in the shape of a demon in the hallucinations her granddaughter experienced as part of the shamanic trances she induced in herself by taking *datura*. She kept coming back because she was the source of Krisnja's suffering, and the object of both her love and her hatred.

Krisnja had only been trying to protect herself, to save herself, but now she would for ever have to pay the price Ewa had demanded, like a bounty on her own head.

Marini sat up again, one arm outstretched as if to point at something. He was mumbling incomprehensibly.

Teresa stuck out a hand and pushed him right back onto the bed.

She was thinking of Aniza, of the *Sleeping Nymph* who had led her all the way here. *Would she find peace, now?* Teresa hoped so. She could almost feel it: there would be no more sorrow for her now, only calm. She hoped the same might be true of Alessio Andrian.

Marini woke up again.

'Is it morning already?' he asked, with a bewildered look at the needle in his arm.

She glanced at the lock of hair sticking up from his forehead, like the comb on a dishevelled rooster's head.

'Good morning, handsome,' she said, holding back a laugh.

He looked scruffy, dirty and singed around the edges. If he could have seen himself in the mirror just then, he would probably have recoiled at the sight.

He turned over to lie on his side.

'I feel sick.'

Teresa moved away and pulled her coat tight around her. All she wanted to do now was to go home and turn her thoughts off until at least the morning.

She heard him muttering something behind her and noticed that he was holding a crumpled piece of paper. It looked familiar. Teresa rifled through her pockets and realised she'd lost the page from her diary that she had found in Emmanuel's home.

'Give that back!' she barked.

'Shame on you, Superintendent. Shouldn't this be with all the rest of the evidence?' he murmured.

For someone who'd been drugged, it seemed he could still see pretty clearly.

'It's none of your fucking business, Marini.'

'But it is. It's about me.' He looked at the page, his eyes widening. 'A *son?*'

'Sons can be arseholes, too,' she snapped, trying and failing to snatch the note back.

He folded it up and offered it to her, purposely missing her hand a couple of times. He seemed not so much poisoned as outrageously drunk.

'I'm sorry. I couldn't resist,' he said with a sigh.

His voice seemed gentle, as did his expression – or perhaps it was just the drugs in his system.

'I won't tell anyone.'

She pulled the diary page from his hand.

'Speaking of sons . . .' he said, trying to get up. 'I've got one of my own to claim, assuming his mother's not completely ruled me out by now.'

'She'd be better off if she did.'

'I know.'

Teresa looked at him.

'Are you sure about this?'

'I've never been so sure about anything.'

'Marini, you're still high.'

He pulled himself into a sitting position, pulled the needle out of his arm with a whimper and after several attempts, finally managed to get to his feet.

'Where do you think you're going?' Teresa demanded. 'You can't even stand.'

He managed a few yards, reciting her diary entry as he went. Teresa removed one of her scorched shoes, took aim and threw it at him, hitting him square in the back. He fell flat on his face and stayed there. A paramedic spotted him and together with a colleague, they picked him up and put him back on the bed. This time they strapped him in, though by then he was fast asleep anyway, his mouth hanging open.

Teresa watched the firefighters and the police working to extinguish the last of the flames. Her memories had been destroyed, lost for ever. It hurt, but at least death had been kept at bay that night.

A man approached her. She didn't think she'd ever met him before, though by now she no longer trusted herself.

'Superintendent Battaglia,' he said.

It wasn't a question.

'Do I know you?' Teresa replied, too tired to worry about hiding a possible lapse.

The man smiled politely.

'No, we don't know each other.'

His accent didn't belong to the valley. She had only just noticed that his clothes smelt of smoke and that there was a black soot mark on his cheek. She glanced instinctively at the charred remains of the house, then back at him.

The man brought out a blackened object from the folds of his coat.

'I wanted to thank you,' he said, handing it over.

Teresa took her diary. It was in poor shape, the cover reduced to ashes, but the pages seemed to have been left almost entirely intact.

'How did you get this?' she asked him as she leafed through the pages.

The man didn't reply and she felt her disquiet grow.

'Thank me for what?' she said when he continued to remain silent.

'You've helped me to find a treasure I had assumed had been lost for ever.'

Teresa glimpsed the outline of something wrapped inside his coat and a sudden glint of gold in the light of the dying flames.

The *Virgen Nigra*. It had always been hidden in the home where Ewa had lived with her heir.

'Who are you?' she asked him.

The man's smile vanished.

'A friend who brings a warning: be careful. Be very careful. The *Mother of Bones* is far, but not too far, and now that she knows the *Virgen* survived, she will not rest.'

Teresa was about to reply, but the man turned round and quickly disappeared in the throng of rescue vehicles. She tried to stand up but fell back again, her breath catching, her heart beating madly in her chest.

De Carli and Parisi arrived soon after that, bearing her discarded shoe. Blanca and Smoky threw themselves at her.

De Carli took a video of Marini snoring in his sleep, but Teresa didn't have the heart to tell him off. They could all do with some levity, after all.

'What are you looking at, Superintendent?' Parisi asked, following the direction of her gaze into the darkness.

'A stranger,' she replied, lost in her thoughts.

'What stranger?'

Teresa put her shoe back on, held her hands out for Parisi to grab them and was soon back on her feet.

'A man who found something he'd long been looking for,' she murmured, still peering into the night.

But that was another story and she was no longer a superintendent.

'Lona told me to give you this,' said de Carli. 'It must have fallen off.'

It was her holster with her service pistol.

Teresa looked at it but didn't move. Taking it would mean a lot more than just having her job back. It would also mean that she would have to start hiding again.

'You hold on to it for now,' she murmured.

She looked for Albert among the rescue personnel. He was standing not too far from where she was. He stopped for a moment to glance at her before getting into his car.

He seemed tired, or perhaps he just looked like someone who'd narrowly avoided death. He'd threatened her with vengeance and loneliness, but he had thrown himself into the fire, too.

He'd thrown himself into the fire for her.

Teresa mouthed a thank you and thought she saw him give her a quick nod before he disappeared behind the car's tinted windows.

'Everything OK, Superintendent?'

Parisi's voice seemed to come from far away. Teresa nodded distractedly, her mind already racing ahead, following a new lead.

She was tired. She had just come face to face with death and she was afraid that she might not be able to rise up to the challenge she was about to accept; but in spite of everything, she pulled out a pen from her pocket and opened her diary. She wrote down a few words, then looked back up at the night sky.

Mother of Bones. Be careful.

Epilogue

The valley turned pink. Sky and earth had merged into one, suffused in a copper-coloured mist that seemed at once to be falling from the heavens and rising from the depths of the earth. It blurred the outline of things, mixed them up into pastel hues of translucence and dust that gifted an opalescent gleam to the tiny particles of water vapour suspended in the air. In that field of earthbound clouds, the *Wöda* emerged like a sinewy silver dragon sliding sinuously down the valley through karst caves and all the way to the flatlands at the bottom of the valley.

Teresa climbed slowly up the hill, where the men were waiting for her. Marini, Francesco, Raffaello Andrian and his uncle Alessio were all observing the view in silence. The meeting between the elderly painter and the nephew of the *Sleeping Nymph* had been an intense encounter: no words had been exchanged – none had been required. They had merely clasped each other's hands, a tear running down Francesco's face.

Andrian had recovered from his heart attack, but he hadn't said a word. He never would. Teresa suspected that the mysterious visitor Raffaello had seen sneaking out of Alessio's room that day the painter had fallen ill must have been Krisnja. She wondered what he must have thought when he saw her. Perhaps he had believed for a moment that it might actually be Aniza, or her ghost. His heart hadn't been able to bear it, but he was so resilient that he had managed to overcome death once more.

Teresa was sure that Alessio knew where the *Sleeping Nymph* had been laid to rest, and equally sure that he would never tell them. He was keeping her safe, somewhere in his heart, and in the earth that had given her life.

Teresa had returned to the valley with peace in her heart, to find a community grateful for what she had done and wrapped around Francesco. He had tried to thank her, too, but she'd deflected.

'I had to be tough on you,' she'd told him as if to apologise.

'And I was being stubborn,' he'd replied, taking her hand.

But the strangest moment had been the meeting with the shaman Matriona and her special band of women. Rarely had Teresa been so unsure of how to handle a situation.

Matriona had approached her with a smile and allayed any misgivings Teresa may have had by giving her a hug, which was so much more than a simple gesture of reconciliation: it was also a knot that tied them together, a meeting between sisters who were also mothers and daughters. Matriona had slipped a small pouch in Teresa's hand.

'Black cumin – two grams a day. It reduces fasting glucose and counteracts insulin resistance.' She had leant closer then and lowered her voice to a whisper. 'And for the other thing – curcuma, ginkgo leaves and huperzia.'

She had responded to the shock on Teresa's face with a sly smile.

'Improved vascular function helps the mind,' she'd explained quietly. 'Ask your doctor, if you're not sure. They'll confirm that these plants will help.'

Teresa had decided not to ask Matriona how she had figured it out. She was sure the answer would unsettle her. She had seen in that woman's eyes something that reached beyond mere reason, something that came from a place far away, an ancient wisdom.

Teresa joined the men upon the hill. Andrian was ensconced in his wheelchair, looking frailer than ever before, but his gaze burned with tenderness now that he was close to the woman he loved. His eyes were fixed on a spot in the valley somewhere in the woods below and there was an intensity in his expression that transfixed Teresa. Aniza must be there, protected by the mountains and adorned with flowers. She lay under the Musi mountain range, whose ridges traced the profile of a woman asleep, her face turned towards the sky. In the valley, they called her 'the sleeping beauty'.

Alessio was holding the baby shoes Aniza had knitted for their unborn child and Teresa watched as he nudged them towards Marini, who stood next to him. Slipping out of his reverie, Marini took a moment to understand. He looked at Teresa, his face vibrating with emotion, as if hoping for advice.

She gave him a decisive nod. It was right. Life went on. It was hope.

The moment Marini took the gift in his hands, the whole forest seemed to stir, traversed by the vast ripple of a warm breeze scented with blossoms and budding seeds.

Teresa closed her eyes and let it all course through her, a powerful wave of feeling igniting her soul.

She wasn't religious; life had robbed her of faith. But right there, in that very moment, she could have sworn she had felt the presence of something bigger.

A woman who had never left the valley, nor the man she still loved.

Now, Aniza was a flower among flowers. She was earth in the earth. She lived on in other creatures, in that interconnection of life, but a part of her, some vivid, impalpable part, was right there, by Alessio's side.

Seven months later

When Massimo had thought of his child, he had always imagined a boy, some part of himself replicated in his own image.

He hadn't been prepared for the wonder of cradling that fragile and formidable goddess in his arms. She'd made him her slave from the moment she had come into the Earth. The universe and all the perfect balance of its laws gravitated around her, and her pull was so overwhelming that he was powerless to resist it.

Aniza would be the north and the south, the east and the west of his life, until the day he breathed his last breath as a father.

He wrapped her in her blanket, never tired of feeling her weight over his heart.

He handed her to the woman standing in front of him now, and watched her take the baby in her arms with an instinctive and immediate love that would never cease to amaze him. It seemed to be a feeling that transcended memory and required no experience.

After all the months he'd spent with her, he'd thought he'd found out all there was to know about her, but when the woman looked up at him, he was surprised once again by what he saw in her expression.

There was a phrase he'd been thinking about a lot recently, though he couldn't remember where he'd heard it: where there is a helpless creature to be nurtured, there you will find a mother.

He had proof of it now, standing right in front of him.

The past didn't matter. Age didn't matter. The life she had chosen, the life she had chosen *not* to choose, none of that mattered. Teresa Battaglia was – and would always be – a Mother.

[. . .] For I am the first and the last
I am the honoured one and the scorned one,
I am the whore and the holy one,
I am the bride and the virgin,
I am the mother and the daughter,
I am the members of my mother,
I am the barren one, yet many are my sons,
I am a wife and I have not taken a husband,
I am She who births and who has never borne,
I am the solace of labour pains,
I am the bride and the bridegroom,
And it is my man who nourished my fertility,
I am the Mother of my father,
I am the sister of my husband,
And he is the son I have rejected. [. . .]
[. . .] Honour me always,
For I am she who brings Scandal, and she who Sanctifies [. . .]

Hymn to Isis
The Thunder, Perfect Mind, The Nag Hammadi Library, VI.2;
Egypt; third century BC.

Author's Note

The *Sleeping Nymph*, with its interconnected stories and its back-drop of history, has been with me for many years, ever since the day I stumbled upon an article about the Resia Valley. Although the valley isn't far from where I live, I didn't know much about the origins of its people. I'd heard that people there spoke a kind of Russian dialect and that all Resians looked a bit alike. On the former point, I mistakenly believed that the Cossack invasion during the Second World War must have left behind some kind of cultural legacy. And as for the supposed recurrence of certain specific physical traits, resulting perhaps from the valley's geo-graphical isolation – which had moulded its people, its culture and its landscape – it may perhaps have once been true. But that ancient inheritance had certainly been diluted with the influx of new genetic material brought about by the valley's opening up to the world. The same can't be said of the origins inscribed in the Resian people's DNA, however, which tell us of a history that spans centuries, of journeys from and to faraway lands.

If I have been able to tell at least part of the story of the Resian people, I owe it to the patience and kindness of Gilberto Barba-rino, custodian of the valley's historical memory, who let me into his home, passing on his knowledge and sharing his childhood memories with such enthusiasm. I 'stole' one such memory and turned it into one of the paintings in the novel: as a boy, Gilberto was present when a partisan's rifle fired a bullet that hit the bridle of a horse that had been taking a German soldier to the bakery in San Giorgio. Luckily, the Germans' response wasn't as bloody: only volleys of machine-gun fire into the village, and fear.

It wasn't my intention to wade into the historical and political debate raging among Resians on the question of their origins. I listened to one version, the majority's version, and I found it to be uncommonly persuasive. To all Resians, I would simply say to take care of their identity – whatever they think it might be – because the cultural legacy and natural landscape they are called upon to preserve is extraordinary, and widely admired. But all this, they already know.

I filled real places with fictional events, but the opposite is also true: in addition to the story of the origins of the Resian population, there are many other truths nestling between the lines of the *Sleeping Nymph*.

We have a Black Madonna in Friuli. She is kept in the Sanctuary of the Blessed Virgin in Castelmonte. Of course, she is very different from the *Virgen Nigra* described in the novel and as far as I know, she isn't hiding any secrets. Or perhaps they simply have yet to be revealed . . .

Blanca and Smoky are real, and they are called Cristina and Ice. I am deeply grateful to them for introducing me to the fascinating world of HRD. All that is written in the *Sleeping Nymph* about their work is true (so much so that Cristina was a little worried about giving away professional secrets) and in the explanatory passages of the novel I have tried as much as possible to preserve the exact wording used by my source. Any deviations are down to narrative imperatives or my own lapses. And when I say it is all true, I mean all of it: even Mr Skinny and his adventures in the pot (a pressure cooker acquired specifically for that purpose, using supermarket vouchers).

The figure of Christian Neri owes much to Cristian Copetti, a friend in Udine's gendarmerie, working in the unit devoted to the preservation of cultural artefacts. He was the one who first told me, and with such great pride, of the database of stolen artefacts, which contains the 'identity cards' of millions of works of art thus made accessible to law enforcement officials throughout the world.

When I begin to write about a story that I care deeply about,

I often find myself meeting people whose own experiences – so generously shared – enrich and elevate my work: that is what happened with Gilberto, Cristina and Cristian.

But there are also people who contribute to the writing of a novel unknowingly, and yet their contribution, too, is fundamental. *Painted in Blood* owes a great debt to writers such as Daniele Zovi (whose book on consciousness in the plant kingdom, *Alberi sapienti, antiche foreste*, has been illuminating), Marija Gimbutas (author of *The Living Goddesses* and many more, whose theories on ancient Europe and on the Great Mother are the central inspirations for this novel), Morena Luciani (author of *Shaman Women*), Leda Bearnè (*The Ancient Virgins*), Massimo Recalcati (to whom we owe Massimo Marini's beautiful thought: 'A mother is formed every time a helpless creature is taken in and nurtured') . . . and of course Plutarch, that extraordinary philosopher, writer, priest and biographer, whose testimony still has the power to extend our knowledge – and my imagination – far back across the millennia of human history, his descriptions so vivid as to create burning, glimmering scenes in our minds.

So he writes in his *Isis and Osiris*:

'They say that the Sun, when he became aware of Rhea's intercourse with Cronus, invoked a curse upon her that she should not give birth to a child in any month or year; but Hermes, being enamoured of the goddess, consorted with her. Later, playing at draughts with the moon, he won from her the seventieth part of each of her periods of illumination, and from all the winnings he composed five days, and intercalated them as an addition to the three hundred and sixty days.'

In these days of light won in the name of love, Osiris was born, and Isis was born, and 'Isis and Osiris were enamoured of each other and consorted together in the darkness of the womb before their birth.'

Acknowledgements

I will never tire of saying that writing a story is a private and solitary act, but to have it published requires the work and the efforts – and often the patience – of many people. To all those people goes my deepest gratitude: thank you for having loved *Painted in Blood*.

Stefano and Cristina Mauri, who have been so much more than just publishers, and who have put their heart into this.

Giuseppe Strazzeri, a strong and gentle guide who has always known how to comfort me when tiredness seemed about to get the better of me.

Fabrizio Cocco for his friendship and the extraordinary professional skills he has devoted to my stories, for having believed so strongly in getting Teresa Battaglia to her readers, for continuing to believe in her – and in me. And most of all – and I quote – for the 'customary verbal sobriety' with which he knows to encourage me when I need it most.

Viviana Vuscovich, who has sent Teresa far and wide into the world. For her kindness and her sensitivity, and her contagious enthusiasm. A friend.

Elena Pavanetto, for her support and the beautiful words she has written about *The Man in the Woods* and *Painted in Blood*.

Raffaello Roncato, Tommaso Gobbi and Diana Volonté: the exceptional press team who has helped me to overcome barriers that existed only in my own mind.

Antonio Moro: thank you for the scrupulous care you have taken over my stories.

The amazing Graziella Cerutti, Giuseppe Somenzi and all the other agents at Pro Libro, who believed in *The Man in the Woods* from the very beginning and who have now shown the same enthusiasm – and fondness – for *Painted in Blood*.

Thank you to all the international publishers and editors who have embraced my words and my dreams around the world, and to the translators who have lent me their voices.

A heartfelt thanks to Gilberto Barbarino: it's been a long wait, but 'our' Nymph has finally seen the light!

To Cristina and Ice, for their kindness, for their openness, for all the laughter – and for their emotion now in seeing the novel published. I hope I have managed to render at least in some measure the special bond that unites you.

Thank you, Cristian Copetti, for allowing me to add an important element to the story, and to Tiziano Quaglia for his invaluable help in matters concerning the Resian language.

To Michele Scoppetta, who has always been there, ready to banish any doubts, and to all of my friends who never tire of supporting me.

A loving thanks to my family, for the emotional – and logistical! – support.

Thank you, Jasmine and Paolo, for your love and your patience, and for accompanying me on this crazy adventure.

And finally, thank you, with all my heart, to the booksellers, the bloggers and the readers, who have made all of this possible.

THE MAN IN THE WOODS

ILARIA TUTI

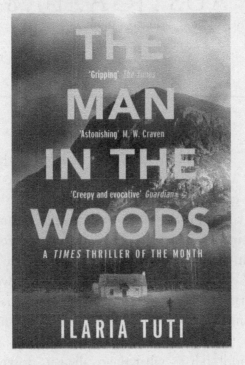

THE FIRST INSPECTOR TERESA BATTAGLIA NOVEL
A *TIMES* CRIME BOOK OF THE MONTH

An idyllic village in the Alps.
A legacy of sin.
An evil hiding in the shadows.

Read an extract of *The Man in the Woods* here . . .

AUSTRIA, 1978

There was a legend that haunted that place, the kind that clings like a persistent odour. It was rumoured that in late autumn every year – before the rain turned to snow – the mountain lake would begin to exhale sinister murmurs.

They came from the water like steam and rose over the banks with the morning mist when the surface of the lake reflected the sky, heaven mirrored in hell. That was when the hissing began, a protracted sound, like a howl, that enveloped the late-nineteenth-century building on the eastern shore of the lake.

The School. That's what they called it, down in the village, though the purpose and the description of the building had shifted through the years, from imperial hunting lodge, to Nazi command centre, to a sanatorium for consumptive children.

Now there was only silence along its corridors, only peeling walls, crumbling plaster, and the echoes of solitary footsteps – and in November, that howling that unfurled through the fog, rising to the top-floor windows and onto the pitched roof glistening with frost.

But legends were for children, the elderly and nostalgic, and for the faint of heart. This much, Agnes Braun knew. The School had been her home for long enough that she wouldn't let something like nocturnal whispers get to her. She had memorised the creak of each floorboard and every rusty pipe winding through the entrails of those walls – even though most of the building's floors were closed off now, and many rooms boarded shut.

Ever since the School had been converted into an orphanage, public funding had dwindled and no private benefactor had come forward with a donation.

Agnes walked across the kitchen, which was situated in the basement between the pantry and the laundry room. Pushing her trolley, she wove her way through cooking pots that would soon be steaming with greasy vapours. She was alone, at that hour suspended between night and day: her only companions were the shadow of a furtive rat and the shapes of slaughtered animals left to hang inside what used to be an ice box.

She took the service lift up to the first floor: this part of the building was her responsibility, but recently this task had begun to fill her with a nameless dread, like a latent fever that never quite flared up.

The lift groaned under the combined weight of her body and the trolley, the chains and the cables began to squeal, and the cage rattled as it rose, coming to a shaky halt a few metres above. Agnes pulled the metal grate open. The damp-stained first-floor corridor was a long narrow band of dull blue, with a constellation of large panelled windows on one side.

A windowpane was banging against its frame in a steady rhythm. She left her trolley and went over to close the window. The glass was cold and fogged over; she wiped at it with one hand and made a porthole of sorts. Down in the valley, the light of dawn had begun to illuminate the village. The roofs of the houses looked like tiny lead-coloured tiles. Further up, at 1,700 metres above sea level and between the settlement and the School, the motionless expanse of the lake was beginning to turn pink beneath the mist. The sky was clear. But Agnes knew that the sun that day wouldn't bring any warmth to their steep, sloping clearing – by now she had learned to interpret the migraines that plagued her the moment she stepped out of bed.

The fog rose to engulf everything in its path: light, sounds, even smells became imbued with its stagnating presence, that essence of ancient bones. It seemed to come to life as it climbed over the frostbitten grass, and from its tendrils came forth those laments.

The sighs of the dead, thought Agnes.

It was the Buran, a fierce north-easterly wind. From its source in distant steppes, it had journeyed thousands of kilo-metres and forced its way into this valley, roaring against the river banks below the tree line, whirling across the flood-plains, and howling as it emerged on the other side, only to crash against the rock wall of the mountain.

It's just the wind, she kept telling herself.

The pendulum clock in the atrium chimed six times. It was getting late, but Agnes stood still. She was conscious that she was tarrying, and she also knew exactly why.

It's all in your head. All in your head.

She gripped the trolley's metal handle, and the bowls on it clattered as she finally willed herself to take a few steps towards the door at the end of the corridor.

The Hive.

Her stomach contracted with the abrupt realisation that it really was a hive. That's what it had become over the past few weeks. There was a subtle, mysterious buzz of activity about the place, like a diligent insect preparing for metamorphosis. Agnes was sure of it, though she wouldn't have been able to explain what was happening in there. She hadn't said a word to anyone, not even the principal: he would have thought she was going mad.

She put her hand in the pocket of her uniform and her fingers found the coarse material of her hood. She took it out and pulled it over her head. A thin veil covered her face and eyes, obscuring the outside world. That was the rule.

She walked in.

The room was completely silent. A few embers from inside the large cast-iron stove near the door were emitting a pleasant warmth. There were forty cots in the room, arranged in four rows of ten. No names to mark them: only numbers.

There were no cries or calls. Agnes knew what she would have seen if only she'd looked: blank, vacant gazes.

With one exception.

Now that she'd become accustomed to the silence, she could hear him kicking at the far end of the room, building his strength. He was preparing for something, although she couldn't say what. Maybe she really was insane.

Her footsteps brought her closer to cot number 39.

Unlike the others, this subject was thriving. His eyes, which were so unusual, were alert and darted about following her movements. Agnes knew that the subject was seeking out her eyes behind the veil of her hood, but she kept looking away, embarrassed. Subject 39 shouldn't have been aware of her presence, and yet . . .

She checked to make sure that no member of staff was looking through the door, and then she extended a finger. The subject bit it, squeezing her flesh tight between its gums. The expression in its eyes was different now, electric. Agnes pulled back, cursing, and it let out a short, anxious moan.

That's its true nature, she thought. *A carnivore.*

What happened next convinced her that she could no longer keep her suspicions private: the cots next to number 39 were no longer quiet. The other subjects' breathing had turned agitated, as if they were responding to a call.

The Hive was buzzing.